COLD DARK MATTER

For my parents,
Joan and Peter,
with gratitude and love.

COLD DARK MATTER

A Morgan O'Brien Mystery

Alex Brett

A Castle Street Mystery

THE DUNDURN GROUP
TORONTO

Editor: Barry Jowett
Copy-editor: Andrea Pruss
Design: Andrew Roberts
Printer: Webcom

National Library of Canada Cataloguing in Publication

Brett, Alex
  Cold dark matter / Alex Brett.

ISBN-10: 1-55002-494-9
!SBN-13: 978-1-55002-494-4

  I. Title.

PS8553.R3869C54 2004   C813'.6   C2004-901389-0

  2   3   4   5   09   08   07   06   05

Conseil des Arts du Canada   Canada Council for the Arts   Canadä   ONTARIO ARTS COUNCIL CONSEIL DES ARTS DE L'ONTARIO

We acknowledge the support of the Canada Council for the Arts and the Ontario Arts Council for our publishing program. We also acknowledge the financial support of the Government of Canada through the Book Publishing Industry Development Program and The Association for the Export of Canadian Books, and the Government of Ontario through the Ontario Book Publishers Tax Credit program.

Care has been taken to trace the ownership of copyright material used in this book. The author and the publisher welcome any information enabling them to rectify any references or credits in subsequent editions.

                                                    J. Kirk Howard, President

Printed and bound in Canada
Printed on recycled paper☻
www.dundurn.com

Dundurn Press   Gazelle Book Services Limited   Dundurn Press
8 Market Street   White Cross Mills   2250 Military Road
Suite 200   Hightown, Lancaster, England   Tonawanda, NY
Toronto, Ontario, Canada   LA1 4X5   U.S.A. 14150
M5E 1M6

Author's Note

Truth is stranger than fiction. One of the greatest challenges in writing fiction is to take those aspects of a story based on fact and make them believable to the reader. *Cold Dark Matter* is a work of fiction. The people in this book do not exist. Although many of the book's locations appear similar to real places, they are not. All my locations have been purposely distorted through the lens of fiction. The underpinnings of *Cold Dark Matter*, though, and the most unbelievable aspects of the story are based on fact. The summit of Mauna Kea *is* one of the world's foremost sites for optical astronomy. Dark matter *was* discovered by the method described in this book, albeit by Dr. Vera Rubin, an intrepid woman astronomer from the United States. And the Fruit Machine *was* built and used. Real science. Real events. Real technology. Perhaps we can learn from our errors.

Though my soul may set in darkness, it will rise
in perfect light;
I have loved the stars too fondly to be fearful
of the night.

Sarah Williams
"The Old Astronomer to His Pupil"

chapter one

In the world of science to see is to believe. To observe is to know. That which is tangible, which can be recorded and measured, is defined as the truth. Yet over 90 percent of the universe is completely invisible to us. Astronomers know that this dark matter exists because they observe its effect on all visible objects, but where the dark matter resides, and what it might be made of, remains a mystery.

Yves Grenier had been working on dark matter.

I remember thinking, as I glanced through the reprints, that this must somehow connect, it must be important, but the drone of the jet engines, the Merlot served with dinner, and the stress of my hasty departure from Ottawa had all taken their toll. I could no longer concentrate on anything but sleep. I closed the folder, tucked it into the pocket under my tray table, and extended my seat back the few centimetres that it was willing to go. If I was lucky I might get a few hours of cramped, stale slumber before the plane landed in Kona on the Big Island of Hawaii. I closed my eyes and tried to relax, but instead of falling into dreams my mind moved inexorably back to Ottawa and the gruesome image of Yves Grenier that had put me on this plane.

chapter two

The body was not celestial. There was no flicker of ancient light, no rings or orbiting moons, just a dark, lifeless form dangling from a cable high in the telescope's struts. From this angle, from the observing floor some twenty metres below, it looked like the corpse was bowing its head in a final tribute to the giant mirror at its feet. I pushed the photograph back across the table.

"I take it he's one of ours."

Duncan took the picture and, studiously avoiding the image, slipped it back into a plain brown envelope. I'd forgotten he was squeamish. When it was safely back inside he slouched forward, wrapped his hands around his coffee cup, and stared into the black liquid. The deep lines and dark bags beneath his eyes were thrown into high relief.

A customer squeezed by our table making for the door. It was an odd place for a meeting, a rundown café on the wrong end of Wellington Street, but it was also far from the hustle and prying ears of Parliament Hill, which was, I assumed, why Duncan had chosen it. Finally he looked up.

"He *was* one of ours. That," he motioned to the envelope, "happened yesterday. Dr. Yves Grenier, resident astronomer at one of our telescopes in Hawaii. Bright, young, and talented. What an unbelievable waste." He shook his head and, with a weariness I don't remember ever seeing before, slowly lifted his cup. This was not a social call. Duncan had phoned me just around noon with an urgent request to meet him at this out-of-the-way location. He'd arrived at our rendezvous looking shockingly rattled for a guy who approached all drama with analytical calm.

"At Gemini?" I asked, referring to the jewel in our astronomy crown.

Duncan shook his head vaguely. "FCT — the FrancoCanadian Telescope." Then he seemed to pull himself together. "The day before yesterday Grenier goes to work as usual. He arrives at the telescope in the early evening, then spends the night working with one of the French astronomers and the telescope operator on duty that night. By all accounts they have a stellar night of observing, if you'll forgive the pun, and neither Mellier, the French astronomer, nor Aimes, the telescope operator, notice anything amiss. Mellier leaves first, around 3:00 a.m., with a massive high-altitude headache. Grenier and Aimes finish up around 4:30 a.m. and leave together, but in separate vehicles. Aimes checks in at the Astronomy Centre halfway down from the summit but is off the next night so decides to continue on home instead of sleeping at the Centre. Grenier never arrives. Half an hour later he sends a farewell note by e-mail to all the staff, takes the maintenance lift up to the peak of the dome, puts a loop of cable around his neck, and takes a dive."

"A suicide."

"So it would seem." At this point Duncan lifted his coffee again and took another painfully slow sip. The stuff was grey slosh, so I knew the goal of the drinking was to buy time, give him space to formulate. He took a few more moments then carefully placed the cup back in its saucer and looked at me directly. He searched my face then said, "We need your help."

Duncan and I used to work together investigating research fraud for the National Council for Science and Technology. That is, until he bailed for a job as special advisor to the powerful Minister of Industry and Science, something I hadn't quite forgiven him for. "We?"

"The minister's office."

Jobs for them usually involved endless hours of paperwork and mountains of bureaucratic crap, so I kept my voice noncommittal. "What's the problem?"

Duncan leaned forward and lowered his voice. "Grenier kept research diaries, and they're gone."

If that was supposed to impress me, it didn't. "Who cares? The dead guy's an astronomer. It's in the public domain."

Duncan leaned over and extracted a file from his briefcase, which he pushed across the table. It was stuffed with reprints from the *Astronomical Journal*, *Astronomy and Astrophysics*, *Proceedings from the American Astronomical Society*, in short, from the most prestigious astronomy publications in the world. I glanced through it while he spoke in a low voice. His gaze kept shifting to the window every time someone walked by, but being Duncan it didn't break his concentration.

"Grenier was a genius at image reconstruction, where they take the electronic data from these huge light-sensor arrays and use it to build a detailed image. That's what he's been doing with the FrancoCanadian

Telescope, developing software to handle a new wide-field imaging camera." He nodded to the file. "It's all in there. Grenier's team was using the camera to detect gravitational lenses and map dark matter, but the point is it has other applications."

I looked up from the file. "You mean military applications."

He nodded. "High-end satellite surveillance. You see the problem."

Actually, I didn't. Military research is always at least ten years ahead of academia, what with all the money, no publishing, and no teaching. Duncan knew this, but I said it anyway. His response caught me off guard.

"We have reason to believe that Grenier was extremely advanced in this area, and much of his work was unpublished. Those diaries may contain algorithms, flow charts, even snatches of code. The fact that they're missing concerns us. We funded the research. It belongs to us, and we want it back."

I looked at him for a second then pushed my chair back and turned to stare out the dirty window. Outside, needles of freezing rain slashed against the glass, and pedestrians scurried by with collars gripped tight against the wind. Welcome to Ottawa's spring. Something didn't add up. For starters Duncan — or at least the Duncan I knew — had disappeared. *We* need your help? *We* are concerned? *We* have reason to believe? Where was the critical, questioning, intelligent Duncan I'd grown to cherish and respect? The Duncan who believed in nothing and trusted no one? The Duncan who was my friend? A year ago I would have trusted him with my life, now I wasn't even sure I knew him. Anyway, this sounded like a spook job, and that didn't turn my crank. I deal with good clean science fraud for good clean reasons, like jealousy, greed, and egomania. I turned back to Duncan and gave him the answer he should have known he'd get if his brain hadn't turned to bureaucratic mush.

"No thank you."

He lifted his head and circled the cup with his hands. His clear hazel eyes looked into mine. "*No* is not an option."

I could feel the heat rise from my gut. "*No* is always an option. There may be consequences attached, but it's always an option."

He stared at me for a moment, then his face collapsed, dropped, as if the skin had suddenly detached from the bone. He leaned forward and covered it with his hands. His voice came out in a hoarse whisper. "For Christ's sake, Morgan, do this one for me. There's no one else I can trust."

Duncan had never, in all our years of working together, made a personal appeal. I took a deep breath. "Look, Duncan, if your theory is correct and someone did steal the diaries they're gone. They're in Washington, or Moscow, or Baghdad, or wherever the hell else you're worried about."

"They're in Hawaii."

"How do you know?"

I could see him struggle with that one for a minute. He laid his hands flat on the table. "Look, I need someone who can get inside, ask the right questions, recognize any discrepancies. Someone who understands the culture."

I thought about that for a minute. Not what he was saying: what he wasn't saying. "You think it was an inside job. Someone on staff."

He gave a noncommittal shrug. "Or an astronomer from another telescope, or a visiting observer, or an engineer, or a technician. There are lots of candidates.

The point is, I need someone who understands the connections." He leaned forward again. "And someone who isn't afraid of what they might find."

That, of course, meant politics.

"Has it been called?" I nodded to the envelope.

I saw just the slightest wince and did a rapid calculation based on a five-hour time difference between Hawaii and Ottawa. When I came up with the number I sat back and laughed. "It hasn't been called, has it? Yves Grenier isn't even cold."

"It's open and shut, a suicide."

"Except that it's not shut, and until it is I'm obstructing a police investigation. People go to jail for that, Duncan, unless you've got a diplomatic passport filed away in my travel papers." He had the grace to look chagrined. "I didn't think so."

The door to the café opened with a blast of icy wind, and Duncan's eyes followed the elderly man as he shuffled to a booth. As far as I was concerned this meeting was over. I gulped down my coffee and started to pull on my coat.

"My ex-wife called," he said suddenly. "She wants custody of Alyssa and Peter."

I stopped with my arm halfway in the sleeve. "When did this happen?"

"Yesterday." His lips trembled, and he clamped them shut.

I slumped back in my chair too stunned to say a word. I was suddenly painfully aware of how little I knew about Duncan's past. He'd been married, I knew that, and rumour had it that his wife had left him suddenly, just more or less disappeared after their second child, Peter, was born four years ago. Duncan had just started his new job as an investigator at the National Council for Science and Technology, and none of us knew him well enough to know what was going on. As I got to know him better, as he went from being a colleague to an acquaintance to a close friend, he never spoke of his ex-wife, and I didn't want to probe. As far as I knew they hadn't been in contact since her departure. Duncan had done some dating — I'd even set him up with a couple of my friends — but for the most part he seemed content to divide his time between his job and the two children. Suddenly, I felt ashamed at my lack of attention to such an important part of his life.

"Is that why you're not going to Hawaii yourself?"

"I can't leave right now, and if you don't go I'll have to." He leaned forward again. "It's my kids, Morgan. Please. Do this one for me."

I looked at his gaunt face, and despite the mental sirens wailing in my head I gave a reluctant, "Fine."

"Thank you," he said. He took a moment to collect himself, then he switched back to business mode. He pulled one more file from his briefcase and pushed it across to me. I flipped it open. There was a pile of paperwork telling me that I'd been temporarily assigned from my normal job in Investigations to the minister's office, and there was a travel itinerary and tickets. I closed it, gave myself a mental kick for saying yes, and tucked it into my briefcase.

Once outside, we stood for a moment on the sidewalk. It was still grey and dark, the freezing rain driven by blasts of wind.

"Do the kids know about their mom?" I asked.

He shook his head. "They were too young when she left. What do you tell them? Sorry kids, but your mom preferred a job to having you so she took off without a word? I don't think so." He put his hand on my arm. "If you need to get in touch, land lines only. And don't call me at home."

I stood for a minute trying to work out what this all meant, but he'd turned and was now at his car. I watched as he pulled the keys from his pocket, unlocked the door. He was just climbing in when he caught sight of me observing him. We locked eyes, his slender hand resting on the roof of the car. "Morgan ..." He hesitated then said, "Watch your back."

A moment later he'd pulled into the traffic and was headed to Parliament Hill.

The first thing I did when I got home was pick up the phone and call Lydia. I caught her just before she was leaving for class.

"I have your first assignment. You interested?"

Lydia had recently left the Council on early retirement and, at my suggestion, had gone back to school to get a diploma in policing and public safety. From there she would write her PI exams. Even over the phone I could feel her BS sensors homing in on me. She'd be a good investigator. She answered carefully.

"That would depend on the nature of the work. I am not yet licensed, as you know, and the examiners look unkindly upon an applicant with a criminal record."

"It's completely aboveboard. Some searching of public records, maybe making some use of your old friends in the minister's office. Good practice really."

I could hear the smile in her voice. "What, pray tell, are you up to now?"

This was the hard part. "I need information," I paused briefly, "on Duncan."

Her voice sagged with disappointment. "Morgan. How could you?"

"It's not what you think. His ex-wife. Do you know anything about her?"

"He never spoke of her to me. And frankly, Morgan, I didn't ask."

"Well, it's too bad we didn't, because now she's back in the picture and she's suing him for custody." I hurled that like a barb.

"Oh," was her only response.

"So we have to help him out, whether he wants it or not."

"And how do you propose to do that?"

"By hiring you. I want to know who she is, where she's living, and what she's been doing for the past four years, and if any of it doesn't feel right — if any of it could be used against her in a custody hearing — then *we* decide, both of us together, what to do with the information."

She was silent for a minute, obviously mulling it over. Then she said quietly, "Are you sure you've thought this through? Duncan's life is none of your business, not unless he wants it to be. I'm wondering if, perhaps, your interest in the situation is more … personal."

Of course it was personal. Duncan was my friend, and his kids were a gas. I even had their picture in my wallet, a goofy portrait of the three of us taken at the Children's Museum. Then the implied meaning caught me. "You mean am I interested in Duncan, as in romantically interested in Duncan? Lydia! Of course not."

Her voice was still quiet. "And the children? You're awfully fond of them, I know. Are you sure — "

"I'm worried about Duncan. End of story."

"And I suppose if I don't do it you'll find another way."

"I suppose I will."

She sighed. "All right then, I'll do it, but on one condition. You hold to your promise that *we* decide together how best to use any information I obtain."

"Agreed." I was a little miffed that she'd question my integrity, but the tone of my voice was lost on her.

"One more question, Morgan. Have you stopped to consider what might be in the best interests of the children? My ex-husband Ralph was, in my opinion, a worthless husband and a useless father, but the girls love him and I have no business intruding on their relationship with him. Think about that."

I promised I would, mumbled something about missing my plane to Hawaii, and promised to give her a call in a couple of days to see what she'd dug up. We'd almost completed our goodbyes when I remembered the other thing.

"Do you still have contacts in the minister's office?"

"His executive assistant and I are still on excellent terms."

"Could you take her out for lunch? Find out what's going on with the FrancoCanadian Telescope? Just the general scuttlebutt."

"Do I bill you for that one separately?"

"Ingrate."

chapter three

I'd just managed to drop off to sleep when the cabin attendant bustled by to collect the pillows and blankets. I checked my watch, and she informed me that it was almost 7:00 a.m. local time. Beneath us was still an endless turquoise blue, but as the nose of the plane dipped to begin the descent I caught my first glimpse ahead of the chain of emerald islands erupting from the sea.

Twenty minutes later when I finally arrived at the airplane's open door I couldn't help but stop and gape. I'd left Ottawa in sleet and snow with the temperature hovering below zero. Here, even in the early morning, the waves of heat were so intense that the background behind was a blur of greens.

I took the steps down to the tarmac slowly, trying to take it all in. The airport itself was small with the planes landing out on the tarmac. The buildings resembled a series of attached Polynesian huts right down to the simulated thatch roofs, but there were no walls to enclose the structure, something incomprehensible to my Canadian sensibility. And everywhere around me clumps of palms rattled and swished in the wind. I moved my bag to the other shoulder. There was no doubt about it. If one had to work this was the place to do it.

Detective Donald Benson of the Hawaii County Police Department leaned back in his chair. His legs stretched out so far that his shiny brown loafers poked out from beneath the desk and almost touched my feet. With his hands laced behind his head he observed me with what appeared to be casual interest, but I suspected was anything but.

"O'Brien, right?" I nodded. "Where'd you say you were from?"

I'd called Benson from the Kona airport just before picking up my rental car. As the lead investigator on Grenier's death he'd have more useful information than all the astronomers combined, and he'd been surprisingly helpful. Instead of the usual suspicion, stonewalling, and runaround, Benson had told me to come right over. He'd even offered me a cup of coffee. His behaviour put me on edge.

I pulled out my passport and my National Council for Science and Technology ID card, identifying me as an investigator. He pulled them over and glanced at them but didn't look impressed.

"So you investigate what exactly?"

"Research fraud, embezzlement, occasionally murder or manslaughter if it's related in some way to research." Then I added carefully, emphasizing theory over practice, "But in those cases I'm there to help the police."

He tossed my papers on the desk, leaned back again, and ran his hands over the fine bristle of dark hair that barely obscured his scalp. As he lifted his arms the olive T-shirt beneath his pale linen jacket stretched across muscle. "You got law enforcement experience?"

"RCMP."

His face brightened. I had connections to the brotherhood. "I know a couple of Mounties. Good guys. I met them at a conference in Atlanta a couple years back."

I leaned forward, pulled a Post-it off his desk, wrote down the names of two officers — one a detective with the local Ottawa police, the other a sergeant with the RCMP — and pushed it across the table.

"Give them a call." I nodded to the paper. "They'll tell you I'm legit."

He picked up the paper and fingered it, obviously trying to decide if he should make the calls before giving me any information. Finally he looked up. "So you understand all this science shit?"

"That's my job. And if I don't understand it and it seems relevant, I have contacts who help me out."

"And this Grenier guy, he was one of yours?"

"We paid his salary."

He gave a little shrug. "So what's the problem? People commit suicide all the time. They don't send in the government troops."

I'd thought about this, how to explain my presence. Benson was the fastest route to information. With him on my side I wouldn't have to waste time on preliminaries. He would have done that for me. He could also give me access to sources of information that would otherwise be closed to me as a foreign national, so to make this work I had to cast myself as an asset, not a liability. But how to do that without mentioning the research diaries? If he didn't know about them I wasn't about to tip him off. The best route, I reasoned, was a partial truth, which is so much easier to weasel out of than an outright lie if things begin to fall apart.

"Some of Grenier's data is missing," I said, keeping my voice neutral, "and it belongs to us."

He came forward in his chair. "Really. Now why didn't any of those pointy heads let me in on that?"

So they hadn't mentioned the diaries. That in itself was interesting. "Maybe you didn't ask the right questions, or maybe you asked the wrong person. Not everyone would know."

"Why the interest?"

"His work represents a substantial investment on the part of the Canadian government."

He'd picked up a pencil and absently tapped the eraser on his blotter while his eyes stayed riveted to mine. "It must, to send you all the way here to get it."

He was analyzing my every twitch, tick, and squirm, and I was careful to keep my eyes level with his and my hands neatly folded in my lap, but I felt the heat. I needed a diversion. "How solid is your suicide?"

It took a second, then Benson frowned and threw down his pencil. "I hate friggin' suicides. This one? I've got a note, I've got no physical evidence to back up anything else, and I've got several witnesses saying that Grenier'd been a bit bizarre over the past two weeks. Add to that no motive for murder, not that we could dig up anyway. Let's just say it's hard to commit resources on that basis."

"But the case isn't closed."

He sighed, and shook his head. "Unless something else comes up," he motioned to the pile of folders on his desk, "I've got other cases, and the brass wants it shut."

I smiled to myself. Any self-respecting detective would rather solve a murder than declare a case a suicide. I lowered my voice a couple of tones, giving it seductive edge. "Maybe we can make a deal."

I could see the corners of his mouth turn up, almost against his will. "And what kind of deal would that be?"

I leaned in a bit and tilted my head down, so I was looking up at him through my lashes. In wolves this would be called a submissive posture, designed to reduce any sense of threat. It usually worked, particularly on men. "You tell me what you've got and whatever I find I turn over to you. Consider me the hired help, except you don't pay a thing."

He broke out into a smile of brilliant white teeth. "Simple as that, huh?"

I nodded.

He eyed me for a minute, his teeth almost glinting against the tan, then he gave a little nod in my direction. "The Hawaii County Police Department is always happy to help a neighbour." He leaned forward and reached for the phone. "How are you with pretty pictures?"

"It's not my first choice of entertainment, but I won't puke on your floor."

"Good," he said, banging in a number, "because Bunny wouldn't like that." Then he turned slightly away from me. "Bunny, get me Star Boy's forensic file to interview 6 please."

Benson led me down a corridor lined with interview rooms. He was a pleasing sight to follow, tall and nicely muscled, but not overdone, ostentatious. I knew we'd struck a deal, and I also knew that Benson didn't trust me any more than I did him: a good cop's instincts. But even with the flow of information censored it would still be better than what I could get working it alone.

The door to interview room 6 was open when we got there. Whoever Bunny was, she was efficient. There was a file on the table and a video player and monitor beside it. Benson sat in one chair, I sat down beside him. He pulled a video from the file, shoved it in the machine.

Then he unbuttoned his jacket, crossed his legs, and hit play on the remote. His belt, I noted, matched his shoes.

"No narration," he said, his eyes on the screen. "But I'll lead you through it."

The video began from a small dirt parking area that faced the FrancoCanadian observatory dome. It was a mammoth structure, like a giant golf ball sitting on a squat tee, glistening white against a deep blue sky. Even more imposing than the dome, though, was the terrain around it. The camera panned slowly to the left through a landscape so desolate, so bereft of life, that it could have been an image relayed back to Earth from the Mars lander. We appeared to be standing on an island of red rubble poking through an endless sea of soft white cloud. The camera picked up several more domes in the distance, majestic on their contours of rock, then the image shuddered and the camera switched direction, this time moving to the right of FrancoCanadian observatory. On a hill just above it sat an even bigger dome, silver, with a rough track connecting the two. The road followed the narrow spine of a ridge, and it dropped on one side into the bowl of the ancient volcano, on the other into the clouds. That image held briefly, then the camera shuddered and jerked, as if the cameraman himself teetered on the edge of the cliff.

"That's the wind," said Benson. He glanced over at me. "Hope you brought those Canadian long johns."

Then he hit fast-forward, and the camera moved along into the observatory, picking up details of the entryway and first set of doors. We were now in a small foyer with two doors at its base, one leading to the right, one to the left.

"What time was this?" I asked.

"We got the 911 at around 5:00 a.m. By the time we got up there it was 6:00, and the Ident guys didn't arrive until 7:00." He hit the slow button as the camera came through the first set of doors into a narrow corridor. It panned to the left getting a full shot of an in/out board with all the staff members listed. Grenier's magnet was "out."

"And that's how you found it?" I asked.

"No. We pushed it to 'out' when we knew he was dead."

I twisted around. His face was blank and his eyes were studying the screen. Just when I began to wonder if I'd actually heard him correctly, his glance slid from the screen to me; he raised an eyebrow, then went back to the screen. He was jerking my chain. "It tallies with what Aimes, the telescope operator, told us. Grenier left with him but must have returned alone. Since he was alone he didn't bother moving his magnet."

I watched carefully as the camera slowly made its way up a tiny, cramped elevator. Benson, too, was leaning forward as if hoping to catch some detail he'd missed.

"Who called in the 911?"

He kept his eyes on the screen. "A guy named Pexa. Native Hawaiian. Good guy. He's head of maintenance up there. He was at the Astronomy Centre halfway up the mountain getting ready to start his day when he got a call from an astronomer who'd seen the suicide note. Star Boy sent it by e-mail. Can you believe it? So Pexa goes right up and sure enough finds Grenier hanging from the telescope. Fortunately for us he's a sensible guy, ex-Navy. He didn't try to get him down, didn't tamper with the scene, just backed out and called us." He leaned forward, elbows on his knees. "This is where it gets interesting."

The camera had arrived at a set of swinging doors labelled "Observing Floor." They were pushed open by an unseen hand to reveal a vestibule painted flat black and another set of doors. These swung open onto a concrete floor. The camera stopped dead and began a slow and careful pan of the vast open space. It was like a cave, dim and lifeless, with unfamiliar shapes looming in the shadows. I moved forward to get a better look. "What's all that stuff?"

"Equipment. There's junk everywhere. You can't move without tripping over a cable or some piece of crap." I felt Benson turn and look at me. "You ever been up there? You know why there's no narration on this tape?" I shook my head. "Because the Ident guy didn't have the breath to walk, talk, and carry the camera all at the same time. It's a friggin' nightmare. There's not enough oxygen to keep you thinking straight, and it's so goddamned cold you start to shiver ten minutes after arriving. So I ask this Pexa to turn up the heat. I mean, how the hell are we supposed to work? And you know what he tells me? No can do. There is no heat. And the friggin' floor's refrigerated. No joke. Something about heat rising up and affecting their whatever." He shook his head. "It's a nightmare." Then he pointed again with the remote. "Here comes your boy."

The camera had arrived at a huge cylindrical mass suspended from the floor. I knew from the pictures in the file that this was the base of the telescope, and within that cylinder lay several tons of mirror, the pride of the observatory. The image climbed slowly upward, moving over a lattice of metal struts constructed around the mirror. At the top end of this open tube a large black box sat suspended in the centre, and below this hung Yves Grenier, lifeless as a sack of grain. The camera continued upward. Benson tapped the screen with the corner of the remote. "The lift is there."

I could see the vague shadow of a box in the peak of the dome. I leaned forward, trying to peer through the darkness. "If somebody else was with him —"

"We have no evidence of that."

"But if somebody was, could they get the lift back in position?"

"Easy. It can be controlled from inside or from the ground."

"And you dusted inside?"

He rolled his eyes then shook his head. "You think we're hicks? Everything and everywhere. We're still doing eliminations."

The camera now moved slowly down from the peak following the cable back to Grenier's body. When it got there Benson hit pause, letting the gruesome image hang in the middle of the screen. He turned to me. "It's real easy to fall up there. You walk up three steps and in that thin atmosphere your head starts to spin. If it hadn't been for the note I would have said death by misadventure. Still, I don't like the feel of it."

"There are no other leads?"

He clicked the machine back on and the camera continued its slow descent along the struts of the telescopes, down across its base, and around the floor once again. Then the image disappeared into a flat blue screen.

Benson laid the remote on the table and turned to face me. He adjusted his pant leg, maintaining the perfect crease. "I've shown you mine, now you show me yours."

"What about the ligature?"

"Inconclusive."

"No wife or girlfriend?"

"Not that we could find."

I paused and thought it over. "You could have a bad case of researcher envy."

He tilted his head with interest. "Go on."

I gave a shrug. "I'm not saying that's what happened, just that it's a possibility." I opened up my briefcase and

extracted all the reprints Duncan had given me and
thumped them onto the desk. "Yves Grenier was both
talented and prolific. Maybe somebody didn't like that.
Maybe someone thought he was stealing their ideas or
trespassing on their research domain. Maybe someone
needed to eliminate the competition for a big grant. Who
knows. It's a cutthroat business."

"None of my witnesses mentioned anything like
that."

"Because if they did the investigation might veer too
close to home. You might even disrupt their work."

His eyes narrowed. "I'll follow up on it."

That's what I was hoping he'd say. This red herring
would keep him busy for at least a few days. "If you
want I can get you some names," I said helpfully.
"Astronomers who would be in direct competition
with Grenier for money or telescope time. We've got a
librarian on staff who specializes in that kind of data-
base search. Then we can cross-check and see who was
in Hawaii at the time of Grenier's death."

He considered my proposal for a moment then nodded. "I'd appreciate that, and in the meantime I'll follow
up the old-fashioned way." That meant interviews and
cross-checking statements.

"That'll work. Two independent methods. Let's see
if we come up with the same information."

Benson ejected the video and put it back in the
accordion file. "You got a cellphone?" I pulled a business card from my pocket and passed it to him. He read
it and dropped it into his breast pocket. "And I do have
to ask, are you armed?"

"No. But I have a credit card. I'll just go down to 7-
11 and get a Glock if I feel the urge to kill."

"You and every other tourist. This place isn't safe
for Hawaiians anymore."

I began loading the reprints back in my briefcase. I kept my voice casual for the next question. "Can I check out Grenier's house?"

He raised his eyebrow and gave a slight smile. "That's off limits."

I nodded and snapped my briefcase shut. "Have your crime scene guys gone through it?"

"What do you think?"

"Find anything interesting?"

He held the door of the interview room open for me. "Should they have?"

I gave him a wry smile to let him know I understood the game. "Only you would know, Benson."

At the front door I took his hand. He gave mine a sharp squeeze.

"Stay in touch."

It was an order, not a request.

I stepped outside into an oven of burning sun and searing heat without even a breath of wind to rattle the palms. I crossed to my vehicle quickly — a silver Toyota SUV — opened the door, and slid in. The heat was suffocating, and it took me a moment to find my keys, get the engine running, and jam the air conditioner on high. When I finally looked up I caught sight of Benson back at his office window, watching me leave. As I pulled out of the parking spot I saw him turn away and lift the phone. By the time I left the lot he was deep in conversation.

chapter four

The office building spread across the ground like low, grey lichen, insinuating itself into the folds of the land. High above, a heavy mist poured over the cliffs and settled into the valley, making it hard to see where the building ended and the atmosphere began. In fact, I would have missed it altogether had it not been for the impressive sign at the base of the drive, "The FrancoCanadian Telescope/Le Télescope FrancoCanadien," in red and white.

If the observatory dome was the heart of operation, then this building was surely the brain. Within these offices astronomers managed the complex night-to-night operation of the telescope, engineers built new instruments for it, and computer scientists developed the software needed to eke out and analyze every photon of light that touched that mirror. If I was looking for answers this is where they'd be.

From Benson's office I'd taken the only road that leads into the island's interior, a narrow highway that follows a ridge right up into the mountains. It rose through a landscape of arid, long-grass meadows cut every few miles by rivers of solid lava, obsidian black and devoid of vegetation. Some of the flows looked like roiling rivers of tar with surfaces as smooth and taut as skin. Others were vast plains of angry pinnacles, razor sharp and glistening in the heat of the sun. As I climbed, though, the sky paled from blue to grey, and I could feel the temperature drop. I switched off the air conditioning and started the heat. By the time I reached the telescope offices in the village of Waimea the countryside was shrouded in fog and curtains of rain lashed the road.

In the parking lot I sat for a minute, preparing a strategy for the next few hours. When I'd called Dr. Edwin Eales, the observatory's director, from the airport he'd flatly refused to see me and I'd had to pull rank, telling him he was an employee of the Crown, this was a government investigation, and he didn't have a choice.

Of course, he *did* have a choice. I had absolutely no jurisdiction in Hawaii, but if he wasn't aware of that I wasn't about to let him in on the secret. When I was ready to go I turned, rooted around in my suitcase, and pulled out my leather jacket. So much for a Hawaiian vacation. When it was all zipped up, I hopped down from the truck and ran for the building.

The receptionist behind the counter wasn't pleased to see me. "Can I help you?" she said, making an effort to avoid my eyes.

"I'm here to see Dr. Eales. We have a meeting."

Her hands skittered across the desk as if she was trying to locate a paper that had suddenly gone missing. She kept her eyes lowered. "I'm sorry, but Dr. Eales is …" She hesitated but kept the hands moving. "Dr. Eales has been called away. If you'd care to leave your number …"

I checked my watch. I was already five minutes late for our meeting. "No thanks," I said, and I pushed through the swinging door beside her, past the astonished faces of the clerical staff, and continued on down the hall until I arrived at the door labelled "Director." I gave two sharp knocks then let myself in.

The two men in the room turned in surprise.

"Dr. Eales, I presume." I headed for the one behind the desk with hand outstretched.

Eales was compact and wiry — a runner by physique — with bristly fair hair and an alpha personality. It took him a moment to connect, to figure out who I was. When he did he shot from his chair. His face went from tan to deep pink in a timeframe that couldn't be healthy. "Who the hell are you? Get out of my office. You can't just walk in here without, without … " He was quick enough to realize that he'd moved onto slippery ground, so I finished the sentence for him.

"An appointment." I looked at my watch. "Yes, I am sorry. It took me a little longer to get here than I thought it would. That's quite a drive." I slipped into the chair next to the slightly rumpled, older man.

Still standing, Eales banged his open palm hard on the desk's surface, a good display behaviour if you happen to be simian, but it didn't have much effect on me. "You can't just —"

The man next to me raised his hand slightly from where it lay on the arm of his chair. "Edwin." Although it was said gently there was no mistaking the warning.

Eales glanced at him, and the older man gave a slight tip of his head toward Eales's chair. The director glared at him for a moment, then reluctantly sat back. The guest turned to me.

"I'm Anthony St. James. You must be the investigator." His voice carried a distinct note of disapproval.

For my part, I had to hide my surprise. Even I knew the name Anthony St. James, and astronomy wasn't my usual beat. St. James was one of Canada's most renowned astronomers, although I couldn't for the life of me remember why. Something big, I vaguely recalled, that he discovered in the late 1950s or early '60s near the beginning of his career. I'd have to ask Duncan about that. What I did recall, though, was that instead of fleeing south to bigger salaries, more prestige, and access to high-end telescopes, St. James had resolutely stayed in Canada. He was now credited with helping to build an astronomy community in a country that, at that time, had no history and little appreciation for cosmic gazing. Suddenly the exchange between him and Eales became clear. Eales might be the director of the observatory, but St. James was a founding father.

I took his hand. At the first physical contact his demeanor changed, as if he'd resigned himself to my presence and was determined to be a gentleman, despite my profession. "A terrible tragedy, Ms. O'Brien. You must forgive us. We are all still reeling from the shock, and ...," here he slowed and chose his words carefully, "it is difficult for us to understand what possible benefit could be derived from an investigation. Surely the police will handle that."

Then he withdrew his hand and sat back to wait for an answer.

"Are you here because of Dr. Grenier?"

He showed a moment of surprise — he was a man used to being answered, not questioned — then recovered. "A most unfortunate coincidence, I'm afraid. I'm observing the next few days." He must have seen my eyebrows raise and looked amused. "Oh yes, Ms. O'Brien,

I still carry out an active research program, much of it on this telescope. Without the observing, why live?"

"So you knew Dr. Grenier then."

He made a display of shifting to face me, giving himself just enough time to frame an answer. "I did, yes, rather well. Dr. Grenier's death is a tragedy, not just for his family and friends, but for Canadian astronomy as well. He was a gifted researcher, and you can't just replace someone of that calibre. In Yves's case I don't think he can be replaced at all."

"I wouldn't go that far, Tony. We're all replaceable." Eales's voice was cool.

St. James, who seemed to have momentarily forgotten Eales, let his gaze drift back to his face and rest there, but before he could respond I did.

"You didn't get along with Dr. Grenier?"

"Don't put words in my mouth," Eales snapped. "I simply said we are all replaceable, a principle I'm sure Tony will support, in practice if not in theory. Now what do you want?"

"Edwin." This time the warning had more force, but so did Eales's response. He leaned forward, his hands flat on the desk, and glared at St. James. "This is still my office and still my observatory. And it is *still* my responsibility to run it as I see fit, regardless of your opinion." Then he switched his gaze to me. "I, for one, am overwhelmed with work since Yves managed to do considerable damage to the prime focus in his final asinine act. And every night of observing we lose represents thousands of dollars, a figure I'm sure Dr. St. James would be happy to confirm. So what the hell do you want?"

I let a beat pass, and when I was good and ready I said, "Dr. Grenier's research diaries."

Eales pulled back, and out of the corner of my eye I saw St. James's hand drop limply to the side of his chair.

Eales, however, a pugnacious alpha male, hopped right back in the ring. "By what authority?"

Again I let a moment pass, just to let him know I wouldn't be bullied. "The Government of Canada, who, after all, owns them."

At this point I heard the door to the office open. "I'll take it from here."

I turned to see a cross between a leprechaun and Leif the Red standing, arms crossed, in the doorway. With his balding head of red hair and close-cropped auburn beard, he held himself like a Celtic chieftain, albeit in pinstripe grey. The only flaw was the bow tie. It's hard to take a man seriously who sports a bow tie. *Although*, I thought as he stepped in the room and shut the door behind him, *I might have to revise that opinion.*

He locked eyes briefly with Eales, then with St. James, before moving to me. He thrust out his hand. "Gunnar McNabb, Public Relations."

I didn't take it. "I'm not the public." I turned back to Eales. "I want the diaries, Dr. Eales. If you —"

Gunnar leaned over and gripped my arm. "This meeting is over."

I turned, looked at his hand on my arm, then looked up at him. "This meeting is over when I say it is." I snapped my arm out of his grip and turned back to the director. "Dr. Eales?"

St. James had bent his head and was now massaging his temples as if to ward off a major migraine.

"Don't say anything," said Gunnar.

I stood and turned on Gunnar. He wasn't any taller than me, but he was built like a brick wall: broad shoulders, big chest, all muscle. If he knew how to use that muscle, and it looked like he did, he could flatten me in seconds, but it wouldn't come to that. I poked him hard on the chest.

"You're obstructing an investigation. If you want to keep your job and your hefty government pension, back off."

He didn't. Back off, that is. In fact, he moved in closer. A little red light went off in my head, but before I could make the connection he was in my face. "I'd like to see your identification." His hand was out, waiting. For a smallish man he had big, beefy fingers.

"Gunnar, please." That was St. James. Gunnar's eyes, a lively blue, flicked toward him. St. James must have signalled something because Gunnar took a small step back, although he clearly wasn't happy about it. I felt myself relax slightly, but Gunnar still had his hand out. "How do we know you're not a reporter?"

I pulled out my ID and handed it to him.

He read out my name, position, and affiliation then handed my ID back. "You have no authority here. I'll have to ask you to leave." He stepped aside and motioned to the door. "Now."

"Authority? We fund this operation."

Eales cut in. "We're incorporated, Ms. O'Brien. Although our funds come from Canada and France, we exist as a separate corporation under the laws and statutes of the State of Hawaii. Thank you, Gunnar. You're quite right. She has no authority here."

Gunnar reached for my elbow. For a PR guy he had very bad manners. I put up my hand in acquiescence. "You're right Gunnar, Dr. Eales. I have no authority. Not technically anyway." I dipped down and picked up my briefcase. "So I'll just fly on home to Ottawa and write up my report for the Minister of Industry and Science telling him that the Canadian staff of this telescope refused to cooperate in his investigation, right from the director, down." I held out my hand to Dr. Eales just to show that there were no hard feelings. "By the way, Dr. Eales, when *is* your next funding review?"

"All of you, stop this." It was the quiet voice of Anthony St. James. He raised his head from where it had lain cradled in his hand. "I think we should cooperate. Edwin, we have nothing to hide. We've done nothing wrong. Tell me, what can it hurt?"

Gunnar moved forward a step. "I wouldn't advise that, sir."

"No," said St. James, barely suppressing his annoyance. "I'm sure you wouldn't, but I think you'll take orders from me on this one." He sat up straighter and seemed to rally his strength. "Sit back down, Ms. O'Brien. Let's get this over with. What is it you want?"

"The diaries, and the sooner I find them, the quicker I leave you alone."

"But we have no idea where they are. How can we possibly help?"

"So they *have* disappeared? You don't have them, or one of your astronomers?"

He glanced at Edwin, and Edwin gave a barely perceptible shake of his head.

St. James turned back to me. "Not that we know of."

"But you didn't notify the police. Not one of you." A complete silence greeted my statement, and I let it hang in the room for a good minute. Outside, the rain splashed against the window. Eales had his head turned and was staring at the bushes outside, as if he'd disengaged entirely from our conversation. McNabb's shoes squeaked as he shifted his weight from one leg to the other. Finally St. James leaned forward, balancing his elbows on his knees, his eyes focused on his hands.

"But we don't know they've been stolen. Maybe Yves hid them. Maybe he destroyed them. How do we know what was going on in his mind before —" He stopped abruptly. "Well, obviously he wasn't thinking rationally." A piece of his sparse grey hair fell forward, and he pushed it back with a weary gesture.

"I want to search Grenier's office, then I want access to all the staff records and any staff members who saw him or worked with him the day he died."

Eales reconnected and snapped his head around. "This is not Ottawa, Ms. O'Brien. People actually work here. You may search the office, yes, but you may interview the staff only through me. And no records."

"I can insist."

"Not without a subpoena, you can't, and I don't think even the minister wants to breach Hawaii's privacy laws."

I could just imagine Duncan's reaction if I landed him in that kind of toxic water so I figured it was time to cut my losses. I'd work around the other problems later. I pulled my briefcase to my lap. "I'll check his office now." I stood. "If you can think of anything that might help me locate the diaries, call me." I gave them both a card with my cellphone number on it. Gunnar moved to the door and opened it. I gave first Eales, then St. James, a penetrating look. "The sooner I find these things the sooner I'm out of here, and the less I disrupt your work." At the door I turned once more. "Think about it." Then to Gunnar. "I don't need an escort. I can find my own way."

It was Eales who responded. "There are limits to my patience. Don't try them." And he nodded to Gunnar.

"Are you normally stationed here?"

Unlike most PR professionals, Gunnar made no attempt to be social. "Ottawa," was all he said, but it was exactly the answer I wanted. I'd been pretty sure he wasn't from here. He didn't have a tan, his accent was Ottawa Valley, and his grey suit and bow tie just didn't say Hawaii.

"Which department?"

"Astronomy Institute. Director of Communications — Acting." He pulled out a business card and handed it to me.

I tucked it in my pocket. "So you'd know Amanda Sims."

He gave me a sideways glance. "I doubt it."

"Science reporter for the *Ottawa Citizen*?"

"I work at the policy level. My staff would know her."

Not likely, since Amanda Sims didn't exist. "If you work in Ottawa what are you doing here?"

We'd gone around a corner and had now arrived at Grenier's office door. McNabb unlocked it and motioned me through first. "Containment." He stepped in behind me and shut the door.

Grenier's office was small, neat, and in shades of grey. The wall directly in front of me was ceiling to floor glass, with a door that led outside to a lawn the colour of Astroturf. Grenier's desk sat almost in the middle of the room with a computer arm off to the side and two guest chairs in front. Behind these was a wall of books.

I swung around. "I thought you did policy?"

Gunnar crossed to the windows and opened glass louvres to let some much-needed fresh air into the room, then turned around backlit by the windows. It was, I noted, a cop trick, putting your conversational partner at an immediate disadvantage. Where had he picked that up?

"We're concerned about media fallout. I'm here to keep an eye on things until they settle down. A bit of a perk for me, really."

I looked at the monsoon outside. Some perk. It was probably warmer and drier in Ottawa right now. As for media fallout, what was the Institute expecting? Most Canadians didn't even know we had a telescope in Hawaii, and unless Grenier's death involved sex, drugs, or reality TV, they couldn't care less. "Have any reporters been sniffing around?"

"I'm afraid I've just arrived so I haven't been fully apprised."

I almost smiled. This guy was not only an excellent liar but also a master of half-truth and evasion, the exact set of qualifications that allowed him to excel in the field of public relations. I watched as he crossed back toward the door, but instead of leaving, as I'd hoped he would, he took up a position directly in front of the desk. With his back against the bookcases, he crossed his arms and prepared to watch my every move. It was supposed to intimidate me, make me hurry through my task, but I had all the time in the world. Probably a lot more than Gunnar McNabb. I moseyed over to Grenier's desk, pulled out his chair, and sat down with a sigh of comfort. I tried a few drawers, which were all open, and then I smiled over to Gunnar.

"Might as well sit down. You're going to be here for a while."

He gave me no facial reaction whatsoever. He pulled one of the guest chairs over and sank into it. Then he sat, back straight, arms crossed over his chest, and watched me. He wasn't going to make this easy.

When he was firmly seated I stood, walked over to the door, and opened it. "It's a little stuffy in here," I said. *And I want every single staff member to see me going through Grenier's desk*. But that, I didn't say. I wondered if Gunnar would get up and close the door, but, as I'd hoped, he didn't. He obviously figured I couldn't get into too much trouble under his watchful eye. Unfortunately, he was right.

Duncan had given me a description of the diaries — bound blue notebooks just like we used to use in chemistry lab — so I knew what I was looking for. I also knew I probably wouldn't find them in Grenier's office, but that wasn't why I was here. I pulled out my notebook, laid it on the desk, and pulled the first drawer out onto the desk. I carefully removed, examined, and catalogued every item in the drawer. When I'd finished that, I moved on to drawer number two. At my current rate, it would take me approximately three hours just to complete his desk.

As I worked, I saw several people pass the office in the hall outside. By the time I'd finished the second drawer word had gotten out that someone was rifling Grenier's desk and traffic had picked up considerably. Some people stopped and stared. A few even approached the door, but they backed off when they saw McNabb seated like a prison guard on the chair across from me. McNabb, I noted with satisfaction, had begun to squirm, and that was my cue. I pulled out the third drawer and put it on the desk, then I lifted my briefcase onto the chair, opened it, and made it look like I was pulling something out and stuffing it in the pocket of my jeans.

"I'll be back in a minute. I just need to use the ladies'." We'd passed it on the way here, so I didn't wait for a response. I just breezed out the door.

At the bathroom door I gave a quick glance up and down the hall, saw no one, and pushed the door open, letting it bang shut, then I scooted across the hall into an empty seminar room, leaving the lights off but the door wide open. I leaned on the wall just inside the door and waited. It took seven minutes. I heard a light step coming down the hall. It stopped outside the ladies' room, then shuffled impatiently. Finally, the staccato click of high heels approached from the direction of the office. McNabb directed the woman to check the stalls. A minute later she was out with the unfortunate news. They were empty.

"Shit," said McNabb, and the sound of his footfalls diminished as he took off in the direction of the office. There was no sound for a moment, then the heels clicked into the bathroom and the door swished shut. McNabb had left Grenier's office door open, but the instant I was back inside I closed it. I didn't have much time.

The first thing I did was grab an agenda from Grenier's desk and stuff it in my leather jacket. Next, I hit the callers button on his phone and scrolled to the day before his death. I wrote down the names of the people who'd called Grenier that day, the following day, and the day after he died. I would have liked to get the names of all the callers, but my time was limited. Next I moved on to his speed-dial and copied down the ten names there. I'd just gotten into his directory when I heard a soft knock at the door. I froze. Was it locked or not? There was another soft tap, the door opened, and a small, round man slipped inside and shut the door quietly behind him.

"They are looking all over for you," he remarked in a beautifully articulated French accent. Then he stepped forward, took a furtive glance over his shoulder, and said, "Andreas Mellier, at your service. I was thinking that maybe you might like an escape route."

Actually, I'd planned to let myself out Grenier's back door, but Mellier was offering me an intriguing alternative.

He glanced at his watch. "And it is lunchtime. Perhaps you would care to — " There was a shuffle outside and the door swung open. Mellier did a quick pirouette, which brought him face to face with McNabb, or face to shoulder, to be more accurate. "Ah! It is Monsieur McNabb," he said with a grin. Then he motioned to me. "You see? I have found your fugitive and she has agreed to have lunch with me at the Ranch House Restaurant. I am a very lucky man." He put out his arm. "Shall we?"

I linked my arm through his, gave McNabb a dazzling smile, and waltzed out the door on Mellier's arm.

chapter five

The waitress showed the bottle of pinot noir to Mellier, and he nodded. She poured a bit in his glass. He smelled it, swirled it, sniffed, and finally took a sip before giving her a nod of approval. I put my hand over my own glass. I was already feeling the effects of jet lag compounded with a lost night of sleep. The last thing I needed was to pour alcohol on top of that.

Mellier gave a *tsk tsk* and poured himself a big glass. "You will go up to the observatory after this?" he asked. I nodded. "Then you have the steak. You will need the hemoglobin. Shelley." The waitress was already halfway across the open floor headed for the kitchen, but she turned at the sound of Mellier's voice. He was obviously a regular. He raised two fingers, and she gave a nod. Good thing I wasn't a vegetarian. He turned back to me. "Why were you in Yves's office? I would like to know this, please."

We'd come in separate cars down the main street of Waimea to a restaurant more reminiscent of Little Joe and the Ponderosa than tropical Hawaii. The exterior of the Ranch House Restaurant was log surrounded by a wide, covered porch. The inside was sombre: rough planks; heavy, dark wood furniture; and a decor of wagon wheels, oil lamps, saddles, and bullwhips. The only thing that didn't fit was the damp chill, and I'd been relieved when the waitress led Mellier to a table in front of a huge field-stone fireplace, complete with blazing fire. I'd pulled my chair right up to the hearth and was now trying to absorb the dry heat through my leather jacket.

This was my first chance to really observe Mellier, and I'd quickly realized that he was no buffoon despite first impressions. Given the adroit way he'd just avoided the question I'd asked him, I suspected his bumptious style was a ruse to hide the razor sharp mind behind the glasses. I needed to keep my wits about me.

"My question first," I responded.

He lifted his glass and took a sip, keeping his eyes level on mine. He was assessing me, much as I was him. Finally he put it down. "Why did I help you? This is what you want to know? It is very simple. I helped you because you piss everybody off and I like that. It means we perhaps have compatible interests."

"And what interests are those?"

"But you did not answer *my* question. Why were you in Yves's office?"

It was too early in the investigation to trust anyone, especially Andreas Mellier. Mellier was, in fact, the French astronomer that Grenier had worked with the night of his death, and this made Mellier a prime candidate for pilfering the diaries. I needed to play him carefully, giving out just enough information to get something useful back in return, at least until I could figure out what he was up to. I started with what he probably already knew, or what he would know by the end of the afternoon when the gossip train had finished its run through the telescope headquarters.

"I'm an investigator. I've been sent by the Canadian government to tie up some loose ends around Dr. Grenier's death."

"An investigator? Really? Why should I believe you?"

I pulled out my ID card and passed it over to him. He examined it, then handed it back. "In Paris I can go down a back alley, I pay someone fifty euros, and they make me a card like this in less than one hour. It doesn't mean much."

"Do you know anything about Dr. Grenier's diaries?"

Mellier raised an eyebrow. "Perhaps."

"So you know they're missing."

"I've heard this, yes."

"I've been sent to bring them back. If you don't believe me, call the Minister of Industry and Science. The number's on the Internet."

His expression changed. "That makes me really angry. That makes me really, *really* angry." He hit the table with his fist. "Don't you people care about what happened to Yves?" Several diners glanced uneasily in our direction. "A good man is dead for no reason, and you goddamned Canadians, Edwin, St. James, that idiot McNabb, all you care about is to cover up what happened. What is the matter with you people?" He threw his napkin on the table. "I was hoping that maybe you are different. That you come from Canada ready to ask some real questions rather than hide the truth." He gave a Gallic shrug. "You pissed off the others so much I think that maybe you are not working with them, but obviously I am wrong." He started to get up. "You will have to eat alone, I am afraid."

I put out my hand to restrain him. "Are you saying that Eales and St. James are trying to hide the circumstances around Grenier's death?"

"I'm saying they're lying, yes. Everyone is lying. Perhaps even the police."

I remembered Benson's willingness to *help a neighbour*, an almost inexplicable behaviour in a cop. "Did you voice your concerns to the police?"

"They don't want to hear. They think I'm some crazy Frenchman who sees aliens and the CIA under my bed, but I can tell you something. I work with Yves for many years. He did not jump that night. I know this for sure."

"Suicide is notoriously unpredictable. It's possible you wouldn't have known."

"Then why is Shelton lying? What is he afraid of?"

"Shelton Aimes? The telescope operator?" And the last person to see Grenier alive.

"Sure. You want to see for yourself? He works at the telescope tonight. I take you there and we have a little talk with Shelton." He poked the air in my direction. "You're the investigator. You see if he's telling the truth."

I sat back in my chair and took a moment to weigh the pros and cons. The waitress arrived with two plates, although they were barely visible beneath the huge slabs of meat on each one. When she was gone I leaned toward Mellier and said quietly, "It's a police investigation. I can't just waltz in."

At that his dark eyes twinkled. "Ah! You mean like you did in Yves's office."

He let me squirm under that for a few seconds, then he reached out and put his hand on my arm. "I know more about Yves Grenier and those diaries than anyone else in Hawaii. You help me find who pushed him, I help you find the diaries. Perhaps we will, what is the expression in English? Kill the two birds with one stone."

Driving is my meditation, a time when I can let my mind detach from the rational world and move into a deep subconscious process that sorts and organizes information in entirely new ways. When I left Mellier on the porch of the restaurant, with an agreement to meet him later at the Astronomy Centre, I needed a long drive. My subconscious was writhing with little worms of information that refused to be stilled. Maybe by the time I reached Hale Pohaku and the Astronomy Centre, I'd have a few of those worms under control.

I was about to turn the key in the SUV when I remembered something and checked my watch. It was just past two o'clock here in Hawaii, making it five hours later, around seven o'clock, in Ottawa. Lydia might be home. I reached for my cellphone and hit the speed-dial. If I was really lucky, I could stamp out a few of these wrigglers before I even got started. After a series of buzzes and clicks the line connected.

"Hey, Lyd, no classes tonight? No Firearms 101 or Interviewing 302?"

"I am trying to study for my final exams," she said pointedly, "in between your assignment, of course. Are you settled in Hawaii?"

"Settled wouldn't quite describe it. You turned up anything yet?"

"You mean in the brief time I've had since you called?" She let that hang for a minute. "Interestingly no, although not for want of trying. I did have an excellent lunch today with the minister's personal assistant. Like so many of our public servants she does enjoy The Canal Ritz, but then you'll see that when you get the bill."

Hey, I wasn't paying. I couldn't care less. Duncan's budget came from the minister, so the minister had just taken Lydia and his own secretary out to lunch. As far as I was concerned, they both deserved it. "You asked her about the telescope, discreetly I presume?"

"Really, Morgan, I've been at this a long time one way or the other. Yes, I did mention the telescope, and that's what's interesting. I am quite sure she's never heard of it, much less any controversy surrounding your astronomer's death. Just to verify I made a few other calls on your behalf — all very discreet of course — and they confirm my first impression. The rank and file know nothing of it, which, you must admit, is curious."

Both curious and unusual. It meant that this investigation was "need to know" only, even within the minister's office. It seemed a bit extreme. "What about the other thing? Did you get a lead on Duncan's wife?"

There was a pause just long enough to let me know that Lydia still didn't approve. "Not as yet. I should have something by the end of the day tomorrow."

Something in her tone caught me. "You're not holding out on me, are you? You haven't talked to Duncan?"

"That, Morgan, would be unethical, and I, at least, try to avoid that. Now I really must go and study. I have forensic science tomorrow." The line went dead.

I pressed the "end" button and pushed the phone aerial in, then laid the phone on the console between the two seats, all the while replaying that last exchange. Lydia hadn't actually answered my question, so that left it hanging. Had she been in contact with Duncan?

With a sigh I started the truck, pulled out of the parking lot, and headed back toward the telescope headquarters. Just beyond the headquarters there was a turnoff to the Saddle Road. On my map the Saddle Road appeared as a narrow squiggly line that cut right across the centre of the island, crossing the high mountains through a pass between the peaks of Mauna Kea and Mauna Loa. At the highest point on the Saddle Road, just before it began its descent into Hilo, there was a faint broken line that snaked up to the summit of Mauna Kea. Halfway up this line was a little dot labelled Hale Pohaku, the location of the Astronomy Centre, and my home for the next few days.

By the time I reached the turnoff the rain had let up but a heavy mist still poured from the cliffs above, hiding the terrain around me. The Saddle Road began with about the width of a driveway, and by a few metres in it had degraded to a track of broken asphalt. The first turn was a blind twist, then the road shot straight up. I scrambled to gear down and the truck lurched forward. With my hands gripping the wheel and my foot on the gas, I gave up any idea of disengaging. If someone came barrelling down the road we'd both be dead.

After ten minutes of what felt like a vertical climb the mist began to thin, and I saw light above. I came around another corner, then I unexpectedly shot out of the fog into clear blue sky and an intense and dazzling sun. I was in a high chaparral of rock, stunted Ponderosa pine, sage bush, and low, spreading cacti. A few long-horn cattle lifted their heads as the truck rumbled by, but they quickly went back to pulling at the tufts of grass that poked out between the cacti. Then the road levelled and opened up into a wide, flat valley of yellow grasses and low shrub. Mauna Loa rose on my right like a soft green swell. On the left, the peak of Mauna Kea loomed above me, a fortress of rock.

With the road flat and wide enough to see oncoming traffic, I now could let my mind wander. I began with Mellier. What was he up to? Was he only interested in the death of his friend, or was there something else? I ran through our conversation from several directions, dissecting it for inconsistencies and possible untruths, but I could find nothing glaring. Still, something wasn't right. Why, for starters, would Mellier trust me? He didn't trust anyone else, so why had he waltzed me out of Grenier's office? What did he know, and what was in it for him? I mulled that over and didn't get anywhere, so I filed it away for more work. Maybe I'd know more after our trip to the telescope.

Then there was the problem of Duncan; too many little things that didn't add up. How did the minister's office find out about Grenier's death so quickly? Benson didn't tell them, unless his surprise at seeing me was feigned. And it wouldn't have been Eales or St. James, since they obviously didn't want outside interference. So who was it?

Then I realized that two of the worms were related.

Someone had sent the minister's office a photograph of Yves Grenier hanging off the telescope, and it must have been taken a very short time after his death to arrive in Ottawa so early. That meant several things. Someone on-site in Hawaii knew of the minister's interest in Yves Grenier. And, whoever this person was, he or she had either police connections or unauthorized access to the crime scene. I gave myself a good, swift mental kick. If I hadn't been so damned preoccupied with Duncan's personal problems I would never have left that café without the name of the Hawaiian source. I filed away another mental note. Squeeze Duncan, and squeeze him good. He was withholding information, and that's not allowed.

I was just moving on to Edwin Eales when I saw a turnoff whiz by in my peripheral vision. It had been hidden behind a low bush. I jammed on the brakes, pulled a three-point turn in the middle of the road, and aimed myself up the switchback with my subconscious firmly switched off. My first destination was the Astronomy Centre halfway up to the summit. After a little nap I'd continue up to the dome.

I slept like the dead. A few hours later, with no idea where I was, I opened my eyes a crack. I was in a bed, which was good, and the bed was comfy and warm, but my eyes felt like sand and my sinuses had hardened to a crust. My nose and ears were also numb with cold. I lifted my head, the room came into focus, and my mind kicked in.

I was in the Astronomy Centre in my monastic single room, a small box decorated in shades of white, grey, and pale wood. A neat little desk was built into the corner, and beside it were a dresser and an armoire. The only luxury was a private bathroom with shower. And, I seemed to remember, a drinking glass for water. I struggled a little higher. If I made a dash for the bathroom I could jack up the electric heat on my way back then snuggle up in bed until the temperature climbed above freezing. I took a deep breath, threw off the cover, and three seconds later was back under the blanket guzzling fluid. The heater had already begun to buzz and creak, and moments later waves of heat rose through the air.

When I'd arrived here a few hours earlier I'd been so exhausted that I hadn't even bothered to change. I'd just dropped into bed in the same clothes I'd worn since I got off the plane. Part of my exhaustion was jet lag. Part was from the short walk uphill between the parking lot and the Centre. At home I would have taken those forty stone steps at a run, jogging up them two at a time. Here, I'd only been able to manage three risers before putting down my bag to rest. Then three more steps, and another rest. Even standing still it felt like I was breathing through a straw. No matter how hard I sucked there was never enough air.

I gulped down more of the water and felt my nose rehydrate and my ears begin to thaw. The bedside clock blinked 6:12 p.m. in red LED numbers, and outside dusk was falling. Mellier might be downstairs already, but I had a few things to take care of before I could meet him, and the first of these was to take a shower. I braved the cold and leapt out of bed.

Fifteen minutes later I was a new woman, dressed and ready to go, including wool socks, long underwear, and a down vest. If it was this cold here at the lower elevation it was going to be brutal on the summit. I checked the clock again and did a rapid calculation. In Ottawa it would be near midnight, too late to call Duncan with his young children, but Vancouver was three hours earlier. Sylvia would just be warming up. I picked up the phone.

As usual, she was already connected to the Internet. I could hear her tapping away even as she lifted the phone to her ear. "Hey babe," she said, before I even had a chance to say hello. "Duncan said you'd call."

Sylvia is the best science librarian in the federal government system, and both Duncan and I make use of her services often. Still, it was curious that Duncan would have called and mentioned me. "When was this?"

"Yesterday. He called me and asked for a search then told me to send it by e-mail to you. Said you'd be requesting it anyway when you got around to it. He knows you too well. How's Hawaii?"

I looked around at the spartan room and felt the itch of my long johns. "It's not your scene. Trust me on that."

"Yeah right. Try again." There was a clatter of tapping in the background. "Are you online?"

"Not right now. What's up?"

"I just sent it off. You have a complete reference search on Yves Grenier." Then I heard another burst of rapid-fire typing. "And there goes Andreas Mellier. Anything else?"

"Duncan requested a search on Andreas Mellier?"

"You bet. Looks like most of his work is co-published with Yves Grenier. Quite the publishing record, the two of them. What are they up to? Cooking the books? Creative data management?"

I didn't answer. My mind was preoccupied with another question. Why would Duncan have asked for that search? What was behind it? Then I came back to reality. "Can you add two more to the list?"

"Fire away."

"Edwin Eales and Anthony St. James. But there's something else."

"If I charge for it, it's yours."

"Physics is more your line than mine. Can you look over the stuff when it comes in? See if anything juicy hops off the page?"

"Give me a hint. What are we looking for? Fraud? Data theft? It helps if I know."

I thought about that for a minute, but the answer that came out of my mouth surprised even me. "A motive for murder."

There was silence at the other end. Even the tapping ceased. "What has Duncan gotten you into?"

Sylvia had become a little too maternal since my last brush with death, and I didn't like it. I'd already had one mother, and she'd been one too many. "It's my job, remember?"

"A homicide investigation? Last time I checked you did research fraud and embezzlement. When did your job description change?"

"Just find me anyone whose research might benefit from Grenier's death, or at the very least from his research notes." Once I had a list of possible competitors I could cross-check the names against the list of people on Mauna Kea the night of Grenier's death. If nothing else, I could pass the information on to Benson in fulfillment of the agreement I'd made with him.

There was a long-suffering sigh on the other end. "Just watch your back, O'Brien. I prefer my friends alive."

So do I, I thought, *but some of us don't have that choice.* I, however, kept those thoughts to myself. Sylvia hates maudlin, particularly when it's directed at her, and given the tumour growing in her brain — the result of high levels of estrogen used to transform her from a David to a Sylvia Delgado — it often is. I gave a rather too abrupt goodbye and hung up the phone.

My second order of business was a quick check of the e-mail just to make sure nothing urgent had come in. I plugged my laptop into the high-speed connection and within seconds my account was before me. There were the usual reams of crap: messages on the new interpretations of the workforce adjustment policy, nomination forms for brown-noser — that would be employee — of the year, and several contributions to the office humour file. I whacked it all without reading. Sylvia's e-mail reference searches popped up, and I downloaded them to my hard drive. I'd get to those as soon as I could.

Finally, and with trepidation, I opened an e-mail from my boss, Bob. He would be seriously ticked at my temporary appointment to the prestigious Minister's Office, and really out of whack if he knew the assignment was in Hawaii. The e-mail, I was sure, would be a written harangue ordering me to stay in touch (meaning tell Bob everything about the case, whether it was his business or not), a list of five additional files I should handle while I was away, and an order to be back in the office by the end of the week. Instead, this is what he wrote.

Morgan:

Don't worry about the office. Everything is taken care of here. Get lots of rest and come back when you're fit as a fiddle.

Bob

Get lots of rest? He thought this was a Hawaiian vacation. I looked outside at the sun setting low over desolate rock. If only he knew.

"I have not good news. I don't think they'll talk." That was Mellier, speaking for the first time on the entire ride up to the summit. I'd wondered if he was preoccupied with Grenier's death or just scared speechless by my driving.

From the Astronomy Centre there was only one road up to the summit, and it ran in a series of abrupt switchbacks up a steep slope of rubble. The road itself seemed to have been scraped out of loose rock. The outer edge was ragged as if ready to crumble at the weight of the truck, and if it did give way there was nothing to stop us tumbling from here to the Saddle Road miles below. As if that weren't enough, each turn of the switchback was so tight I had to fight with the lumbering four-by-four to bring it around in time. When we finally arrived near the summit the road flattened onto what looked at first like a wide plateau but was in fact a broad bowl. Like a scene from an apocalyptic thriller, it was an endless vista of lifeless rubble housing an enchanted city of pale domes. Cast against the blackness of the sky and crescent moon it was an eerie sight. Mellier told me to turn off the headlights.

"Who is 'they'?" I said, slowing and keeping my eyes on the road.

"Shelton. And Elizabeth Martin. She is the staff astronomer on duty tonight."

Mellier directed me to the last dome at the end of the road, the FrancoCanadian Telescope, and I pulled into the small parking area. Two FCT trucks were already there. The truck rocked, buffeted by the wind.

When the motor was off he said with an apologetic tone. "It's possible they don't even let you in." Then he turned to the landscape and spoke without looking at me. If his sadness was feigned he was a world-class actor. "You know, Shelton I understand. He has something to hide. But Elizabeth? She and Yves were very close friends. Why will she not help?" He let that hang for a good minute, then he seemed to return to himself. "Oh well." He gave a shrug and an impish grin. "Why don't we at least see how far we can get. Maybe we will make it right to the observing room and surprise them both."

"What are they going to do, physically remove me?"

"Ah," he said, "you have not met Pexa." Then he opened his door and hopped out of the truck.

I ran through my mental files. Pexa. The guy who found Yves Grenier hanging from the telescope and called 911. I smiled to myself. No, I hadn't met him yet, but I was looking forward to the moment I did. With that thought I tucked my briefcase under the driver's seat and swung the door open. The wind hit me like a solid wall, and I had to throw my weight against the door to get it shut. Then, eyes watering, I fought my way step by step to the observatory doors. Between the sound of the gale and the snap of my jacket in the wind it was bedlam out there. By the time I reached the doors Mellier was already inside. He held the door open and I moved into blessed silence and gulped down air. I felt like I'd run a 5 k.

"Come this way," said Mellier quietly.

We were standing in a small foyer, and at the end of it were two steel doors, one leading to the left, the other to the right. He pulled open the left-hand door.

"*Merde,*" he said loudly and leapt back. On the other side of the door, leaning against the wall, stood a big, dark-skinned man with a beautifully chiselled face and short black hair. He had his arms across his chest. He'd been waiting in ambush.

"Andreas," he said with a slight nod of his head.

Mellier moved forward and flicked the guy's arm with his hand. "You almost give me a heart attack. What are you doing here? Your shift is over." Then to me. "This is Pexa. He is the building manager, but only by day." He spoke up to Pexa. "At night the astronomers take over. Okay, Pexa, now we go in."

Mellier began to walk around him, but Pexa moved to the middle of the narrow hall. "I'm sorry, Andreas."

Despite his size he moved with an agile grace, and I had the impression it would take bulldozer to move him, but Mellier took him on.

"You're blocking me? This is absurd. I'm the senior astronomer here. You can't block me from my own observatory."

At that Pexa moved slightly aside. "You're right. You stay, but she goes."

Now it was my turn. I kept my voice like his: low, commanding, and calm. "I don't know who the hell you think you are, but I'm an here on an official investigation. I go where I want."

I started to move forward, but he took a step toward me. "Not up here, you don't."

I took a step closer to him. "You're the one who found Grenier, aren't you?"

He gave a nod but didn't answer.

I pulled out my notebook and flipped it open to a new page. "Who was it who called you?"

He was watching me with a veiled expression. "Elizabeth Martin."

"And what time would that have been precisely?"

His response was cool. "I've told the police everything they need to know."

"The police investigation is still open, and as long as I'm in Hawaii I'll make damn sure it stays open." I took another step forward so I was now within inches of Pexa's face. "And you know what that means? That means you're going to be questioned again, and again, and again, either here or down at police headquarters. You'll be questioned until both Detective Benson and I are satisfied with your answers. So what time did you say you got that call?" Then a light went on in my head. "Now isn't that interesting. Look who we have in the dome tonight: Shelton Aimes, the last person to see Yves Grenier alive; Elizabeth Martin, the first person to see Grenier's suicide note; and Pexa, the first person on the scene. I can see why you don't want me around."

Pexa put his hand on my shoulder and firmly turned me in the direction of the door. He maintained the dead calm in his voice, but my last statement seemed to have hit a nerve. "Under the safety statutes and laws of the FrancoCanadian Telescope Corporation, the telescope operator has absolute authority to determine who may be in the dome. You've been ordered off the mountain for your own safety."

He'd gotten me as far as the foyer. "For my own safety? That's a load of crap."

"Don't be fooled, Ms O'Brien," he said. "It's a dangerous place up here. Real easy to get hurt."

Mellier stepped around Pexa and puffed himself up to his full five foot two. "This isn't over. I walk her first to her truck then I come back here and we settle this once and for all. First with you, then Shelton and Elizabeth. This is an abomination."

I smiled to myself. If I didn't know better I'd say that Mellier had been at this game as long as I had. Then I stopped up short. For all I knew maybe he had.

chapter six

When we were back outside and I was seated in the truck I asked, "How long can you keep him busy?"

Mellier leaned in the truck window. He glanced briefly at Pexa standing in the doorway then turned back to me. With the howling wind there was no way that Pexa could overhear our conversation. "Long enough. I will try to get Elizabeth too. Then you'll have Shelton all to yourself. I can't guarantee, but perhaps."

"The two of them together I can handle. Just get Rambo out of the way."

He told me quickly where to hide the truck and, once back inside the dome, how to find my way to the observing room. When he was finished he straightened and stepped away from the SUV, his sparse hair standing upright in the wind. He glanced uneasily at the dome, then back at me, as if he were trying to decide something. He took a decisive step forward and tapped on the glass. I brought the window back down. This time he put his head right in and spoke more softly.

"What Pexa said about the dome being dangerous, it is not a joke. Just remember when you're inside, there are bottles of oxygen everywhere. If you feel dizzy or sick, you stop, you use the oxygen. Don't take a chance if you're alone." He tapped his watch. "Nine o'clock here. I don't see you, I notify the others and we begin to search."

It wasn't a cheering thought, but I gave him a nod and reached for the headlight switch. His hand shot forward. "No headlights on the hill. You'll screw up the observations." He moved his hand to my arm and gave it a squeeze. "Be careful."

When he was back inside I reversed the truck and swung around onto the trail that would take me up a rise to the Gemini Telescope. I got my last view of Mellier poking his finger accusingly into Pexa's solid chest. I hoped he could keep Pexa occupied for at least half an hour. It might take me that long to huff and puff my way back down the three hundred metres that separated the two telescopes.

When I reached the Gemini Telescope I slowed and came cautiously around the base of the dome. It was a massive structure, one of the biggest on the mountain, and tucked into the base was a large loading dock just as Mellier had described. The loading dock bay was huge, the length of a semi and twice as wide. With no outside lighting on the summit, and no headlights either, it would be impossible to see even a large truck parked in its recesses. And, as Mellier had explained, Gemini used remote observing. Tonight's Gemini astronomers were sipping coffee in a warm office somewhere down in Hilo while the remote-controlled telescope streamed images back to them. There would be nobody up here to notice my truck.

I reversed and backed into the furthest corner, turned off the engine, and checked my watch. Five minutes, on top of the time it would take me to get back down to the FrancoCanadian Telescope, should give Mellier enough time to move Pexa out of the way and start a good yelling match somewhere else in the dome.

With the engine cut a vicious cold seeped into the vehicle, and despite all the clothing my teeth began to chatter. It was bizarre. I'd lived through much colder weather in Canada, but this cold was so penetrating that it seemed to cut right to the vital organs, possibly a consequence of oxygen deprivation. I checked the inner pockets of my leather jacket for my flashlight, lock picks, and other tools, zipped my coat back up, and slid out of the truck. I closed the door quietly behind me and crunched my way across the gravel to the entry of the loading dock. The land around me stood in relief: looming pillars of rock black against the deep blue sky and the huge ghost-like domes pale against the rock. I moved a bit further out and strained to hear, but with the wind buffeting the metal above I wouldn't hear a Sherman tank coming up this road. I had no choice. I pulled up my collar, regretted that I hadn't brought a toque, and headed down the hill.

Fifteen minutes later I was back in the FrancoCanadian observatory hallway sucking back air as if I'd just scaled Everest. I stood still long enough to run through Mellier's instructions in my mind then pushed myself off the wall and got moving. I took the same door Mellier had earlier, only this time there was no Pexa to stop me. An in/out board, the one I'd seen on Benson's video, was just inside the door. According to the magnets, four people were presently in the dome: Mellier, Pexa, Martin, and Aimes.

That, at least, was a relief. There were no other itinerant astronomers that I might bump into.

At the end of the hallway I found the door to the stairwell and slipped inside. I was standing in a dark narrow chute with metal walls, the claustrophobic's nightmare. The steep, open risers seemed to disappear into the gloom above. Like everything else I'd seen so far — riveted metal walls, the round portals in doors, dim lights, and no windows — this place felt more like a submarine sitting in the Mariana Trench than an observatory perched on top of the world.

It was a brutal climb to the fifth floor, and I had to stop every few steps to gasp. By the time I reached the top my legs wobbled and my head spun. I sank down on the landing and noticed an oxygen bottle hanging on the wall. It was tempting, but I had no idea if the things made noise, so I decided to wait it out. When I could finally breathe again I stood, moved forward, and peeked through the portal. There was no movement or noise, but as Mellier had promised my destination was in sight: a pair of swinging doors just to my left had "Observing Room" written above them. This, Mellier had told me, was the telescope's control room. Within this small, heated space the telescope operator monitored and controlled the telescope, and observing astronomers watched as their images and data flowed from the telescope through the computer to the monitors inside. I crossed the hall, pushed open the doors, and stepped inside.

A lanky young man sat in a swivel chair with his back to me. "We're ready to roll," he said, not turning around. He was facing what looked like the console of a NASA shuttle. In addition to watching an array of buttons, switches, gauges, and flashing indicator lights, his gaze seemed to dance over three computer screens arranged around him on an L-shaped counter. Each displayed a different image. "I'd say we're good," he confirmed, then he twirled around to face me.

"Hello, Shelton," I said.

I revised my first impression. Shelton Aimes wasn't lanky, he was thin to the point of gauntness and looked like he needed a Hawaiian vacation. His hair was greasy and parted haphazardly on the side, his skin pale and his cheeks hollow. The eyes, though, were huge and luminous, magnified by the lenses in his aviator glasses. It gave him a look of permanent surprise.

I stepped forward. With a thrust of his legs he backed his chair against the counter. "Who are you?"

"I think you know that already. May I sit down?"

He didn't say anything, but didn't move either. Then one hand darted for the phone. I crossed the room in an instant and snatched it before he could lift the receiver. I put it back on the desk, unplugged it, then pulled up a chair. Mellier has been right about one thing. Shelton Aimes was scared, but I wondered if it was a chronic state.

"I don't have to talk to you," he said.

"But why wouldn't you? One of your colleagues is dead, and all I have is a few simple questions. Nothing difficult, nothing incriminating. Not that you have anything to hide, but there are some details that just don't add up. Did you know I'm working with Detective Benson?"

I could see sweat on the fuzz above his lip. "I already spoke to him."

"And he told me you were very helpful, but there are a few things that have cropped up and you're the only person who can help us."

"I'm working tonight. I'm busy here. Look." He twisted around and poked the monitor to his left. "Do you know what that is?"

It looked like a swirling blob of red and blue. I shook my head.

"It's a front coming in. We have four, maybe five hours to get in a whole night of observations because when that thing hits everybody's off the mountain." He seemed to gain a little confidence. "I don't have time to piss around with questions."

"Fair enough, but either we do it here or Benson and I bring you into the station, and I can promise you it'll be way more convenient to do it here. So what do you say, Shelton? Just a few quick questions?" His leg was vibrating with tension, but he didn't say no, so I continued. "The night that Yves died —"

"That he committed suicide."

"The night that he died —"

The door swished open behind me. "What about that night?" A woman strode forward, yanked the telephone line from my hand, and jammed it back in the phone, then swung around on me, effectively blocking Shelton from my view. "What the fuck do you think you're doing. I've been trying to call him. Get out of here."

It was a powerful entrance, and even though they were on the same team Shelton cowered. Despite her physical presence the woman was tiny, not more than five feet tall, and even in the bulky clothes she'd be lucky to weigh in at a hundred pounds. Her blonde hair was tied back in a neat ponytail.

"You must be Elizabeth Martin. It's a pleasure." Then I moved my chair over so I could see Shelton and continued as if she'd never arrived. "The night of Dr. Grenier's death, did he have his research diary with him?"

He pushed his glasses up on his nose and glanced at Elizabeth. I looked meaningfully at her, then back at him. "It's a simple question, Shelton. It doesn't require Dr. Martin to get an answer."

"He doesn't have to answer you," she said. "You're not a cop."

I ignored her again and kept my eyes locked on Shelton. "Just tell me the truth, Shelton."

"I don't remember."

"That's odd, because Andreas Mellier told me that at one point in the evening you asked Dr. Grenier to check in his diary for a telescope positioning from the week before."

"I'm calling Pexa," said Elizabeth, and she reached for the phone.

I finally looked at her. "It won't change a thing. I'm staying until Shelton answers."

"He doesn't want to talk to you. Can't you see that?"

Shelton had paled considerably since I'd arrived. "Did Yves have his current diary in the dome that night? Yes or no."

Shelton nodded reluctantly.

"And did he have the diary with him when he left the building?"

He turned away and fiddled with his computer mouse. "I don't know." Then he said louder. "I don't know." He stood abruptly. "I think I'm going to be sick," he said and bolted from the room.

Elizabeth watched him leave then turned on me. "You complete asshole. If I lose Shelton tonight, if he's not here to operate the telescope, I lose a whole night of observing. Do you know what that means? No, of course you don't, because you're from Ottawa. So let me explain. I have five nights." She jammed her fingers in my face in case I couldn't count. "Five nights. That's five nights all year booked to observe on this telescope. That's all I can get, that's all anyone can get, and thanks to you I've just lost one of them. Goddamnit." She turned away from me and wrapped her arms around herself. "Goddamnit!"

The outburst seemed to calm her slightly, and she turned. "What do you want? Just tell me. I'll help you if you promise to leave."

"Deal. What's Shelton hiding?"

"You need me to tell you that?" She flopped into the chair he'd vacated. "What the hell do you think? Guilt."

"Guilt? Why?"

"Because the telescope operator is responsible for the safety of everyone in the building. They can order someone off the mountain if they think they're too sick to stay and they ensure that everything is closed up and turned off at the end of the night. It's their responsibility to make sure that everyone gets out safely, then they lock up. Yves died on Shelton's watch. That's hard to get over."

"So it was Shelton who ordered Mellier off the mountain the night Yves died."

She glared at me. "I'm not going anywhere with that."

"Nor am I. I just need to understand." She barely nodded. I continued. "So if Shelton is responsible why didn't he check and make sure Yves got down?"

"He's not a babysitter. His responsibility ends when everyone's out and the doors are locked."

"Did Yves have his own key?"

"We all have keys, but you're not allowed in here alone, not under any circumstances. It voids our insurance." She stood up. "I've done my part. It's time for you to leave."

I stood. "You know it's not over. I'll get to Shelton eventually."

"But by the time you do —" Then she stopped herself.

"What?" Mellier stepped from a hidden door on the other side of the room. Where had he come from, and how long had he been there? He continued. "By the time she does, what, Elizabeth?"

She seemed less surprised to see him than I was. "Why are you helping her, Andreas?"

"Why are you *not* helping her? Yves was our friend."

"Exactly. Yves was our friend. And who do you think cares more about Yves? Her or me?" She kept her eyes on Andreas, but spoke to me. "Why don't you tell Andreas who sent you?"

"He already knows."

"Tell him anyway."

She said it as if she knew something that I didn't, and that made me uneasy. "The Minister of Industry and Science," I said carefully.

She'd taken on the tone of a TV lawyer. "And he's interested in what, exactly?"

She was pushing me toward some hidden trap, I could feel it. "They want the diaries. They belong to the government."

She swung around to me. "A tautology, Morgan O'Brien. They sent you here because they want the diaries. They want the diaries so they sent you here. But *why* do they want the diaries?"

The trap door swung open and I began to fall. She caught the momentary panic in my face and laughed. "They didn't tell you, did they?" She turned to Mellier. "They didn't tell her, Andreas. Do you know why? Because this isn't about Yves. They don't care about him. They only want the diaries. If they cared about Yves, how he died, do you think they would have sent …," and she gave me a look of disdain, "… her?"

I drove my truck back down alone. Mellier decided to stay up at the dome and help Elizabeth since Shelton had collapsed in the staff lounge and was attached to an oxygen mask. I took one peek in and even I didn't have the heart to question him, he looked so pitiful huddled in a down jacket with the mask plastered to his face. But as I'd said to Elizabeth, it wasn't over. I needed to know where that diary was when Grenier'd left the building, and Shelton was the only one who knew.

I'd also have another go at Elizabeth Martin, but I'd wait until my anger died down. She'd as much as told me I was being used, and that infuriated me, but the fury was fuelled by fear. Somewhere deep in the recesses of my mind a little voice was saying the same thing, and whether the interpretation of the facts held up under scrutiny, there was no denying the facts were solid. Bottom line, I didn't know why I was here, not the underlying reason why these diaries were so important, and that pissed me off. Not knowing the bigger picture was like walking in the forest without a map: I'd stumble blindly from tree to tree ending up in the same place that I began. It was no way to run an investigation.

Back at the Astronomy Centre I headed directly for the cafeteria. It was open all night, with the staff there sending up sandwiches and hot meals to the telescopes for a midnight "lunch." I ordered the daily special, some kind of congealed flesh in a glutinous liquid. The counter guy plucked it from the hot tray with tongs and it slid across my plate on a greasy emulsion. Perfect. I was ravenous and wouldn't get another chance to eat for some time. Given the cholesterol load, though, I opted for the salad bar over the French fries, along with a big glass of juice followed by coffee. I chose a table in the far corner of the room that looked across to the summit of Mauna Loa. Far below on the Saddle Road a set of headlights seemed to slither through the darkness. I poked the meat with my fork and four little geysers of fat spurted from the holes. A second later I was savouring what turned out to be a deliciously juicy pork chop in a sublime and delicate sauce. It's true, you can't always judge a book by its cover. I turned off my rational brain and let my primitive senses prevail.

Half an hour later, revived, I crossed the stone floor of the foyer and went slowly up the stairs that led to my room. At the door I stood for a moment. Earlier that evening the hallway had been bustling: doors opening and closing, astronomers, technicians, and engineers hurrying along the hall with heavy briefcases and down jackets slung over their arms. Now all I could hear were the occasional low voice and the clicking of a computer keyboard somewhere nearby.

I put the key in the lock and opened the door but stopped abruptly. It was the smell that caught me first, faint but unmistakable: the manly odour of a deodorant soap. I scanned the room. Nothing seemed to be out of place. I listened intently, then, keeping my head high, I edged over to the bathroom. I pushed the door open with my foot, edged my hand inside, and flicked on the light.

It was empty.

I crossed to my room door and closed it, then I looked around again. Someone had been here, but nothing seemed to be disturbed. I turned on all the lights and began a methodical search for anything out of place. My clothes were hanging as I'd left them; the bed may have been further rumpled, but it was hard to say. I bent down and pulled my suitcase out from under the bed. It was still locked, but there were telltale scratches around the locks. I pulled out my key and opened it. Everything was as I'd left it.

At the bathroom door I stood for a moment and studied the position of my hairbrush, the placement of my shampoo, the exact angle of my toothbrush, all those things that I make myself aware of before I leave a hotel room. Nothing was out of place, and that made me nervous. Whoever had been in here was no amateur. Still, Locard's Law of Exchange had to apply. Whoever had been in my room must have left something behind and taken something away. Hopefully they would have left something behind more macroscopic than a carpet fibre, a strand of hair, or a trace of DNA. I didn't exactly have a crime lab at my disposal.

I pulled out my flashlight, returned to the main room, and threw my leather jacket on the bed. I was sure my suitcase had been opened so I started there. With the flashlight held obliquely to carpet, I ran it over the area where the suitcase had been, then swept out from that point. I'd arrived at the base of the bedside table when I found something: a few flecks of a fine silver powder just around its base. I kept my breathing even. I didn't want to jump to conclusions. I ran the flashlight beam up the side and caught a few flecks there as well. Now I was sure enough to cut to the chase. I pulled myself up so I was kneeling in front of the bedside table. There were two obvious choices: the phone and the water glass. Given the colour of the powder, a pale silver-grey, it had to be the glass. I pulled out my geologist's loupe, held the flashlight to the glass, and did a careful examination. I could see the smears where it had been wiped. I looked more carefully. There were no prints on the sides and no lip marks on the rim, just a few silver flecks around the base. Dusting powder: lightning grey. Someone had lifted my prints.

I switched off the flashlight and sagged against the bed. If they wanted my prints it could mean only one thing. They had official status and access to the fingerprint databanks. Whether they could get into the ones where my prints were stored would depend entirely on who and what they were.

I didn't even bother checking my watch. I needed some answers now.

Duncan picked up on the first ring. "Yes," he said abruptly.

"It's me."

He hesitated. "I can't talk. I'm waiting for a call."

"Who's on the ground here, Duncan?"

There was silence for a minute, then he said, "I'm not sure."

"Well I've had unexpected company and they lifted my prints. And while we're at it, where did you —"

Then I heard little Peter cry in the background and the plaintive voice of Alyssa calling for her father. His voice changed back into Duncan my friend. "Morgan, I'm sorry, but I just can't talk right now."

The connection went dead.

I sat there for a moment, stunned. I'd just been abandoned in Hawaii on some screwball mission for the minister without all the cards. On the other hand, Duncan had his own problems right now and I was a big girl. I'd have to work it out myself. I struggled to my feet. Best to stick to the plan, and the plan for now was to take a little ride.

I headed back down the Saddle Road and at its base turned toward Kona. About halfway down I took the turnoff to Waikoloa Village. It was dark as all get-out, no lights at all along the road, but as I neared the development I could smell the change in vegetation. The dry grassland transformed into swaying palms, lush gardens, and perfectly manicured lawns, the joys of irrigation. Behind the tropical paradise, though, were the same condos and double-car garages seen in every development across North America.

Grenier, I could see from my map, lived on a crescent. As I came up to his street I slowed and made the turn.

It was a street of detached single dwellings with the houses nicely separated by vegetation or high fences. Grenier's house was a two-storey detached with fencing on either side. I kept moving slowly along and took in the neighbourhood. The only light from the houses was the occasional blue glow of late-night TV, and the driveways were packed with cars, often three or four to a house. There were some cars parked on the street, so my vehicle wouldn't look out of place.

When I reached the end of the crescent, I didn't loop back immediately but took some time to cruise the area and work out several escape routes. Occasionally another car pulled in behind me, but it inevitably deked around to pass. Other than that, the neighbourhood was dead. I drove back to the main street that fed onto Grenier's crescent and parked my car. I slipped my briefcase out of sight, did a final check of my tools, and quietly shut the car door behind me.

At this elevation, close to sea level, it felt more like postcard Hawaii. It wasn't brutally hot, but hot enough for me to start sweating in my leather jacket. And the air was damp and fecund, smelling like a mixture of chlorophyll and peat. I did one slow walk by Grenier's house to test the dog barking potential, which, fortunately, turned out to be low, then I looped back around, crossed his lawn, and moved into the shadow of the recessed door.

Through the sidelight the hallway looked dark and abandoned with a pile of mail lying on the carpet beneath the door. A set of stairs ran up the right-hand wall, and the hallway itself continued back to what looked like a kitchen in behind. I could see the edge of a glass door that must open onto a patio in the backyard.

Somewhere down the street a dog barked, then two cones of light appeared. I moved into the corner, confident that I couldn't be seen. The car didn't slow, just continued out the other side of the crescent. Maybe it was a security guard or, for that matter, a cop. It was time to move. I stepped off the portico and crossed to the side of the house. A narrow path squeezed between the house and the high fence next door. Halfway down I heard a siren wail somewhere in the distance, and it added to the eerie cacophony of night sounds: birds screeching, the rustle of big-leafed plants, the clicks and croaks of the lower phyla.

At the end of the path I stopped and glanced around the corner. A grouping of cheap outdoor furniture sat on a small cement patio, and this was surrounded by a border of ill-kept greenery. A high fence enclosed it all. I pulled out my flashlight but kept it off. After another minute of listening I left my corner and crossed the cement, aiming for the door. It wouldn't take me more than a minute to pick that lock and walk inside.

Then I felt something crunch underfoot, glass being ground into cement. I flicked my flashlight on, ran it across the patio door, and quickly turned it off. I wouldn't be needing those lock picks after all. Someone had been here before me, but they'd used a crowbar instead. I wondered, as I crouched low, if they were still inside.

I waited ten, fifteen minutes, straining to hear any noise from the house. Finally, when I was confident that I was alone, I stood and stepped into the kitchen. Pots and pans were scattered across the floor, drawers were upturned, even bags of food had been dumped out on the counter. What once were light fixtures were now gaping holes. The fixtures themselves dangled below, an uncanny reminder of Grenier's death. Despite the crowbar entry this didn't look like a smash and grab. This looked like someone searching for drugs. Or money. Or hidden diaries.

In the hallway I stopped again and listened. Straight ahead was the front door, to my left the staircase and open archway, and to my right a closed door. Grenier's home office, where, Mellier had told me, Yves Grenier had kept a neat row of his old diaries. I started to move forward then saw something in my peripheral vision, a movement in front of the stairs. I froze. It was near the floor, then without warning it burst up the stairs, white and fluffy and scared. Then I connected something I'd smelled in the kitchen: the odour of drying cat food.

I forced myself to relax and moved forward. At the door to Grenier's office I caught a glimpse of the street through the sidelight. There were way more cars out there now than when I came in. I'd have to be careful with lights. I gave the knob a tentative wiggle. It wasn't locked, so I pushed it open with caution, and when I was sure I was still alone I stepped inside.

The office had been searched with no attempt to hide it. Drawers were pulled open, but not emptied as they had been elsewhere. Books had been pulled out of the bookcase but some still remained standing. I did a quick scan just to confirm that the diaries weren't there, then started with the phone. Who was on Grenier's speed-dial, and who was listed in his directory. I clicked through the speed-dial and wasn't surprised to see Elizabeth Martin, Andreas Mellier, and several other astronomers from the observatory. Shelton Aimes wasn't there, nor was Edwin Eales. The other numbers were for the computer room, the observing room, and the doctor, dentist, and InfoSurf line.

I moved on to the directory. Would I find Eales under E? St. James under S? But the very first entry under C stopped me cold. *Carmichael, Duncan*, at home and at work. My heart missed a beat and I reached forward to brace myself against the desk. Duncan never told me he

chapter seven

"**ID?**" Benson put out his hand. As if he didn't know who I was.

Officer Morita handed him my wallet. Benson made a show of holding up the various cards for examination. He glanced up to see me glaring at him then went back to the job without a flicker of response. I was seated at Grenier's desk with my hands cuffed behind me. Benson finished and threw the wallet on the desk.

"So," he said, then he looked pointedly at the mess in the room. "What's a nice girl like you is doing in a place like this?"

Benson had taken his own sweet time arriving at the scene — over an hour to be precise — during which I'd been sitting in this chair trussed up like the Christmas turkey. I was in no mood to play games. "Not what it looks like. Obviously."

"It's not so obvious to me." With a pencil he lifted my lock picks from the desk where the uniform had dumped the contents of my pockets. He dangled them in front of my face. "These are nice."

"Does it look like I used them? Go check the back door."

"Maybe you were in a hurry."

"You think I could have done all this damage and not have a speck of dust on me? Come on, Benson, you know better than that."

"You were making a call when my officers came in. Mind telling me where?"

"It didn't go through."

He watched me for a second then he clicked his tongue and shook his head. "You'd think with all that technology they'd be able to connect two people in a conversation, wouldn't you. But there you have it. It didn't go through."

I shrugged, as much as one can shrug when confined with handcuffs. "It happens."

"It sure does, but I'll tell you what. Why don't we see if it happens twice." He pulled latex gloves from his pocket, snapped them on, and pressed the speakerphone button so we could both hear the progress of the call. He poked redial, crossed his hands in his lap, and settled in to get comfortable

I was liking Benson less and less. The call began in the usual way with a series of beeps as the number dialed.

"Area code 613. Where's that at?" Benson asked affably.

The phone was now in the click and buzz stage as the signal connected over land, space, and sea. I was having trouble concentrating on Benson's questions. "Ottawa."

"A friend of yours?"

The phone connected and began to ring. I could feel my underarms start to seep. "Something like that."

Benson leaned over the phone. "Duncan Carmichael. It says so right here on the call display. Now there's an amazing coincidence. Both you and Yves Grenier know a Duncan Carmichael, and here you are in Dr. Grenier's house, a restricted crime scene I might add, dialing Duncan Carmichael on Dr. Grenier's phone." Then he dropped the good-cop act. "Care to tell me what's going on?"

The phone continued to ring. Where the hell was Duncan? Why wasn't he picking up? "Did you call my contacts?" I could see from his face he hadn't. "Jesus, Benson."

But that just ticked him off. "Guess your guy isn't home." I felt myself relax ... a moment too soon. Benson gave his head a regretful shake. "And that is really unfortunate."

I didn't want to ask, but I knew the longer I put it off the longer I'd be sitting here in cuffs. I sighed. "Okay Benson. Why is it unfortunate?"

"Because that was your one call. Now we're going for a ride."

The doors clanged open down the hall and I pulled myself upright. I hadn't slept a wink. Between the noise of college boys on March Break puking out their double Mai Tais and a seriously pissed-off pickpocket railing against the state of American justice, it was hard to just float off into the nether regions. That, and the fact that I had to go to the bathroom but was damned if I was going to pee on video, was enough to keep my eyes open and my brain running on overload throughout the night. I only hoped the person coming down the hall was going to spring me before I wet my pants.

It was a uniform, and she stopped at my cell. She put the key in the lock and swung in open. I was already off the bed and heading for the open door when Benson came around behind her. "Leave it open," he said with a dismissive nod. He had a package of stuff in his hands.

"Have a seat," he said to me.

I did. I was better off sitting anyway. Benson opened the large zip-lock bag. He carefully removed a sheet of fingerprinting ink and laid it on the edge of the desk. That was followed by a folded piece of paper, which he opened and smoothed out right next to the ink: a fingerprinting form.

The bastard. He was going to print me, and that meant I was going to be formally charged. The good thing is that I'd had lots of time to think in the past few hours, so I was ready for this.

He surveyed the table, gave a satisfied nod, then looked up at me. "How'd you sleep?"

That would have been pretty obvious from the state of my face, but we were both playing a game. "Like a baby."

"The beds aren't too bad," he said, and he took a seat next to me, too close for comfort in my opinion.

I shifted back toward the wall. "Did you make those calls?"

"To your police buddies? I sure did."

"And?"

He gave a shrug. "They think you're okay. You don't play by the rules, but I'd kind of figured that one out on my own. Problem is, I still have a B&E on my hands and you're my best suspect."

The moment of truth had arrived. It's not that I trusted Benson, but I was running out of options. "Duncan Carmichael," I said. "The guy I called last night?"

"The one in Grenier's directory?"

"Did you call him again?"

He shook his head.

Duncan had sold me down the river. He'd lied about Grenier, and then when I needed him most he'd abandoned me without a word. I didn't owe Duncan anything other than a good swift kick in the ass, which I planned to deliver personally when I got on the next flight back to Canada. So now it was my turn.

"He works for the Minister of Industry and Science. That's who sent me out here."

He gave a whistle of appreciation, although the sarcasm managed to sneak its way in. "The Minister of Industry and Science. Is that like a congressman?"

"More like a senator — a federal politician who heads up a big department. Duncan is the special policy advisor on scientific affairs. He's the one who briefed me."

"Big mucky-muck, huh? So he briefed you on what?"

"Why don't you ask him?" I reeled off Duncan's office number.

He pulled out his cellphone. "You must know this guy well. I mean, you know his number off by heart."

"Not as well I thought," I said just under my breath.

He'd poked in the number and now he had the phone up to his ear. "Technology works." He ran his hand over his bristle. I could hear a woman's voice pick up in the background. That would be Duncan's assistant. Benson introduced himself and asked to be put through to Mr. Carmichael. "He hasn't." He said it as a statement, then he glanced at me. "I have a woman here named Morgan O'Brien. She says she's working a case for your department, something to do with an astronomer named Yves Grenier. Does that ring a bell?" There was a pause and he put his hand over the phone and gave me a reassuring wink. "She's going to check around." It took a minute or two then the voice came back on. "I see," said Benson. He nodded firmly. "I understand. Thank you so much. The weather? Hot and sunny, just like always. You too. You have a good day, you hear." He bleeped off the phone and put it on the desk beside the fingerprinting kit. "Duncan Carmichael is on an extended leave of absence, and they've never heard of Morgan O'Brien. Looks like you're on your own."

My stomach suddenly felt shaky, or was it the pressure of my bladder pushing up against it? At some hidden level I'd been expecting this, but that didn't make it any easier to hear the words. I looked over at Benson. For a guy who couldn't have gotten much more sleep than I did he looked pretty good. This morning the suit was a pale olive green, the T-shirt a dark topaz. It brought out the amber flecks in his eyes, something I'm sure he was well aware of. To put it bluntly, he looked good and I was out of chips. I had nothing left to lose.

"Grenier kept diaries. They're missing. That's why Duncan sent me here."

Benson's eyes narrowed momentarily as he processed that information, then his expression opened and he gave me a radiant smile. "You know, O'Brien, you look a little uncomfortable. Do you need to use the bathroom? I'll tell you what. There's a nice private ladies' room right down the hall. Officer Yates will take you down there, then you come back and maybe we can finish up this conversation."

He got up and walked right beneath the video camera. "Can you come in here?" he said up to it. Then he turned to me. "You won't try to run off, will you? It's a small island."

"Show me a toilet with a door, and you have me in the palm of your hand." *Just as you knew you did, you prick*, I thought.

When I came back Benson was still sitting on the bed. Now, though, he looked more at ease. He was leaning back on his elbows and had one leg crossed over the other. When he saw me he stood up and met me halfway across the floor. Then he did something unexpected. He discreetly put his hand on my forearm, a silent warning to trust him. He waited until the uniform had disappeared out of the cells then turned quickly to me. He pulled something from his pocket and pressed it into my hand. "I found this in a sweep of your car."

It was a small black disk: a listening device, also known as a bug. What the hell was it doing in my car? I looked up at him completely baffled, but he gave me a warning glance and stepped back. The uniform came through the door and stopped below the video camera. She reached up.

"I've lost video." She fished around the back. There was a click and the red light above the electric eye went back on. "What the hell?" The question was addressed half to Benson and half to herself.

"End of tape," he said, his voice offhand. "It does that sometimes, triggers the automatic turnoff."

She cocked her head and looked at him. "It's a loop."

"It still clicks over. Sometimes the mechanism just gets confused."

Man, this guy could lie without even a quiver. When the uniform had gone back out I asked in a neutral voice. "So where do we go from here?"

He turned and started to gather up the stuff on the desk. "You go wherever you want. I go back upstairs to my desk."

I stood there stupidly, not comprehending. Minutes ago I was about to be charged. "I'm free?"

He slipped the ink strip in the bag. Then he looked at it, then me, with innocent surprise. "You didn't think

it was for you, did you? It's for the guy next door. You?"
He slipped the form into the bag as well. He let a beat
pass then looked me directly in the eye. "You have
friends in high places. You've been sprung, no charges
laid. Have an excellent day."

Outside in the car I gave myself a nanosecond to think.
First the disappearing Duncan, then a bug in my car,
then being sprung by a mystery phone call from someone with pull. It didn't make sense, particularly on zero
hours of sleep. Still, there were a few little details I
needed to confirm. I pulled out my cellphone and dialed
Duncan's house. There was no answer and no voice
mail. The second call was to the director of the school
that Duncan's children, Alyssa and Peter, attended. I
was listed as an emergency contact for the kids so I
knew that she'd talk to me.

"Alyssa and Peter?" she said, surprised. "But they're
not here. I understand they'll be away for some time."

I felt my chest constrict. "Since when?"

"Dr. Carmichael called in this morning. Some sort
of family emergency. He didn't say when they'd be back.
I do hope it's nothing too serious."

I looked out the window. A palm tree next to the car
rustled and bent in the wind.

The first thing I did was hit a bank machine. I took out
the maximum daily limit and walked away. Next, I
took the SUV, which now felt like it had a giant neon
flag waving above its roof, and wove through the
streets of Kona, first driving conspicuously down the
main tourist drag along the beach, then climbing onto
the smaller streets above. There I spent half an hour

slinking down alleys, squeezing through one-way lanes, and pulling around blind corners to see what might follow me up. When I was sure I didn't have a tail I pulled into a vast public parking lot behind the tourist strip, pulled my briefcase and all other personal items out of the car, and descended into the clots of humanity on the sidewalk below. I did a little shopping, bought shades, a sun hat, and a few different T-shirts. I moseyed along the street, stopping frequently to survey the human throng, and made several abrupt changes in direction and destination. Paranoia was driving my actions.

Finally, after several trips along the strip I settled on a nice little cappuccino bar nestled between a mini-mall and a sushi house. It was perfect. Long and narrow, dark inside, with a beautiful terrace overlooking the street and the vast Pacific beyond. I was the only patron inside. I chose a table at the back, sipped my cappuccino, and studied every pedestrian who so much as hesitated in front of the café. Had I seen them before? Was there anything familiar there?

I took my time with the coffee. Eventually the waitress came over and I ordered a second. When it arrived I paid my bill and settled in for a leisurely second cup, but I'd barely started it when nature called. I picked up my briefcase and headed for the bathroom in the back. There I pulled open the bathroom door. It blocked me from the view outside. By the time it had swung shut I was in the back alley outside jogging to the low-rise motel half a block down. I paid in cash using a false name, and five minutes later I was letting myself into the third-floor room.

It was 1950s tacky with matching orange plastic patio furniture on the balcony and inside. The double bed was draped with a faded quilt and the air conditioner rattled in the corner, giving the room that distinct odour of chemical cold. I crossed the room and switched it off, then, staying behind the sheer drapes, I pulled open the patio doors. A hot, dry breeze pushed them against me and I stepped back quickly. I couldn't risk being seen, but fresh air, the rhythmic sound of waves washing up on sand, and the happy babble of the tourists below was a relief after my night in Kona's lock-up.

I had some thinking to do, some notes to assemble, and some calls to make, but all of that was useless without a functioning brain. I pulled the quilt back, flopped on the bed, and felt the warm outside wind flow across my skin. A minute later I was asleep, but with the comforting sound of the tourists below mingling with my dreams. Two hours later the lizard brain woke me. I lay there, my eyes suddenly wide open, my heart racing, then I heard it again, and this time it registered in the cortex. A noise at the door.

Nobody knew I was here, so who was it? The knob slowly turned. Someone was testing to see if it was open. I rolled off the bed in one fluid movement and landed next to the desk chair. I heard a card being slipped in the lock outside, the door opened just a slit, and a thin metal strip slid through it and flipped the security lock open. I lifted the chair and torqued it around. The door banged open and the bore of a handgun swung toward me. I launched the chair with enough force to put it through the wall.

Good thing Benson was quick.

chapter eight

"Frig!" he yelled.

He threw the handgun into the centre of the room and yanked the door in front of himself as a shield. The chair bounced off it, taking out a chunk. I dove for the gun, rolled, and a second later was on my feet with it aimed at Benson. He stepped inside, slumped against the wall, and put his hand to his heart. "Jesus, O'Brien, next time just answer the door."

"Next time call up. Shut it." I motioned to the door.

He reached out with his foot and flicked it closed. "You can put that away. If I didn't want you in circulation you'd still be in jail."

I kept the gun level. "How did you know I was here?"

"A lucky guess."

"Bullshit." My heart rate dropped slightly but my hands still shook. I hoped Benson wouldn't notice. "You followed me."

He gave me a level gaze, challenging me to pull the trigger, then pushed himself off the wall. "Mind if I —" and he nodded to the balcony doors. When I didn't say no or blow his brains out he sauntered across the room. At the sliding doors he parted the nylon sheers just enough to see out and surveyed the human traffic below. "I didn't have to," he said, still looking out. "I just asked myself what I'd do if I had a serious tail. I'd come down here to the tourist strip, get lost in the crowds, then hole up in some motel until I could figure out what was going down. I wouldn't use a credit card because whoever can place a bug can trace that too damned fast, and I sure as hell wouldn't park that honking SUV in the hotel lot." He let the curtain fall and swung around to face me directly. "I've just spent the last two hours schlepping around every hotel on the strip asking if anyone of your description paid cash for a hotel room in the past few hours." Then he gave me a boyish grin. "Not that many tall, dark-haired, blue-eyed women pay for hotels in cash these days. In Honolulu maybe, but we're a bit of a backwater here." He looked at the gun. "Put that thing away."

I didn't. With the gun still trained on him I let his information sit for a minute in my brain. It sat there solidly, not tipping or jiggling, not crumbling to the floor, but then Benson was a skilled liar. I'd already seen that.

"Sit," I said, and pointed the barrel of the gun towards the edge of the bed. As he sat I lifted the projectile chair — one leg now slightly bent — and placed it across from Benson with enough distance between us for me to raise the gun and fire if I had to. I sat down and laid the gun conspicuously on my lap. "What do you want, Benson?"

He sat with his hands splayed on his knees. "The same thing as you. To find out what happened to Yves

Grenier. Getting you out of Hawaii in one piece would be a bonus."

"You always enter a room barrel first?"

"Someone planted a bug on you, O'Brien. This doesn't instill confidence. You didn't answer my knock so I had no idea what I'd find in here." His dark brown eyes gazed calmly and openly into mine.

I gave an abrupt laugh. "You came to save me?"

"If the shoe fits ..." He shrugged.

"That's sweet, Benson. Considering you just threw me in jail."

"You got yourself thrown in jail, but you had a little help, and that's what interests me."

That caught my attention. "The 911?"

He nodded. "It came from the payphone at the grocery store down the street. Somebody was following you, but it wasn't me." Then he leaned forward and put out his hand. "Can I have my gun back? It was a peace offering. We're really not supposed to lend them out."

I looked at the handgun then back at Benson. I still didn't trust him, but I was pretty sure he wasn't here to shoot me in the back. Either he was on the level or his game was more subtle than a bullet in the spine. I passed it over. As he was stuffing it in the holster I threw out a question to catch his reaction.

"Did you search my room at the Astronomy Centre?"

He looked up, surprised. "When was this?"

"So it wasn't you?" He shook his head, but slowly, thoughtfully, calculating something. "Where were you yesterday evening, Benson?"

He calmly snapped the holster shut, making me wait for an answer, then he gave me his full, exasperated attention. "What is it about *no* you don't understand? Where was I yesterday evening? The same place I've been every minute of the day since I got this friggin' case. At my goddamned desk. You want to know why? Because ever since Grenier's death I've been assigned a shitload of work, and I *do* mean a shitload of work, if you get my drift."

I felt a tingle run up my spine. "Too much work."

He nodded without joy. "Too much work to focus on a complicated case involving a foreign national that may or may not be suicide, that's for sure. And I'm getting a hell of a lot of pressure to wrap things up: call it and close the file. Then I haul you out of Grenier's place and find a bug on your car. If I were paranoid —"

"— which of course you're not."

"Which I definitely am, but not usually this bad." A breeze parted the curtains to reveal a strip of the thoroughfare below: a slice of jostling colour as Hawaiian shirts and neon sundresses flowed by. Benson glanced out. "If I were being paranoid I might wonder if someone in my own organization doesn't have something to hide."

I leaned forward in my chair and gazed at him, studying his face and body position. He was avoiding my gaze. "Like what?"

He sniffed, paused for a moment, then looked directly in my eyes. "You tell me. You're the one with the bug."

I did a rapid mental calculation. To trust or not to trust, that was the question. Now Benson was watching me. He knew precisely what was going on in my mind, although he wasn't party to the detail. It was pretty clear that Duncan had cut me loose. Worse than that he'd lied to me, and at this point I had to consider the unsavoury possibility that he knew more about Grenier's death than I did. It was hard to swallow, but why else would he lie? In comparison to Duncan, Benson was an extremely attractive option. He was connected, he had status here in Hawaii, and his intentions appeared to be honourable, as long as I could trust what I saw. So I made a decision. The only way to figure out what was going on with Duncan was to crack this case, and Benson could help me do that. The trick would be to stay one step ahead of him, and that wouldn't be easy. I needed him more than he needed me, but he couldn't be allowed to see that.

"Okay, Benson, but only as equal partners. You give me all the forensic reports, witness statements, the whole shebang. You withhold and the deal's off."

"And I have access to all your supplementary information, including interview notes and anything out of Ottawa. I find out you lie," he paused for an instant and gave me that boyish grin, "I shoot you. Of course, this is all off the record. Officially I can't go near you."

That suited me fine. It meant that nothing could be traced. "I'll live with that. So, when do we start?"

"What? Are you stupid, O'Brien?" He reached into his inside jacket pocket and pulled out a thick envelope, which he threw on the desk. "Why do you think I'm here?"

Benson took my laptop, sat on the bed, and reviewed my incomplete notes as I sat at the desk and went over his witness statements, forensic reports, and notes. He was finished before I was even halfway through. He stretched out on the bed, put his hands behind his head, and promptly fell asleep. Outside the tourist traffic had increased and the undertones of conversation were now mixed with the rhythms of sidewalk music. I looked at Benson with more than a touch of longing. It had been a long time since I'd hopped into bed with anyone, and him lying there like that, so open, so inviting, it was all

I could do to keep my eyes on the paper and my hands on the desk. I allowed myself one more wistful glance then forced my mind into logical mode and trained my eyes on the police reports. It took me almost an hour to go through everything, and when I finally finished I turned, waited just a little longer than was absolutely necessary, then cleared my throat.

Benson snapped awake and swung his legs over the side of the bed. He gave his head a shake and ran his hands over the bristle. "That felt good."

If he was uncomfortable about having fallen asleep in the intimacy of a hotel room with a total stranger sitting five feet away he sure didn't show it. He stretched, then pulled up one of the chairs way too close to mine and sat down. "So what have you got?"

I moved away slightly. Before waking Benson up I'd done a mental sifting of everything I'd read, and although I felt there was something in there, I just couldn't pull it out. We needed to go back to square one. "What's your take on Grenier's death?"

"My gut? It doesn't feel right. But evidence? Motive? Opportunity? I'm not working with much."

"Plenty of people had opportunity. It's easy to hide up there. As for motive, there's always the diaries."

"Sure." He gave me a sideways glance. "Now that I know about them." He sat back in his chair and crossed his legs. "So let's play a game, O'Brien, since you obviously like playing games. Let's assume that Grenier was killed for the diaries. What does that mean in concrete terms? According to Mellier, Grenier had a diary with him the night he died."

"And the rest of them were back at his house," I added.

"Exactly. So how did it go down? The killer offs him, hops in his car, speeds down here, breaks into Grenier's house, and lifts the rest of the diaries?" He shook his head. "It can't be done. We had that house sealed off within half an hour of the call."

"There was no sign of forced entry?"

"Nope."

"So the killer had an accomplice."

Benson mulled that over for a second. "With a key?"

I pulled out the bug and laid it on the table. "I don't think we're dealing with amateurs here."

Benson hesitated, then pulled out his notebook and flipped it open. "I'll pull some phone records. Maybe someone of interest placed or received a call at just the right time."

He started to jot something down, then stopped abruptly and looked up. "What do these diaries look like? Would you recognize them?"

"Sure."

He'd connected something and his voice quickened. "Think about it, O'Brien. We got one diary up top with Grenier and a bunch down at his house. That's what Mellier said, right?"

I nodded. "All lined up in the office. There was quite a little row of them, upper shelf, left-hand corner."

Benson almost leapt up. He reached for the envelope he'd given me and pulled a CD from it. He pushed it into my laptop. He had one hand on the back of my chair, the other on the trackball, and as he leaned forward to manoeuvre through the screens I could feel his arm press against my back. Benson, however, was oblivious. His attention was completely focused on the screen, which now showed a series of thumbnail-sized photographs. "These are the forensic photos taken when we sealed the house." He clicked on the first one. "You got to remember, our mindset was suicide, not homicide, and we'd have no idea what these things were." He clicked through the numbered photographs, going from the kitchen to the living room to the bedroom, until finally we hit the office. His face was almost next to mine, and if I turned even slightly my nostrils were flooded with that subtle odour of soap and skin.

"Here?" he said abruptly.

I forced myself back to the present. "They'd be up there." I pointed to the bookcase on the wall behind the desk.

Benson clicked forward to an image of the bookcase and leaned even closer to me. "Can you see them?"

Then, in a flash, I understood where we were going with this and my mind slipped into gear. I brushed Benson's hand off the trackball and took over, enlarged the area that Mellier had told me contained the diaries, and slowly scanned it. Benson pressed up against me, literally breathing down my neck.

"Can I get some space here?"

It took him a minute to pull his gaze away from the screen, and he let it rest on me for a few seconds. "Gee, O'Brien," he finally said. "I didn't know I could rattle you."

I kept my eyes on the screen. "Don't flatter yourself, Benson."

He smiled and moved back a step. "What's this?" He jabbed his finger at the screen.

I leaned forward. It was a space of maybe thirty centimetres with the books flopped down around it. "That's it. That's where they were." I swung around to Benson. "So if Grenier was killed for the diaries — if he didn't hide them himself — either someone had an accomplice or they got in there *before* Grenier was killed." I turned back to the picture and studied it again. There was something there that bothered me, something that wasn't right. Then I realized what it was. "Where are all the other books?"

"What other books?"

I magnified and scanned the shelves. "Did you guys remove anything from this room?"

"I'll check with the Ident guys, but not that I know of."

"Those books packed tight on the shelves." I turned to Benson. "That's not what I saw in Grenier's place."

Benson sat back down in his chair and studied the screen, but his question was rhetorical, directed to the great unknown. "Who uses a crowbar to break into a house and steal a bunch of books on astronomy?" Then he turned to me. "You busy tonight, O'Brien?"

"I assume this isn't a date."

"Sure it is. You, me, Grenier's place, around nine-thirty. I'll bring takeout Chinese —"

"— and we'll sit and catalogue books."

"You got it. And maybe we'll take another canvas of the neighbourhood, see if anyone can remember seeing someone remove boxes from the house early that morning."

As Benson said this I remembered the flicker of curtains as he'd shoved my head in the cruiser the night before. "I'm sure the neighbours will appreciate a felon knocking on their door at ten o'clock at night. Good plan, Benson."

"Not to worry. You'll be with me." Benson stood up, stretched again, and reached for his jacket on the back of his chair. "I'll go pull some phone records, make some calls, see if I can get a list of everyone on the mountain that night. What about you?"

I checked my watch. "I owe Shelton Aimes a wake-up call."

Benson stood there for a moment ready to go, hesitated, then decided to go for it. "Duncan Carmichael.

What's going on there? He knew Grenier, he knows you, he disappears."

I grimaced slightly, then I went for selective truth. "I don't know, but I'm working on it. I have someone checking out things in Ottawa." Then I thought of something. "Who sprung me, Benson?"

"I got a call from the top, so someone put pressure on them but they wouldn't tell me who." He watched me for a moment then said, "Did you ever consider we're being played for chumps. You on your side, me on mine?"

"And what if we are?"

Benson's eyes narrowed slightly. "No one murders on my watch and walks away. I don't care who it is. Remember that."

Then he turned and walked out the door.

When I was sure he was gone I brought up the photos of the bookshelf on my laptop screen and stared at the large gap where the diaries had been. It didn't make sense, and without Benson breathing down my neck I allowed my mind to frame the question. If this was about research and competition, if that's why Grenier was killed and the diaries taken, why steal research diaries that are ten years old? The information would be obsolete, so what else had Grenier put in those diaries? I filed that uneasiness deep in my mind. Given my concerns about Duncan it was not a question I wanted Benson to even consider.

After leaving the motel in Kona I'd meandered along the tourist boardwalk stopping every block or so and looping back to make sure I still wasn't being followed. I picked up a big order of takeout sushi along the way and gobbled it down standing, then ordered an industrial-strength cappuccino that I sipped while (seemingly) taking in the sights. In a crowded boutique I changed hats, pulled on a new shirt, and rejoined the human stream. People who plant listening devices are usually expert at physical surveillance too, so I couldn't afford to take any chances.

Finally, after a good hour of what seemed like aimless wandering I arrived at my destination: the big resort hotel at the end of the strip. I went into the car rental office and rented another vehicle, but this time a little economy job, silver, and with no defining characteristics. I'd seen plenty of this model around, which made my new transportation as inconspicuous as possible. I hoped my parked SUV would keep one surveillance team occupied for at least twenty-four hours.

In my new rental car I drove right back up to Waimea where I knew Shelton lived. My plan was simple. Roust him out of bed and refuse to leave until I got the answers I needed. If he wasn't at home I'd just make myself comfortable and wait.

At the telescope headquarters I took a right down a little side street instead of turning left into the headquarters' driveway. I passed an elementary school and a rundown low-rise apartment, then spotted Shelton's street and turned left onto it. It was a scrappy little cul-de-sac lined with clapboard bungalows, dirt patch lawns, and rusted-out vehicles suspended on blocks. I cruised slowly down the street checking for activity in the surrounding houses.

Shelton's house was a peculiar shade of robin's egg blue that was peeling in strips around the windows. Inside, the window treatments revealed his profession. The smaller window to the right was covered in tinfoil. The large picture window displayed limp curtains closed up tight despite the early hour. Next to the house the driveway sat empty, but one of the cars parked on the street could be his. I finished my loop, turned out onto the main street, and parked my car. I checked the pockets of my leather jacket, not that I was expecting a problem, turned my cellphone off, and walked slowly back to Shelton's house keeping an eye out for neighbours. Instead of knocking on the front door I peered in the sidelight. The hallway was dark, but I could see sports shoes and hiking boots strewn across the tile. Shelton's rust-coloured down jacket was hanging on a hook next to the door, so he'd definitely returned from the observatory the night before. I leaned over but couldn't see in the archway to my right, although I assumed it led to the living room, with the bedroom beyond that. Down at the end of the dark hallway I could see through to the kitchen where the back door stood ajar, light streaming through the crack. I smiled. This was not Shelton's lucky day.

I balled up my fist and pounded on the door, then stepped back and watched the living room curtains. There was no movement. I stepped forward and banged again. This time I saw a slight shiver in the edge of the curtain, as if it had been brushed by wind. So he was there but had the sense not to answer the door. Not that that presented a problem. I walked forlornly down the stairs, making it seem as though I was about to leave, but at the last minute I turned and sprinted to the back of the house. I was up those back stairs and into the kitchen before Shelton would have realized the back door was open.

"Shelton?" I called. There was no answer, so I let the screen door slam behind me. "I'm inside and I'm not leaving until we talk. You might as well get it over with now."

There was a whimper and a shuffle from the living room. I headed across the kitchen and trotted up the hall. Just as I arrived at the arch a door banged shut: the bedroom door at the end of the living room. I lunged for it, hoping to force it open before Shelton had time to wedge something against it, but halfway across the room my legs hit something, I pitched forward, and a black plastic bag was pulled over my head. I landed hard on my forearms, but not as hard as the guy who landed on my back a second later and pinned me to the floor. He'd knocked the wind out of me, and as I gasped for breath my mouth and nostrils were sealed by plastic.

I was going to die in a garbage bag.

My head began to spin, and I knew I only had seconds before I blacked out, not that I'd likely notice since it was already so dark in the bag. When I'd just begun to run through all the things I hadn't accomplished in life there was a voice near my ear. "Stop struggling and I make a hole." The weight pressed down harder on top of me.

I stopped moving. The truth is I would have done anything for oxygen. I would have sold God, queen, and country right down the river for a lung full of air. I just prayed he'd get the hole in there before I died. The plastic was pulled away from my face, a gloved finger poked through, and light and air rushed in. Not much of either, but enough so that if I lay absolutely still I figured I could maintain my vital systems. When I felt my hands and feet being bound with duct tape I did nothing to resist.

The next few minutes passed as a blur. The guy on top of me lifted his weight but kept a knee planted in my back, pinning me like a bug to the carpet. The air in the bag was hot, humid, and laden with CO_2, making my head light, and the sound of my own breathing muffled the activity around me. There were no voices, I'm sure of that, and someone snapped his or her fingers several times as if wordlessly directing other people. Then the activity seemed to cease and there was another jab of pressure on my back. Someone grabbed the bag, which was firmly tied around my neck, and jerked it up, wrenching my head back.

"Struggle and I tape the hole." He let my head fall back on the floor. I was then hoisted to my feet and, with one person on either side of me, dragged down the hallway toward the kitchen. We stopped, and I heard a vehicle reverse and approach the door. I was hustled down the stairs and thrown unceremoniously onto a cold metal floor. The doors clanged shut — two of them, so I knew I was in a cube van — and the doors up front opened and slammed shut. A moment later the vehicle lurched forward and I lay quietly on my side thankful to be alive.

I was positioned more or less in line with the direction of the van, and by concentrating on the movement and sound of the tires I was able to conjure up a kind of mental GPS to keep track of our position. Just like a real Global Positioning System, I visualized the van as a little glowing dot moving against a map of Waimea. I knew we'd come out onto the main road, and after about ten minutes I felt us take a sharp turn to the left. The engine strained as we began a steep uphill climb, which could only mean we'd taken the Saddle Road, but heading for where?

Some twenty to twenty-five minutes later I had a partial answer. The van plateaued in the upper valley and the driver braked suddenly then swung to the right. The sound of the tires changed and the van rocked as we drove along more slowly. We must be on a dirt track, I realized, heading slightly downhill. This went on for at least five minutes until the van came to an abrupt stop. Up until that moment I'd been completely focused on the progress of our voyage, but with the van so suddenly stopped, I now had to look to the future, and I was paralyzed with fear. I heard the key go in the lock and the back doors open.

I tried to keep my voice calm and controlled. "Look, I don't know what's going on but maybe if we could have a conversation we could work something out."

Someone grabbed my legs and jerked me toward the back of the van. I heard a ripping noise as the tape around my feet was cut. I felt a moment of hope. Maybe they'd take the bag off my head. But then I was pulled to my feet, again with someone on either side of me, and I was marched forward. We seemed to follow a rough, narrow trail that wove downward. We arrived on a flat area of dirt and I was fed through what I assumed was a door. The next thing I knew I was thrown to the floor.

"If you want information —" I started to say, but then there was the tear of duct tape and I shut up. I didn't want to risk my breathing hole. My ankles were bound up tightly, brought up behind me, and bound to my hands in the most uncomfortable position humanly possible.

"Nice job," said one voice. The other one laughed. Then I heard the scuffle of footsteps recede down the path. The van doors banged, the engine caught and engaged, and the van made a three-point turn and lumbered back down the road.

I lay there in silence utterly alone.

Or so I thought.

chapter nine

When I was sure the truck had left I began to work at the small hole in the plastic bag, trying to catch it and tear it on the rough floor. I'd been at it a few minutes when I heard a match strike. I stopped moving, but what I felt by now was more akin to fury than terror. "What do you want?"

"A little chat. That's all."

I knew the voice. "With a bag over my head? I don't think so."

I heard him stand and approach me. A cold blade touched my skin and cut the tape that attached my hands to my feet. I eased myself back into a normal position, but before I had time to enjoy it he hauled me to my feet and pushed me down into a hard chair. With my hands and feet still bound I had to balance on the edge of the seat.

He came around behind me, cut the bag loose at the bottom, and pulled it off. It was like rising from the bottom of a swamp to glorious light and air. I took several deep breaths and shook my head. Gunnar McNabb sat back down on a rickety chair in front of me. He crossed his leg, took a pull on his cigarette, then watched me for a moment through the haze of smoke. He wasn't wearing his bow tie.

"Sorry for the drama," he said without conviction. "But it's hard to get good help these days, especially on short notice."

I was sitting in a stone hut that looked prehistoric. There was a single room, dirt floor, and low ceiling. The door and two windows were open holes. Outside the sun was low in the sky, and a brisk wind blew over scrubby bushes and tall, yellow grass. There were only two pieces of furniture in the room, both broken wooden chairs. McNabb sat in one, me in the other.

"This is a little off the science beat, isn't it, Gunnar?"

He tapped the ash of his cigarette onto the floor. "You're in very deep shit here, O'Brien, but I'm going to give you the benefit of the doubt. I'm going to assume that you don't know what you've walked into, and once you do you'll be more than happy to cooperate. What do think? Can I give you the benefit of the doubt?"

"By all means, but you're going to have to tell me what you're talking about first."

He observed me for a moment longer then dropped his cigarette on the floor and ground it out beneath his shoe. "Duncan Carmichael." He leaned over, picked up the butt and dropped it in his pocket.

"Is that a question?"

"When were you last in contact with him?"

"Yesterday? A couple of days ago? I'm having trouble keeping track, what with the oxygen deprivation and lack of sleep."

"That's unfortunate, because he's taken a runner with his kids and that makes things real bad for you."

A runner with his kids? "That's got nothing to do with my job here."

"Maybe you'll recognize these." He reached into his pocket and pulled out a sheaf of papers, which he held under my nose long enough for me to examine. They were the forms approving my temporary transfer to the Office of the Minister of Industry and Science. I could feel my mouth go dry.

"Where did you get those?"

Gunnar smiled and slipped them back in his pocket. "Where I got them is irrelevant. What is relevant is the fact that they're forged. Or did you know that already?"

My heart missed a beat. The whole transfer thing had happened so fast: too fast for the plodding bureaucracy of the federal government. But Duncan forging papers? "I don't believe you."

He shrugged and pulled another paper from his pocket. "'Take as long as you need,'" he read from the paper. "This is from your supervisor, Robert Gregory. Of course you already know that since you accessed it sometime ago. 'Don't come back until you're ready.' Does that sound like a transfer to you?" He folded it up and slipped it back in his pocket as well. "What did Carmichael tell you? That you were working for the minister?" I didn't answer. I couldn't. I was trying to get my heart out of my throat and back in my ribcage. He pulled a pack of Players Light from his pocket, a good Canadian cigarette, extracted one, and tapped it thoughtfully on the box. "Is that what he told you, O'Brien?"

"I'm here to recover the diaries. You already know that."

He pulled his chair closer to mine. "You're just being a good citizen, right?"

I raised my voice. "I'm just doing my job. The paperwork looked legitimate. If someone offers to send you to Hawaii you don't ask a lot of detailed questions. Anyway, why should I believe you over Duncan? He didn't bag my head."

"True, he didn't bag your head, he just left you dangling so you could take the fall." He lit the cigarette and, just like the butt, put the extinguished match in his coat pocket. "And by the way, it's one hell of a fall."

My feet, which had already been cold, now felt like ice. My hands too, as if all the blood had drained from my extremities. "I still don't know what you're talking about."

"Those diaries contain classified information. This is a national security issue. Your friend Carmichael ...," he hesitated for a moment, "... is working for the other side."

"That's not possible. I know Duncan. I've worked with him for years. There's no way."

"It's easy to compromise someone, O'Brien. You threaten their family, you offer them large sums of money, you blackmail them around some hidden secret or vice. We all have a weak spot, a point of vulnerability, it's just a question of finding it." He took another drag of the cigarette then said in very different tone of voice. "You know, I considered you for my unit." He caught my look of surprise and smiled. "Sure, I've seen your file. I even watched you in training. Too bad you didn't stay with the Mounties, but then," he smirked, "other things got in the way. You know why we didn't approach you?" He flicked the ash on the ground. "You're a hothead, don't know when to hold it in. You don't know when to shut up." He tapped his head with his index figure. "You don't think things through. And now here we are." He took another drag of the cigarette. "Sometimes I hate being right."

I knew he'd felt familiar, that ex-cop demeanor, the moustache and upright stance. Had he really watched me during my training? Assessed me for work with presumably CSIS — the Canadian Security Intelligence Service? Did he really know about Suzette? But then I realized that the truth of what he said didn't matter. The speech was designed to throw me, to get under my skin. His job was to rattle me, then once rattled, to deconstruct my reality brick by brick. Once in rubble he could then rebuild it with his official version of the truth. The problem was that my reality at that moment *was* pretty damn fragile. Isolated, deprived of sleep, and in physical discomfort, not to mention reconsidering the loyalty of one of my closest friends, I wouldn't be able to hold out for long. The sooner we cut to the chase the better. "What's on the table, McNabb?"

The smile touched the corners of his mouth. "Pursuant to the Anti-Terrorism Act, Bill C-36, Subsection 83.3, I can arrest you and detain you indefinitely without a warrant. You'd lose your job, what friends you have would abandon you, and by the time you finally got out your life would be in shambles. And that's if you're *not* convicted."

I tried to keep the sarcasm out of my voice. "And the alternative?"

"Cooperation. You're in our way, O'Brien. You leave, we expunge any record of you ever being in Hawaii, and you go back to your cushy little government job having had a wonderful sick leave."

"That's it?"

There was a pause as McNabb considered how to present the next item. "Carmichael trusts you."

It was a dubious assertion at this point, but I let that go. "I don't know where he is."

"But he will contact you, we're sure of it. And when he does you'll contact us."

"You want me to rat on Duncan?"

"We want you to inform the authorities in the best interests of your country."

"Right. Duncan, that threat to national security."

I turned to look out the open door at the fading light beyond. I hoped McNabb would think I was mulling over his deal. In fact, I was desperately running over the past two days trying to make sense of the chaos. At least part of what McNabb was saying was true. The forms were probably forged, Duncan hadn't given me all the information, and he couldn't have known everything he did through official channels alone. Things were terribly wrong, but did they add up to McNabb's conclusion? Could Duncan be involved in smuggling sensitive intellectual property? I thought about that dispassionately. Duncan would certainly make a desirable intelligence target. He was smart, knowledgeable, and, as a policy advisor to a powerful minister, had access to classified information. But could he be compromised? I ran over our last meeting in this new light. Maybe it wasn't his ex-wife that had threatened to take the kids. Maybe the threat came from someone or somewhere else. Or maybe he needed money for the custody battle? Or to start a new life somewhere else? It could all fit. If I believed McNabb. But there were several disparate pieces of information that didn't fall neatly into place. Grenier knew Duncan well enough to have him in his personal phone directory. How did that fit? And if neither the good guys nor the bad guys had the diaries, then who did? I turned back to McNabb.

"How did Grenier die?"

He gave an offhand shrug. "We don't know for sure, but Carmichael may be involved."

At that moment McNabb's careful reconstruction of the truth came crashing to the ground. I had no doubt that Duncan was into something way over his head. I had no doubt that he'd jerked me around big time. But murder? Not a chance. If McNabb was lying about that, what other lies was he telling?

I smiled, nodded my head as if we were moving toward an agreement, then said sweetly, "Fuck you, McNabb. When we're back in Canada I'm going to hunt you down and have your balls for this."

I saw a flicker of surprise in his eyes, then he gave an enigmatic smile. "I see you haven't lost your edge, but maybe you'll change your mind by morning." He stood up and came around behind me. The bag went over my head, and I had to clamp my jaw shut to stop myself from saying I'd do anything, sell any friend or family member, to avoid that bag.

He taped it so tight that I could hardly swallow, then he leaned in close to my ear. "We'll find him anyway. We always do, and with two kids in tow he can't last long." He pulled the bag back so it tightened over my face. "And since he doesn't have those diaries in hand, you just better hope we find him before the competition. See you tomorrow." I heard him walk to the door, then stop. "Unless I get busy with other things."

Then the sound of his footsteps receded up the path.

I waited just long enough to hear McNabb's car disappear, then I went to work. In all his security-service arrogance McNabb had gotten cocky. He was so sure he could intimidate me, so convinced he could subdue me, that he hadn't bothered to re-tape my hands to my feet, and that was a big mistake.

My first order of business was to get the bag off my head, and I knew from my brief glimpse at the back of my chair that one of the supports stood free and broken, like a spike. If I could hook the bag over it I would be able to slice it or tear it. The trick would be doing so without losing an eye.

I got to my feet and, keeping my legs in contact with the wood, minced and bunny-hopped my way around the seat. When I could feel the back of the chair I bent down ever so slowly until my forehead contacted wood, then I moved my head to the right until I found the furthest — the broken — support. I then held my breath, pushed my breathing hole over the point, turned my head, and pulled down. The point grabbed the plastic and pulled it tight over my face, blocking off all air, but I felt it pierce the bag to create a second hole. I pulled back, and the bag tore open. With a blast of outgoing breath I pushed the plastic away from my face. I must have looked like the Grim Reaper staring faceless from a dark hood. I bent down again and used the back of the chair to tear the bag apart and push the tattered pieces over my head so they hung around my neck like a collar.

From there I hopped over to the open doorway, leaned against the door jamb, and began to saw the duct tape on the rough stone corner. It wasn't precision work, and for every bit of duct tape I tore I removed a piece of skin. After a few minutes I had to stop and take a break from the pain, but I was making progress. I could feel a loosening in the tape.

The sun had now set, and out beyond me the only piece of the day that remained was a faint orange glow toward Kona. I wondered briefly what time it was, and whether I'd be meeting Benson after all, when I heard the sound of a car passing on the main road. I was about to start sawing again when the sound of the car changed, slowed. This was followed by the high-pitched whine of a car reversing. The sound of tires on asphalt became the thump of rubber on a rough dirt track.

I pressed my wrists hard to the rock edge, pulled them taut, and sawed. I felt the tape split and I jerked my wrists apart. A second later I'd pulled out my pocketknife, slit the tape at my feet, and was sprinting up the slope in front of the hut. The car stopped somewhere on the dirt road, but no door slammed. I slipped behind a rock outcrop, hunkered down, and waited.

My visitor moved silently over the path and I heard nothing at all until a branch snapped in the clearing below. By now the slope behind me was in shadow and it would be difficult to spot me against the dark backdrop. Unfortunately, the same applied to the clearing in front of the hut. When I glanced over the outcrop all I could see was a dark shadow moving against the paler rock toward the hut's door. He stood for a moment by the door, then a flashlight went on. The beam swung first over the floor then slowly up the door jamb. He moved in closer and knelt in front of it, holding the beam close to the stone, then ran his fingers over the area where I'd sawed my tape apart. He brought them close to his face and shone the light directly on them. A squarish head, chiselled features, and a short brush of black hair. Pexa. How better to keep tabs on sensitive research than to have one of your own working inside.

He stood abruptly and stepped inside the door. I could see him run the flashlight over the two chairs and floor, then he was out again sweeping the beam over the slope. I ducked behind my rock. A pebble dislodged and tumbled a few feet. The flashlight beam engulfed my rock and I held my breath. Then it was over. The light switched off and Pexa disappeared down the path, making no attempt to be silent. He slammed the car door, and the sound of the tires disappeared in the direction of Hale Pohaku.

I slumped down and took several deep breaths. I was shivering with cold, hungry, and exhausted. The adrenaline rushes had left me spent, but I also couldn't lie here for long. If hypothermia didn't get me, Pexa might be back with reinforcements. I zipped up my leather jacket, managed to get to my feet, and clambered down the slope. On the walk to the road I would figure out what to do next.

At the side of the road, hidden in the underbrush, I sat on a rock and turned on my cellphone. I had three messages waiting. Two were from Mellier, but I didn't want to risk calling in to get them. If someone was monitoring the wireless networks I needed to make my call as short as possible. From where I sat I could see the dim lights of the Astronomy Centre halfway up to the summit. With any luck Mellier would be there. I dialed his cellphone, and when he answered I cut him off. We had less than a minute to do this.

"Don't say my name," I ordered. "Where are you?"

"In the Astronomy Centre waiting for you. Didn't you get my message?"

"Is there anyone with you right now?"

"I am alone."

"Can you pick me up on the Saddle Road? I'm a couple of miles beyond the turnoff in the direction of Waimea. You'll see a dirt track going off just there."

There was silence as he absorbed the information. "Sure. It will take me maybe ten minutes, but I don't understand. You'll just be there at the side of the road?"

"I'll explain when I see you, and Andreas, if anyone asks, say you're heading for Waimea. Don't say anything about me." He was just about to hang up when I added, "Water and a coffee would be great."

Then I turned off my phone, huddled on the rock, and waited.

Above me the clouds had cleared and a crescent moon hung above the summit. The Milky Way was a bright smudge across the sky and the blackness around it was bejewelled with a million brilliant stars. I stared upward knowing that I might never again see the heavens so clearly from anywhere on Earth, and then I let my mind drift. Not surprisingly it drifted to Duncan. Was he all right? Where was he now? And why had he fled with the children? I briefly considered abandoning the search for the diaries. Wouldn't I be better to leave here and get back to Ottawa where I could try to find him? That might yield more in the end.

I registered movement in my peripheral vision. Two pinprick headlights had swung out onto the road near the Astronomy Centre and they were weaving their way down the switchback road. I went back to my contemplation. If I left now McNabb would believe he'd won. He'd pat himself on the back thinking that he'd scared me into running home, and I was damned if I'd give him that. Then an image materialized in my head, the haunted face of Duncan in that rundown café. *We need someone who can get inside*, he'd said. *And someone who isn't afraid of what they might find.*

Like Gunnar McNabb and the people behind him?

The headlights arrived at the turnoff and aimed themselves in my direction.

I stood. That had been Duncan's coded message to me, perhaps the only one he had been able to give. That no matter what I thought was going on, no matter what I was being told, I had to stay and crack the case. *Watch your back*, he'd said, and now I knew why.

The FrancoCanadian Telescope truck, a hulking Suburban, passed me and pulled onto the shoulder. The passenger door was pushed open from inside. I jogged up to it. Mellier gave me a surprised look, and I realized that the tattered bag still hung around my neck. I pulled myself into the seat and slammed the door.

"Can you take me to the FCT headquarters in Waimea?"

"I think I should take you to the hospital. I'm just not sure what section."

There was a sandwich, coffee, and bottled water in a cardboard tray on the floor. I picked the whole thing up and put it in my lap. My hands, I noted, were dirty, torn, and bloodied, but I'd already made a decision. I didn't want Mellier to know too much, particularly with Pexa so close at hand. I popped open the water. "You called me twice." I took a few gulps. "What's up?"

Mellier kept his eyes on the road. There was none of the impishness I'd seen earlier. "Shelton has disappeared."

This wasn't exactly news to me, but what did the observatory staff know? "Does anyone know where?"

"He called in sick and said he wouldn't be in for some time. I went around to see if he was all right and he was gone. I mean really gone. The neighbour saw him leave with a suitcase." He turned and glanced at me. "Ham with Dijon mustard. My family sends it to me from France." I took a bite. Sublime was an inadequate word. "Are you going to tell me what's going on?"

With the water and food I could feel some heat and energy seep back into my body. At least Shelton had left upright and not with a bag over his head. "Was anyone with him when he left?"

"I don't think so, but I didn't ask directly. I'm an astronomer, not a detective."

"So you didn't check the airlines?"

Mellier shook his head. "Not yet."

"I'll do it." I crammed another bite of sandwich in my mouth and took a minute to chew and wash it down with water before going on. "I think he's safe,

Andreas, but somebody's scared him off. Somebody doesn't want him talking. Do you know where his family lives?"

We'd hit the steep decline where the Saddle Road dropped off the cliff. "Somewhere in Canada, I think." Then he said in an offhand voice, "I can get a contact for you if you need that. Next of kin or something like that."

I smiled. "You're going to pull the personnel files? That sounds like a detective to me."

He glanced at me then back at the road. "I don't want Shelton to end up like Yves."

That wiped the smile off my face, and I moved to the coffee. It wasn't exactly hot, and it wasn't exactly strong, but it was the best damn coffee I'd ever drunk in my life. I let his morbid comment dissipate then asked, "What else, Andreas? Why the second call?"

He swallowed. "I tried to talk to Elizabeth." He took a deep breath. "You must try to talk to her again."

"What makes you think she'll talk to me now?"

"Someone went through her house, and she thinks it was you."

I stopped the coffee mid-gulp and turned to look at Andreas. "When did this happen?"

"Last night when she was at the telescope. She thinks you left and went directly to her house knowing she wouldn't be there. It's absolutely crazy, *non*? But she is crazy these days. I know she was very close with Yves, but I truly don't understand her behaviours. I am, as I believe you would say in English, baffled."

"Did Elizabeth call the police?"

He shook his head.

"Why not? Did you ask her?"

We'd arrived at the end of the Saddle Road and Mellier turned right, heading for Waimea and the telescope office building. "Sure I did, and she said that there wasn't any point. Nothing was taken. I told her it couldn't be you. That it just wasn't possible."

He was absolutely right. How could I be doing a B&E at Elizabeth's house when I was busy burgling Grenier's? "I have an airtight alibi, Andreas. Maybe you'd like to pass it on."

"She'll be working at headquarters most of the night. I'll stop in and see her."

"Tell her I was in jail. She can call Detective Benson if she wants verification."

He almost laughed. "I thought this was a bad rumour."

Then I realized there was something else that didn't fit. Benson said I had friends in high places. I'd been assuming it was Mellier who'd somehow found out I was in the slammer and had called and put pressure on them to let me out, but that piece of the puzzle was rapidly re-forming itself. "So it wasn't you who got me out?"

He shook his head. The coffee had perked me up, and by the time Mellier parked the vehicle I was ready to get back to work. That meant meeting Benson at Grenier's place, and if I was lucky I might even get there before him. It would give me time to clean up my hands.

Mellier had his fingers on the ignition key and I stopped him. "I need the truck, Andreas. I'll have it back tomorrow."

I'd expected an argument, but he just shrugged. "You're a government employee. There's a sign-out sheet inside."

Hopefully I'd be able to retrieve my rental car tomorrow, but it was too risky right now. McNabb might have it staked out to ensure that I was leaving the island. I was concerned about my laptop, but given that McNabb could intercept e-mail he'd probably already taken it and copied everything on the hard drive.

I shook my head slowly and silently.

Understanding lit his face. "I see. Then you better not crash it up if it's signed out in my name." He climbed out of the truck and turned from the pavement to address me. I could just see his head above the seat. "Where are you going now?"

"I have a meeting with Detective Benson. I'm still trying to convince him that there's more here than meets the eye." Mellier nodded his approval, as I knew he would. I needed all the friends I could get. "Andreas, if you see Elizabeth —"

"I will for sure. She's inside crunching data. Knowing Elizabeth she'll be there all night. Me?" He looked at his watch. "I'll be gone in an hour or two."

"When you see her tell her what I said. That I couldn't have done that break-in." Mellier gave a nod and started to close the door. "And, Andreas," my voice was now more insistent, "if she knows something it could be dangerous for her. Tell her I said that. This isn't a game."

chapter ten

By the time I reached Grenier's house it was almost
nine-thirty. I'd hoped to beat Benson there and take
some time rifling through Grenier's personal stuff in
search of that elusive connection between Grenier and
Duncan, but Benson's white cruiser was already parked
in the driveway. At least I didn't have to use my lock
picks to get in. I parked beside his car and climbed out
of the truck. Inside the house, all the lights were on, but
when I banged on the door no one answered. I followed
up with the doorbell, waited, then tried the knob. The
door swung open. A white cat scowled at me from the
hallway then streaked up the stairs.

"Benson?" I called.

No one answered, but the luscious odour of Chinese
food filled the air. I stepped in then heard steps coming up
the driveway. It was Benson, his linen jacket flapping as
he jogged. He stopped short when he was close enough to
get a good look at me. "What the hell happened to you?"

I had managed to remove all the plastic and duct tape from my body, but I'd also taken off my leather jacket, leaving my wrists and hands exposed. I clasped them nonchalantly behind me.

"I had a little accident."

His eyes narrowed. "Accidents seem to find you, O'Brien." He nodded toward the kitchen. "Go sit down, but no food until that's all cleaned up."

In the kitchen I immediately went to the sink. The warm water and soap were brutal on the abrasions but I knew it had to be done. Benson returned with a huge first aid kit and opened it on the kitchen's centre island. I took one stool, he pulled up another in front of me.

His knees touched mine as he took one of my hands, turned it palm up, and examined the wounds. "Nothing deep," he said, not looking at my face, "but the cuts are dirty." He reached into the first aid kit and pulled out a pair of latex gloves, which he snapped on. "You up to date with your tetanus shots?" He picked up my hand again.

I didn't say yes or no because at that moment I couldn't remember. I was too distracted by his gentle touch and his face so close to mine. Damn those hormones to hell. Benson, however, was oblivious. Apparently the odour of pheromones couldn't override the sharp smell of disinfectant. "Interesting accident," he said. He daubed my wounds without looking up. "Is this related to Grenier or did you just piss someone off?"

The antiseptic seared my wrists and I had to close my eyes to speak. "Someone tried to scare me off."

"Just someone, or someone specific?"

"That's hard to say. I had a bag over my head."

He glanced up. I could see concern in his eyes, but he bent back over my hand. "So you don't know who?"

"Someone who's after the diaries," I said carefully, trying not to commit a blatant lie. With Benson it was too dangerous — he'd feel it in my hands — but until I knew how Duncan fit in I had no intention of divulging the whole truth.

Benson finished with the one hand then moved on to the next, scrutinizing the damage before beginning. "Could they have played a role in Grenier's death?" he asked a little too casually.

I had a brief image of bending over and nuzzling that brush of dark hair but thankfully he started probing with the gauze and pain overrode the lust. I spoke through clenched teeth. "I don't think so but I can't say for sure. They scared Shelton Aimes off, though." Benson looked up abruptly, and I nodded. "We can find him no problem, but it does mean they have something to hide." I winced and shifted as he daubed another cut.

It was now my turn for studied nonchalance. "Is there any chance your federal agents are involved?"

I felt a pause, a tightening, in his hands. "FBI?"

"Or the CIA, since Grenier was a foreign national."

"Interesting question." He put down the bloodied gauze and pulled out a bandage. "Why would the feds be involved?"

"Just a thought."

He worked silently, meticulously bandaging every nick and cut, then he packed up the bandages, closed the first aid kit, sat up straight and looked me right in the eye. "Just a thought? You're lying to me, O'Brien, I can smell it, and that's not part of our deal."

I was careful to keep my eyes level with his and raised my chin slightly. "According to Mellier some of Grenier's work had military applications. I get a bug attached to my car, you're getting pressure to wrap up your investigation, and people seem more concerned about those diaries than Grenier's death. Add to that that everyone's afraid to talk, and now I've been warned off in no uncertain terms. There has to be more to this than some guy's research notes." Benson crossed his arms and turned his head to the side so he was looking down the hall. He was processing. That much was evident. "Now you're holding out on me, Benson. What's going down?"

He turned back to me. His eyes were dark and hard. "I told you once, I'll tell you again. Nobody kills on my watch and walks away. I don't care who the hell it is. Now let's eat."

The food wasn't as hot as it might have been, but it didn't really matter. I was still in a calorie deficit and the spice of the Kung Poa chicken and Singapore noodles made up for the lack of thermal heat. The Heineken that Benson passed me negated some of the effect, but after the stress of the day a touch of mellow was welcome. As it turned out, we weren't the only ones in the house attracted by the food. I was just popping a sesame shrimp in my mouth when the white cat padded down the hall and stood in the doorway eyeing the end of my chopsticks. She was a handsome animal, pure white with orange eyes. She watched me accusingly, as if the shrimp really belonged to her. Benson followed my gaze.

"I wouldn't worry. She looks well fed." He went back to the Kung Poa chicken.

Well fed? I froze. The shrimp dangled like a question mark in front of my open mouth. It was a classic cartoon moment when the proverbial light bulb suspended above the head clicks on. "By whom?" I asked no one in particular.

Benson's chopsticks also stopped in mid-air. I put the shrimp back on my plate, hopped off my seat, and began to scan the kitchen floor. I found what I was looking for near the boarded-up patio door: a double stainless steel bowl, one side filled with clean water, the other with kitty kibble. A plastic bowl next to it contained the remains of a canned cat dinner. I picked it up. It was still moist: definitely not two days old.

I turned to see Benson watching me and I gave him a nod. We both knew what it meant. Someone had a key. And if that someone was on the recipient list of Grenier's suicide note — in other words, if they were on staff at the observatory — they could have gotten in here, taken those diaries, and been out before the police shut the house. And someone having a key made perfect sense. Astronomers travel. They're forever going to conferences, seminars, and various telescopes for specialized observing. Grenier must have had someone who regularly cared for the cat. I pulled out my cellphone and dialed Mellier. Benson took another swig of his beer but kept his eyes trained on my face.

"Andreas," I said when he picked up. "Who takes care of Yves's cat?"

The question obviously caught him off guard. "Is there a problem?"

"I just need to know. When Grenier travelled who fed the cat?"

"Elizabeth. She lives just a few blocks over. If she couldn't do it I did."

"Do you have a key?"

"*Non*, Elizabeth. I get it from her if I need to, but right now she's feeding the cat until we can find a home for her. Would you like a cat? She's very nice."

"No thanks. I just needed to know she was being cared for." I didn't want him mentioning the key to Elizabeth so I created a diversion. "That family contact you promised me for Shelton Aimes. Have you come up with anything?"

He lowered his voice in a conspiratorial tone. "I'm just waiting for Edwin to leave. When he's gone I can go in. Then I go home."

"When you get it give me a call. An address and phone number would be great." I pressed "end."

I looked at Benson. "Elizabeth Martin."

He took a final swig of his beer, stood, and stretched, displaying that flat stomach and broad chest. Was he doing it on purpose? Then he relaxed and tucked the T-shirt back into his pants, leaving not a wrinkle out of place. "Tell you what. I'll go canvas, see if anyone saw Martin here in the early morning of the day Grenier died. You take a crack at the book break-in. See if you can come up with anything."

I nodded. I was happy to stay here. It would give me time alone in Grenier's office, and I planned to make use of that.

When Benson was gone I closed the curtains and shut the office door. Benson's laptop was now open on the desk. The forensic photographs that were taken just after Grenier's death were up as thumbnail images on the screen. I was assuming that McNabb and the boys had done the second break-in and conveniently framed me for it. The use of the crowbar on the back patio door was a nice touch. Nobody would view it as a professional job. That question was, had they taken anything with them? From the forensic photographs Benson and I already knew that the diaries weren't there when the second break-in occurred. They'd either been taken or hidden by Grenier sometime before the house was sealed, but the fact that the intruders had taken other books intrigued me. Why? What was in those books? And would any of it connect back to Duncan?

I began by standing over the mess in Grenier's office to get the gestalt of it. Was there some kind of overall pattern? It looked like there was. Most of the books pulled to the floor had come from the furthest of the three bookcases, the last one in the left-hand corner of the room. It was the same bookcase that had held the diaries. The other bookcases had been gone through, but only a few sections had been pulled out, leaving the books on the shelves listing to the side.

I turned then, leaned into the laptop, and clicked on the photograph of the left-hand bookcase. Once it was up on the screen the dog work began. Checking back and forth between what was on the photograph and what was on the floor, I replaced as many books as I could to their original position. As I worked the pattern emerged. Grenier's diaries had been in the top left-hand corner of the bookshelf. Most of the missing books came from the top two shelves with several having been taken from the bottom shelf. In all, around fifteen books were gone. Now for the big question. Did the missing books have something in common?

I sat down at the desk. If the images had been shot with a high-resolution camera I would be able to magnify specific sections of the photograph and read the titles of the missing volumes. *If* the resolution was high enough.

I scrolled to the upper left corner of the photograph and magnified. There was a space where the diaries had been, then a series of old journals. I turned back to check the bookshelf. They were definitely gone. I hadn't picked up any old journals in my search. I held my breath and magnified further. The *Astronomical Journal*, seven issues dating from 1960 to 1964. I jotted down everything I could from the spines including dates and volume numbers. I continued on, jotting down missing titles, then decided that, since I was sitting at Grenier's desk anyway, I might as well take a gander through the desk drawers. Keeping an ear out for Benson I opened the middle drawer and sifted through it, but found nothing of interest. I then moved on to the side drawers. The left-hand drawer was devoted to personal items including bills, statements, and reminders. The other side was reserved for research. There were several reprints on wide-field imaging cameras, detectors, and optics as well as printouts of tables and graphs.

I heard Benson open the outside door and come in. I shut the drawer and tapped the laptop to bring the photos back up. He waltzed into the office without knocking. "Photon," he said, and smiled widely.

"Is that your word for the day?"

"It could be, but it's also the name of the cat. I know because Mr. Ogilvie across the street likes to feed the birds and Photon likes to eat them. He doesn't want to speak ill of the dead, but he's glad the girl who feeds Photon doesn't let her out as much as Grenier did. He did tell me 'the girl' fed the cat whenever Grenier was away and she let herself in with a key. He assumed they were more than just friends."

"That's all you got in an hour?"

He gave me a superior look. "Well, there's also Mrs. Mahuna next door." Benson came over and leaned on the desk next to where I sat. He was a little too close for comfort. "She gets up early to let out her dog, one of those yappy little things the size of a rat. Turns out the dog doesn't like Photon either."

I felt a tingle of anticipation. "I don't suppose she let the dog out early on the morning that Grenier died."

"Funny you should ask. As a matter of fact she did. She remembers that day because five minutes after she let it out — the dog's name is Lester — it was barking its little head off and she had to go outside to see what was going on. The blonde girl — the one who always feeds the cat — was chasing Photon and trying to get her back in the house. Apparently the cat escaped when the door was open."

"Did Mrs. Mahuna see Elizabeth carry anything out of the house?"

He shook his head. "She brought the dog in and went back to CNN."

That was a biggy. Elizabeth Martin had a key and she was here early that morning. She had opportunity, but what was the motive? "It's a good start."

"A good start? I thought you'd be ecstatic."

"It's a good start," I said emphatically. "The problem is we know that Martin didn't kill Grenier. She couldn't have if she was down here. And we still don't know if she took the diaries or Grenier hid them himself before she ever arrived. Maybe she just came over to feed the cat."

"After getting a suicide note from her friend? She came over for a reason, O'Brien, and it wasn't to feed the cat."

"Then you better go and shake her down."

He gave me a questioning look. "You don't want to be in on this?"

"It's okay. I've got some stuff to finish up here. Anyway, I'm not a cop, and this is your investigation. Once we've found those diaries I'm gone."

He gave me a calculated look, one that said he wasn't sure he bought in. "You find anything in here?"

I handed him the list of all the titles of all the missing books I'd gotten so far. He picked it up, scanned it and handed it back.

"Shit," he said, and I agreed. With the exception of the *Astronomical Journal* they were all books on Cold War military technology and satellite surveillance.

"I'm going to make a call," I said, taking back the list, "a librarian I know who's familiar with stuff. She might be able to tell us something." I turned off the laptop, closed it, and pushed it across the table. "Elizabeth Martin is up on the summit at the telescope tonight. If you want to talk to her I think you'd better take her by surprise. Either that or wait until she comes down."

"And when will that be?"

"Around six tomorrow morning, give or take an hour."

Benson looked at his watch and considered his options. It was an unappealing option to drive all the way up the mountain at this time of night. He leaned over and pulled the laptop toward him. "You need help here?"

"You're not going up?"

"This is an island, O'Brien. Martin's not going anywhere unless I say she is, and I need a good night's sleep. Anyway," he said, trying to justify his action, "she may be more forthcoming when she's exhausted and ready for bed tomorrow morning. I'll threaten to drag her down to the station and force her to drink our coffee."

I smiled. "I'm pretty well finished here. I'll just make my call and we'll leave together."

Benson disappeared back into the kitchen to clean up any evidence of his triage and our dinner. I considered using my cellphone but picked up Grenier's phone instead. I dialed Sylvia in Vancouver. It would be past 1:00 a.m. — two hours later than Hawaii — but she tended to do her best work late at night, and sure enough she picked up. "Yeah," she said.

"It's Morgan."

"I thought you'd be calling sooner."

The nuance wasn't lost on me.

"It's been busy."

"Hey, babe, the guilt's all yours. That's not what I meant. Duncan called again. He gave me a charge-code and said you'd be in touch."

I felt a little jolt of adrenaline. "When was this?"

"This morning at some ridiculous hour. He woke me from my beauty sleep."

"Can you be more precise?"

"Just after six. I'd only been asleep an hour."

That would be around nine o'clock in Ottawa, about three hours after I last heard Duncan's voice on that fateful call from Grenier's house. The one where I ended up arrested and in jail. "What did he say? I mean exactly, Sylvia. What did he say?"

She'd caught the urgency in my voice; I could now hear caution in hers. "He gave me the mother of all charge-codes and said if you needed anything I was to help you without question. That even includes travel. I could be in Hawaii by morning."

I ignored the humour. "Where was he calling from?"

"What's going on, Morgan?"

"Duncan's disappeared with his children. When he called you he was obviously setting things up so that he could vanish. I need to know where he is and why he disappeared." I let the next thought form slowly in my mind, then I voiced it. "I need to know he's okay."

I could hear Sylvia clicking through something. When she spoke again she was professional and matter-of-fact. All the humour was gone. "His call came in listed as *unknown name, long distance* so he must have been calling from his cellphone."

Damn. Another dead end. "Can you do something for me?"

"Yeah, anything. Those are my instructions direct from the Minister's Office."

I doubted that, but it would take months for her billing department to connect with the minister's billing department and realize that something was amiss. "I have references for a series of old journals here, specific volumes of the *Astronomical Journal* from the early sixties. I need to know what this group of journals has in common. There has to be something, a reason why Grenier had them." And a reason why someone would want to steal them.

"That's all you got? You need a medium, not a librarian."

"I can't go into it now, but there has to be a common factor. Maybe they all have articles on a specific celestial body, maybe a particular technology or instrument, maybe something to do with some kind of imaging. He had an interest in satellite surveillance. Maybe that ties in."

I could already hear her fingers flying over the keyboard. "Early sixties. Satellite surveillance. That stuff was pretty primitive back then, but I'll see what I can do. I'll need a bit of time. I can't pull these old journals direct off the net so I'll have to, God forbid, go to the library."

As a database expert Sylvia stayed as far away from ink and paper as she possibly could. "It'll be good for you," I said. "You'll remember how a library works."

"You want the results by e-mail?"

"No." My voice was emphatic. Between my e-mail being monitored and my laptop being lifted, it didn't seem like the wisest option. "I'll call you near the end of your day, see what you've found. And if Duncan calls find out where he's holed up and tell him to call me."

She clicked her tongue. "Forget it Morgan. I know Duncan. If he's gone to ground you're not going to find him."

I sighed and hung up.

"Is that Carmichael you're talking about? The guy on Grenier's speed-dial?" It was Benson and I wondered how long he'd been standing there. "So he's really missing."

I nodded.

"How do you read that?" he asked, drilling me with his eyes.

I have two rules about lying. First, I try not to do it. Selective truth is so much harder to detect. Second, I try not to fidget when forced into a situation where a blatant lie is necessary. It's a natural tendency, but people like Benson and me are trained to zero in on body language, and I already knew Benson was good. I couldn't afford to slip up. Still, under the pressure it was hard to resist. I let my hand stray to Grenier's blotter and I toyed with it, lifted the corner and pushed it back. "I think it's related to his custody battle, not this case."

He took in a slow, measured breath and narrowed his eyes, trying to sense what was going on. I kept my eyes on the blotter. There were several papers underneath, children's drawings by the look of it. I pulled one out, hoping to distract Benson. It was a crayon picture of a space rocket with a large round window in the front. In the sky above hung a big yellow moon. Below, on the ground, was a stick figure looking at the rocket through a telescope. Inside the rocket were two stick-figure faces with childishly wide stick-figure smiles, and everyone was labelled. *Uncle Yves* looked through the telescope. *Alyssa* peered through the rocket window with a crown of yellow curls. *Peter* waved a gargantuan hand at the astronomer below. Uncle Yves, Alyssa, and Peter. I felt my breath catch, and my face may have paled, but I laid the picture on the desk without comment.

"Custody cases," Benson said, and shook his head in disgust. "They're the only thing I hate worse than suicides, dealing with parents who abduct their children. What people do in the name of their kids …" He shook his head and let the sentence trail. "If Carmichael pulled that kind of stunt he deserves to be thrown in jail."

It took me a moment to answer, and when I did my voice seemed to come from somewhere far away. "Sometimes," I said slowly, "things aren't all that clear. I think we should go now."

Before switching off the light to Grenier's office I took one last look at the drawing sitting on his desk. *Alyssa, Peter, and Uncle Yves.* At least now I had my connection. Damn Duncan. Why didn't he tell me?

I'd noted on my drive in a few scattered lights inside, and as I parked the truck in the line of corporate vehicles I wondered who was still working. Mellier hadn't called me with the contact information on Shelton Aimes so he might be inside, and if he was still hanging around the chances were that Edwin Eales, the director, hadn't left his office. Even Gunnar McNabb might be skulking about, and that was not an appealing thought. I wondered if Pexa had let him know I was on the loose.

With my truck hidden amongst all the others I pulled out my cellphone and dialed Mellier's number. An electronic voice informed me that the cellular customer I was trying to reach was not available at this time. I suppressed a jab of annoyance: if Mellier had been inside it would have made my life much easier, and where the hell was he? At that I pushed "end," turned off my cellphone, and slid out of the truck. Outside, I did a quick check of the inside pockets of my leather jacket to make sure I had all the tools I needed, then I edged my way along the back of the building, keeping to the shadows. My destination was the side of the building where Grenier's office was located. I planned to let myself in his door and find Elizabeth's office from there, but there was one problem. Since both Elizabeth and Yves Grenier were staff astronomers there was a good chance that her office would be along the same corridor as Grenier's, only she would be in it. I might have to walk right by her windows to reach Grenier's office.

At the corner of the building I peeked around. Sure enough, light flooded out of the office just beside me. I glanced around trying to work out an alternative plan. The lawn, I could see, was cut out of what looked almost like a jungle, big-leafed plants that stood like an impenetrable green wall around the perimeter. Beyond the shaft of light from the corner office the lawn was perfectly dark. If I could skirt around the edge unseen I could cross the lawn in darkness on the other side.

I angled away from the building, looped around a maintenance shed, and a minute later was edging my way along the backdrop of leaves. When I was in position almost diagonally across from the lighted office I dropped to a squat and studied the building. All the offices, with the exception of the corner office, were dark. In the corner office Elizabeth Martin sat hunched over a computer, her back to me. I shivered slightly. The perfect target.

I started across the lawn, staying low. I was at the halfway mark when Elizabeth's office door opened and Gunnar McNabb stepped in the room. I froze and dropped to a crouch. Elizabeth stood belligerently. It was like viewing a silent film. McNabb's hands rested on the back of a chair as he leaned forward and spoke to Elizabeth. She stood behind her desk, her back to me, responding to his words with a vehement shake of her head. He came around and took the chair. He was now almost facing me. I sank cross-legged onto the damp grass and watched. McNabb's mouth moved and he poked the surface of the desk with his finger. Elizabeth sat but pushed her chair back from the desk and crossed her arms. She gave her head an occasional sullen shake.

As I watched I mentally ran through my options and came up with surprisingly few. I could wait it out and risk a bad bout of hemorrhoids; I could retreat and try again tomorrow; or I could try to roust McNabb. I rejected the first two with little trouble. If I was this close to finding those damn diaries McNabb was too, only he wouldn't hesitate to abduct and intimidate Elizabeth to get what he wanted, and I had no doubt she'd cave. Bottom line, I had to get there before he did.

Making as few movements as possible I pulled out my cellphone, then rooted around until I found the business card McNabb had given me on our first meeting. I turned on the phone but hid it under my coat and hoped there would be no telltale flash of blue light. I poked in McNabb's number.

From the lawn I could see his hand dip in his jacket pocket and pull out his phone. He glanced at Elizabeth, flipped it open, and answered.

"You're too late, asshole," I said.

"Who is this?"

"You don't recognize my voice? I'm crushed. Let me see if I can find a garbage bag. That might help."

"And I thought you were all tied up elsewhere."

"Not anymore, and guess what McNabb? I win, you lose. I've got the diaries."

He stood and turned his back to Elizabeth. "Bullshit."

"Believe what you want but I can tell you one thing. I've taken a peek, and it sure ain't me who's gonna get hung out to dry. See you back in Canada, chump."

I pressed "end" and watched. McNabb snapped his phone shut and swung around to Elizabeth. He said something accusatory, jabbing his finger in the air. She sat quiet for a moment, then nodded her head. Smart girl. He stormed out of the office. Seconds later I heard the back door open and slam shut; the car reversed, and a moment later it squealed down the driveway. Elizabeth slumped forward, her head in her hands.

I'd taken a lucky shot at McNabb and won, but the victory would be short-lived. He'd tear down to the airport hoping to intercept me, but it wouldn't take him long to figure out he'd been duped, and once he did, he was going to be ticked. I had to get both Elizabeth and myself out of there fast.

It only took me a minute to open Grenier's door, and a second later I walked into Elizabeth's office. Her eyes popped open. "I thought you —" Then she caught herself. "How did you get in?"

I placed my hands flat on her desk. "Look at my hands." I wanted her to see the bandages. Despite her hard exterior there was a flash first of concern then of something else. Fear.

"What happened?"

"Gunnar McNabb. That's what happened. I just saved your butt, but we have to leave now. We can talk in the car."

"I've got nothing to hide. I told him that."

"Except you agreed when he asked if I had the diaries." At that she paled. "We know, Elizabeth. Both Benson and I know. There was a witness."

Her voice was considerably less sure. "I don't know what you're talking about."

"Grenier's neighbour saw you that morning putting the diaries in your car." Sure it was a lie, but it had the desired effect. She suddenly looked both pale and ill, so I pressed my advantage. "You can either come with me now or Benson picks you up tomorrow morning. That is, if McNabb doesn't get you first." I held up my hands. "For your sake I hope he doesn't. You've got to trust someone, Elizabeth. Who is it going to be?"

"Even if I had the diaries, and I'm not saying I do, then I'd have them because that's what Yves wanted. I can't just ..." She hesitated. "I can't just hand them over."

At that I pulled out my wallet and flipped it to the photograph of Alyssa and Peter. She squeezed her eyes shut. "Why are you showing me this?"

I pushed it into her face. "Look at it. These children and their father have vanished, and I know it's connected to Yves Grenier. I don't know how, I don't know why, but the answer is in those diaries. For God's sake, Elizabeth, let me have them. Would Grenier have wanted these children to die?" She turned her face away. I could see the muscles around her mouth tighten. "Just come to Hale Pohaku with me. Stay in the Astronomy Centre tonight. Please. You're going to have to trust someone. You can think it over, decide in the morning." I looked at my watch. "It's your choice, but you have to make it now."

She took a deep breath. "How do I know you're telling the truth?" She motioned to the photo. "About them. How do I know you're not lying?"

"I'll tell you on the drive up, anything you want to know."

Somewhere in the distance I heard a door open and slam shut. So did Elizabeth. She glanced at the door. "All right, but I'm not promising anything. Do you understand?"

I nodded, then I reached over, locked her door, and turned out the light. For an instant we stood in silence with the pale gleam of the moon casting ghostly shadows across the floor, then the light was extinguished by churning clouds and we dropped into total black. I pulled out my flashlight, and in silence we collected Elizabeth's things and slipped out the back door onto the lawn. Behind the building there was still a space where McNabb's car had been, so it had been someone else coming in, but I kept that information to myself. I finally had Elizabeth Martin exactly where I wanted her.

We made the trip to the Astronomy Centre largely in silence. I let her stew. In the end I couldn't force her to do anything. She had to come to me, and right now I could almost feel the conflict and confusion spinning in her head. She had to sort it out alone.

At the Astronomy Centre I tried to book a double room so she wouldn't be out of my sight, but she adamantly refused, although she did finally accept the room directly across from mine. I escorted her in and set up the small portable alarm system I carry with me on her window and door, then I told her to keep them armed. It wasn't much, but it was the best that I could do. Anyway, I planned to be up early before Benson was on the trail, so it was only a matter of a few hours.

Back in my own room I jacked up the heat and took a hot, and much needed, shower. I'd had the same clothes on for so long that as I peeled them off I wanted to burn them. At the very least I'd have to bag them in plastic to make sure they didn't contaminate everything else. When I was all dry, and the room was toasty and warm, I fell into bed. I wondered briefly if I'd have trouble falling asleep given my extreme state of fatigue, but before the idea was even complete I was in free fall through a dark and endless pit. I couldn't have pulled myself out even if I'd tried. And I didn't.

A hand came down through the water and I reached up, tried to grab it, tried to reach the surface for air, but the dark waters kept dragging me back down. I fought with them, struggled upward, but slipped further and further away. I knew I had to get to the surface, that the sounds of the sirens were the rescue workers coming to save me. I had to be close enough for them to pull me out. I reached and grasped the hand. Light flooded my eyes and I forced them open. Brilliant high-altitude sun streamed through the windows, and I heard a real siren wail just outside. I wanted so badly to close my eyes that I forced my legs over the side of the bed and sat up.

Another siren followed the first, and I hoped it wasn't some poor slob in the throes of altitude sickness.

I started for the shower, but something crackled under my foot. I looked down to see a piece of paper that someone had pushed beneath my door. I scooped it up, sat back down on the bed, and opened it. It was a note from Elizabeth Martin. She'd reached her decision. The diaries were hidden in the dome. She would retrieve them and give them to me this morning if I would personally promise to find those children.

I threw the paper on the table and muttered a thank you to whatever great goddess lurked in the ancient volcano of Mauna Kea and stumbled to the shower. With any luck Elizabeth would be back with the diaries before I was dressed. I was just drying my hair when my cellphone rang. I snatched it up and flipped it open.

"Where the hell are you?" Benson had to yell against the noise behind him.

"At the Astronomy Centre. Where are you?"

There was a pause. "You don't know what's going on outside?" He gave me a moment to answer, and when I didn't he said, "You better get your butt up here fast."

I stepped out the front door and was stopped in my tracks. It was a midway of flashing lights — red, yellow, and blue — halfway up the summit switchbacks. Just off one of the switchbacks an ominous plume of black smoke curled into the air. I hopped into the same truck I'd had the night before, jacked it into all-wheel drive, and started to grind up the hill. With all the activity the dust had risen like smog, and by the time I got to the scene my truck was covered with a fine red powder. I pulled in below the other vehicles and hopped out.

A group of people, a mix of rescue workers and observatory staff from the different telescopes, huddled at the edge of the switchback. I picked out Benson from the crowd, taller than the others and wearing a linen suit, albeit with a down puff jacket over it. I hurried toward him. When I got there he said nothing for a minute, giving me time to absorb the scene. The most salient feature was the signature smell of death-by-vehicle-impact: gasoline vapour mixed with the angry stench of burning rubber. I'd seen enough of the resulting blood, dismemberment, and smashed bodies in my time with the RCMP to gag at the mere hint of that smell, and I hoped my olfactory nerves would habituate before I embarrassed myself.

Not wanting to, but knowing I had to, I stepped forward and looked over the edge. The truck lay on its roof. Columns of steam hissed from rents in the undercarriage and liquid oozed from broken tubes. It looked like a giant beetle overturned and helpless between two rocks, but instead of broken legs, twisted wheels dangled from struts and wires. Rescue workers were climbing down the treacherous slope, building a human chain, and fire extinguishers had already started down the line. I knew without asking who was in the truck. I turned away.

"When did this happen?" I finally asked.

"About twenty minutes ago." Benson nodded to the rescue trucks. "Not bad when you consider they had to come up from Hilo."

I turned around and looked behind us, following Elizabeth's route down. Benson seemed to read my mind and turned as well, then he confirmed my thoughts. "No skid marks, no brakes." His eyes seemed to follow the trajectory she would have taken. "She went off that edge like a rocket."

I had to grit my teeth to ask the next question. "Is she alive?"

Benson glanced down at the truck. "We're about to find out."

The first crew of burly firefighters had reached the wreck. Two went to work with fire extinguishers, the third pulled off his heavy work glove, slipped on a latex glove, and bent down beside the broken passenger window. His arm disappeared inside. He groped, pulled his hand out, then hopped back to his feet. The glove was covered in blood. He spoke to the guy next to him, and the walkie-talkies around us crackled. Benson put his to his ear, listened, then pulled it away. "She's alive, but barely. They're bringing in a chopper."

Below, the firefighter put his heavy gloves back on and picked up a crowbar, which he wedged between the truck body and the door. A moment later another man, a big civilian dressed head to toe in black, pushed past the other rescue workers and added his weight to the crowbar. It was Pexa, conveniently at the scene. There was a screech of metal as the door bent open a crack. A big circular saw was now making its way slowly down the chain of people. They were going to have to cut her out. This wouldn't be quick.

I turned away and suddenly Mellier was in my face. "What has happened?" His hair was all askew and his voice close to panic. "I thought you were with her? That's what she told me when she called me last night. Why weren't you with her?"

Benson swung around and stared at Mellier. My mouth opened to say something but nothing came out.

"What do you mean?" Benson's voice was glacial.

Mellier for his part was almost bouncing on his toes. "Elizabeth called me late last night from the Astronomy Centre. She told me she had the diaries and she had decided to give them to Morgan. I told her that that was the right thing to do." He flung his arm toward the scene below. "Now what in the name of God has happened?"

Benson took a step toward me and squeezed my arm. "Is that true?"

I didn't even try to break loose. Instead I closed my eyes, willing this to be a bad dream but knowing that was futile. I pulled Elizabeth's note from my pocket. He let go of my arm, and I handed it to him. He read it over once, then a second time, his face like stone, then he folded it carefully and placed it in his pocket.

"Get out of my sight," he said, and he wheeled around and walked away.

Back in my room I packed quickly, called the airport, and booked a flight out for late that afternoon. I grabbed a coffee and a muffin in the cafeteria and met Mellier in the parking lot below. The medevac helicopter passed over our heads.

Mellier took the Saddle Road with the élan of a French rally driver, literally going airborne over the bumps. To his credit he was no longer angry at me, and even tried to assuage my guilt. When I explained what had happened, that I hadn't heard Elizabeth leave or push the note under my door, he gave a quiet shrug.

"But astronomers are very good at that. We are always sneaking around when other people are asleep so we get used to being very quiet. Really, you cannot blame yourself."

But of course I could, and I did.

Halfway down the Saddle Road the chopper passed above us once again, this time heading down to Hilo, just as we were.

At the emergency entrance we went directly to the front desk. After almost five minutes of waiting a receptionist in a white lab coat finally appeared.

"Can I help you?" she asked in an officious voice that said, in fact, she didn't really want to help us at all.

"Elizabeth Martin," I said. "She was just brought in by helicopter. Is there any news?"

I saw a slight softening in her face and my stomach dropped. I knew what that meant. "Have a seat," she said with institutionalized kindness. "I'll go find the doctor."

Ten minutes later a young woman in scrubs with a stethoscope dangling around her neck pushed through the swinging doors. The receptionist tipped her head to Mellier and myself. I could see the doctor steel herself, then she came forward and took the chair beside mine. She had a clipboard in her hands.

"Are you family?" she said softly.

Mellier started to say something. "Yes," I said firmly.

The doctor placed her hand on my arm. "I'm very sorry to tell you that Elizabeth Martin died in transport. The medics did everything they could but the injuries were too severe. Even if they'd managed to bring her in alive we still couldn't have saved her. If it's any consolation, she never regained consciousness after the initial impact. I'm very sorry."

Mellier had reached over and was now crushing my hand in his. It made the wounds on my hands sear, but I didn't mind the pain. It helped me stay focused. I took a deep breath. "May I see her?" I said. "It would mean a lot."

The doctor gave a nod and stood up. Mellier stayed seated and began to cry in that awkward, repressed way men do. He covered his eyes with his hand.

Elizabeth was still strapped to the gurney they'd wheeled her in on. Her coat had obviously been opened for an attempt to jump-start her heart, but it was now closed. Her face was smashed, her blonde hair bloodied, and all that intelligence and beauty were nothing now but death. I put my hand on her forehead hoping, I suppose, to feel some heat, some spark of life, but I felt only a clammy coolness.

I glanced up at the doctor. The tears in my eyes were real. "Could I have a minute?"

The door swished shut behind her. "Why," I said aloud. Even more than guilt and grief what I felt was seething anger. "Why the hell didn't you wait for me? Why did you go up there alone?" I moved to position myself between the door and the body. "You asked me to do something, to find those kids, and I'm damn well going to do it whether you like it or not."

I took a quick glance through the door then searched all of Elizabeth's Martin's pockets. Other than her keys, which I took, there was nothing to find. I was about to turn and walk away when I had an unpleasant thought. If a woman had to hide a piece of paper in a hurry would she put it in her pocket? No. She'd jam it in sock or, if she was really in a hurry, down her pants. I didn't want to go there but had no choice. I hoped nobody would walk in and misinterpret my actions.

I tried the shoes first, but there was nothing, then I pushed my hand down the front of her pants. I felt a folded paper, pulled it out, and stuffed it in my pocket without even looking at it. All I wanted to do was get out of that room.

The doctor came up beside me in the corridor outside. She still had the clipboard in hand. "Do you know the next of kin?"

"Sorry," I mumbled. "I'm not sure who she'd list."

"No, no," she shook her head. "We have the name of the next of kin, the HMO sent us all that information, but I was hoping you knew her husband personally. Sometimes a tragedy like this is easier to absorb if you speak to someone who was there. Someone who can tell you more than just an unknown doctor."

Her husband? I pulled out my notebook. "I've met him once or twice but I'm terrible with names. So many cousins, then their spouses and children too! If you can remind me of his name and give me the phone number I'd be happy to call."

She flipped through several pages on her clipboard until she found what she was looking for. "Here it is. Next of kin. Husband. Lives in Ottawa. A Dr. Duncan Carmichael."

For just a moment everything in my world stopped, as if the molecules themselves suddenly froze, then I slowly closed my notebook.

"You don't need a number?" she asked.

I shook my head. "Not to worry. I'll track him down."

chapter twelve

After leaving the hospital Andreas Mellier and I drove back over the Saddle Road to the headquarters in Waimea or, to be more exact, I drove Mellier in his car. He was in no condition to drive. Once at the telescope headquarters I'd hefted my bag and walked the few blocks to Shelton's house and my abandoned rental car. My briefcase and laptop were still in the trunk. I threw my suitcase in with them then took a stroll by Shelton's place. The curtains were drawn and the day's mail sat piled on the other side of the front door. I did a quick check up and down the street. It was tempting, the thought of breaking into Shelton's place, but in the end I decided against it. I didn't have time to do his house and Elizabeth Martin's and still catch my flight out. Reluctantly I walked back down the stairs and climbed into my car.

At the turnoff to Waikoloa Village I checked the map, located Elizabeth's street, and parked on the connecting road below her house. A quick reconnaissance on foot told me that I'd just received my first lucky break on an otherwise rotten day. Benson's team hadn't yet arrived to seal off her house. Looking more confident than I felt I strode up the driveway.

Elizabeth's neighbourhood was dingier than Yves Grenier's, the houses smaller and older. Most looked like they'd originally been built as cottages, but with the boom in Hawaiian real estate the owners had haphazardly converted them to permanent dwellings. Elizabeth's house was a small bungalow in need of a coat of white paint. An ill-kept hedge ran along the front and behind was a ratty little lawn, chipped concrete patio, and standard back door. I took out the keys I'd pulled from her body and let myself into a small, dark kitchen. Despite the exterior she kept the inside tidy and clean. Ahead of me was a pass through to a dining/living room. On my left a narrow hallway opened onto two small bedrooms, one used for sleeping, the other for an office. I heard a car drive by on the street outside. I had to move.

At her desk I pulled open drawers looking for personal files. The filing drawer on the right contained mortgage papers, tax files, banking information, and a file labelled "A&P." I pulled it out. It was filled with photographs of Peter and Alyssa at various family gatherings, usually with Duncan hovering in the background. Duncan's handwriting inscribed the details on the back. *Peter and Alyssa with Grandma at Christmas. Peter and Alyssa in daycare Easter play. Alyssa at her first piano recital.* I felt my heart squeeze and fought to stay in control. I'd taken that picture, and I wondered suddenly how Elizabeth had come to have it. I couldn't imagine Duncan sending her pictures, so it must have come from Yves Grenier, which would explain the close bond between them. I closed the folder and slipped it back in the drawer.

Beyond the children's file I found D for Divorce. All the legal back and forth was there, although it looked like a pretty straightforward, uncontested break. The custody papers were there as well, again uncontested, giving full custody to Duncan Carmichael.

I heard a car pull into the driveway out front. I jammed the divorce file back in the drawer and pulled out a file labelled "Will." A car door slammed. I flipped through the file. At the back was a sealed white envelope, which I pulled out. Someone tried the front door knob, and this was followed by a commanding voice.

"Let's try the back. It'll be easier to open."

I shoved the file back in place, shut the drawer, and vaulted out of the chair. At the front door I stopped and waited a moment. Footsteps disappeared around the side of the house. I held my breath, hoped they hadn't left someone sitting in the car, and stepped out onto the front stoop. A police cruiser sat in the middle of the driveway. I shut the door behind me, and just as I heard the back door open I sprinted down the driveway, then continued on walking casually down the street with my heart banging in my chest. In my car I took a second to check the envelope. *To be delivered to my children, Alyssa and Peter Carmichael of Ottawa, Canada,* it said on the cover, *in the event of my death.*

It was all I could do not to lay my head on the steering wheel and weep, but I didn't have time for grief. I had a plane leaving in less than an hour, and I could do more for Elizabeth by finding her children and delivering this letter in person than by sitting and crying in my car. And, I vowed as I slipped the letter inside my jacket, I would deliver the damn letter whether Duncan liked it or not. I took one last look at Elizabeth's house and pulled out onto the road.

At the airport I settled up for my two rental cars, telling them to charge me for the inconvenience of not having one actually with me, then I climbed on the plane with only moments to spare. I nipped into my seat, hastily fastened the seat belt, then sank back and closed my eyes, relaxing for the first time in hours. The plane jerked, pulled forward, and swung in a wide arc. It bumped along the runway then began to pick up speed and finally lurched into the air. Only then did I open my eyes. Below me the asphalt dropped away, the palm trees shrunk like startled anemones, and the paradise below was reduced to a ribbon of sand rising out of a turquoise sea.

As the plane climbed we came level with the stark peak of Mauna Kea, its domes glistening in the fierce sun. Just a few hours before Elizabeth Martin had been alive, stepping out of her car onto the summit's rubble. Where had she gone? What had taken place on that barren landscape? And who had the diaries now? Presumably the same person who'd cut her brake lines and sent her hurtling off the road.

The seat belt sign flickered off but I left myself firmly belted up, my leather jacket zipped to the collar. As I gazed at the summit I could almost feel Benson up there interviewing witnesses, snooping around the domes. At the thought of him, the memory of his scent, I felt even emptier than I had a moment before, as if, like the land below, my future had suddenly dropped away.

The plane banked left and headed out across the Pacific for Honolulu. Just as well. I'd burned my bridges and there was nothing for me here. After what I'd done Benson wouldn't let me anywhere near the case. I touched the chest of my leather jacket and felt the reassuring crackle of paper beneath. But it didn't really matter. Whoever had killed Elizabeth Martin was a puppet in a bigger game, and one that had nothing to do with palm trees and tropical sun. The root of this case — the motive — lay hidden somewhere beneath Canada's slush and snow. I was willing to bet my life on it.

The flight attendant appeared with coffee and a small bag of macadamia nuts, both of which I accepted. When she was gone I did a quick survey of my fellow passengers. The plane was about the size of a bus and no one looked familiar, which was a good sign. In fact, most of the passengers looked like Hawaiian housewives flying to Honolulu to shop. Still, I couldn't risk pulling out my treasures now. The space was too confined. At my stopover in Honolulu I'd find a private corner and see what I'd hauled in.

I glanced around, confirming once more that no one could see me here, nor could they approach without being seen. Despite the size of the Honolulu airport and the crowds near the airline gates, I'd managed to find a nook with a single bench where I was hidden and alone. I hauled my briefcase up beside me, pulled out a pair of tweezers, a small paper bag, and latex gloves, then carefully removed the scrunched-up paper I'd found on Elizabeth's body. I flattened it and, using the tweezers, placed it in on top of the bag. The lined paper certainly could have been torn from a lab notebook, and there was a date written across the top: the last day of Grenier's life. Below that it read:

> 0530 rc Daniel Marcotte (613) 789-4571:
>   Confirmed testing 1960 to 1964.
>   Gov't labs. Call Friday for contacts.
> 0623 tel SB/no.
> 0635 tel HK/no.
> 1700 AM @ HP
> 1823 AM, SA @ FCT

The writing ended abruptly following the entry at 1823.

I read the information over several times, trying to make sense of it. At least one thing was clear. Yves Grenier had made the last entry sitting in the FrancoCanadian Telescope the night he died. Both AM — Andreas Mellier — and SA — Shelton Aimes — had been present, and this piece of paper gave no indication that Grenier was planning to take his own life.

I went back to the top of the note and looked at the name Daniel Marcotte followed by an Ottawa phone number, then the years 1960 to 1964, the same period covered by the missing journals. Coincidence? I pulled out my notebook and meticulously copied everything from the tattered page. Tomorrow I could follow up with this Daniel Marcotte. Maybe he'd blow the whole thing open. I popped the note in the paper bag, sealed it, and put it in my briefcase.

With my first task finished I pulled Elizabeth's letter from my pocket. *To be delivered to my children, Alyssa and Peter Carmichael of Ottawa, Canada, in the event of my death.* I stared at it and felt a shiver rise through my body. Had Elizabeth known she was at risk, or was this just the precaution of an estranged mother working in a dangerous profession? I gave the flap a speculative tug, but it remained firmly adhered. Usually I have no compunction about opening someone else's mail, but this was different. How could I justify my actions to the wide, innocent eyes of Alyssa and Peter? I slipped the envelope back into my jacket pocket.

I checked my watch. I still had a little time left. It was just past two in Honolulu, making it around four in Vancouver. I found a payphone and dialed Sylvia's office.

"Dr. Delgado?" the receptionist answered. "She's on long-term leave. Can I direct your call elsewhere?"

I felt an unpleasant jolt of adrenaline. "Since when?"

There was the hesitation of a well-trained employee at the other end, so I pushed. "It's Morgan O'Brien from the National Council for Science and Technology, and it's urgent. When did she go on leave?"

"A week ago at least." Then the young woman lowered her voice. "I think it's some kind of medical thing so I'm not sure when she'll be back."

So Sylvia was out of remission. The tumour nestled deep in her brain had decided to start growing again. I thanked the receptionist, hung up, and poked in Sylvia's home number. She picked up on the first ring. "Delgado."

"Why didn't you tell me?"

"Oh, it's you. I should have known. Who else calls from a payphone? Where the hell are you?"

I wasn't going to let her weasel out of it. "Why didn't you tell me?"

"Oh for Christ's sake, you didn't ask."

"Why should I? You were in remission."

"And what would you have done? Climbed on your tall white steed and ridden out here to save me? It doesn't work that way, babe. I'm on enforced R&R. Beyond that there's not much else can be done. A little chemo, a few zaps of radiation, then we wait and see."

"If I'd known you were on R&R I wouldn't have sent you work."

"You don't think I'm offline? Please, there are limits. I promised I wouldn't go into the office. Am I in the office? Nope. Anyway, this isn't work, it's fun, and without a little fun a girl might as well be dead, if you catch my drift."

I hated Sylvia's gallows humour and I didn't laugh. Six months ago she'd been feeling perky and things were looking good. Now I wondered now how long she'd be alive. "The case is all wrapped up," I lied. "I'm on my way home. When I'm back in Ottawa I'll —

"Good try, O'Brien, but can it. The case isn't all wrapped up. You're calling to follow up on those journals, so here it is. I've scanned the complete contents of each issue, I'm running that through a text recognition program, and once I have everything in digital format I can begin to play, start doing keyword searches, and see what I come up with, but I'll need another day, maybe two."

I ran that over in my mind. Sylvia was going to do what Sylvia was going to do whether I liked it or not. She certainly wasn't going to go offline for R&R, so I might as well give her something to keep her occupied. "Okay," I said with resignation. "The truth is something has come up that might help."

"The case isn't closed? Surprise, surprise." I heard paper rustle on her desk. "What have you got?"

"In Grenier's last diary entry —"

"You found the diaries?"

"Just the last page. I can't explain it now, but the day he died Grenier may have spoken to someone in Ottawa about something being tested, possibly in government labs, between 1960 and 1964."

"So I should be looking at technology, something to do with optics or instrument development from Canadian government labs?"

"It's possible. On the other hand this may have nothing to do with the journals." But I sure as hell hoped it did.

"It's a place to start. When are you back in Ottawa?"

"Early, so don't call tomorrow before noon. With any luck I'll be asleep."

"Hey, I'm on R&R and that's nine in the morning here. Anyway, like I said, this may take me a day or two. When I find something I'll be in touch."

I lay in bed and groaned. A river of light spilled through the gap in my curtains, flooding my eyes with hot, red light. I rolled over and covered my head with the blankets. It felt like I'd been asleep less than an hour, but when I peeked out from beneath the covers my bedside clock read just after eleven. Better than I'd thought but still way too early. My caffeine addiction, though, didn't agree. It said it was time to get up or risk a headache, so I forced my legs over the side of the bed.

I'd arrived at Ottawa's Macdonald-Cartier airport in what felt like the dead of night, but was really just after dawn. As I'd pushed my way out the revolving door my face had been stung by needles of freezing rain, and by the time I'd reached the car I was shivering and wet. My car, after several days in the lot, was encased in solid ice several inches thick. I managed to chip a hole around the lock, get the key inside, and yank open the door, but the effort was so exhausting that I couldn't imagine getting out and hacking the ice off all the windows. Instead I decided to just sit in the car with the heat on high until the ice slid off in glacial sheets. By the time I left the parking lot the sky had lightened enough to consider it day and rush hour traffic clogged the streets.

When I finally got to my apartment I didn't even bother to shower. I ignored the message light blinking on my phone, peeled off my clothes, and hopped into bed. Within seconds I was comatose. That was less than three hours ago.

As my feet touched the cold of the floor it jerked me awake just enough to consider my options for the day. The first thing I had to do was get coffee. Next on the agenda was a shower, followed by a cleanup of the cuts on my wrists. They were healing nicely, but a big glob of antibiotic cream and new bandages would be a wise decision. Beyond that I needed breakfast. Once the caffeine and food had done their job I'd work out the rest of the day. I had a transient thought of calling Bob, my boss, to let him know I was back, but nixed that idea quickly. He'd want me back in the office, and I didn't have time for that right now. I'd just have to keep my head down and hope our paths didn't cross. Half an hour later, briefcase in hand and with my first cup of coffee beginning to kick in, I locked my apartment door and headed out to eat.

I live in the downtown core off a funky little strip called Elgin Street, just down the road from Parliament Hill. My street is part of a rectangle of old brick mansions that front onto a small park, complete with a children's playground enclosed in a wrought iron fence. A hundred years ago this was a high-class neighbourhood housing members of Parliament, business tycoons, and well-placed judges and lawyers, but then times changed. During the Depression the luxury mansions were chopped up into apartments and rooming houses, and the park became a haven for the homeless, which it remains today. But times have changed again. The twenty-something dot-com cappuccino crowd discovered the neighbourhood and started to buy up the old mansions and restore them to their former glory. I just hoped I'd be able to keep my apartment, the second floor of one of the old houses, another couple of years before it was sold or condo-ized.

At the bottom of my walkway I turned right and strolled down the sidewalk toward Elgin. At Elgin I turned right again and made my way up the street, hardly glancing at the restaurants, bars, boutiques, and cafés. It was a refreshing walk. After the bleakness of dawn the sun had managed to burn through the clouds and now shone upon the ice with the force of spring. Everything sparkled, and the sound of ice-melt filled the air. Water poured off roofs, streamed across the sidewalk, and cascaded down the storm drains in a symphony of sound. I was happy to be home, happy to be in a place where I could depend on backup and knew the rules.

At the Mayflower, my usual breakfast spot, I pulled open the door to the luscious aroma of the all-day cholesterol special — eggs, waffles, and sausages — and slipped into my favourite booth. I gave the waiter my order then got up and went to the pay-phone. I put my quarter in and dialed. The voice that answered was low and wary.

"Yeah?" he said.

I'd been hoping for a secretary or at the very least a business greeting. "I'd like to speak to Daniel Marcotte."

"You've got him."

"I'm a friend of Yves Grenier's." With that hook in the water I waited to see if I'd get a strike, but there was no response. He let the bait dangle. I decided to take a chance. "I'm calling about the contacts."

"Who am I speaking with?"

"My name is Morgan O'Brien. Yves couldn't make the call, I was in town, he asked me to make it for him."

"He did, did he?" Skepticism dripped from his voice. Best to forge ahead.

"Did you manage to get those contacts?"

There was a pause. "Morgan O'Brien? That's what you said your name was?" He gave an abrupt laugh. "Well, listen up, Morgan O'Brien, or whatever your name really is. I don't know who the hell you are or what you're talking about. Now if you'll excuse me, I've got work to do." He banged down the phone.

I could see my waffles, eggs, and sausages had arrived at the table so I gave a mental shrug and returned to the booth. You win some, you lose some.

Under normal circumstances I would have fired up my laptop, done a quick search on the guy, and known more about him than he'd like in a very short time, but my laptop and cellphone were off limits. Cellphones are too damn easy to monitor, and as for my laptop, Gunnar had doubtless installed some spy-ware while he had it in his possession, so until I could get the hard drive wiped and everything reinstalled I couldn't use it.

I slowly munched through my breakfast, adding an extra big dose of maple syrup to remind me I was home, and considered my options. I could call Lydia, but I still felt uneasy about our last conversation. She was too close to Duncan to trust. I could always ask Sylvia and have her do the search for me, but that would take a few hours, or I could — I smiled — support my public library. I altered my leisurely pace and gobbled down the rest of my breakfast.

Half an hour later I left the library with everything I needed to know about Daniel Marcotte, at least for now, specifically his address and his occupation. Daniel Marcotte, the Internet had revealed, was a freelance investigative journalist with a particular interest in Ottawa scandals. It certainly explained his refusal to divulge his contacts, but his contacts on what? Why had Grenier called him? Now that I had his address I planned on paying a visit, but not right away. I had a more pressing engagement.

Duncan's house is located in a quiet residential neighbourhood on the west side of Ottawa. The heart of Westboro, as the area is known, is a strip that runs along Richmond Road and varies from politically correct cafés to upscale outdoor stores. In behind is a neighbourhood of big trees, older houses, and landscaped yards.

Duncan's house is on a narrow street about two blocks up from Richmond Road. With the lack of sidewalks and open ditches the place had the feel of a country road, and the street was so narrow that parking was a challenge, but this made my job easier. Staking out Duncan's place would be damn near impossible. If someone was running surveillance I'd spot them pretty quick.

I parked my car in a public lot on Richmond Road then began what looked like a meandering stroll on the streets around Duncan's. I crisscrossed the area above and below his house looking for anything unusual. I carefully noted the dog walkers, making sure that I saw no one more than once, and I passed his place twice, looking for any houses nearby with the curtains drawn in the middle of the day.

When I was sure there was nothing out of the ordinary I cut across the street and jogged up the stairs of the house directly across from his. The large porch was littered with outdoor toys: hockey nets, plastic sleds, and small trucks of various sizes and shapes. I pressed the doorbell. A moment later a woman arrived at the door with a toddler on her hip. The child regarded me with large, blank eyes.

"Yes," she said abruptly. She looked harried and probably assumed that I was selling something door to door.

"I'm a friend of Duncan's," I said, pointing to his house across the street. "I met you at Peter's birthday party last year."

Her expression softened. "Right. Morgan. Sorry, I've got one home sick and the other teething. Will it never end?" She pushed open the screen door and I stepped into the vestibule. The voice of SpongeBob SquarePants came from somewhere inside. "What can I do for you?" she asked. The baby started to wriggle. She set him down, and he toddled off in the direction of the living room, but she kept her eye on his retreating back.

"I'm looking for Duncan. Do you know where he is?"

"He went to see family I think." She pushed a strand of hair over her ear, half attending to me, half keeping an ear on the activity in living room. "Is there a problem?"

"I've been away and I have some urgent business that I need to discuss with him. You've no idea where he went?"

She thought for a minute. "It was a bit odd."

I felt a surge of anticipation but hid it. "What do you mean?"

"I was out with the dog the morning they left. Duncan said it was a family emergency but —" She hesitated as if she didn't want to implicate Duncan in a lie.

"It's important," I said.

"Well, it looked more like a family vacation. Skis, toboggan, snowshoes, the whole kit and caboodle. I thought maybe they were headed for Mont-Tremblant."

I smiled. "That makes sense. I'll try some of the places I know he stays up there, see what I can dig up." I was halfway out the door when I turned. "You haven't noticed anything unusual in the neighbourhood, have you?"

A child wailed in the background and she started to retreat. "Just the usual. Door-to-door solicitors, tele-marketers, and two household surveys, usually at nap time. Mine," she nodded in the direction of the living room, "not theirs."

I gave a nod of thanks and walked down the road. I thought briefly of breaking into Duncan's house just to see what was missing, but from what his neighbour had just told me I probably didn't have to. I had a pretty good idea where he'd gone.

snowshoes or skis, and the tracks would quickly disappear in the relentless blowing snow. Would Duncan have a key? It didn't matter. At this time of year the lake was all but deserted. He'd just jack open the padlock and no one would be the wiser until the cottagers returned on the twenty-fourth of May.

I started my car. It was a long way to go on a hunch, but I had Elizabeth's letter to deliver and some questions that needed immediate answers. Whether I'd ask Duncan my questions before or after I throttled him was yet to be decided.

I drove through downtown Ottawa, crossed the river, and traversed the core of Hull. As I passed through to the other side of the city the tightly packed government buildings stretched into sprawling suburbs, which, as I headed further north, gave way to pastoral farms. The highway then ended abruptly, forcing me onto a two-lane municipal route that, itself, finally narrowed into a twisting rural road. Up here a heavy blanket of snow still covered the land, broken only by the dark rocks and trees that pushed through it. As I drove on I willed my mind to wander, to free associate, but it remained firmly fixed on Duncan, playing and replaying the possible scenarios of our upcoming meeting. None of them were pleasant.

After more than an hour of driving I slowed and began to watch the left side of the road until I saw a hand-painted sign hanging askew from a large birch. "Lac au Sable" it read with an arrow pointing down a narrow lane. I turned and geared down as my car half slid, half rolled down the icy track. The road levelled further down and a lake appeared, an open sweep of white. Dépanneur Réjean sat on the shore, a decrepit little store and marina that I had assumed would be closed in winter, but to my surprise a neon bottle of Labatt's beer glowed in the window. I pulled into the makeshift parking lot. If Duncan were around, Réjean, the old guy who ran the place, would know.

On the stoop I caught the rich overtones of hardwood smoke floating in the breeze. I pushed open the door and a bell tinkled. There was a shuffling from somewhere in the back. The time I'd visited Duncan it had been in the middle of summer and the dark interior of Dépanneur Réjean had been cluttered with cans, dried goods, and junk food of all descriptions. Now, at the end of winter, the shelves were almost bare except for staples. The cooler glowed with at least ten different brands of beer, the case behind the cash was piled high with cartons of cigarettes, and a new Lotto machine hummed quietly beside the aging cash register.

"*Je peux vous aider?*"

I looked up to see a young man, definitely not Réjean, standing in the back doorway. He was short and stocky with a moustache and crew cut. He looked out of place in the plaid shirt and jeans, especially standing "at-ease" like that. I made a rapid change of plans. "I just need some milk for my tea," I said, and I headed for a container of UHT milk sitting next to the beer.

He strolled over and stood behind the cash register. "You from around here?"

I kept my voice casual. "Where's Réjean?"

"Florida. I am Charles, his grandson." He pronounced his name *Sharl* in the French way. "I come up here so they can go away."

"We have a chalet down the road." I waved vaguely in the direction of the lake. "I try to get up here once a year to ski. Is the lake still solid?" I slid the money for the milk across the counter.

He shrugged. "I don't ski myself."

"Too bad. It's good for the cardiovascular. Is there anyone else around?"

"Some snowmobiles on the weekend, a little bit of ice fishing, but during the week you'll be all alone. How far down is your cabin?"

"Just over the first hill."

"That's good. If the weather turns bad you shouldn't have any trouble getting out." He put the milk in a used plastic grocery bag. "You stay long?"

I picked up the bag. "Just in for the day."

"You should stop by when you leave. That way I know you made it out safe."

I smiled. "I'll do that. Thanks for the milk."

I could feel him watch my back as I left the store.

Outside I got back in my car and pulled onto the road. From Réjean's store it wove around the edge of the lake in two icy ruts giving access to the cottages scattered along that side of the lake. The other side was water access only. Just beyond Réjean's the road entered the woods again, a forest of hardwoods, old fir and pine. Even with the deciduous trees stripped of leaves only slashes of sun managed to cut through the canopy above and they glowed against the shadows on the snow.

I came over the first rise, slowed, and turned to look through my rear window. Charles, or whoever he was, couldn't see me from here. I turned into the first cottage and parked my car in plain view. I then walked up the stairs, knelt down to conserve heat, and waited. At first the world seemed utterly quiet with no movement or noise, but slowly the subtle sounds of nature emerged. The wind swished through firs, chickadees cheeped and flitted in the low brush, a red squirrel rushed up the stairs toward me only to be brought up short by my unexpected presence. She scurried up a nearby pine and scolded me from an overhanging branch. By the end of twenty minutes I could no longer feel my toes. I also hadn't heard a single thing that I could identify as human, so I stood back up, my joints protesting the sudden movement, and went back to the car. At least Charles wasn't on my tail. I started the car and backed out onto the road.

I moved slowly down the lake, searching for landmarks on the far shore. Duncan's cabin was hidden somewhere in behind, but would I recognize where? The shoreline looked so different covered in heavy snow. Then, just ahead, I saw a movement, a feeble wisp of smoke curling about the trees. I pulled into the nearest cottage and a minute later was lumbering down to the shore with my skis on my shoulder and my snowshoes strapped to my back.

At least a foot of snow covered the ice, grainy beneath but with a heavy crust across the top. I carefully placed my weight on one ski. I had a moment of hope that the crust would hold, that I'd be able to fly across the top, but the ski broke through. What could have been a simple crossing would be a slow and painful slog, with my skis sinking at every stride. I considered using my snowshoes but then decided against it. The skis, I reasoned, would still be faster. Anyway, I could change in the middle if I had to.

I wasn't thirty metres from shore when I felt prickles of sweat run down my neck. I stopped to unzip my jacket and at the same time glanced down toward Réjean's. Out here, out on the ice, the world was a featureless grey, the lake blending with shore, the shore melding with an overcast sky. Only the trees stood out in contrast, dark spikes against the luminescent grey. I put my hand above my dark glasses to cut out more light and turned to study the shore ahead. It took me a moment to find it but in a clump of spruce I saw the glint of a window. With that as a point of reference I could then make out the broken outline of the roof amongst the trees. I followed an imaginary line down to the shore where a finger of land jutted into the lake. In my mind I could now see the altered shoreline of summer, with the floating dock bobbing off the end of that point. I pulled out a compass, took a heading, and started to ski. If the weather came up in a sudden whiteout I'd still make my destination.

I reached the point of land soaked with sweat and my chest heaving. I took a minute to catch my breath, then turned parallel to the shore and started around the point. Behind it lay a little bay, and at the base of this was a small beach with a path running up to the cabin. As I rounded the point, though, I stopped. A set of footprints — snowshoes to be exact — crossed the bay, climbed up the shore, and headed up the path to the cabin. There'd been no other tracks on the lake, at least not from the direction I'd come. I turned back to the lake and squinted. These tracks seemed to come out of nowhere, as if the wearer had risen up from the lake itself. And it couldn't be Duncan. He would never leave the children alone with a burning wood stove. With my eyes I followed the tracks up the path. The fact that they went in only one direction — up, and not down — was particularly disconcerting.

I sidestepped into a stand of spruce and considered my situation. I was unarmed, out in the middle of nowhere, and entirely alone. Common sense told me to get the hell out of here, but Duncan might be up there alone with two small children. Duncan could take care of himself, and damn well should after what he'd put me through, but the children were quite another matter. Then I thought of my promise to Elizabeth Martin. If they needed help, I had to go.

I slipped off my skis, hid them beneath a tree, and strapped on the snowshoes. Then, crouching, I made my way to the other side of the spruce stand. So far I'd heard no human noise, no high-pitched little voices, no resonant tones of an adult male. Was that a good sign or not? I could see the outline of cabin above and knew if I kept low and followed the line of trees I could get close to the front door without being seen — at least I could in the middle of summer. What the terrain was like covered in ice and snow I had no idea, but I also had no other options.

I edged my way upward, and when I was close enough to see the door I crouched beneath another spruce and waited, hoping to see movement or hear something inside. The snow in front of the door was compacted with footprints, both big and small, so I had been right, this was Duncan's hideaway, but I didn't feel any sense of victory. All I felt was dread.

I unstrapped my snowshoes and leaned them against the tree then quietly crossed to the stairs. My boots squeaked on the packed snow. I hesitated a minute, trying to prepare myself for whatever I might see, then I leaned over and peered in the small window next to the door. In the dim light all I could see was a mess, but an inanimate mess. Clothes, blankets, and toys on the floor.

I put my hand on the knob and the door swung open. I waited a moment then stepped inside. The place smelled of human habitation — of food recently cooked, of wet wool. Something snapped and I jumped, but I realized it was only a piece of wood smouldering in the stove.

"Shit," I muttered, trying to shake the fear from my body.

In front of me a ladder led to an open trap door in the floor above. Upon the rungs hung little woolen mittens and toques. I looked up. The second floor, I knew, was divided into two rough rooms, one for guests and one for the children, but what was up there now? I pulled the ladder down and laid it on the floor. I didn't want any surprises descending from above. Outside, the pines trembled in the wind and I turned to look out. Would I feel safer, I wondered, with the door wide open or shut up tight? Then I realized it didn't matter. I wouldn't feel safe until I was away from this place, the faster the better.

The first thing I did was examine the main-floor bedroom. It was hardly more than an alcove with a built-in bed and a small window that let in little light. A sleeping bag lay crumpled on the bed and the room had the musty smell of sweat. Feeling just a tad silly I bent down and checked beneath the bed. There were lots of dust bunnies roaming around but the only signs of a true mammalian species were the pellets left behind by a family of mice.

I moved from there to the kitchen. The sink was filled with dirty dishes and the remnants of what looked like canned beans. It wasn't like Duncan to leave dishes undone, especially not here in the cabin. The smell would attract bears, and hungry as they were at this time of year they'd go through that front door like a toddler through gift wrap.

In front of the wood stove I knelt and peered inside. A heavy layer of ash lay across the bottom with only a single black crescent of log that sputtered and glowed on top. How long would it have taken to burn that log down? Two hours? Four? I banged the stove-door shut, stood, and looked uneasily at the trap door. So far I'd heard nothing from up there, not even a whisper or a creak. I dreaded it, but I had to go up.

I lifted the ladder, braced it against the edge of the opening, then began a slow and quiet ascent up the rungs. At even the hint of a noise I'd drop off that ladder faster than a tick off a dead dog. When I was just below the hatch I waited a moment, held my breath then sprung through the opening like a missile. I flattened myself against the wall and waited to see what would happen. When nothing did, I edged my way along the wall until I came to the door of the guest room. I flicked it with my foot and it swung open with an ominous squeak. Through the murky light I could see that the bed was made, the room was tidy and there was nowhere to hide. That left the children's room.

I crossed the hall, took the knob in my hand, turned it slowly then banged the door open. There was no movement, no sound at all, just two unmoving mounds in sleeping bags, one on each twin bed. I crossed the room in an instant, peeled down the zipper, and pulled open one of the bags. I had fully expected a body, my only hope being that the body would still be alive, so it took me a minute to integrate what I was seeing. I whipped around and yanked the zipper down on the other sleeping bag. Pillows. Somebody had stuffed the sleeping bags full of pillows to make it look like there was someone inside. What the hell was going on?

I began my search at the base of the outside stairs and moved like a pendulum, but swinging further down with each arc. I found what I was looking for just beyond the hard-packed snow underneath a tree. Duncan must have been a Boy Scout. The surface had been disturbed, brushed over with a branch. Ten metres away a set of tracks emerged from the swept snow and disappeared into the brush. I strapped on my snowshoes and prepared to follow.

When I got to the undisguised trail I could make out a set of snowshoe tracks, but running on top of them was the unmistakable skid mark of a toboggan holding a fair bit of weight. I followed on, keeping to the side of the track. Duncan seemed to have followed a rough trail, a game trail perhaps, then another ten metres up my heart missed a beat. Coming in from my right some-one else — also travelling on snowshoes — had picked up the trail. I crossed over to get a better view.

It was a high-tech snowshoe, more like mine than the traditional wood and leather style Duncan used. I placed my foot inside for comparison. Whoever owned those prints was big. The length of the imprint and depth of displacement was considerably larger than mine. I'd have to check this imprint against the ones coming up from the lake. I was pretty sure they were the same, but I hadn't taken a lot of time to carefully examine the others.

I turned back to the trail and started forward again. Where the hell was Duncan going, leaving all the supplies back in the cabin while heading into the back-woods with two small kids? Was he crazy? Up ahead the trail rose up a steep bank to a clearing above. As I approached I could see that the children had gotten off the toboggan and clambered up the hill on all fours. Mr. Snowshoe on the other side had gone up sideways, keeping to the right of Duncan's trail. I went up side-ways too, making a third trail beside the other two.

As I stepped over the rise my quest came to an end. A car had been parked in the clearing, which wasn't a clearing at all but a summer-use logging road so new it probably wasn't here when I visited. This was how Duncan got in. And he obviously got out the same way.

I looked around. The footprints led up to four neat depressions that marked the place where the car had been parked. The car had done a three-point turn and taken off down the road. The only one not to get in was Mr. Snowshoe. Like me he had cased the area, his tracks overlaying some of the tire tracks, then he followed the tire tracks a few metres before veering off over the edge of the road and disappearing into the forest. Whoever he was, he knew the territory well enough to take a secondary route back to the lake. I sure couldn't do that, and with that thought I turned around and began the shuffling jog that would take me back down the slope to the cabin and my skis.

Back in my car I felt only exhaustion. When I passed Réjean's the neon beer bottle was no longer lit and my intuition told me to keep right on going. About thirty kilometres down the road I found a *casse-croûte*, a roadside snack bar, and ordered a coffee and poutine to go. Normally I avoid poutine, a heart-stopping combination of French fries, cheddar cheese curds, and thick gravy, but right now, on the verge of hypothermia, I craved the calories and fat. The coffee, I hoped, would keep me awake when all that food hit my bloodstream.

By now, the day was beginning to fade, and as I sat in the driver's seat forking fries into my mouth I considered my next move. Duncan had been in that cabin. More important, Duncan had fled, leaving behind clothes, dirty dishes, and sleeping bags. Someone else was on his tail and they were a step ahead of me. I checked my watch. I was tired, grumpy, and becoming totally pissed off with my lack of progress. Bottom line, I had only one strong lead, a certain journalist named Daniel Marcotte who was playing hard to get. Grenier had called him the day he died, and I wanted to know why. It was time to pay Marcotte a visit.

With the rush hour traffic clogging the bridges it took me an hour and half to get back to the city. Along the way I'd stopped for another coffee, and by the time I reached Marcotte's I was in fighting form. Daniel Marcotte lived in a house on the west side of Ottawa near the Parkdale Farmers Market. His house, like the others on the street, was an old, narrow, wooden structure, but Marcotte's house was nicely done up in pale yellow with clean, white trim. Flower boxes hung from the porch railing, and I could imagine them in summer spilling with blooms. Marcotte's house was wedged between two of a similar vintage, but without the same pride of ownership. They were ramshackle affairs with peeling paint and bits of trim hanging off at odd angles. Plastic toys lay scattered across the melting snow.

A light went on in one of Marcotte's windows. That was excellent news. It might be a wife or a roommate, but at least it would get me in the door. I left my car parked a few houses down, crossed the street, and strode up the stairs. The top half of the door was a glass window looking down a dark, narrow hall. At the end of the hall was the bright light of the kitchen. I banged hard. It took a moment, but I heard a thump from the floor above and someone barrelled down the stairs that stood at the side of the hall. A man appeared in the glass window, gave me the once-over, assumed as a woman I posed no threat, then pulled open the front door. Big mistake.

"Daniel Marcotte?" His eyes widened, but before he had time to react I had my foot in the door. "We need to talk. About Yves Grenier."

He tried to slam the door shut, but I threw my shoulder against the wood and gave a sharp push. He staggered back. A moment later I was inside with the door closed firmly behind me. At the sound of the ruckus, though, a form had appeared at the other end of the hall, back-lit by the lights beyond. He wasn't tall, shorter than me, but he was built like a tank: broad shoulders, biceps like loaves of bread, and a shaved head. He didn't come forward. He just stood there like something in a bad movie, a bulked-up shadow against a halo of light.

As Marcotte gathered himself up I was faced with a new reality. Marcotte himself was no pipsqueak. It was just that he dressed like a writer geek — button-down shirt and cargo pants — so he looked less intimidating. Suddenly, between the weightlifter at the end of the hall and Marcotte at my side, barging in didn't seem like such a bright idea.

Marcotte seemed to read my mind. He leaned against the wall and brushed himself off. The big guy took a step forward. I backed myself into the corner, placed one leg slightly behind the other, and lowered my centre of gravity. I planned to inflict at least a bit of damage before being squashed like a fly, but when the big guy — dressed head to toe in black — got within range, Marcotte stepped between us and put up his hand.

"Don't," he said.

Mr. Muscle eyed me then gave a little shrug. "I'll go finish dinner," he said, and he turned and walked away. Halfway down the hall, though, he stopped. The jeans and T-shirt were so tight I could see every muscle contract. "Will your guest be staying for dinner?"

"She's on her way out," said Marcotte, and he reached for the door.

"Yves Grenier is dead."

He stood for a moment, his eyes on mine, then he dropped his hand.

"Who are you? Not your name. I already know that."

"I'm an investigator." I fumbled in my pocket and held out my ID. "Yves Grenier died in Hawaii about twenty-four hours after he called you. I think he was murdered."

He reached across and took my ID. He examined it, but I could see his mind was elsewhere, and I was pretty sure I knew where. He was a reporter, I was an investigator, and the mix, for him, was like oil and water: it never really took. He flicked the edge of the card on the palm of his hand. I stepped back and leaned against the wall. It was a tough call for Marcotte. He didn't trust me, he didn't want to trust me, but his journalistic nose smelled something spicy. "What happened?" he said, almost reluctantly.

"As far as the Hawaiian police are concerned he hung himself, sent a suicide note and everything. I'm not so sure."

He let that register then turned and stared out the window behind me. After what seemed like forever he turned and called down the hall.

"Freddy," he said. "You better set another place."

The breath I'd been holding escaped in a quiet rush of air. I hoped to hell these boys served wine.

chapter fourteen

We ate in the kitchen at a table set with china, candles and all. Frederick sat across from me. Up close he wasn't a monster at all. In fact he was excessively polite, had impeccable manners, and spoke with a quiet confidence. But then, when you're carrying that much extra muscle you don't need to press the point. Frederick was also an excellent chef. We were eating, he told me, a *daube*, a stew from the south of France flavoured with orange and wine. It was accompanied by a hearty red Syrah that Marcotte applied liberally to my glass.

I had no illusions about what he was up to. Marcotte didn't plan to cooperate, but he smelled a story and he wasn't going to let it slither away. I, though, was exhausted from my day of skiing, preoccupied by Duncan's disappearance, and suffering from creeping jet lag. Without thinking I guzzled the first glass. It flooded my brain like an injectable drug, and I realized, sadly too late, that I was now going to have to fight to stay ahead of Marcotte's game. I let him fill my glass a second time but was careful to take minuscule sips.

And Marcotte, I discovered while eating, was a good reporter. He spent the first half of dinner making no mention of Grenier at all. Instead he gently grilled me, probing where I worked, how I accomplished my job, and who I knew. I answered as truthfully as I could while omitting any reference to the dubious provenance of this particular case.

After the *daube*, which was so tender that the meat melted on the tongue, Frederick got up and brought a simple green salad to the table, but instead of sitting down he disappeared. I heard him climb the stairs and a few minutes later there was the murmur of conversation above. Marcotte was watching me.

"What does he do for a living?" I asked.

"Frederick?" He gave me an amused smile. "He's a cop." He lifted his glass and eyed me over the rim. "I hope you've been telling the truth."

I raised my glass. "Here's to the cops. Now it's your turn. Tell me about your call from Yves Grenier."

"Not until you're in the clear."

A few minutes later Frederick came back downstairs and gave a single nod in Marcotte's direction, then he turned and left the room. Apparently I'd been vetted and passed. "So now," said Marcotte, "we make a deal."

"What kind of deal?"

"You tell me what you know, I tell you what I know."

"I'm investigating a murder."

He shrugged. "Have it your way."

"I could have you subpoenaed."

"I'm protecting my sources. It's gone to court before and you'd never win."

I considered that. He was right. Anyway, it was all bluff on my part since there was no murder investigation here in Canada, just me off on a wild goose chase, but Marcotte didn't need to know that. "Do I have your word that you'll hold off on publishing until the investigation is over?"

"It depends."

"That's not good enough." I stood up. "Looks like we can't do business."

"Why should I trust you?"

I gave a snort. "You trust Frederick and he's a cop."

"How did you know Grenier called me?"

I let that question hang in the air for a minute. "Does that mean we have a deal?"

"I won't be part of a cover-up. You understand what I'm saying?"

I felt a little zing go up my spine. "Then we must be on the same side because I won't be part of one either." I pulled out a photocopy of Grenier's diary from the last day of his life and laid it flat in front of Marcotte. "Grenier wrote that the day he died."

He examined it for a minute without speaking then looked at me. "Where'd you get this?"

"A gift from the Hawaii County Police Department." I reached out for the paper, but he pulled it toward him.

"What's this?" he said. He pointed to the other entries. "Who's SB? HK? AM?"

I gave a little *tsk tsk* and pulled the paper back. "You share first."

Marcotte looked away, and I could see him calculating how much he'd have to say to get me to reciprocate. In the warm glow of the candles, shadows played across the planes of his face. He was a good-looking man, dark, with a moustache that gave him a Latin look, almost Middle Eastern. He seemed to reach a conclusion and turned back to me.

"Have you ever heard of the Fruit Machine?"

It rang a bell, but I couldn't place it. I shook my head.

"And you, working for the National Council for Science and Technology. What is this country coming to?" Then he dropped the sarcasm. "In the late 1950s and early '60s the RCMP and National Defence contracted secretly with your organization — the Council for Science and Technology — to develop a 'homosexual detector,' fondly referred to as the Fruit Machine. We were at the height of the Cold War, the CIA was putting pressure on the RCMP to clean up Canadian security leaks, and the RCMP Security Services promised they would. The first thing they did was create a special investigative unit — known as Section A-3 — which was devoted entirely to investigating, identifying, and removing homosexuals from the civil service, based on the belief that homosexuals were not only weak individuals, they were vulnerable to blackmail by Soviet agents. But, as A-3 began their work, they made a terrible discovery. It was hard to tell who was bent and who wasn't, so they decided to develop a fag detector and they contracted with a group of university and government scientists to do it. The outcome was the Fruit Machine. Before Trudeau became prime minister and reminded us all that the government has no business in the bedrooms of the nation, the RCMP managed to purge between three and five hundred men from their jobs under the guise of national security." Then he gave me a nasty smile. "I broke the story a couple of years ago and not everyone was thrilled. That's why he called me. Grenier wanted information on the Fruit Machine."

"Did he say why?"

Marcotte gave a shrug. "I presumed he was gay, sort of a reclaiming history thing."

I watched him for a moment. He was telling me the truth, just not all of it. "What about this reference to contacts. It says 'Will call with contacts Friday.' What's that about?"

Marcotte shifted, becoming cagey. He twirled his wineglass and watched the liquid swirl as he spoke. "I'd interviewed a few guys for my article, men who'd been tested and lost their jobs, but none of them wanted their names in print. Old wounds. Grenier wanted to speak to them. I couldn't give him the names without their permission."

"And?"

He leaned his chair back so it was balanced on two legs. "They all refused."

"This isn't a game, Marcotte. Two people are dead."

"Two? Now who's holding out?"

Marcotte was ticking me off. "What does this mean?" I said abruptly. "'Tested from 1960 to 1964. Volunteers gov't labs.'"

He thumped forward on the chair and pulled the paper toward him. "Grenier wanted details on how the machine was tested. The thing is, the Fruit Machine never officially existed. It was kept secret even from the Prime Minister's Office, so the history's a little sketchy, but from what I could establish the RCMP started developing this thing sometime in the late fifties. By 1964 it still didn't work, one reason being that they couldn't get enough volunteers to test and debug the damned thing. In the end the researchers had to recruit volunteers from the government labs."

"And Grenier? What was he after?"

"He wanted the names of people used in the testing. That's why he wanted to talk to my contacts."

"But why?"

He shrugged. "I don't know and that was the last I heard from him."

I sighed and looked at the page of Grenier's diary again. Was I wasting my time here? Was this all just a sidebar or did it have something to do with his death? "Do you have copies of those articles you wrote?"

"Yeah. Yeah, sure I do."

When he'd headed up the stairs I went to the sink and dumped the rest of my wine. I was filling the empty glass with water when Frederick came into the kitchen, ostensibly to make coffee but probably to keep an eye on me.

"You a uniform?" I said.

He shook his head. "Ident officer." Jesus. That was way up there. It required lots of study and dedication. I wondered if he was out. I couldn't imagine the local police promoting a known gay man into the higher ranks.

"It must be a challenge," I said. "Living with a reporter."

He was at the sink filling the coffee pot. When it was full he turned around and gave me a slow smile. "Let's just say I don't bring work home. The price you pay for love."

"Did Dan ever mention Yves Grenier?"

"Never heard of him."

"Just as well, seeing as he's dead."

I could see Frederick's eyes light up. "Natural or assisted?"

"You ever done a scene where all the physical evidence points to suicide but you just know that's not it? You know in your gut that somebody killed him, but you don't know who or why?"

The coffee brewed behind us. Frederick came over to the table, flipped a chair around, and sank into it. He crossed his arms over the back and laid his chin on them, looking surprisingly cat-like for a man of his bulk.

"Suicides. Definitely the worst. We did a scene last week, the girl calls 911 and says her boyfriend has just blown his brains out with a rifle. Bullet wound at close range, lots of aerosol spraying, blew the inside of the guy's head right out the back. She was freaking out, covered in blood and brains. We went in there, checked the angle of the shot, analyzed the blood spatter, checked her hands and his for powder residue. No question he pulled the trigger, but when we asked around you know what? Not one of his friends could believe it was suicide. Not one."

The coffee was done and he got up and poured one for me, one for Marcotte, which he placed at the empty chair, and one for himself. Then he turned and started to leave.

I leaned forward. "Hey, Frederick, don't leave me hanging."

He shrugged, his big shoulders straining at the fabric of his shirt. "Two days later she spilled. The idiot was fooling around with the rifle pointing it at himself but at the same time trying to hand it to her saying, 'Shoot me, shoot me. Go ahead and shoot me.' His finger slipped and bang. Lights out. The moral? Only two people at a murder scene know what happened: the guy who gets it and the guy who did it. Everything else is speculation. I never forget that." Then he gave me a nod and left.

A minute later Marcotte came thumping down the stairs and swung back into his chair. He handed me a thick brown envelope. "Thanks, Freddy," he yelled toward the front of the house as he grabbed the coffee mug. He took a swig then leaned forward.

"Now it's your turn," he said. "What's all that other stuff mean? SB? HK? TJ?"

"So those initials aren't connected with your Fruit Machine?"

"It's not *my* Fruit Machine, but no, he didn't have any names, not that I know of anyway." He gaze slid away from mine. "So how'd he die?"

"He was found hanging from the struts of the tele-scope. There was a suicide note sent by e-mail."

"Shit," he said. He pushed his chair back and crossed his legs over the side of it. "If I still smoked," he said, "I'd have one now."

"You talked to him that morning. Was he upset?"

He shook his head. "Pumped."

"What do you mean?"

"He was pumped like he was onto something, just like I am when I'm following a story and things are falling into place. He was, I don't know how to put it, com-pletely engaged in what I was saying. He kept asking for details and saying, 'You're sure? You're sure?' And I kept telling him yes." He looked into my eyes for the next ques-tion. "Why would he have made the arrangements to get information on volunteers if he didn't plan to be alive?"

Why indeed. I folded the photocopy and slipped it back into my pocket. "Do you think it's related? Does anyone care after all these years?"

Marcotte shook his head. "I don't see why. It's all out there. After I broke the story it was picked up by the mainstream press right across Canada. It's no big secret anymore. Unless ..." His voice trailed off.

"Unless what, Marcotte?"

"Unless," he said, "there's something I missed."

"Like what?" But I could see I'd lost him. He was miles away reviewing and assessing, just as I'd be doing if I were in his shoes. Still, I had no intention of letting him off the hook. I stood. "I need those names."

"Yeah, sure thing," he said absently.

"Tomorrow."

He nodded, but I wasn't sure he even heard me. As I left I thanked Frederick for the wonderful dinner. He looked up from the book he was reading. "Cooking takes my mind off work."

I nodded. "I owe you."

He smiled. "I plan to collect."

"Not without my knowledge." Marcotte had suddenly appeared beside me.

A look flashed between Frederick and me. As fellow investigators we had an understanding.

When I left Marcotte's it was dark and the wind had picked up. I stopped at the end of his walkway and glanced down the street to the Parkdale Market. In less than six weeks this deserted corner would be a bustling farmers' market overflowing with flowers and local produce, but right now the only sign of habitation was a naked metal frame and shreds of rope and canvas that snapped in the wind. Across the street a single bulb lit the swinging sign of the Black Horse Tavern, a forlorn-looking neighbourhood pub. So much for gentrification. I turned and headed down the street to my car. In the dim light the houses seemed to crowd against the sidewalk like a bad set of teeth.

I'd just opened my car door when I noticed a small pickup truck half a block down with the windows fogged over. Lovers in a huddle? Or some local kid having a toke before returning home. Of course, these days it was just as likely to be a new dad forced out into the cold for an after-dinner smoke. I threw Marcotte's envelope onto the passenger seat and thought of the articles sitting inside, then of Frederick working Ident with the local police. It was reassuring to know that things do change. There is some point to it all.

I took the scenic route home, heading down Parkdale Avenue to the Ottawa River Parkway. Usually I feel a calm set upon me as I look across the vast river to the shore of Quebec, but tonight even the river could do nothing for me as Duncan, Grenier, and Elizabeth Martin crowded my mind.

When I got to Elgin Street I took the back alley behind my building and pulled into my parking space, two dirt ruts cut out of the tiny weed patch the landlord advertises as a back lawn. In winter the yard looks like a refuse dump with empty bottles of Canadian sherry, dog shit, and paper bags scattered across the snow. Mint, my downstairs neighbour, is pushing Mr. Oinik to fence it and clean it up so her son, Amadeus, can play outside, but both Mint and I know the truth. Amadeus is happier at the computer. It's the two of us who yearn for a deck chair and a patch of grass.

As I pulled in I saw someone skitter behind the house and disappear next door. I didn't think much about it. The back alley is a hangout for people wanting activity a little more illegal than what they can accomplish on the park bench out front. There was rarely any violence, but I reminded myself to stay alert. I didn't have a wallet full of money, but my visitor didn't know that.

I waited for a moment in the car. When I didn't see any more activity I slid out, went around to the rear, and opened the Subaru's back door. The snowshoes could stay in the car — they were hidden beneath some old blankets — but the skies poked out over one of the folded back seats. They'd have to come in. Anything that looked like it could be pawned was too much of a temptation for the local lads.

I reached forward, and two things happened at once. An upstairs light flicked on — my bathroom light to be precise — and an arm snapped around my throat, jerked me off my feet, and started to drag me back. The skis clattered to the ground. I scrabbled for a foothold, but my feet slipped on the icy lane. I was being pulled toward a narrow gap between two commercial buildings. As I struggled, the grip — a very professional hold designed to compress my jugular vein — tightened. I heard a disembodied gasp and realized it was me. My vision began to swim and the mythical tunnel appeared, the light at the end beckoning me to a purer, a holier place.

So this was it. It was over. I felt an overwhelming sense of calm, a gratitude that I was headed up instead of down. The light expanded to fill the narrow tunnel — the pitiful remains of my life — then something else, another stimulus, was added to the light. The trumpets of heaven so soon? Then someone yelled, my assailant let go, and I collapsed like a sack onto the lane. As blood was released from my brain, the tunnel of light resolved into two distinct sources, the headlights of a car, and the trumpets became a horn that continued to blare. Two of the usual hang-abouts came barrelling around the corner to see what the racket was all about and saw me crumpled on the ground.

"Holy shit," said one of them. "Are you okay?"

It was a silly question. As they came forward the car reversed.

"Wait a minute." I waved my arm and tried to get up. Whoever was in that car had just saved my life and they might have seen my attacker, but the car didn't slow. It swerved onto the road. By this time John-John and Animal were helping me up, clucking like mother hens. They stank of Aqua Velva although neither had shaved in at least a week. As the car squealed off down Elgin I saw what I'd missed before. It wasn't a car at all. It was a compact model pickup truck, the same one I'd seen at Daniel Marcotte's. I turned and glanced at my bathroom window. The light was off.

Inside the hallway I tapped softly on Mint's door. She opened it with a smile that faded when she saw me. "What happened?"

I felt bad making the next request. I didn't want Mint or Amadeus messed up in my affairs, but I didn't have a choice. I stepped inside and shut the door quietly behind me. Amadeus gave me a wave from the TV. He — at ten — was watching the late-night business news. I kept my voice low.

"I need a favour. If I don't come downstairs in the next ten minutes to tell you I'm okay, call 911. Don't open the door for anyone. Just call the police and keep your door locked until they arrive, no matter what you hear." She started to protest but I cut her off. "I don't have time to explain. Just do as I say."

She gave a reluctant nod. Being an anarchist, right down to the head-to-toe black and multiple piercings, the thought of doing anything she was told went against the grain, but I heard the deadbolt slide shut and the chain lock clink into place as I left.

At the top of the stairs I tried the knob. It was locked. I slowly inserted my key, eased it through the clicks, then opened the door a crack. The lights in the living room were off, but my bedside lamp was on, and it had been off when I'd left with my skis. There was also a smell in the room, the light odour of musk. I stepped inside, reminding myself that Mint would call the police if I couldn't get back down. I just hoped they'd get here quickly enough.

I started to cross the room, heading for a lamp, when I heard a rustle on my couch. I crept forward and glanced over the back. A body lay across it shrouded head to toe in blankets. What the hell was going on? I reached for a blanket and yanked it back.

She sat up, rubbed her eyes, and gave me a groggy look. "If the mountain won't come to Mohammed," she said. "Then Mohammed ..." she waved her painted nails. "You know the rest."

"Jesus," I said, clutching my throat.

Sylvia had come for a visit.

"Don't you ever answer your phone?"

Sylvia had the blanket wrapped around her shoulders and a glass of Irish whiskey balanced on her knee. She looked like shit, even worse than me. Her hair was perfect, but then it always was. Between chemo and radiation she had an excellent selection of wigs. Her eyes, though, were ringed with gray and her skin hung pale on those beautiful bones. Beneath the blanket she was still fully dressed in tight black jeans and a red cashmere sweater. The high black boots lay beneath the coffee table.

Once I'd recovered from the initial shock and contacted Mint to tell her everything was fine I'd poured us both a big belt of whiskey. It had been one hell of a day. I didn't want to sound churlish, but entertaining company wasn't quite what I had on my agenda. "What are you doing here?"

She gave me a bright smile. "R&R. Just what the doctor ordered."

"How did you get into my apartment?"

She pulled my extra key out of her pocket and threw it on the coffee table. "You really should change your cache from time to time. So, babe, how goes the investigation?"

At the tone of her voice my ears perked up. "You've found something."

She gave me a foxy smile. "Houston, we have liftoff. And if you'd answered your goddamned phone I might not be here now, but as things began to fall into place I figured you'd need me. I'm just following Duncan's instructions."

And using his charge-code, I thought, *but what the hell*. He deserved it.

Sylvia popped open the laptop sitting on the coffee table and patted the cushion beside her. "Fasten your seat belt, babe, because we are going for a ride."

Despite the horrors of the day I was now fully alert. I got up and moved over beside her. She gave me a sideways glance. "By the way, O'Brien, you need to get more sleep." She went back to the computer, tapped a few buttons, and tilted the screen toward me. On it was the information I'd given her from Hawaii: the list of journals stolen from Yves Grenier's.

She leaned back and crossed her arms, but kept her eyes on the screen. "When you gave me this list I thought you were nuts. I mean, it was like you were asking me to understand the thoughts and motivations of a dead man, and one I never knew, but being a good girl and a dedicated employee — and being bored out of my skull on this friggin' R&R — I started at square one. I pulled every paper of Yves Grenier's and I read the abstracts, sometimes whole papers, trying to get a sense of who the guy was. They were nice papers, by the way. Clean and succinct, which is pretty rare in a field like astrophysics. Then I pulled all the journals you specified — those old volumes of the *Astronomical Journal* ranging from 1960 to 1964 — and I went through them article by article looking for any obvious connections to Grenier's work."

She reached out and hit the return button. "First I searched celestial objects, thinking that maybe I'd get a match to some object of interest to Grenier." She shook her head and hit return again. "Nothing. Then I checked technologies. Instruments. You'd mentioned something about a technology being tested. Maybe, I thought, I could find the precursors for Grenier's large-array cameras, sensor technology, something like that, but still nothing. I was this close to calling you up and telling you that you were full of crap when I thought I'd try one more thing. Ironically, the easiest thing. Maybe, I thought, he's collecting someone's work — someone he admires."

She leaned over and hit return again. "I started with the last journal, 1964, and for every author in the journal I ran a citation list for the period between 1959 and 1965, then I filtered by the specific volumes you gave me. If an author had seven hits then they appeared in every journal. It was a tedious job and showed me how small the community was back then, with the same names appearing in multiple journals, which of course confounds the process."

She gave me a moment to study the screen. I was having trouble making sense of what I saw there. Sylvia watched my confusion with a bemused expression.

"So?" I said finally, as much to satisfy Sylvia as get the bloody information. "What's it all mean?"

"Only one guy appears in every journal." She leaned forward, scrolled down to a citation and hit return. The first page of an article came up. She highlighted the second author. "Dr. Peter Aarons. He's your common denominator."

"Does it give his affiliation?"

"You bet. In 1964 Dr. Peter Aarons was an astronomer with the Canadian Astronomy Institute, Ottawa, Canada."

I felt a great weight lift from my shoulders. I knew it. I knew it all led back to here. "And his newer stuff? Can we get his most recent affiliation?"

"Hey, babe, don't crowd the artist. That was just the appetizer." She raised her hands and wiggled the fingers like a magician preparing to conjure, then she leaned over and began rapid-fire typing. From what I could follow she was logging into an astronomy and astrophysics data-base, and seconds later she was searching on the author P. Aarons. A list of publications came up.

"*Voila*," she said with a look of triumph.

I leaned forward and examined it. It didn't make sense. "That's identical to the list I gave you. The same seven journals."

"It's more than that." She was watching my face. "It's the life work of Dr. Peter Aarons. Everything he ever published is contained in those journals."

I felt my stomach drop. "He's dead."

"It's a bit more complicated than that." She paused dramatically. "According to the records he never lived."

I sat back and stared at the blank screen. My brain wasn't exactly firing on all neurons, especially with my adrenaline titre falling and the whiskey kicking in. Is this what Grenier discovered? But what did it all mean? I looked back at Sylvia. "Did he have co-authors on those papers?"

"I'm with you babe." She leaned down and pulled copies of Aarons's papers out of her briefcase. "And three of them are still alive and kicking right here in Ottawa. Well, maybe not kicking. They're probably all retired now. I've marked down the addresses."

I pulled the papers toward me. Three names were highlighted in yellow. Simon Batters, Helen Keeler, and, my breath caught, Anthony St. James. *There is*, I thought, *a God in heaven*. I could go to sleep in peace.

The next morning I slipped out the door around nine leaving Sylvia fast asleep in my guest room. On the coffee table I left her two things: my laptop, with instructions to wipe the hard drive and reinstall my software, and the envelope of articles from Daniel Marcotte. On a Post-it note stuck to the front I asked her to read every scrap of paper inside and trace anything she could on the so-called homosexual detector. Maybe we'd find some connection between Marcotte's Fruit Machine and Peter Aarons, or, for that matter, a line to Yves Grenier. In the meantime I'd see what I could dig up elsewhere on the elusive Peter Aarons. If he'd worked at a federal government lab in Ottawa — as his articles claimed — there had to be a paper trail.

I stepped from the front porch into a surprise weather turnaround typical of Ottawa. The sun shone hot in a cloudless sky and the ice of the night before now lay in big, flat puddles across the park. Pigeons fluttered at the edges cooing and dipping to celebrate what they believed was the beginning of spring. I took the steps slowly and considered my next destination. It was Saturday morning and the Mayflower was out of the question. The double-income-no-kids crowd would be holed up there for brunch, each half of the happy couple perusing a section of the *New York Times* while picking at the low-carb special. I wouldn't get a booth until sometime after three. Still, coffee was a must, and the sooner the better. I headed out to Elgin Street and turned into the first café that I knew had decent coffee. I ordered a large latte to go and, just to be contrary, pointed to the gooiest, most carb-laced muffin in the place, then took my takeout order and headed for my car.

In the back lane I took a few minutes to survey the area, looking for any evidence of my attacker the night before. There were partial boot prints and a scrape in the mud from my heel when I was being pulled back, but nothing more. The lane, where my attacker had finally fled, was now a swamp of dirty slush and any evidence of him had, quite literally, melted away. I took a sip of the coffee and thought back to the evening before. Was it a random attack? He'd used a deadly military chokehold. Anything less and I would have broken it in seconds. Still, there were nutcases on the street with that kind of training. And what was with the pickup truck? Why did it take off? Another puzzle to file away for subconscious processing. I got into my car, and while it warmed up I gobbled down the muffin and gulped the coffee, then I pulled out of the lane and headed for Sussex Drive.

Sussex Drive hugs a high bluff that juts out over the Ottawa River, and it boasts some of the capital's most prestigious addresses including the prime minister's residence, the National Gallery, and the new American embassy. Nestled between the official residences of the British High Commissioner and the French ambassador sits 100 Sussex Drive, also known as the Temple of Science. The building itself is impressive: a solid grey block faced in sandstone and granite with a sweeping front entry dwarfed by huge Doric pillars. This was the original seat of Canadian science — the first government research labs. With the huge expansion of science and technology during the Second World War, 100 Sussex became too small to house the burgeoning research, and the laboratories were moved out to a large campus in the east end of the city where they remain to this day. A few laboratories, however, stayed in the old building, and one was the head office of the Canadian Astronomy Institute. But even more important to my current inquiry were the science archives housed at the Sussex library, and this was my destination.

I pulled into the parking lot at the side of the building and stepped out of the car. To my right a walkway wove along the edge of a high cliff taking tourists to the Rideau Falls some half a kilometre beyond. Below me the vast expanse of the Ottawa River sparkled in the sun. I didn't relish spending the morning in a dark, dusty archive, but with luck I'd have time for a run later on.

Inside the foyer I approached the commissionaire's desk and pulled out my ID.

"Do you have an appointment?" he asked.

"I don't need one," I said, and I pocketed my ID. "Do researchers sign in on the weekend?"

He shifted uneasily. "Well, usually they —"

I reached over his desk and flipped the sign-in book around, then I ran my finger down the list of names. Most government departments are devoid of life on the weekend, but the government labs are an exception. Publish or perish is still the rule, and government researchers are just as compulsive and driven as their colleagues in academia. I smiled to myself and pushed the book back around. It was better than I'd hoped. Anthony St. James was back from Hawaii and somewhere in the building. Dr. Simon Batters had arrived at nine that morning, but I'd save them for later. I gave the commissionaire a curt nod and headed for the library.

Even the smell of the Sussex library evoked another century, a soft mélange of wax, Persian carpets, and leather-bound books. It was impossible not to stop just inside the door and gawk at the beauty of the place, its walls, shelves, and long, monastic tables glowing in dark, polished wood. The real centrepiece, though, was above: a high cupola of deep blue that swirled with galaxies and stars luminous in gilt. It was a beautiful sight, evocative, like walking into the private library of an Italian renaissance prince. Even the librarian seemed from another time. His shock of heavy white hair matched a crisp white dress shirt, and he sat hunched over a large volume behind an imposing oak desk. A pair of tortoiseshell reading glasses balanced on the end of his nose. With the exception of the librarian, though, the library seemed empty.

I moved into the room, and the librarian looked up, momentarily startled. "So sorry," he said with a distinct English accent. "Have you been there long? Can I be of some assistance?"

"I'm not sure."

He looked at me for a moment, then took off his glasses and laid them on the open book. "I'm afraid you'll have to be a little more precise."

"Would you have a record of all the researchers who worked at the Canadian Astronomy Institute throughout its history? Something with pictures?"

Despite the white hair his eyebrows were a dense black, and at the question they twitched upward. "May I inquire as to the nature of your interest? Are you writing a book? Researching a particular individual?"

"Genealogy. I'm trying to trace a great-uncle who we think might have ended up here."

He seemed relieved by that answer. "And what time period would this have been?"

"Somewhere between 1960 and 1964. I can't be sure."

At that he gave me a broad smile. "In that case I can help." He got up, came around the desk, and extended his hand. His skin was dry and papery. "Dr. Simon Batters, Emeritus, obviously." He gave a distracted wave toward the stacks. "Used to work here as a research officer but now I take care of this. Cutbacks, you know. Librarian laid off, shocking really. Shocking. But good for me. I'm more interested in history now, history of astronomy; who did what when, that sort of thing, particularly in Canada. Not much done in that area, you know. Quite a gap, really, despite our dominance in some fields. So I thought I'd fill in the gap in my retirement." He reached out and patted my arm. "Glad to hear you're not writing a book on the Astronomy Institute, scooping me. I couldn't have that now, could I?" He chuckled to himself and headed off toward the stacks, expecting me to follow. He half turned as he walked. "Noble sort of work, genealogy. Tracing your family tree. It is possible I knew your uncle, great-uncle did you say? But if not — " He led me toward a shelf of reference books. He was a surprisingly tall man, well over six feet, but his back was curved and he walked with the fragility of someone in poor health.

He turned into an aisle and stopped in front of a row of identical hardcover volumes. He pulled one out and flipped it open. In front it had a black and white picture of a group of men sitting posed on the Sussex steps. He looked at the photo, then patted his breast pocket. "Bother. Give me a minute." He handed me the book. "This is 1959. Look up there and you'll find our annual reports for all the subsequent years. Should be a photo at the front of each, names below. That should help you out."

Then he left in search of his glasses.

I shelved 1959 and pulled down 1962. The group photo had been taken on the front steps in summer. The men were a rag-tag lot, short hair, but few with ties. Most wore white dress shirts with the collars open and sleeves rolled up. The few women looked distinctly clerical: conservative skirts, white blouses, and cat's-eye specs. They were in the front row surrounding the director like a harem, their ankles crossed and tucked neatly under the chairs. The only exception was one woman in the back row. I went over to one of the long tables and pulled up a seat. Dr. Batters, I noted, had found his glasses but was now distracted by a pile of papers. Just as well. I needed to see what I had before I approached him.

I turned back to the book on the table. Batters had told me it was an annual report but it looked more like a college yearbook. Granted, there were news items on the various articles published by the staff and visiting scientists and notes on the progress of instruments being developed, but there were also pictures of social functions: the staff whooping it up at the Christmas party, a summer picnic, several symposiums. They looked like a small, close-knit group. I went back to the formal photograph at the front and examined the names one by one. Peter Aarons wasn't there. I felt a pang of disappointment. According to his research papers he was at the institute in 1962, but maybe he'd been sick that day or away at one of the observatories.

I left the book open and returned to the shelves where I pulled out the volumes covering 1960 through to 1964. Back at the table I arranged them in chronological order in a semi-circle around me, all open to the group photograph. I began with 1960.

Simon Batters was there, looking handsome and debonair if a bit preoccupied. In 1961 a very young, earnest-looking Anthony St. James appeared in the crowd. By 1962 a woman — Helen Keeler — had joined the group, a rather obvious addition as the only woman standing amongst the astronomers. I moved on to the next year, 1963. Keeler, Batters, and St. James were all there, but still without Peter Aarons. That didn't make sense. I was about to move onto the next year when something caught my eye. I leaned over and examined the faces just to make sure and felt a zing go up my spine. In this picture Keeler and Batters stood in the back row on the far left. Helen Keeler stood on the end, an unknown researcher stood beside her, and Simon Batters stood next to him. Keeler was leaning over saying something to her neighbour. I looked at the legend again. The names listed left to right were Helen Keeler, Simon Batters, George Standing, David Silver ...

I pulled out my magnifying glass and examined the face of Keeler's neighbour, then I moved back a year. Sure enough there he was, this time standing between Keeler and St. James. I carefully counted the number of heads in the back row, then counted the number of names in the legend. Fifteen names, but sixteen people.

I peered again at the intent young face next to Helen Keeler's, took a deep breath, and said a silent hello to Peter Aarons.

Simon Batters had settled back at his desk reabsorbed in his weighty tome. I picked up the yearbook and carried it over to his desk.

He looked up. "Excellent. You've found something. I can see it from your face. Let's have a look then."

I slid the book onto the desk and pointed to the man standing between Keeler and himself. He tilted his head upward to get a better view through his bifocals. "It's always possible that I don't ..." He jerked back and in an abrupt movement pushed the book away. "Good God."

I leaned forward, my hands on the desk. "Who is he, Dr. Batters?"

He pushed his chair back and started to rise. "I'm afraid you'll have to leave now." Then a voice came from behind me. "Not to worry, Simon, I'll handle it from here." Anthony St. James reached around and whisked the book off the desk. "The commissionaire called me. I think it's time we had a little chat."

"Your great-uncle?" He shut the book and pushed it aside. "That was unkind. Simon isn't well."

From where I sat on the other side of his enormous desk I could see the hive of External Affairs looking strangely deserted on this Saturday morning. I turned back to St. James. He seemed to have aged five years since I'd seen him in Hawaii. Was it just the travel or something else? "Kindness wasn't the first thing on my mind."

"And what was?"

"The truth."

"The truth? How simple that sounds. And which truth would you like?"

I leaned over the desk and opened the book. I pointed to the man standing between Keeler and Batters. "This man. Who is he?"

St. James examined the photograph carefully, bringing it up close to his face. "I have no idea," he said, and he put the book back down. "I was, what, twenty-five, twenty-six, when this photograph was taken? We had post-docs and visiting scientists coming from all over the world. Some stayed for two months, some stayed for two weeks, some never left. Perhaps when you're my age your memory will be better than mine. For your sake I certainly hope so, but I couldn't name …," he pursed his lips reflectively, "… at least a third of the people in that picture. I'm sorry to disappoint you."

"Does the name Peter Aarons jog your memory?"

St. James leaned back and gave me a blank look. "It doesn't ring a bell, no."

"Do you remember Gunnar McNabb?"

"Don't be ridiculous. Of course I do."

"And that's odd, Dr. St. James. I mean, usually with age we *can* recall the past, often in vivid detail, but recent events disappear. You, on the other hand, have no trouble with what happened yesterday. It's the 1960s that draw a blank." I let that hang in the air for a minute. "You published several papers with Peter Aarons. Is your memory really that bad?"

I saw him swallow as if his throat had suddenly gone dry. "Apparently it is."

I stood up. "Then I guess I'll have to get my information elsewhere."

I reached for the book but his hand came down on it. "This can't leave the building."

"I'll take a photocopy."

He pulled it onto his lap. "I can't allow that."

"By whose authority?"

"If you don't leave the building at once I'll call the commissionaire."

The commissionaire was, if anything, older that St. James so it wasn't much of a threat. Still, I didn't want to create too much of a ruckus. "I'm not going to disappear, Dr. St. James. Not until I have what I want."

He clutched the book to his chest. "This has nothing to do with Yves Grenier. That's all I can tell you." He looked up. "And I've said too much already."

"I will get the information in the end."

He gazed at me, his eyes tired and sad. "I have no doubt you will, but it won't be from me."

From 100 Sussex Drive I headed south into an upscale residential neighbourhood nestled between Sussex Drive and Beechwood Avenue. While Lindenlea was certainly an exclusive address, the houses were by no means mansions: mainly older three- and four-bedroom family houses with smallish yards. The residents here paid a premium for location, location, location — specifically the proximity next door of the ultra-exclusive hamlet of Rockcliffe, Ottawa's point source for millionaires.

I found the address I needed and parked just out front. At the door I pressed the bell hard, letting it ring three or four times just in case her hearing was bad, then I turned and waited. I looked across the porch to a small park ringed by pretty stucco and wood houses. The park was now mostly puddles, but a month ago it would have been the local hockey rink. In the middle was a ring of boards enclosing a flattened patch of mud, and temporary spotlights still hung on poles around the perimeter. I heard the latch and turned to see an elderly woman pulling open the door. She wore a matching sweater and skirt, and her hair was wrapped around her head in a perfect chignon. Despite a distinct stoop she snapped open the heavy wood door.

"My hearing is just fine," she said. "Whatever happened to patience?"

"Dr. Keeler?" I reached for my photo ID to display it through the glass of the screen door. She gave me a withering look. "I already know who you are. You might as well come in."

As I crossed the threshold I caught sight of her hand on the knob, her fingers pulled painfully across the knuckles from chronic arthritis. No wonder it took her some time to get to the door. "Dr. St. James didn't waste any time," I remarked as she closed the door behind me.

She looked at me with sharp blue eyes. "What did you expect? We're not entirely stupid, you know."

"Nor am I. The picture is of Peter Aarons."

We stood for a moment eyeing each other, a Mexican standoff, then she sighed and said, with just the hint of a smile: "I suppose you're expecting me to offer you tea. It's what one seems to expect of women my age."

"Actually, I'd prefer coffee."

"Well that," she said, "is at least one point in your favour." She turned and headed down the hall. I wondered, as I noted her hair again, how those crippled hands could produce such perfection. She waved at the living room as she passed by. "You may take a seat."

Instead I followed her into the kitchen. She pulled down a jar of ground coffee and an old-fashioned percolator. I leaned against the counter. The kitchen was tiled in a peculiar shade of green not seen since the early 1960s. I let her fiddle with the coffee for a minute then said, "You knew Peter Aarons."

She gave me an assessing look then took the pot over to the sink and filled it with water. How many cups did she plan to drink? When she got back to the counter she slipped the basket into the pot and started to slowly spoon in the grounds. Between a marked tremor and her stiff fingers they didn't all make it in. It broke my heart, but I couldn't let her get under my skin.

"Is that what you've heard?" she said, not breaking the rhythm of her task.

"You co-authored four papers with Peter Aarons. The first in 1961, two in 1963, and another one in 1964. Would you like me to give you the titles?"

She put down the spoon and turned to me. "That won't be necessary. I quite remember Peter."

"Exactly my point, so let's not waste your time or mine. You tell me about Peter Aarons and I walk out of here happy. Otherwise I keep coming back until I get what I want."

"A threat? But they do say that old ladies love company. I suppose I could just keep you coming back for the pleasure of it."

I'd glanced into the living room on my way down the hall. A computer screen glowed in the corner on a desk piled high with papers and books. She couldn't fool me. I knew the truth. "I'm not nearly as interesting as your journals and papers, as I'm sure you'll agree."

She gave me a laser stare, her eyes the colour of an indoor pool, then said, "The cups are in the cupboard. When the coffee's ready I'll send you in for it."

In the living room she took a large recliner across from the couch. There was a soft whirring and a footrest came up as the chair tilted back. As she got herself settled I moved over to the wall of photographs that surrounded the chimney mantle. It was like a history of modern astronomy with Keeler standing beside various telescopes. As the telescopes got bigger, the clothes became more modern, going from the sweater sets of the fifties to the pantsuits of the sixties through to the loose, casual dress of the eighties and nineties. There were pictures of her shaking hands with various luminaries, including … I leaned in closer to see if it was true … both Gerhard Herzberg and Albert Einstein. I turned back to her with surprise.

She was watching me with disarming intensity. "What is it you want?"

"Is Peter here?" I motioned to the photographs.

"No, he is not."

"But you admit he existed."

She twisted slightly, winced, then settled back. "That, as you pointed out yourself, is evident."

"Then why can't I find an official record?"

She turned and stared out the window, formulating an answer. When she turned back it was with that slight smile. "The coffee's ready. Black, no sugar, for me."

When I got back I set the mug down beside her. "You didn't fill it too full," she remarked. "That was very thoughtful. Thank you." She picked it up, but with the tremor the mug seemed to rock in her hands. She managed a careful sip and laid the cup back on the table, but kept her hands around it. "I'm not supposed to tell you anything about him. None of us are."

"By whose authority? Dr. St. James?"

"Heavens no. Tony couldn't — well, Tony was involved but he couldn't *command* us in that way. No. It was — " She hesitated, then diverted. "It was so very long ago. Another time. Another era in every sense of the word." She looked out the large front window again and her voice changed, detached, as if it were coming from a different person. "Peter Aarons was my graduate student, and from the moment I set eyes on him I knew he was destined for great things." She looked down at her hands around the mug. "I started my career as a professor at the University of Toronto after getting a Ph.D. in England. I would have preferred to stay here for my graduate work but at the time there was no one who would take me as a student." She gave me a self-deprecating smile. "England has a history of eccentric women so it was a little easier there, and I did rather well, which is why the University of Toronto offered me a position. And of course at that time they were losing so many trained astronomers and physicists to the U.S.: Princeton, Harvard, MIT. A few years after I arrived at the University of Toronto a young man, Peter Aarons, applied to do graduate work with me. He was just finishing up his bachelors at McGill, the youngest person to ever graduate with an honours degree in physics, and it was a coup for me to get him. He could have gone anywhere. Needless to say I accepted him, and that September he came to work in my lab. Of course, Tony was at U of T at the same time."

"Dr. St. James?"

She nodded. "He was a few years ahead of Peter, but the two became inseparable — a case of opposites attracting I suppose. Like Peter, Tony was a brilliant student but he was much more ...," she considered the next word, "... human, I suppose you'd say. Peter had only one interest in life and that was astrophysics. I never heard him speak of family, never saw him socialize except with other physicists, and as far as I know he never had a date. He was insatiable, working night and day on research, developing instruments, but with no interest in the kind of politics that one needs to survive in academia. Tony recognized Peter's genius and took him under his wing. They worked well together, Peter obsessive about the work and Tony able to negotiate all the politics needed to keep projects funded and granting bodies happy. When Tony graduated from U of T he was hired immediately by the Canadian Astronomy Institute, which was, I must point out, quite an accomplishment, to go directly from graduate school to the Institute. Not long after I was offered a position — the fact that Tony was there to sing my praises must have helped — then we saw to it that Peter was hired when he graduated. It was, as I'm sure you're aware, a heady period. The space race was on and there was significant money available for astronomy and physics. Einstein's theories were being probed and tested, quantum physics was changing our understanding of fundamental physical processes, and there were major advances in areas like optics and signal processing that were letting us see deeper into space than we'd ever thought possible. The rate of discovery was breathtaking." She turned back to me and pursed her lips in a dry smile. "Now, of course, that's all changed. Where once there was a fertile field now there is a desert." She picked up her coffee cup and slowly lifted it to her lips. She took a minuscule sip off the surface and placed it back on the table. "One of the reasons Peter was so desirable to the Institute was his ability in instrumentation. Peter could design and build anything, but spectrographs were his specialty. As you've already pointed out I did several papers with him, Simon Batters did as well, and of course he and Tony continued a fruitful collaboration. Then one day Peter simply disappeared."

"Just like that?"

"More or less, yes, or so it seemed at the time."

"There must have been an investigation."

She gave a deep sigh. "I did try." At this point she looked out the window again, her eyes focused on the past. When she finally turned back to me her expression had changed. "Why dig this up now?"

"Did you know Elizabeth Martin?"

"I know Dr. Martin, yes."

I could have pussyfooted around but I wanted maximum impact. "She's dead, Dr. Keeler."

I saw her fingers tighten around the mug. "When?"

"Elizabeth Martin was killed the day before yesterday in Hawaii, an apparent accident. That makes two astronomers dead in unclear circumstances in less than a week. From a purely statistical point of view how likely is it that the events are not connected?"

She'd gotten hold of the recliner's remote and the backrest whirred forward as the foot support disappeared beneath the seat. "I was told that Yves committed suicide."

"Who told you that?"

She didn't answer. Her feet were now on the floor. "What about Elizabeth?"

"It was no accident." Then I decided to take a risk. "Yves Grenier called you the day he died." There was no verbal response, but the tremor in her hands seemed to travel up her spine, and now her head shook slightly. I hardened my voice. "What did he want?"

"I can't tell you."

"Two young people are dead and you can't tell me?" I stood. "Then I'll lean on Simon Batters and I'll lean hard. You leave me no other choice."

"No," she said quickly. "Leave Simon alone. He's not well."

I gave a small shrug, letting her know where I stood. She raised her chin, pulled herself painfully forward in the chair, and turned to face me. "Peter Aarons defected to the Soviet Union in 1964." Then she stopped and looked briefly out the window. I waited without a movement or a word. She turned back. "Yves was trying to find him."

"Did Grenier know he'd defected?"

"No, he did not."

"And what did you tell him?"

"I told him nothing at all." Then the chin dropped and she shook her head. "Peter Aarons betrayed us all."

chapter sixteen

———————

As I got into my car in front of Helen Keeler's house her final statement stayed lodged in my brain. *Peter Aarons betrayed us all*. It wasn't so much the words that caught me — they made perfect sense — it was the way she'd said them. The tone. A mixture of grief, defiance, and something else. Something I couldn't quite capture. I started my car and turned off my rational brain, just letting the words loop through my mind without analysis. At the bottom of Springfield Road I turned right onto Beechwood, the main artery that would take me back into the downtown core. Even on a Saturday the route was jammed with traffic.

We crawled along, stopping and starting in time with the streetlights. The Chinese Embassy came into view with its high concrete walls and surveillance cameras positioned on every post, a relic from the Cold War. *Another era*, Helen Keeler had said, but one, I thought as I looked at the fortifications, that had lingering effects on the present.

I'd just finished that thought when an orange BMW cut in front of me, forcing my attention back to the road. I jammed on the brakes and hit the horn. I heard the squeal of tires behind me and prepared for impact. Fortunately that driver had managed to hit her brakes as well and when I glanced into the rearview mirror she was sitting, her hand on her chest, looking shaken. Then another commotion caught my eye. Several cars down a compact pickup truck was trying to force its way into my lane. Why would someone move into the lane that was standing still? I felt a jolt of recognition. So it wouldn't have to pass me, of course. I started forward, but kept an eye on the truck behind.

We continued in stop-and-go traffic until the main intersection at King Edward Avenue. Here the traffic slowed even more as we entered the narrow streets of the Byward Market, the oldest section of Ottawa. Thai bistros and small French cafés crowded the sidewalk while parked cars lined either side of the road, further restricting the traffic. I kept my fingers crossed. I'd reached the second block when a parking space miraculously opened up a few cars down. No one ahead of me took it and I nipped in.

The traffic streamed along beside me, the roof of the little pickup moving inexorably forward. He was, I noted with satisfaction, completely boxed in. There was no escape. Then it struck me. Helen Keeler's words. In addition to grief and defiance, they'd held disbelief. As if, at some deep level, she didn't, or couldn't, believe that Peter Aarons *had* betrayed them all, despite the evidence.

The light ahead turned red and the traffic came to a halt, but a van just behind me blocked my view of the pickup truck. I wondered briefly if I should make some attempt to hide but nixed that idea. I wanted the driver to see me and I wanted him to know that I'd seen his face.

The light changed and the traffic lurched forward. The van moved slowly by, then the pickup truck came into view. Sunlight bounced off the windshield and I couldn't see inside until the little truck pulled up right beside me. I looked across into the cab to see two young women in ball caps and ponytails laughing up a storm. They looked like college kids on their way to a ball game. The traffic surged forward and the truck disappeared through the other side the intersection. I slumped back in my seat. I was becoming paranoid, and that didn't bode well for the investigation.

I took a minute to collect myself — chastise myself would be a more accurate description — then I signalled left and started to nose my way out of the space. I glanced over my shoulder hoping that some nice person would let me in. A young man in the car behind waved me into the line, but as my head swung around there was a gap in the traffic across from me. There, at the side of the road, sitting parked in a compact pickup, was Pexa, eyes straight ahead. A cube van pulled beside me and cut off my view. The Good Samaritan honked, now regretting his decision to let me in. I jerked forward but craned my neck around. I caught one brief glimpse of the truck before being forced to move ahead.

The front seat was empty.

Back in my apartment I found a note from Sylvia saying that my computer was clean and she'd gone to the National Archives in search of information. I changed into running gear and headed out the door for the Rideau Canal just at the end of the block. In all honesty I didn't want to go for a run. My leg muscles ached from a combination of yesterday's ski trip, too many time changes in too short a time, and generally not enough exercise to keep everything in working order. I would have to get back to the dojo soon or my body would seize up.

I walked to the pedestrian path that follows the canal and once on it fell into a steady pace despite the dog walkers, weekend bikers, and university students strolling hand in hand. My plan was to go as far as the Dow's Lake pavilion then turn around and jog back. It wasn't a tremendously long run, but for today it would do the trick.

As I ambled along I let my mind wander, taking in the sunshine and weekend crowds. Seeing Pexa had unnerved me. I'd have to call Andreas Mellier at the telescope to see if he knew what was going on. I detoured around a large puddle. A month ago I'd been skating on the canal, the surface concrete hard. Now, I noted, the ice was almost gone leaving the mud flats exposed on the edges. Soon the locks would be shut, the water would rise to summer levels flush with the pedestrian path, and the pleasure boats would reappear. With bikini-clad crew draped across the decks they would cruise through Ottawa's downtown, giving the city an almost European feel.

I'd just passed the Ritz Canal restaurant when I felt someone come up on my left. I glanced behind me. A man with salt and pepper hair but the physique of thirty-year-old jogged along beside me. When he made no move to pass I turned to look at him fully. He had a pair of headphones dangling from his neck.

"We'd like to have a little chat," he said, keeping his eyes forward.

Suddenly my muscles didn't ache anymore. The adrenaline took care of that. Then I felt someone come up on my right, this time a woman who, like the guy, was dressed for serious jogging and extremely fit. I said nothing, kept my pace even, and did a rapid assessment of the situation. I couldn't outrun them both, that was for sure. On the other hand there were lots of people around. They couldn't make me go anywhere I didn't want to. Not without a fight.

"So chat," I said.

"There's a car up ahead. We'll take you for a ride."

"No thanks." The woman reached for my elbow, but I jerked it away. "I wouldn't do that if I were you. Not unless you want one hell of a scene."

She glanced at her partner, he gave an almost imperceptible nod, and she fell back.

I continued. "Anything you have to say to me you can say out here or not at all."

The man took the set of headphones and handed them to me, keeping pace. "This might interest you."

I slipped them on and he pressed play. At first all I could hear was the low hum of a car engine then a voice cut in. "It's all right," said Duncan. "They're not going to hurt us. They're just taking us for a ride."

I stopped and pressed the headphones to my ears.

"But Poof got left in the car," said Alyssa. "She'll be lonely." Poof was a stuffed animal, a white Persian cat, that I'd given her for Easter the year before. I strained to hear more.

"I want to go home," whined Peter. "Why can't we go home?"

I felt the blood rising to my brain and I glared at the man in front of me.

"Poof will be fine," said Duncan, his voice tight. "Now we need to be quiet and enjoy the ride."

The tape clicked off. I yanked off the earphones, snapped them in half, and hurled them at that bastard, then I moved into his personal space. "Who the fuck are you?" I wanted to kill him, but he stood solid not even taking a defensive stance. I felt the woman, though, come up behind me. The dog walkers gave us wide berth.

"We'd just like to talk," he said calmly. "It would help your friends."

My arm was itching to jab up hard into his solar plexus and the woman must have felt this because she draped her arm around my shoulder and gave me what anyone would interpret as a warm smile. "If you touch my partner," she said sweetly, "I'll take you. I have handcuffs in my pocket. Please step back."

I did but I was breathing hard. A maroon sedan with tinted windows slid up beside the curb. The man spoke. "Would we bother with this charade if we wanted to hurt you? How many people have seen us? How many people could describe what they saw? You'll be back in the same spot, very much alive, in an hour. You have my guarantee."

Like that was worth shit? They started toward the car.

"We're giving you the option to help those kids," the woman said over her shoulder. "Take it or leave it." He climbed into the front, she took the back.

I stood there for a moment too stunned to react, but when a hand reached from the dark interior to pull the back door shut, I sprinted forward and jumped in just as the car pulled out from the curb.

A black Plexiglas divider with a sliding window cut off my view of the front. My companion showed no interest in conversation, and that was fine with me. I preferred to monitor our route while silently saying my prayers. I knew I shouldn't have gotten into the car, but with the sound of Peter and Alyssa ringing in my ears I decided it was a risk I had to take. Just as my companions knew I would. I just hoped to hell that tape was real.

At the end of Queen Elizabeth Drive the car took the ramp up to Laurier and continued across town eventually funneling onto the Ottawa River Parkway. I was at first reassured by the route, taking us as it did through the downtown core, but by the time we hit the Parkway I began to feel uneasy. There were isolated spots along the river, especially at this time of year. My stomach gave a definite jolt when we turned into a barred service road that disappeared into the woods. A man in an official-looking brown jumpsuit appeared from nowhere, unlocked the gate, and swung it open. We bumped down the road and I watched in the rear window as he re-closed the gate, locked it, and disappeared back into the woods. This was not a good sign. At the end of the service road a small clearing opened out onto the river. Along its edge ran a popular bicycle path but it was still too early in the season for much activity.

Our sedan pulled up next to another similar car, this one black. Mr. Jogger hopped out of the front passenger seat and swung open my door. He then opened the back door of the black sedan and nodded to it. I took a deep breath, slid out, and slid into the other car. The door shut firmly behind me. I found myself alone on powder blue leather seats with, once again, a dark Plexiglas shield between the driver and me. Was this the end? Were they now going to dispose of me in this new and untraceable car?

A door opened up front and a moment later a dapper man slipped into the seat beside me. He was small, trim, and lean, with a clean-shaven, disciplined face, and he was dressed with obsessive perfection: a sport jacket of a subtle tweed, brown dress pants that blended perfectly with it, and brown wingtip shoes that could be forty years old or bought yesterday at premium prices. He turned his head slightly toward me.

"You've discovered Peter Aarons. I'm very impressed."

"Where's Duncan?"

"Safe. Well taken care of." He had his hands folded comfortably in his lap. "But let's talk about Peter Aarons first."

"Who are you?"

"I think you know who I am."

"I think I know who you work for. And I think I already met one of your associates — the charming Gunnar McNabb — but no, I don't know who you are, and I don't do business with nameless people."

He gave me a thin smile. "You're very good. How about Raymond Jones? Will that do?"

"How original. Okay, Raymond Jones, let's talk about Peter Aarons. What's the big secret?"

"If there is a big secret I'm hardly likely to tell you what it is, am I. It would be classified under the Security of Information Act, but surely a woman of your intelligence can speculate."

"No, a woman of my intelligence can't speculate because a woman of my intelligence doesn't play your silly games."

At that he laid his hands flat on his thighs and turned to me fully, but without any discernable expression. "I can assure you that this is anything but silly, and certainly not a game. Peter Aarons disappeared at the height of the Cold War. He was an astrophysicist, an expert in instrument development, and he lived in Ottawa literally next door to the Soviet Embassy. Do you know how many Canadian scientists were approached by Soviet agents between 1950 and 1980? Dozens. In every department. And that's just the ones that we know of. We're talking people with access to high-level military secrets and nuclear facilities, both here and in the United States. Scientific exchanges, conferences, tours, they had access to it all. Do the names Raymond Boyer or Allan Nunn May mean anything to you? Let me reiterate, it's no game."

It was a wonderful speech, impassioned, but I wasn't buying. "I investigate science. I know my history." I leaned forward. "So here's my problem. I *do* know the names Allan Nunn May and Raymond Boyer, and I know that both were convicted of passing secrets to the Eastern Block while working in federal labs right here in Ottawa. But I can trace their histories, find their birth records, see their tax returns. Peter Aarons? *Nada*, or *nyet* if you prefer. Why?"

"For God's sake use your brain."

I was obviously not going to get anywhere with Mr. Raymond Jones unless I played it his way so I sat back in my seat and looked out across the river. The water here was shallow, spilling like an oversized brook across a series of steps, flat tables of rock hidden just beneath the surface. People often thought that because the water looked shallow it must be safe, without understanding the power that lay beneath: thousands of tons of water sweeping up and over those steps. Every year several waders, often children, were simply swept away.

Why, I asked myself. *Why expunge the record?*

To hide Peter Aarons's existence. But why? There were only two reasons I could think of. To cover up a crime or … A light went on in my head with what felt like an audible click. To ensure he couldn't be traced if, for example, he was going into deep cover as a double agent. Raymond Jones must have seen the change in my expression.

"I can see you've arrived at an answer."

"But the Cold War is over. If he's still alive he can walk away. And if he's dead who cares. Tell the truth."

He put up his hand. "Of course, I can't confirm or deny anything. Peter Aarons may be at the bottom of the Ottawa River for all I know, but if he went into the Soviet Union as a double agent we would certainly

want his family and colleagues to believe he defected."
Then he added with emphasis, "We wouldn't want
people trying to trace him."

On the one hand it seemed plausible. It certainly
fit at least some of the data, but it still left unanswered
questions. "All right, let's just say I buy your hypothetical story."

"Hypothetical. An appropriate word."

"Yves Grenier. Place him in the picture, because
right now I can't make him fit."

He gave a nod of agreement. "Yves Grenier is
problematic, especially in a business like ours, where
what appear to be coincidences rarely are."

"We're not in the same business, Mr. Smith. Or was
that Mr. Jones?"

"But we are. We may have a different clientele, but
our goal is the same. My point is that coincidences do
happen although we find them hard to accept. Yves
Grenier committed suicide, an unfortunate event
regardless of what may surround it. And, even more
unfortunately, he was trying to locate Peter Aarons at
about the same time, but the two events are not connected. However, I am willing to concede that if, hypothetically, Peter Aarons had gone into the Eastern Block
as a double agent, then we would stop Yves Grenier, or
anyone else, from tracking him down."

"But why? Why couldn't you allow that? The Wall
fell, in case you missed it."

"Hypothetically?"

I regretted introducing this new word into Mr.
Jones's vocabulary. It was beginning to grate. "Fine.
Hypothetically."

"Because if Peter Aarons did go into the Soviet Union
he might still be alive and useful to us. And don't fool
yourself for a minute. If his cover were blown he'd be a

dead man. And even if he's no longer alive, perhaps we'd prefer to have his presence there remain a secret. Perhaps if his identity were to be revealed the Russians could determine the nature of the information that was leaked. We only have an advantage if they don't know we have it."

I was beginning to feel caught in a time warp. "I thought we were now on the same side?"

"A somewhat narrow view, I'm afraid. There are still significant threats to our way of life."

"To yours, yes, but not to mine, and certainly not to Duncan's. In fact, as far as I can see you're the only significant threat to his way of life."

He gave his head a regretful shake. "Dr. Carmichael is a more complex problem, one we're hoping" — here he turned and looked at me with those expressionless eyes — "you'll help us with."

"Your operative Gunnar McNabb already made me a very persuasive offer." I lifted my healing wrists. "Regardless, I declined."

I could see Jones's jaw tighten. "McNabb acted without authority. He will be disciplined. I hope you'll accept my apologies."

"Where's Duncan?"

His voice remained hard, as if Duncan pissed him off as much as Gunnar McNabb. "Duncan Carmichael has been trying to trace Peter Aarons for several years. We know that he's used his position in the government to his advantage, accessing classified documents that he had no business seeing."

"I don't believe you."

"Don't be naive."

"But why?"

"He has a handler, Ms. O'Brien. He's passing information. We don't think that, we know it. If he cooperates, works with us, that changes everything."

"And you think I have some influence?"

He paused for a moment watching me. "Why did he want those diaries? Did he tell you?"

"He made a vague reference to military secrets, but that's all."

"We think that Yves Grenier had all but located Peter Aarons. There are people who'd kill for that information. We want those diaries, and we're willing to make a trade."

I stared at him for a moment trying to comprehend what he was saying. "Are you offering me Duncan for the diaries?"

"He hired you for a reason. He's a brilliant man."

"And both he and the children would walk away free."

"Without the diaries he has nothing, and his cover's blown. No handler will touch him."

I had to repeat it again. "You're offering me Duncan and his children in exchange for the diaries?"

The corners of his lips turned up in a humourless smile. "Actually, I'm offering you a job, one more suited to your range of talents than the position you currently hold. I'll give you twenty-four hours to decide. We'll be in touch." He reached for the door handle.

"And if I say no?"

He paused for a minute, but kept his hand on the latch. "This is a national security operation. We can hold him as long as we want, and don't think we won't charge him."

True to their word, approximately one hour later, the jogger twins left me precisely where they'd picked me up. The minute their maroon sedan disappeared down the street I pulled out a pen and wrote a licence plate number down on my arm. It wasn't theirs. It was the plate of Raymond Jones, the black sedan. I was sure it was a government vehicle and I should be able to trace it back to a department, and with luck to a specific individual. People do get sloppy. Even control freaks.

I popped the pen back in my pocket and looked around. The faces had changed in the hour I'd been away but the scene remained the same, with dog walkers strolling by yanking at their sniffing pets' chains. I briefly considered turning around and jogging home, but decided that for my brain as well as my body finishing the run was the right thing to do. It would give my thoughts time to percolate.

I have to admit Jones's offer had caught me off guard. *The diaries for Duncan.* It meant, for starters, that Gunnar McNabb didn't have the diaries. And it meant that Jones didn't have much faith in McNabb's ability to retrieve them. But of course that begged the bigger question of whether I could believe anything at all that Jones said. His "hypothetical" version of Peter Aarons's history certainly seemed to fit some of the facts, but not all of them. Or, to be more precise, there were still pieces of information floating about that didn't fit, and for me to buy the theory it had to explain all the facts.

I'd started off my run nice and slow, but as my brain engaged so did my leg muscles and I picked up speed. Grenier's death still nagged me. A coincidence, Jones had said, but I didn't believe him. Neither would Benson if I told him — that is if he'd crawled out from under his huff and was talking to me again. And then there was that call to Daniel Marcotte. Grenier wanted information about the so-called Fruit Machine, but more than that he wanted contacts. People who'd been there. Was that a coincidence too? That he just happened to be searching for information on something that occurred around the same time that Peter Aarons disappeared? One coincidence maybe, but two? Three? The probabilities of that were infinitesimal.

At Dow's Lake I did a 180-degree turn, almost tripped over a standard poodle, and started my run back. Jones wanted me to go back to Hawaii and that didn't make sense either. I mean, he'd spent considerable effort trying to make me leave, now he was sending me back with an offer I couldn't refuse. And his associate Gunnar McNabb wouldn't be thrilled to have me treading on his toes. Then I thought of something else. I'd been assuming all along that Gunnar had a hand in Elizabeth's death — that he had the diaries — but if that wasn't the case then what the hell had happened on the summit the morning that Elizabeth Martin died? It was a chilling question.

As I passed the Ritz Canal my stomach grumbled. When I got home the first order of business was to call Daniel Marcotte and get those contact names. Next I needed to track down Sylvia and see what she'd found on the Fruit Machine. I had exactly twenty-four hours to figure out who Raymond Jones really was and what he was up to. If I didn't know by this time tomorrow then I'd be flying back to Hawaii with no real sense of why I was there. It was no way to run an investigation.

chapter seventeen

Sylvia thumped her briefcase on the table and slid into the booth across from me.

"Exciting day?"

In full light and artful makeup she looked healthier than I did but I still knew the truth. Beneath that carefully laid foundation an insidious little parasite was eating away at her brain. As quickly as the thought came, though, I blocked it. Pity would only tick her off.

I'd managed to reach Sylvia just as she was leaving the National Archives and she'd agreed to meet me at the Mayflower. It was, I thought wryly, just like old times. As I'd watched her enter and scan the crowd every eye in the place — man, woman, straight, gay — turned to admire her.

"It was —" I searched for the right word. "Productive. Yours?"

"Interesting. And disturbing. Do you think Marcotte's Fruit Machine is connected to Peter Aarons?"

The waiter came over, poured Sylvia a cup of coffee, and refilled mine. He said he'd give us ladies a few more minutes to think, although I'm pretty sure he only saw one lady at the table and it wasn't me. When he'd gone I gave Sylvia a brief recap of my morning meetings with the astronomy crowd — Simon Batters, Anthony St. James, and Helen Keeler — then brought the conversation back to the Fruit Machine. "As far as the astronomers are concerned Peter Aarons defected. No one said anything about a Fruit Machine by that or any other name. On the other hand I didn't probe too deeply. I wanted to see what you'd uncover first. And if Raymond Jones is to be believed then the Fruit Machine is not connected."

"Raymond Jones?"

I gave her a coy smile. "I got picked up today."

"Really? A boy or a girl?"

"Both."

"Even better." The waiter arrived at the table with his order pad open. I went for the hamburger platter, Sylvia the all-day breakfast. When he was gone she leaned over. "Did they make you an offer you couldn't refuse?"

"Actually they did." I picked up the cream, poured some into my coffee, and watched as it diffused in a slow rotation, like a spiral galaxy sweeping out in the deep vacuum of space. I looked back up and into Sylvia's eyes. "The diaries for Duncan. They have him and the kids."

All levity dropped from her face. "Who's they?"

"I'm assuming it's CSIS, but Raymond Jones isn't his real name." I pulled out a piece of paper from my pocket and pushed it across the table. "Can you trace this?"

She pulled it over. "An Ontario licence plate? Please."

"It might not be that easy. It's probably part of the government fleet."

"I can trace it to a department, possibly even an office. If you're lucky the car is assigned directly to some big cheese, and if not then someone had to sign it out for those hours of use." She crinkled her nose. "It's Saturday. It might take me a few hours."

"I have twenty-four. Then I have to give the elusive Mr. Jones an answer. Either I accept the deal or not."

"A pact with the devil."

I nodded. "And I'd like it to be a devil I know."

She studied the letters and numbers for a moment, then tucked the paper in the pocket of her jean jacket. "I'll do my best. What about the Fruit Machine? Do you want me to drop that?"

"Did you find anything?"

She gave a non committal shrug. "The archivist thought I was crazy until I showed him Marcotte's articles, then he got all hyped up. It was like a good detective story. One thing I can tell you for sure, the thing existed. The science leader was an eminent university professor — now deceased — with some interesting theories on the differences between straights and gays. Junk science at its best." Sylvia opened her briefcase and pulled out a pile of papers, copies of memos typed up on an old typewriter. She flipped through them until she came to one with a schematic attached. "*Voila*. The Fruit Machine." She passed it over to me.

"It looks like an electric chair."

She waved her long nails in my direction. "It looks gruesome but it wasn't painful, not in the physical sense anyway. What you see here," she pointed at the heavy straps that crossed the arms, "are sensors for measuring stuff like pulse rate, galvanic skin response, pupil dilation. The subject was strapped in and shown a series of images — a mix of neutral images, sexually appropriate images, and sexually inappropriate images — while the tester monitored their physiological responses. If those little pens jerked back and forth when you saw some guy's hairy butt you were in deep shit."

"Did you find any test records?"

"They never actually got the thing to work. Despite years of testing and refinements, costing hundreds of thousands of dollars, the Fruit Machine never could reliably detect a faggot, something, I'd just like to point out, that every gay person can do without thinking.

"The first hitch was the stimulus problem. I mean, show a chemist a test tube and he gets all hot. What does that mean? Is a test tube a sexually appropriate or inappropriate stimulus? Then there was the issue of establishing baselines. To determine who is and who isn't, you need to judge each test subject against reliable baseline data. To get that data you need multiple test subjects of known sexual orientation, and their test results have to be consistent within their group. But guess what? They couldn't get volunteers. The gay boys weren't exactly lining up for the privilege since it was a surefire way to lose your job, and the macho lab studs refused to take the seat, presumably for fear that they might respond inappropriately to the aforementioned test tube. So without volunteers it became impossible to develop the technology, faulty as it was." She pulled out a memo and pointed to a section she'd highlighted. "Phase two refinements held up due to lack of volunteers." She pulled out another. "Phase three refinements held up, testing of new galvanic skin repose sensors held up. And, of course, every holdup cost them time and money. By 1964, the RCMP brass was getting pissed. The thing was finally scrapped in early 1965, but according to Marcotte's article, only after the RCMP had purged several hundred suspected homosexuals from the civil service. There was no compensation, no recourse. They were just driven out."

"But you said it didn't work."

"Who cares? If you spend thousands of dollars of public money then you better show results. Otherwise your job is next."

I leaned back in the booth and tried to integrate all this information. Was it just an interesting sidebar or was it relevant to Grenier's death? And did it connect to Peter Aarons? I knew that Grenier was connected to Peter Aarons, and Grenier was connected to the Fruit Machine, but was there a relationship between the Fruit Machine and Peter Aarons? The million-dollar question.

The waiter arrived with our meals, and as he slid the plates onto the table Sylvia provided the obvious answer to that question. "It's a hideous history," she said, "but between Marcotte and the Archives there's nothing to cover up. It's all out there. There's no motive for murder."

"Until we know precisely what Grenier was after we can't know that for sure." But what the hell was he after?

We both chewed thoughtfully for the next while, me with more gusto than Sylvia. She had, she told me, stopped her chemo but her appetite was still on the skids. Since I was almost finished by the time she was less than halfway through I asked to borrow her cellphone. She pushed it across the table and I dialed Daniel Marcotte. If anyone knew exactly what Yves Grenier was after it was Daniel Marcotte, and he'd promised me those contact names today.

But Marcotte, it seemed, was suddenly scarce. I'd tried him after my run and been diverted to his voice mail. This time was no different. I left him a pointed message with Sylvia's cellphone number and hung up in frustration. He wouldn't be calling me back until he'd milked those contacts for all they were worth. On the other hand, I thought suddenly, there might be another way. I motioned to the pile of photocopies now sitting at the side of the table.

"Are there names in those memos?"

"Sure. All upper echelon RCMP Security Service. Half of them are probably dead and the ones that are alive aren't going to talk to you. Not about classified information."

"It's not classified now." I smiled. "And I can be very persuasive. Do you have Marcotte's articles there?" That's what Grenier had seen, and what had spurred him to call Daniel Marcotte. Maybe there was something in there I could use without Marcotte's help.

As Sylvia picked through her bacon and eggs I read the articles, punctuating each page with a French fry dipped in ketchup. It was not what I'd hoped for. Marcotte's information had come from two sources. One was clearly the same archival material that Sylvia had copied. The other was in-depth interviews with gay men purged during the witch hunt. They, however, refused to allow their names to be used, and that's what Grenier must have been after. The names of homosexual men purged during the 1960s — but why? I took a last swig of coffee. There was only one way to find out.

When I got to Marcotte's neighbourhood I chose a parking space one block down behind a van. I could see his property clearly but he wouldn't see me. I sat for fifteen minutes and watched. There was no activity around his house and all the interior lights were off. Since Sylvia had been heading back to my apartment after the Mayflower I'd borrowed her phone, and I used it to dial Marcotte again. The voice mail clicked through so I hung up.

As I sat waiting the light began to fade and the streetlights flickered pale orange. Inside a nearby house a light went on in the living room window, followed by another next door. Marcotte's house, though, remained dark. I checked my watch again. If I had to wait all night, I would. To pass the time I pulled out my notebook and began to frame questions for my upcoming interview with Simon Batters. He knew more than he was saying and, fragile or not, I intended to get that information. I didn't relish the idea of squeezing a sick and elderly man, but the future of Duncan's children was at stake. And after all, I was just asking the guy to tell the truth.

A car slowed at Parkdale and turned onto Marcotte's street, then swung into his driveway. A moment later Daniel Marcotte stepped out, briefcase in hand, crossed the lawn, and let himself into the house. A few lights went on downstairs, there was a pause, and then a light went on in what I now knew was his upstairs office. I laid the cellphone on the seat beside me and waited to see if he'd call. He didn't. And Sylvia would have called me right away if he'd put the call through to my apartment.

So I'd been right. He was avoiding me. I climbed out of my car.

At his door I leaned on the bell. It buzzed insistently but there was no other sound or movement. I gave the knob a quick twist, but it was locked, then I started banging, but to no response. I was just about to add yelling to my repertoire when the cellphone blurped out the "Maple Leaf Rag." I flipped it open, expecting Marcotte, but it was my name on the screen.

"Hey babe," said Sylvia. "You're needed at home."

"I'm sort of in the middle of something here."

"Whatever it is, I can guarantee you, it isn't as important as this."

I lowered my voice. "What's up?"

"In person only."

That meant it was either too big or too ugly to discuss on the cell, and that had potential. I told her I'd be there as soon as I could. I disconnected the call and jogged across the street to where I knew Marcotte could see me. I faced the house and rang him again. Still no answer, but I'd expected that. "Hey Danny," I said to the voice mail, "I was at your house, but I guess you know that since you were inside. I have new information. A big scoop. Too bad you had to miss it."

I pressed "end",turned off the phone, and laughed all the way back to my car.

Back in the apartment Sylvia looked up and grinned as I came in. Her laptop was open on the coffee table, papers were scattered across the surface, and she had a whiskey in her hand. A stray piece of black hair fell over one eye. Sylvia is usually an abstemious drinker. Alcoholism, she says, is an occupational hazard in the transgendered community since the only safe place to meet is in the bar, so it was a surprise to see her drinking alone, but I kept my thoughts to myself. After all, what was it going to do? Kill her?

I pulled off my coat and hung it up. I have to admit, the whiskey did look inviting, but I had a busy evening ahead and I needed to keep my wits intact.

"Did Marcotte call?"

She shook her head. "But you may not need him. Have a seat." She patted the cushion beside her. "Guess what today is?"

"Saturday."

"Nope. It's two-for-one day."

"Really? Who's paying?"

"Duncan, of course, but today it's a bargain. Where would you like me to start? The car?"

I felt a little jolt of adrenaline and gave her a nod.

"After a little digging, a little downloading, and a few calls I was able to determine that the licence plate number belongs to a government car assigned to" — she raised a finger — "not CSIS, not the RCMP, but ..." She leaned over and, with one hand only, tapped a few keys. A table came up on the screen with licence plate numbers on the left, car information on the right. "... the PMO."

"The Prime Minister's Office?"

She nodded.

I'd expected at her revelation to feel a burst of joy, but instead of a rush of endorphins my brain let out a very definitive *Oh shit.*

Sylvia saw my expression and laughed. "Hey, babe, it gets worse. As you know the Mounties handle most of the security up on the Hill, but what you may not know is that there's also a civilian office attached to the PMO. Their guys develop and assess security plans and generally act as independent security consultants to the Prime Minister's Office. This car," she scrutinized the screen then pointed at a line with her finger, following it along as she spoke, "a black 2003 Grand Marquis LSE, four-door, light blue leather interior, 4.6-litre SOHC V-8 engine with dual exhaust ...," I nodded to confirm that this was indeed the car I'd been in, "... is assigned to the civilian security office."

"How many people work there? Do you have any idea?"

"As a matter of fact I do. Six. Three of them are women — clerical staff. That leaves us with only three possible candidates for Raymond Jones."

I thought about that for a minute. "That's doable. We just have to match a physical description of my

Raymond Jones with one of those names." But could we do it by tomorrow at noon?

Sylvia sat back on the couch. "But you've forgotten what day it is."

"I work on Saturday. Sunday too."

"It's two-for-one day." She threw a memo in my lap and pointed to the yellow highlight. "In 1963 RCMP Constable Joseph Kowalski was named as project supervisor for the Fruit Machine. Joseph Kowalski is now the chief security advisor to the PMO. He heads up the civilian office."

I looked at the memo, then at the organizational chart that now sat on the screen with Joseph Kowalski's name at the top. So Raymond Jones was really Joseph Kowalski, and he was connected to the Fruit Machine.

"You bastard," I said out loud, "I have you."

Sylvia sat beside me with her arms crossed and a look of disapproval on her face. It was an expression that had stubbornly remained in place since we'd left my apartment en route to Simon Batters's condo in Rockcliffe. We were now cruising through Ottawa's most exclusive enclave, passing the palatial mansions of high-tech millionaires, the stately homes of ambassadors, and the huge estate of the Governor General, but Sylvia aimed her glacial stare dead ahead. I'd have to find Simon Batters's address on my own.

At the base of the Governor General's estate I saw a long, low condominium building, red brick, with a beautifully landscaped entrance. I slowed.

"It's here," I said.

"Jesus," said Sylvia, and she turned to face the passenger door window.

I pulled into the curb, grabbed my briefcase, and stepped out onto the road. By the time I reached the sidewalk Sylvia still hadn't moved so I walked back to the car and yanked open her door. "If that's the way you want to be then just stay here." I flung it shut. That got a response. She wrenched the door open and vaulted out, bringing her six-foot frame within inches of me.

"You're going to do this anyway, aren't you, no matter what I say."

"I'm just asking a few questions."

"Which you promised Helen Keeler you wouldn't do. Jesus, Morgan. He's sick, he's elderly, and he doesn't want to talk to you. There has to be another way."

"I have less than twenty-four hours to work this out, and if I mess up, what happens to Duncan's kids? Foster homes? An orphanage? All Batters has to do is tell the truth. How hard can that be?"

She gave me a penetrating look and answered in a quiet voice. "Harder than you can imagine."

With that she strode over to the front door and plunked herself down on the bench across from the intercom. What the hell had gotten into her? Maybe it was the hormones talking. I gave my head a shake and went up to the intercom.

Batters's name was listed next to Unit 3B. I debated giving the button a push, but there was too great a chance that he wouldn't let me in. Someone else was going to have to do that job for me. I leaned against the wall and waited. Sylvia pouted. Eventually a woman came around the corner heading for the door. I turned to the intercom. As she opened the first vestibule door I leaned toward the intercom and spoke.

"It's okay, Dr. Batters, don't get up," I said loudly. "Somebody's just come through. We'll be there in a minute." Then I smiled at the woman and snagged the door before it swung shut.

Sylvia stood. "Oh good. Now we can appear unannounced and scare the poor guy to boot."

"Yeah, and you'd better straighten your wig," I said as she passed through the door. "I wouldn't want him to go into cardiac arrest."

She shot me a cold glare and stalked down the hall. She reached Batters's door before me and once there pushed the bell without waiting for me to arrive. Damn it, I wasn't quite ready. I hurried up beside her just as someone inside turned the doorknob.

Sylvia looked down on me. "You owe me for this big time."

I was just about to ask her why when the door opened a crack as a safety chain snapped taut on the other side. Batters took in Sylvia then saw me. I am not proud to record the look of terror that passed across his face. Sylvia elbowed me out of sight and stood in front of the door.

"Dr. Batters," she said formally. "I am sorry to disturb you at this time of night. I studied with Dr. Bernstein at the University of British Columbia. I —" she started.

"David?" he said.

There was an awkward moment when no one knew what to say. Then Sylvia said, "We need to talk to you. I promise, we won't be long."

His eyes shifted to me, then back to Sylvia. He seemed to search her face, looking for some sort of reassurance, then he pushed the door shut. A moment later the chain rattled and he pulled the door open.

"I didn't think you'd recognize me," she said, almost sheepishly.

"Yes, well," he said. "I never forget a face, really. And I must say you do look, well, remarkable. Of course

I've heard about these sorts of things," he waved vaguely at her body, "but it's what's up here," he tapped his forehead with his index finger, "that counts. And for you I'm sure that hasn't changed. Bernstein was damned angry to lose you, David. Damned lucky to have had you in his lab in the first place, I'd say, but that's history, what? No going back now." Then he glanced over at me. "I've been told not to talk to you. I wouldn't have let you in if you weren't with David."

Sylvia gave me a sour look. "She'll behave."

I glanced at Sylvia. What was going on here? Why hadn't she told me that she knew him? Batters led us down a small passageway. As he walked he bobbed his head and muttered *excellent, excellent*, but more to reassure himself than to communicate with us. He seemed a bit disoriented. Of course, that could be from seeing David Delgado, the prize-winning physics student, transformed into a stunning, dark-haired beauty. It didn't say much for a stable, predictable universe. I just hoped that the shock wouldn't completely unhinge him.

We'd reached the living room and Batters pointed to a couch and chair across from a recliner. "Do sit down. I was just — " He glanced around the room. "Now where is that blasted drink." Both Sylvia and I scanned the room.

I walked over to the sideboard and picked up his half-finished drink from the buffet. "Is this what you were looking for?"

I brought it over to him, then went back to the sideboard and picked up the book that had been lying next to his drink. It was the same book I'd seen that morning, and it was open to the same page — the group photo of the Astronomy Institute staff on the steps of Sussex Drive. I lifted it up and looked at the legend beneath the photo — *Helen Keeler, Peter Aarons, Simon Batters*. I felt a sudden weight of sadness. I looked up at Batters. "They don't know you have this, do they?"

He looked away. After a moment of silence he said, "Are you going to take it?"

I walked toward him and held it out. "I only care about Peter Aarons, how he connects to Yves Grenier, and I desperately need your help."

He put down his drink and took the book from my hands. He closed it and held it in his arms like a sacred relic. He gave deep sigh. "I think we could all use a drink, what?"

A few minutes later he was back from the liquor cabinet with a scotch for both Sylvia and me. Now, I'm not a great fan of scotch. The only time I consume the stuff is as a masochistic ritual when I'm feeling so depressed that nothing could make it worse, except perhaps the astringent taste of mediocre scotch. Or if I'm trying to block out the demons of my mother: a bizarre way to go about it since scotch was her preferred method of self-annihilation. This scotch, however, was of a different class altogether: smooth and silky, pungent and explosively warm. More like cognac than scotch, but without the bite. I rolled it around on my tongue and almost moaned.

Batters sank into the recliner and took a hefty belt of his drink. His face had gone from pale to ruddy, and I wondered uneasily about his health. If he suffered from high blood pressure or diabetes all that alcohol couldn't be good. Best to get this over with as quickly as possible. I sat down on the couch. Sylvia took the arm-chair so she was positioned between Batters and me, ready to intervene if I got out of line.

I took another sip of scotch and cleared my throat. "Who told you not to talk to me?"

"We signed papers, you know, when Peter disappeared. All of us did. And I took an oath not to discuss what happened with anyone ever. I can't break an oath to my country."

"It was a long time ago. The Cold War is over."

"You're quite right about that. I couldn't agree with you more, but I still signed that paper. Not that we had much choice in the matter. Helen told you, I suppose. It was a bloody awful time." He took another a swig of his drink and grimaced. "Beastly. Something you young people can't even imagine." He looked Sylvia in the eye. "One day you're doing your research, analyzing your data, novas, globular clusters, Cepheid variables, that sort of thing, the next day they're in your lab saying you're a Soviet spy. It's a bloody shock, I can tell you, uniformed men in your office pulling apart your files, examining your letters — your personal letters, mind — looking for anything and everything. Then they're in your house." He shook his head and looked down at the hand clutching the drink. "There was no recourse, no lawyers. It was bloody awful, bloody inhumane, but not much to be done about it." He looked away. "Sign the paper or lose my job, it was as simple as that."

"But you're retired, Dr. Batters. There's nothing they can do to you now."

"But why dig it all up? Let sleeping dogs lie. What's to be gained by digging up ...," there was a moment of hesitation, "... poor Peter. Dreadful thing, that."

"Poor Peter? That's not the story I heard. I heard he defected and betrayed you all. Why *poor* Peter?"

"Just an expression, I suppose. Poor Peter. They were difficult times. It was hard to know who was with whom, if you catch my drift. But Peter," he shook his head. His voice held the same disbelief as Helen Keeler's. "He just got in with the wrong crowd. Didn't know what was what. Damned innocent fellow, Peter, but not a traitor." Then he gave a muffled hurumph. "Peter wouldn't have known a communist agent from an Anglican priest, and what's more he couldn't have cared less. If it didn't have to do with astronomy he wasn't interested."

"Dr. Keeler told me that Peter was antisocial."

"She would then, wouldn't she? Don't misunderstand me. Helen is a fine person, a decent astronomer, but she's still a woman, what? Expecting polite conversation and decent manners and all that nonsense. Peter wasn't up to it, no question about that. Had no interest, but he was a brilliant astronomer."

"Were the two of you close?"

He started to struggle out of the chair. "A fellow could use another drink just about now."

Sylvia stood. "I'll get it."

I gave her a warning glance as she passed, hoping she wouldn't fill it too full, but at the sideboard she poured him a double. As she did so Batters continued.

"Close as anyone to Peter, I suppose, and I will tell you this. Thank you, David." He took the drink. "Peter was as honest as the day is long. He could no more tell a lie than I could dance in the Bolshoi. Probably what got him into trouble."

"How do you mean?"

He sidestepped. "Just got in with the wrong crowd. That's all I can say."

Honest as the day is long? That didn't make for a great double agent, so who was telling the truth? It was time to try a different tack. "Yves Grenier called you the day he died."

Batters brought his hand to his face. "How did you know that?"

I opened my diary and pulled out the photocopy of the last page of Grenier's notebook. I handed it to Batters and pointed at his initials. "He called you at 6:23 Hawaii time and asked you something, but got no, or maybe nothing, for an answer. Was it about Peter Aarons?" Batters lifted the glass to his lips and I could see that his hand was trembling but I had to press. "Why did he call you, Dr. Batters?"

"Morgan." That was a warning from Sylvia.

"My conversation with Dr. Grenier is private. What right have you to invade my privacy, and Dr. Grenier's?"

"Yves Grenier is dead. He hasn't a shred of privacy left."

Batters grimaced. "Tragic thing in one so young. Quite bloody awful."

"Dr. Batters …" I let a pause hang in the air. "He was murdered."

Batters slumped back and stared straight ahead. Sylvia stood and approached the chair. She knelt beside it and put her hand on his arm. He absently covered it with his own, but his eyes looked at the wall, as if he was searching for something not there.

"Did Yves Grenier call you about Peter Aarons?" Sylvia asked gently. "We have to know."

Batters seemed suddenly to reconnect. "About Peter? It had nothing to do with Peter."

I felt my stomach drop. It had to be connected. "What then?"

"This is damned embarrassing. Damned embarrassing." He glanced uneasily at Sylvia. "He wanted to know about some infernal contraption called the Fruit Machine."

chapter eighteen

"It might have helped if you'd told me you knew him." I started the car and turned up the heat.

"I didn't think he'd remember me." She lifted her hands. "Especially not like this."

I tapped my head with my finger. "It's what's up here that counts, David. And despite you we scored."

"Are we on the same planet? Batters said that Grenier didn't call him about Peter Aarons."

"Exactly. Grenier called about the Fruit Machine, which means that everything connects back. I just have to figure out how." I turned suddenly to Sylvia. "You think Batters was tested?"

"I can assure you, no." She turned and looked coyly out the window.

"What are you saying?"

"You're the investigator. Do I have to spell it out?"

It took me a moment to absorb the meaning of her statement. "Is that conjecture?"

"Empirical knowledge." She crossed her legs primly. "It was all very subtle, and he was the complete gentleman when rejected. It was as if nothing had happened, as if it was all in my imagination, but I know what went down." She gave a half smile. "And it wasn't me."

"Did anyone else know?"

She gave a shrug. "There may have been rumours but I was pretty removed from all that, being the subject of so many rumours myself. Bottom line, if Batters had been tested he wouldn't be around."

I thought about that for a minute. "Unless they had reason to keep him on, a use for him."

"A repugnant thought. Like what?"

"He could spy on his colleagues, pass information on technology developments to the Security Service. The fear of job loss and public humiliation is a pretty powerful motivator, but why would he be so reticent now?"

"When you've been in the closet that long, babe, the closet begins to feel like home. He may not even be out to himself." She seemed to take a minute to calculate something, then turned to me. "Did Marcotte get back to you with those contacts?"

"It's a dead end."

Her eyes narrowed. The investigation was getting under her skin, I could tell, beginning to eat away at her just as it was me. "Marcotte got those contacts somewhere," she said suddenly. She pulled the seat belt taut across her chest. "Why don't we find out where." She gave me a quick once-over. "You're a little underdressed, but you'll do. What are you waiting for? Drive."

Fifteen minutes later we were heading down an alley just off Bank Street. At the side of an old building a concrete stairwell descended to a steel door. There were no markings on the door, just the indecipherable scrawl of gang graffiti. Sylvia pulled open the door with an assurance that I didn't feel, and we entered a long, dimly lit corridor that resonated with the low thump of dance music. A door opened at the end of the hall to reveal the pulse of disco lights. When we arrived at that door a bouncer the size of an armoire, dressed in head-to-toe leather, gave us a careful once-over then, with a nod, let us in. Sylvia tweaked the woman's cheek as she walked by. The bouncer gave me a wry *go-figure* smile, and I answered with a shrug and a shake of my head.

It was just nearing ten o'clock, way too early, Sylvia informed me, for any real action. The place, however, was packed with a stunning array of buff male bodies and perfect hair. There were a few clusters of women, but they'd retreated to the corner tables. Sylvia surveyed the crowd and more than a few surveyed her back.

"Nice," I said in her ear, referring to the red sequined curtain that hung in front of the stage.

"Wait until you see the costumes," she yelled back. "They make the curtain look positively Mormon. The first show starts at eleven. At ten-thirty we'll go backstage and have a chat with Daisy Mae." Daisy Mae? I gave her a questioning look. "She's been around forever. She'll have more first-hand information on the Fruit Machine than any punk reporter. In the meantime," she said, "I hope you play euchre."

With that she turned right and began to elbow her way through the dense mass of bodies. I made it across the dance floor in Sylvia's wake, then through the tight ring of gawkers that surrounded the dancers. Beyond that the crowd ended abruptly. The music dropped to a tolerable level and we entered a small back room, a sheltered intimate space with five semi-circular alcoves recessed into the wall. Each had a single stained glass lamp that hang over the table. Instead of the coiffed jet black and platinum blond of the meat market beyond, the heads in here ran from salt and pepper to paper white, and the omnipresent black leather was replaced by tweed jackets and turtleneck sweaters. At one booth a cribbage board vied with glasses of ginger ale for space on the table. At another some sort of board game was in progress. At still another there was the relaxed atmosphere of old buddies trading war stories. At the table just in front of me five men were locked in an intense conversation. An aesthetic fellow with a beautiful mop of white hair was speaking, poking the table with his finger. Sylvia turned to me and mouthed the word *librarians*, then she turned and approached the table. The white-haired man looked up and a smile spread across his face.

"Perfect timing," he said. He stood and embraced Sylvia. "Come." He pulled her down next to him. "She'll settle it." He leaned toward the man across from him. "Tell him, Sylvia. When was the last time one of your clients requested a book?"

The man across from him, a bald, heavyset man, leaned forward. "There will always be books, Gordon. Your damned computers can't change that."

"You see?" Gordon beamed at Sylvia. "Nothing's changed." He turned back to his opponent. "Nobody said that books would disappear altogether, but I can assure you they won't be in libraries. They'll be in special collections closed to the public." He turned back to Sylvia and repeated his question. "Tell him, Sylvia. When was the last time you had a request for a book? I mean a real book in paper format. Give the right answer and I pay for your drink."

She looked first at Gordon then at his opponent. "Really. The two of you. A girl would think she'd never been away."

The tension popped like a balloon. There was a round of chuckles followed by a few sly remarks. Sylvia turned to me. "Morgan, meet Gordon Draper, the recently retired Director of Online Services for the National Science Library."

"Your ex-boss," I took his hand.

"And a man," she continued dramatically, "of great vision and taste without whom," she raised her hands in a flourish, "I would not be what I am today."

"Hear! Hear," the table responded, and the men raised their glasses in unison. I slid into the bench across from Sylvia and next to Gordon's debating partner, a man introduced to me as Ken.

Sylvia leaned forward and addressed the table. "I bet you boys think we're here just for the pleasure of your company, but in fact I need a favour. Not for *moi*. My friend Morgan needs help."

The man next to Gordon leaned back to get a better a look at me. "Nice hair, good bones, but the clothes have to go. We're needing something a little more —" he fluffed the air with his hands, "feminine."

"God knows I've tried," said Sylvia. She waved her hand vaguely in my direction. "But for better or for worse, she's a package deal. Anyway, it's not that kind of help." The waiter arrived with his tray. Sylvia ordered a martini while I opted for a glass of red plonk. When he'd moved on to other patrons Sylvia turned back to the table. "She needs information on something that happened in the 1960s, a device some people referred to as the Fruit Machine."

The reaction was immediate. All levity vanished. Two men at the end of the table exchanged an uncomfortable glance. Gordon looked down at his hands, and Ken, sitting next to me, went rigid as stone.

Gordon broke the silence. "Why bring that up again? Leave the past alone."

"It's not that easy," I answered. "It's come up in a murder investigation."

That did nothing to lighten the mood.

"Are you with the police?" That came from a man at the end of the table.

I felt the animosity sweep over me before I could even answer. Sylvia stepped in. "She's on our side and she needs our help."

"I'm leaving," said Ken. He pushed against me and forced me to slide off the bench. I stood and watched as he pulled on his coat. Without even a nod to his friends he disappeared into the gyrating crowd. I sat back down quickly to stop the exodus.

"I need to find some men who were tested. Who know what happened and might be able to identify someone."

"And then what?" asked the man at the end of the table. "The police come for a little chat? We have to testify in court? Tell me, who would be on trial?"

Gordon banged his hand against the table. "Damn. I could use a real drink right about now."

His neighbour took his hand. "It's not worth it, Gordon. That's how they win."

By the time the waiter returned with our drinks only Sylvia and I remained at the table. She took a slug of hers. "Fucking pansies," she said.

"They don't know me. They don't trust me. You can't blame them."

"I can." She gave me a crooked smile. "You can't." Then she stood to her full six feet. With the big hair, tight black jeans, and Cossack boots she looked like a warrior queen. "But there's always Daisy Mae."

And with that she turned and led the troops to battle.

Sylvia took a black door hidden behind the edge of the sequined curtain. We rose up a short flight of stairs to a small stage, turned right, and cut through the wings to a dark corridor. I had a brief moment of wondering how Sylvia, with a Ph.D. in physics and library science, could be so familiar with the backstage of a drag club, but I filed that question away for another time. Halfway down the corridor Sylvia stopped at a closed door. A piece of torn cardboard, with the word *Talent* scrawled across it in black marker, hung from the door. Someone had added a few stars in glitter pen. I heard a sharp laugh inside.

Without knocking Sylvia pulled open the door. The first thing that hit me was the smell: a cross between old gym socks and a chemical spill at Revlon. The next was the almost blinding light: stark white of fluorescent tubes, columns of naked bulbs, and everything magnified by wall-to-wall mirrors. A wardrobe rack bulging with ultra-feminine attire — sequined gowns, merry widows, feather boas — sliced the narrow room in half. On top, a line of Styrofoam heads displayed an assortment of wigs that would make Dolly Parton proud. Black, auburn, and platinum blonde. Blue, green, fire engine red. Performers in cheap plastic chairs leaned into the mirrors with lipstick and eyeshadow in hand.

Sylvia edged her way toward the back. As she squeezed through one of the performers pulled in his chair but glared at her through the mirror. "Hey girl," he said. "We're all booked up here. You're gonna have to sell that booty someplace else."

Sylvia's response was immediate. She leaned into his face. "I'll take my booty and sell it wherever I fucking well please." Then she hooked her finger under the shoulder strap of his red push-up bra and snapped it hard. "Where'd you get those done? Tijuana? Nice job, unless you wanted a matching pair."

I heard someone on the other side of the wardrobe mutter *you tell the bitch* but the bitch in question had started to rise out of his chair. He was smaller than Sylvia, but he had the body of a dancer, solid muscle. I was preparing to grab him when I heard the swish and rustle of taffeta and a head popped out around the rack. It was blonde with big sausage curls, a sort of Little Bo-Peep look, but offset by a heavy grey moustache. The man threw open his arms and pulled Sylvia into a smothering embrace. Over his shoulder he waved a dismissive hand at the performer. Sylvia, he seemed to be saying, wasn't a threat. So this was Daisy Mae.

He pushed Sylvia out to arm's length and scrutinized her head to toe. "Looking good. All done?"

Sylvia raised her arms. "What you see is what you get."

That'll be a first, someone muttered across the room.

"Too bad," Daisy Mae chuckled. "I like surprises." He nodded in my direction. "Is she a surprise?"

Sylvia turned and gave me a considering look. "She's always a surprise. When are you on?"

"Five minutes. A bit of an introduction, maybe a song, then the fresh meat takes over. The vagaries of old age. Can you wait?" His glance slid to me. "I get the feeling this isn't a social call." He reached around, pulled a big stogy off the counter, and jammed it into the corner of his mouth. "It's showtime." He wiggled his eyebrows like Groucho Marx and flounced out of the room.

In the bar there was a sudden burst of ribald laughter as Daisy Mae taunted the crowd. The chords of some sappy music cut in followed by a sublime voice — a high tenor, maybe a contralto — crooning some Judy Garland standard.

"Is that him?" I said to Sylvia. "You mean he really sings?"

The performers all around me stood to make the final adjustments in their costumes and wigs.

"Oh, he can sing, baby," said the performer nearest me. "Voice of an angel and mouth of trash. C'mon girls. Let's roll." And the crowd of them slunk out of the dressing room in one fluid line.

There was wild laughter then cheers from the club outside followed by the sound of thumping music. Daisy Mae reappeared at the door, sweat trickling down his pancake makeup. He yanked off the sausage-curl wig to reveal a surprisingly conservative salt and pepper cut and sank down in his chair.

"Drink?" he asked, but he didn't wait for an answer. He pulled three glasses and a bottle of rye from beneath the counter. I held up my wineglass, which was still half full. Sylvia, though, gave a nod. She might have the body and mind of a woman, but she still metabolized alcohol like a man: a hell of a lot more slowly than me.

I waited until Daisy Mae had taken a slug before launching into *my* routine. "I'm looking for information," I said.

"What kind? People? Places? Events? One hundred surefire ways to improve your sex life?"

"Were you around the bar scene in the early sixties?"

Daisy Mae's glance shifted to Sylvia. She gave a single nod, and he turned back to me. "Honey, I was the bar scene in the early sixties. You know what this town was like back then?"

"Have you ever heard of something called the Fruit Machine?"

He gave me a hooded look. "You a cop or a reporter? I'd place my bets on cop."

"I'm trying to help a friend."

Sylvia put her hand on Daisy Mae's arm. "She's with us." Then she gave me a sideways glance. "And if she isn't I'll kick her butt."

Daisy Mae batted his false eyelashes and looked at the ceiling. "The Fruit Machine. Well, golly me, where should I begin?" Then he cut the camp. "The first I heard about it was at a club I worked in around '61. Back then everyone was in the closet. There was nowhere else to be unless you wanted your head bashed in. And the police? They were doing the bashing." He picked up the glass, drained it, and banged it down on the counter. "The Security Service boys used to storm into the club and take all us girls into the back for a little chat. They wanted names: who we dated, what government department they worked in, where they lived, how many times we'd seen them. If you didn't cooperate you lost a few teeth, and I can tell you, the Mounties enjoyed their work." At that he turned away, reached for the bottle, and poured himself a double. "Then they made the Fruit Machine. I was relieved. What can I tell you? Replaced by technology. But it didn't work that way. They still came in checking ID, taking us all in the back, and trying to pry out names for testing. Shit." He picked up the stogy. "I wish I could light this thing."

I felt a little jolt. "And did you?"

"Did I what?"

"Did you give them names?"

"Oh, honey." He leaned over and tweaked my cheek. "You are so very young. In those days we were all Smith or Jones. No one brought ID to a gay bar."

I felt a pang of disappointment. "So if I gave you a name it wouldn't mean anything?"

"Not unless it was Smith or Jones."

"Did you ever date any astronomers?"

"The men with their eyes on the heavens? Sounds romantic, but they're not much fun. Uptight, as I recall. I like my men a little more down to earth."

"What about a photograph? If we showed you a picture any chance you could identify someone who'd hung out at the club?"

"Sweetie, Daisy Mae doesn't rat, so why don't you just tell me what you're after and I'll tell you if I can help."

"A man disappeared in Ottawa in 1964. We're trying to figure out how and why. It may be tied to a recent murder."

"And you think he was gay?"

"We don't know, but it's one possibility."

Daisy Mae lifted his hand and rubbed the bristles on his cheek, then he looked at Sylvia. She kept her expression impassive. "All right, bring it around. If he was a regular there's a chance. If not, you're out of luck."

"Is there someone else who might know? Could you show the picture around?"

"Don't push your luck, honey." He drained his glass in one swig and stood. "My services are needed on stage, the exciting life of a star. You girls got any other questions?"

"Just one," I said. "You ever run across a guy named Joseph Kowalski?"

Daisy Mae's expression changed and he sat back down. "Kowalski." His gaze shifted to the mirror and he lifted his hand and ran a finger over a small scar on his bottom lip, then he looked at me directly. "Is he involved?"

"I think so, but I need proof."

He stood again, this time abruptly. "Bring me that picture. I'll show it around." He jammed the stogy back in his mouth. "And if you see that fucker Kowalski, knee him in the balls, a special gift from me." He smiled. "You look like you could do it."

As we left the bar Daisy Mae took the stage. The crowd was now packed so tightly that movement was impossible. Daisy Mae stepped forward, took the microphone, and in a voice with the gravel of Marlene Dietrich dedicated a song to all the comrades lost and gone. There was laugher and applause. The music came on, the haunting sound of Celtic flute playing the opening bars of *My Heart Will Go On*. The gravel left his voice and a soft, clear contralto floated into the flute line like a feather on a breeze, as pure and poignant as any sound I'd ever heard. I stopped and looked back. He clutched his hands to his chest in a camp version of Céline Dion, but even the outrageous curves, the blue taffeta, and the ludicrous sausage curls couldn't diminish the beauty and the truth of his voice.

"Jesus," I said partly to Sylvia, but mostly to myself. "He could have been a professional singer."

She stopped and watched him for a moment. "She *is* a professional singer." Then Sylvia turned, took a step forward, and was swallowed by the crowd.

I watched for a moment longer, feeling shivers run up my spine at the sound of that voice. Finally I, too, turned and pushed my way toward the door. I'd almost reached it when something familiar caught my eye, the head of Daniel Marcotte plowing his way through the crowd headed toward the back room. He was on the same trail as me but a few steps behind. With any luck he'd find lots of people back there to keep him busy.

When I got to the car Sylvia was leaning against it waiting for me. I pulled out my keys. "You up for a detour?" I asked.

She held up her hand. "I don't want to know."

"You know what?" I unlocked her car door and swung it open. "You're right. You don't."

chapter nineteen

"**R**emind me what we're looking for?"

Sylvia had two thick files in front of her and a pencil sticking out from behind one ear. She looked almost like a librarian. I was sitting across from her at my dining room table with another thick file in front of me. A guy like Marcotte really should have an alarm system. I'd have to mention it to him the next time we crossed paths.

On the way back from Marcotte's I'd let Sylvia drive while I'd perused the files in the dull light of the car. The first contained articles and clippings from various sources. The second — and the largest one — was filled with what looked like the official documentation: the original research proposal for the development of a "homosexual detector," progress reports sent from the researchers to the RCMP, and blueprints for various components of the chair. Marcotte had also done extensive taped interviews in preparing the story, and the file Sylvia was now leafing through contained the logged transcripts of those interviews. I hoped there would be first-hand accounts of the experiments themselves, and maybe even names.

"We're looking for anything that might link the Fruit Machine to either Grenier or Peter Aarons," I said. It might end up being a futile search, but Grenier had been after something and it had to be hot. Otherwise Marcotte wouldn't bother hiding it from me and Kowalski wouldn't be in my face. I just hoped that Sylvia or I would recognize the critical piece of information buried in all this paper. I suppressed a sigh. It wasn't the first wild goose chase I'd been on, and Sylvia was used to it. She did this for a living.

I flipped open the file of official documentation. It looked mind-numbingly dull, and it would take me several hours to plow through it. I pushed a plastic flag dispenser over to Sylvia.

"Mark anything in those transcripts that we could follow up on: names, dates, places. Anything specific."

So far, Sylvia had been surprisingly silent on her role as an accessory to B&E — the driver of the getaway car to be exact — but I knew she didn't approve and I'd been waiting for the jab that would inevitably come. Without looking up she said, "So, babe, is there a return date on these files or are they on permanent loan?"

"It's a long-term arrangement," I said, studying the names of the researchers on the initial proposal. I didn't recognize any of them.

"I do wonder," she said, vaguely, "if the National Archives have copies of all these documents. They really should, you know." I looked up to see if she was kidding, but she'd pulled the pencil from behind her ear and was putting a tick on one of the sheets in the folder. "They *are* of historical significance," she continued. "I know of at least one archivist that, should these land on his desk, would be most appreciative. And discreet."

So much for unshakable moral values. I smiled. "Stranger things have happened."

"Mmm," she said, and continued her work without looking up.

I shook my head and buckled down to reading.

The first thing I went through was the initial research proposal. According to the background, a team of experts from engineering, psychology, physiology, and psychiatry had been assembled by the RCMP to design the project under the guidance of a professor of psychology at one of the local universities. This group developed the research proposal, but the actual construction of the device was contracted out to the labs of my employer, the National Council for Science and Technology. There were minutes from research committee meetings detailing the project's progress, or lack thereof, and the back-and-forth memos between the RCMP's Section A-3, the psychology professor, and the project supervisor in the NCST labs.

I'd been going through the reams of memos and reports for about forty minutes when Sylvia sat up straight. "1963," she declared, and she pulled the pencil from her ear and circled something on the paper.

"What?"

"1963. This is the transcript from a technician who worked on the chair. He says they were having trouble calibrating the sensors, especially the camera used to measure pupil dilation, and Constable Kowalski would routinely come into the lab and throw fits. It was taking too long, it was costing too much. Apparently the brass were on his case." She pulled the page back. "What's interesting is that the technician mentions a red scare in the NCST labs in '63: a chemist caught passing information to a visiting scientist from Hungary." She paused for a moment, and I could see her scan further down the page, then she started speaking like a translator doing a simultaneous translation, keeping her finger moving down the document. "Kowalski panicked, wanted to fast-track the project, get it up and running whether it worked or not. The pointy heads weren't keen, not enough time, not enough testing, inconclusive results, blah blah blah." Then she stopped, smiled, and looked up. "So the president of NCST agreed to provide ten volunteers from each division, since the lack of test subjects was delaying the project. The prick." She got up and came around the table. "Give me those." She grabbed my file and sat down next to me with it open on her lap. "I bet there's a test schedule in one of these progress reports. The researchers would need it to justify their funding."

She fanned through the papers until she reached the section she wanted and pulled a bunch of the memos out. They started in late 1963. She threw half of them onto the table in front of me. "You check these."

Now it was my turn to ask. "So what are we looking for?"

"The Canadian Astronomy Institute is a division of NCST, so they must have contributed ten volunteers. Let's find out when their group was tested."

We began shuffling through the papers, and ten minutes later Sylvia muttered "Eureka" and pulled a document from her pile. She held it up in the air. "Canadian Astronomy Institute. October 1964."

I felt my heart miss a beat. "The same month Peter Aarons disappeared."

"There's your link."

I thought about that for a minute. It was a connection, but what did it mean? I reached for the paper. "Do they give the names of test subjects?"

"Not here, but maybe in the progress reports covering that period."

Marcotte was a fastidious guy and had kindly organized the file in a chronological sequence. When we reached the progress reports for the autumn of 1964 we could see that they were bulkier than the early reports. I pulled out one, Sylvia another. At the end of mine I found the motherlode of information: individual test results from the volunteer test subjects the month before. The subject's last name and initial were neatly written in the left-hand corner of each data sheet. So much for confidentiality. The researchers even had the gall to make their guinea pigs sign a short release agreeing to volunteer.

The data sheets themselves looked pretty straightforward. A left-hand column listed the physiological responses being monitored, including pulse rate, pupil dilation, and galvanic skin response. For each response being monitored there were three scores: *Stimulus — Appropriate; Stimulus — Inappropriate; Stimulus — Neutral*. It didn't take a genius to interpret the results, but just in case the Security Service got confused there was a summation and recommendation at the bottom of each sheet. *No action required* indicated a high score under *Stimulus — Appropriate. Bar from facilities after regular working hours, monitor all activities* was recommended for test subjects with ambiguous scores. *High risk — not suitable for public service* was marked on those test sheets where the high scores sat in the *Inappropriate* column.

I handed the report to Sylvia. She scanned it, then threw it on the table. "These were supposed to be calibration runs. They didn't even know if the damned thing worked."

But I wasn't listening. I was shifting through the papers looking for the November report. If Kowalski was telling the truth about Aarons being drafted as a double agent, then Aarons must have been tested. When he scored high on the fruit-o-meter they made him an offer he couldn't refuse. All I needed was Peter Aarons's test sheet to prove it. I found the report and flipped to the back. Almost holding my breath I then went through the data sheets one by one. When I was finished I sat there for a moment not comprehending. "He's not here. He has to be."

Sylvia yanked the papers away from me and checked them herself. It was past three in the morning, and I was getting cranky. Sylvia, however, was as focused as a stalking cat. She was studying each sheet individually, and as I waited a terrible thought seeped into my mind. Maybe I'd been wrong all along. Maybe I'd made a faulty assumption early on in the investigation, and that had coloured all my thinking from that point onward, a mistake that would ultimately cost Duncan his family and his job. As Sylvia pored over the data I mentally reviewed the investigation step by step, trying to identify that moment where I'd made my logical error.

Then she pulled the pencil from her ear. "When did Aarons disappear?"

"Mid-October," I said absently.

"Do you know the day?"

"The last time he was seen in his office was October 14."

"So look at this." She pushed a data sheet across to me.

The name S. Batters was written at the top, and his signature sat beneath the release. I shrugged. "So you were wrong. He was tested."

"Look at the date and time."

I looked more closely. Batters's appointment had been on October 14 at 6:00 p.m., the last appointment of the day. I put the paper down and stared at the wall, then I turned to Sylvia. "You think Batters ratted on Aarons to save himself? That's why he's so skittish."

"I think he's crammed so far back in the closet he's afraid of the light. His behaviour may have nothing to do with Peter Aarons. On the other hand ..."

I poked at the data sheet. "Look at his test scores."

She perused it then shook her head. "That can't be right."

"One hundred percent red-blooded heterosexual male. No inappropriate responses."

Sylvia shook her head again. "That's impossible." She looked up at me. "Even if the thing didn't work. You've got to trust me on this one."

"I do, and that's my proof. Someone was protecting Batters. They didn't want him fired. Why?"

"You think Kowalski rigged the test scores? I can't imagine an RCMP officer leaving a known homosexual in a sensitive position."

"Unless they owned him."

Sylvia sat forward. "There is another possibility. We're assuming Batters is the victim, but maybe he had something on someone else. Kowalski, or someone high enough up to protect him."

It was an intriguing theory, but right now there were too many theories and not enough data to support any specific one, and none of this told me what Yves Grenier had been after when he'd telephoned Daniel Marcotte. There was no way around it. I had to talk to Batters again, to confront him with his lies, but before I could do that I needed sleep.

Sylvia was leafing through the data sheets as I got up. "I know you're not thrilled with Marcotte," she said absently, "but most reporters wouldn't have touched this story with a barge pole. I've got to respect the guy for digging it all up."

I looked at the mass of files and papers scattered across my dining room table and felt a brief pang of guilt. It must have taken him months to track all this stuff down. This was his livelihood, and it was now spread across my dining room table. Then the pang fizzled. "Too bad he's being such a jerk." Ten minutes later I was curled up in bed and sound asleep.

At seven the next morning I left Sylvia snoring in the guest room and let myself out quietly. It was Sunday, a big day at the Mayflower, but early enough that I could still probably get in. I considered that a moment then nixed the idea. I needed to talk to Simon Batters as early as possible since I had a date with Joseph Kowalski at noon. I opted for another high-carb muffin and double caffe latte, which I consumed en route to Rockcliffe.

As I came around the curve to Batters's condominium I slowed and pulled over. A police cruiser was parked in the loading zone out front. I took a final swig of coffee and surveyed the scene. It was an ominous start to the day. On the other hand there must be a hundred people living in that complex. The probability that the cruiser had anything to do with Batters was slight. I reached for my briefcase and stepped out of the car.

At the outer door I pressed the buzzer.

"Yes?" said a female voice.

"I'm here to see Dr. Batters."

There was a pause. "I'll be right down." A minute later a policewoman appeared and my stomach lurched. She pushed open the glass door but let it swing shut behind her. We were going to chat outside. "Are you a friend of Dr. Batters?" she asked politely.

"Is he all right?"

She repeated her question, but this time with an edge.

"More of an acquaintance really," I said. "What happened?"

She held out her hand. "May I see some identification?" I pulled out my driver's licence. No point in muddying the water by alerting her to my investigation. She examined it and handed it back. "What's the nature of your business at this time of the morning?"

I had an overwhelming urge to shove her aside and march right in but I had enough sense to know that the only place that would get me was downtown on a charge of assaulting an officer. My patience, however, was wearing thin. "Would you please tell me what's going on?"

"Why don't we sit down," she said, directing me to the bench where Sylvia had pouted the night before.

I shook off her arm. "Because I'm not feeling faint, and frankly, I've got a busy day ahead of me. If you won't tell me I'll just make a call to Detective Lilley downtown." With that I pulled out Sylvia's cellphone and started hitting buttons. Of course, I had no idea off the top of my head what Lilley's phone number was or, for that matter, if he'd give me the information, but it might intimidate a low-ranking officer. It didn't. She reached over, took my cellphone, and snapped it shut.

"We can do this the easy way," she said calmly "or the hard way. Which do you prefer?"

Having used that line myself I made an effort not to roll my eyes and sat down on the bench. She handed the cellphone back and pulled her notebook from her jacket. "When did you last see Dr. Batters?"

My immediate response was to lie, but then I remembered the woman who'd let us in, and the front door likely had video surveillance. "Last night around nine o'clock."

"Was he ill?"

"Frail, but I wouldn't say ill."

She scribbled something in her notebook. "And what was the nature of your business?"

I figured that now was the time to come clean, or at least a little bit cleaner. Hopefully it would keep me out of trouble. I pulled my wallet back out and showed her my NCST ID. "I needed information on a researcher that Batters had worked with in the past."

She took my ID and examined it, scribbled something in her pad, then handed it back. "And he was fine when you left?"

I thought back. A bit agitated perhaps, but as healthy as when we walked in. Or at least I think he was. I looked at her full in the face. "He was fine. Are you going to tell me what happened?"

"Did you notice any bruises on his wrists?"

I felt a sickening jolt in my stomach. "No," I said quietly. "He had no bruises at all."

She gave a nod and snapped her notebook shut. "At least that narrows the time frame. The downstairs neighbour heard a thump early this morning and called up to make sure he was all right. When there was no answer she called the building manager."

I felt the muffin churn undigested in my stomach. "Is he alive?"

She nodded. "Civic Hospital ICU, but it's touch and go."

"What's your take? A B&E gone bad?"

She stood. "There's no sign of forced entry and he was frail. It could be natural causes, but the bruises concern us. Until he wakes up and tells us what happened we're treating it as suspicious."

The Civic is Ottawa's oldest running hospital, a big red monolith in 1920s brick. I parked my car on the street and took the side door in. This brought me down a trendy little concourse lined with boutiques that sold to staff, visitors, and patients alike: everything from plush toys to gourmet ice cream. And, of course, cappuccino. I stopped at the café and ordered a large. I needed some fortification before seeing Simon Batters, and as I waited to be served I wondered if my visit the night before had precipitated an attack. A wave of self-loathing threatened to overwhelm me but I shut it down fast. I couldn't afford to have any regrets. Not until this was over and Duncan and the children walked free.

The man at the information desk located Batters's room number and directed me to the elevators around the corner. "He's just out of ICU," he said. "When you get up there turn right and go to the end of the hall. It's the last door on your left."

A police officer was seated in front of Batters's door. She stood as I approached, but I flashed my NCST identification and she nodded and sat back down. When I opened the door Helen Keeler turned from her chair by the bed. She was holding one of Batters's thin, papery hands. His eyes were closed and his mouth open. He was either unconscious or asleep. An intravenous tube snaked down from the side of his bed creating an ugly bruise where the needle entered his arm. I looked away and wrestled my emotions back into their cupboard. "How is he?"

Keeler shook her head.

"Do you know what happened?"

She sighed. "I'm aware of the possibilities."

Then she removed her hand and I saw the livid bruise around his wrist. I winced, but I only wallowed in guilt for an instant. With Batters out of the picture Keeler was my only hope. "I saw Dr. Batters last night."

Her head turned painfully toward me, the eyes hard. "You promised me you wouldn't. That is unconscionable."

"And you promised to tell me the truth. You didn't. That, too, is unconscionable. How long will you all keep lying?" I looked meaningfully at Batters. The steady wheeze of his breath was painful to hear. "And who's going to be next? You? Anthony St. James?"

She shook her head. "I don't know enough to — "

"But you know more than you're saying."

She turned back to Batters, reached up, and stroked his face. She then took a deep breath, put her hands on the bed, and pushed herself to her feet. "You're right, of course." She leaned over and whispered, "Forgive me, Simon." She gently kissed his forehead, then, in an awkward series of movements, she turned to face me. "It is time to tell the truth, but not here. Simon deserves some peace."

Helen found a seat in the cafeteria, and I went through the line to get her a breakfast of scrambled eggs, dry toast, and black coffee. I got myself a bottled water and left it at that.

Back at the table I slid into the seat across from her. She circled the mug of coffee with her hands and sat there quietly, looking into the cup. I could have directed her, bullied her into talking, but something in her posture, her expression, told me she was remembering and organizing the events of forty years ago. Finally she looked up.

"I'm going to tell you some things that I've never told anyone before. I'm not proud of what I did but it was another era. You can't possibility understand it now, but at that time the fear and paranoia were real."

"I want to know about the Fruit Machine."

She gave me a baffled look. "The what?"

"The homosexual detector. I know that's what Yves Grenier was after, that and information on Peter Aarons. I just don't know how the two connect."

"You are thorough," she said dryly. She raised her chin and took a deep breath. "I was on the selection committee to designate candidates for testing," she said. Her voice was at once firm and subdued, as if she refused to back out of the truth, much as she wanted to. "Of course, nobody truly volunteered. They were named and forced to go. In fact, no one even wanted to serve on the selection committee. We were 'volunteered' for that as well." She took a shaky sip of coffee and replaced it on the tray with only a slight clatter. "I can say in all honesty that there wasn't one person on that committee who approved of what was being done. Not one of us. We couldn't have given a whit about an astronomer's private life as long as their thinking was sound and their research strong, but in those days opposition meant guilt. If we'd even peeped a complaint we would have been next on that list, and the fear of communist infiltration was real. The year before a chemist in our own institution had been caught selling classified research to a visiting scientist, and just after that a post-doc with communist sympathies was caught photographing data. Many of us had been approached in various subtle ways, and anyone with something to hide — whether it was gambling debts or sexual, let us say, peculiarities — was vulnerable to blackmail, and the Soviets were not loath to use it. But things got out of hand, and I was unlucky enough to be put on the committee that allowed that to happen."

"Eat something, Dr. Keeler."

She shook her head slowly, but not at my request. She hadn't even heard that. "The whole thing was disgraceful.

The naming of volunteers, it was hardly a random sampling, you understand. Most divisions sent men that were suspect — unmarried or effeminate — or they sent men they wanted to get rid of. It was appalling, really, the worst in human nature coming to the fore. One man, a sweet fellow in Engineering, disappeared rather than be tested. Another man lost his job and, as far as I know, was never heard from again. There were several suicides.

"When we realized at the Astronomy Institute that we had no choice but to comply we decided that at the very least we could make it fair. Our committee drew names from a hat. All the men had an equal chance of going."

"What about the women?"

The corners of her mouth turned up slightly. "I don't think the Mounties had enough imagination to think a woman might be homosexual. Anyway, there were so few of us it hardly mattered."

"So you chose ten men. Was Peter Aarons on that list?"

"We drew names from a hat," she said tartly. "And no, he was not."

"But Simon Batters was."

She gave an almost imperceptible shake of her head, not as a negative response but as a silent recrimination. She leaned forward and lowered her voice. "I may be an unmarried woman, Ms. O'Brien, but I am not entirely ignorant of the ways of the world. Simon was a bachelor, he avoided the company of women except for me, whom he saw as an astronomer, not a woman. When his name was pulled from the hat I felt ill, but there was nothing I could do. Even expressing my concerns would have been tantamount to voicing a suspicion that he might be homosexual, and I couldn't do that. It was such a shameful and repugnant accusation, and don't forget, homosexuality was illegal. He would have been fired, possibly arrested. I was damned if I did and damned if I didn't. I left things alone and prayed for the best."

"So Simon Batters was tested."

She finally took a small bit of egg on the end of her fork and put it in her mouth. It must have been congealed and cold, but she didn't seem to notice. She chewed it thoughtfully then picked up the toast and nibbled on it before putting it down and continuing.

"That's where things get curious." Batters, she explained, had been scheduled as the last test of the day. They'd brought the chair to Sussex Drive to do the testing there and had set up a test room across from the Director General's suite just down the hall from her office. She made a point, she said, of staying late that evening to lend Batters what support she could.

"I was quite determined," she continued, "to tender my resignation on the spot if Simon was dismissed. It was all so absurd. Can you imagine Simon as a spy? The man can't even find the sugar for his tea unless you hand it to him."

"Did you see Dr. Batters go into the test room?"

She cocked her head slightly. "That's what's so odd. He never did."

"I don't understand."

"Nor do I. My office was a few doors down from the Director General's, and being sick with worry for Simon I had my door open and was keeping an ear out so I'd know when he was finished. On his way to the scheduled appointment Simon stopped by my office briefly." Here she turned away and let her gaze rest on the empty table next to ours. Then she sighed unhappily, shook her head, and went on. "He was terrified but doing his best not to show it. I watched him walk down that hall like a man condemned, but when he arrived at the test room the Director General's door opened and he went in there instead. Five minutes later I heard a door open again and a moment later Simon passed my office. I asked him if everything was all right. He said yes, everything was fine. He looked shaken but also relieved. Within minutes he was out the door, almost as if he fled the building. I remember pulling on my coat — I can't tell you how I felt knowing it was over — but as I stepped out of my office I saw the RCMP officer escorting Peter into the test room." Her eyes narrowed as if searching the past. "I've never understood that. Peter's name hadn't been drawn. I know. I prepared the list. And he was my protegé so I was concerned. I waited in my office, and about half an hour later the officer escorted Peter from the building. I never saw him again."

"And you're sure Batters wasn't tested."

"I know what I saw, Ms. O'Brien. My memory of that night is crystal clear."

I fished a folded paper from my jacket pocket and spread it out in front of her. "Then explain this."

She pulled a pair of reading glasses from her handbag and perched them on the end of her nose. I could see her eyes travel over the paper and then a look of consternation settled on her face. "Where did you get this?"

"Look at the date and time."

"I know what it says." Her voice was sharp. She removed her glasses and laid them on the table. "But it's not true." Then she turned the paper around and pushed it toward me. "I grant you that's Simon's name at the top, but that," she tapped the signature beneath the release, "is not his signature." Her gaze shifted to the table next to ours again and her voice became vague. "It does, though, explain something." She stared at the table reprocessing past information. After a few moments she snapped back and turned to me. "Minutes after Peter was taken away the Director General's door opened and Tony crossed the hall. When I left half an hour later he was still in the test room. I've always puzzled over that." She pulled the paper back, put on her glasses, and stared at the signature. "He must have taken the test for Simon."

"But the Director General would have intervened."

She looked up surprised. "Tony was the Director General. Well, he was Acting Director General to be more precise, a temporary appointment until another could be found. He wanted that position so badly. It was quite sad, really, when the permanent position went to someone else." She gave a rueful smile. "But he really was much too young for the responsibility."

I leaned back in my chair and picked up the bottle of water. With the story off her chest Dr. Keeler went at the cold eggs and toast with a delicate gusto, and I took the time to sort through all the information she'd just supplied. So Kowalski's story held. It sounded like they'd forced Aarons to "defect" as a double agent. But what had led them to Aarons in the first place? Dr. Keeler dabbed her lips with a napkin.

"Do you think," I asked, "Simon sold out Peter to save his skin?"

She refolded the napkin and laid it on the table. "I've asked myself that many times, but you know, I can't believe it. Simon ..." she paused to formulate her words. "Simon cared deeply for Peter, but I don't think in that way, and he was a changed man after that night. So nervous, so reclusive, as if he always had one eye looking over his shoulder. We never spoke of that night again, and it wasn't my place to probe."

"But surely people must have wondered what happened to Peter."

"Two days after that terrible night the RCMP Security Service man came in and told us that Peter had defected. Those of us who knew him well were interviewed over several hours, an extremely frightening and unpleasant experience. We were then forced to sign confidentiality papers, told not to discuss the matter with outsiders or amongst ourselves, and notified that we would all be under scrutiny. We were guilty by association."

"A perfect way to ensure that no one would try to trace him."

She raised an eyebrow. "Precisely."

"So what about Yves Grenier? Why was Grenier interested in Peter Aarons?"

At that she gave a long, slow sigh and shook her head. "I wish I could tell you. Much to my shame I was too afraid to ask."

I offered to give Dr. Keeler a ride home but she declined, saying she wanted to sit with Simon in case he awoke. Upstairs in his room I pulled out the chair and helped her sit down. I'd been reflecting on her story and there was still something that didn't click. A missing piece. Then suddenly I realized what it was.

"It still doesn't answer the question why, does it? Why was Peter brought to the test room? Why not Simon? And why did St. James take the test for Simon?" Then I looked at Keeler. "Do you know the answers?"

She shook her head. "And there's only one person who does." She nodded to Simon Batters's inert form.

"Two," I said.

"Two?"

I nodded. "Simon Batters and the man who forged his name on that release. Anthony St. James."

I was just leaving the room when I remembered the final thing I needed. "The RCMP officer on duty that night, do you remember his name?"

"How could I forget? It was the same fellow who did the interrogations. His name was Kowalski. Constable Joseph Kowalski."

chapter twenty

Outside the hospital the sunlight bounced off the bright roofs of parked cars. Across the street the helipad was quiet. The orange medevac helicopter sat on the asphalt square looking like a dragonfly at rest. It was a sad reminder of Elizabeth Martin. I plunked myself down on a bench, pulled out the cellphone, and dialed St. James at home. A woman answered. When I asked for Dr. St. James she hesitated.

"May I ask who's calling?"

I suddenly wondered if he'd told his wife to screen my calls. I had very little time before meeting Kowalski and I couldn't afford a runaround. "I'm calling from the Civic Hospital," I said officiously. "We wish to inform Dr. St. James that Dr. Simon Batters was admitted to intensive care early this morning."

"Simon? How dreadful. Is he all right?"

"He's out of ICU, but I was hoping to have a brief word with Dr. St. James. It is urgent."

"My husband left for Hawaii early this morning and I don't expect him back for several days. I can get in touch with him but ..."

St. James had gone to Hawaii? He'd just arrived back. Damn it. I needed to see him. "That won't be necessary. I'll follow up with another contact."

"You might try Helen Keeler. She and Simon are very close. If you hold on I'll get you the —"

"I have her number in the file. I'll try her next." I flipped the phone shut.

Why had St. James — the only other person who knew what had happened to Peter Aarons — gone back to Hawaii? Was it motivated by fear or guilt? I pulled out my notebook and found the section on St. James. According to what he'd told me he'd been observing at Gemini the night that Yves Grenier died. Since Gemini was designed for remote observing, that placed him at the Gemini headquarters in Hilo, nowhere near the summit. But, I suddenly wondered, had anyone verified his alibi? I made a note in my book, closed it, and shoved it back in my pocket. I hoped that Benson could be convinced to have a conversation with me. I was going to need his help.

At that discomforting thought I stood. It was just before 10:00 a.m.: time to confront the inevitable before the inevitable confronted me.

I could hear voices inside the house, the sound of a child squealing in mock terror. I pressed the bell again then turned to take in the view. I was standing on the steps of a modern split-level — all right angles, soaring glass, and cedar shakes — on a cul-de-sac in the exclusive east-end neighbourhood of Rothwell Heights. Below me the Ottawa River spread across the landscape like a great muddy plain. Swollen with spring runoff it was now at its most dangerous, sweeping away anything in its path. Out near the middle a huge tree slid through the water as stately as a ship. One year I'd watched a whole deer, its legs poking stiff from the water, swirl silently by.

There was a noise on the other side of the door and a blurry form appeared through the sidelight. Kowalski opened the door. He balanced a child on his hip. When he saw me he took a step back and his eyes widened, but an instant later his face was blank.

"What's his name, Joe?" I said, nodding to the little boy. "He'd be, what? The same age as Duncan's boy?"

Kowalski eased the child to the tile floor. "Go find your mother," he said, and he gave him a careful push on the lower back.

"Joseph?" A woman's voice came from the living room behind. "There's still some tea if your guest would like some." A slim, dark-haired woman, closer to my age than Kowalski's, came around the corner.

Kowalski swung around. "It's all right, Eileen. It's business. We'll talk outside." He gripped my arm, but I snapped it away.

"Actually," I looked him in the eye, "I'd like some tea."

The smile dropped from his wife's face and she glanced uneasily at me, then at Kowalski. He spoke to her with a reassuring smile. "Why don't you take Jonathon to the playroom. I'll be down in a minute."

When her back was turned he blocked me from moving in and pulled the door closed behind us. Now isolated on the stoop he moved toward me. "I don't appreciate you coming here."

Rather than stepping back I moved forward into his space. Kowalski was about an inch shorter then me, giving me an advantage, and I hoped his neighbours, with their *Architectural Digest* homes and upscale government jobs, would enjoy the show. "Well, I don't appreciate having a bag over my head, being picked up by your joggers, and having my friend and his children abducted, so I guess that makes us even. Do you love your son, Kowalski?"

His mouth tightened. "Is that a threat?"

"Actually it's not, because I don't hurt children, nor do I involve them in adult affairs. How could you? Especially when you have one of your own?"

He looked away and squinted slightly, but I knew what was going on. He was calculating, specifically how much he'd have to cooperate to get me away from his house. "Let's walk," he said abruptly. He moved around me to the stairs. I knew where he wanted to take me — down to the band of forest that ran beside the river, far from the prying eyes of his neighbours. I had no intention of moving.

"No tea? I'm devastated. I was hoping to tell your wife about Peter, Alyssa, and Duncan, the great threat to Canadian national security. I can't help noticing she's a bit younger than you. Second time around?" He regarded me but didn't answer so I continued. "I'll tell you one of the problems with a younger wife, Joseph. Just like me, she wasn't around in the sixties and we don't get all this Cold War crap. The persecution of communists, leftists, gays. It's sort of out of fashion now. She might not understand, especially the work of the RCMP's Section A-3. It's pretty unsavoury stuff."

His expression was unreadable. "What do you want?"

Good. That meant I'd scored. I was banking on the fact that he wouldn't want his young wife and son to know the details of his past. It was a brutal axe to wield but it was the only weapon I had against him. I leaned back against the railing and crossed my arms.

"I know who you are. I know what you do. What I don't know is why you're so interested in those diaries, but you know what? I don't care. Not right now, anyway. The only thing I care about is seeing Duncan and those children walk free of this mess. So here's the deal. I'll go to Hawaii to find the diaries, if they're there to be found, but don't for a minute think I'm leaving without insurance. You jerk me around and your wife and son may be surprised at what they read in the Sunday paper. And that, Kowalski, *is* a threat."

Kowalski did an admirable job of hiding his fury, but I could see the muscles in his jaw twitch and a slight flush crept up his neck. His voice, though, remained smooth and calm. "I admire you, Ms. O'Brien," he said. "You're very thorough. You would have made an excellent officer."

"Not really. I don't like taking orders."

"And that would have been a problem." He moved around me and walked down the steps. When he reached the driveway he turned and leaned against one of the cars. He was still trying to draw me away from the house so I plunked myself down on the top step. It was damp, but it was well worth it to see him crawl.

"I have conditions," I said across the space between us. "You meet them or there's no deal."

He crossed his arms, waited for a moment, then reluctantly came to the bottom of the steps. I guess he didn't want me to yell my conditions across the lawn.

"Go ahead," he said quietly.

"Number one: I don't see Gunnar McNabb or any of your other boys on my tail at any time. I get even a whiff of them and I'm out of there."

He gave a nod of his head.

"Is that a yes, Joseph?"

"Agreed," he said curtly. "No tail."

"Number two, you stay away from everything and everybody linked to this case, including Simon Batters and Helen Keeler. If I hear of anyone having an accident, however inconsequential, the deal's off."

"You've being reading too many novels, Ms. O'Brien."

"I'll take that as a yes. Finally, I talk to Duncan." I pulled out Sylvia's cellphone and held it out to him. "Now."

"That might be difficult to arrange."

I stood. "Take it or leave it." I started down the stairs. He put a hand up, then dipped the other hand into his pocket and pulled out a cellphone. He snapped it open and pushed a speed-dial button.

"Carmichael," he said into the phone, then he handed it to me.

"Who is this?" The voice was Duncan's.

"It's me, Morgan."

Suddenly, his tone was wary. "Where are you? How'd you track me down?"

"I need to know if you're all right. If Peter and Alyssa are with you and they're all right." I heard a TV in the background. It sounded like cartoons.

"We've been better," came Duncan's ambiguous reply. There was a pause. "I'll be happy when it's over, one way or another." I heard shuffling and a muffled voice. "I've been told I have to hang up. I'm sorry, Morgan. I'm sorry I got you —" The line went dead.

Kowalski took the phone and snapped it shut. "They won't be hurt. That's not how we operate."

I looked at him with unveiled disgust. "Really? There are a couple of drag queens downtown who might disagree, but those were the good old days, right?"

"You wouldn't understand."

I smiled. "And neither will your wife or son."

He let his head drop for a minute to shield his reaction, then he looked up defiantly. "I may not be with the force anymore but I still have a duty to my country. I don't always like doing it. I don't always agree with what I have to do, but I answer to a higher authority. For what it's worth you have my word. We exchange Carmichael and his children for the diaries, and we all walk away from this tragic affair."

"But what if Duncan doesn't want to walk away? He's stubborn as hell. I have no control over what he says or does."

He considered that for a minute, obviously working to rearrange one of his many lies. "Without the diaries he poses no threat. Let's just leave it at that. Do we have an agreement?"

I hesitated for a moment, then nodded reluctantly.

"Good." He wheeled around, pulled out a remote, and bleeped open the sedan sitting in the driveway. Inside he pulled a white envelope from beneath the seat. With a quick glance at the neighbouring houses he returned and handed it to me. It wasn't sealed, so I opened the flap. There was a big wad of money inside, some Canadian, some U.S., all in twenties and fifties.

"Is this from the government's special national security fund?"

"It's for transportation and expenses. Keep the change. No receipts required."

No paper trail is what he meant. I slipped the envelope in my pocket. "You knew you had me."

"That's my job, Ms. O'Brien. To predict a behaviour before it occurs."

I walked over to my car, opened the door, and spoke to Kowalski over the roof. "Anthony St. James left for Hawaii early this morning. Did you predict that too?" I saw Kowalski blink just a little too quickly. "No, I can see you didn't. That's my job, Kowalski. To discover the truth whether you want me to or not. Don't jerk me around."

"I told you," he snapped. "I'm a man of my word."

I'd have to relay that to Daisy Mae.

Somewhere over the Pacific I finally drifted off to sleep. I awoke to the nasal voice of the cabin attendant instructing us to put our tray tables in the upright position and fasten our seat belts for landing. It had been an arduous and unpleasant trip. With flights cobbled together at the last minute I was stuck with stopovers in both Toronto and Vancouver, where I finally picked up a direct flight to Kona at an ungodly hour of the morning.

I struggled to an upright position and tried to clear my head. I had managed to call Andreas Mellier before leaving, warning him that I was on my way back. Gunnar McNabb, he told me, had suddenly disappeared. Pexa had taken a brief vacation, and Anthony St. James was expected back on the island for a couple of days. Mellier had also been able to track down an address for Shelton Aimes, the telescope operator who had been with Yves Grenier the night he died. Apparently, said Mellier, he'd fled to a sister's house in Toronto where he was now holed up on some sort of stress leave. I'd sent Sylvia on a quest to track him down.

From the airplane window I caught a glimpse of green islands poking from the blue Pacific. The nose of the plane tilted down, my ears popped, and we began to drop, aimed for that tiny strip of tarmac somewhere far below. The flight attendants, relentlessly perky, strolled down the aisles checking our seat belts. An announcement came over the loudspeaker letting us know that the temperature in Kona was 82 degrees, the sun was shining in a cloudless sky, and the local time was just past 7:00 a.m.

As we taxied down the runway I finally allowed my thoughts to drift to Benson. I'd done a pretty good job of blocking him out over the past couple of days, but back on his turf that would be impossible. And, of course, our paths would cross. They had to. I needed his help to finish this off. But how could I get Benson back on-side? I'd stolen Elizabeth Martin out from under him just when he'd been ready to nail her for the missing diaries, and as a result of my action she was now dead, something I'd have to live with for the rest of my life. Still, Benson was a cop. He knew the game and he'd have no compunction about pulling the same stunt on me if it served his interests.

Outside on the tarmac I walked slowly, ruminating on my problem. Heat rose up from the asphalt and radiated down from the sun, a shock to my pale Ottawa skin. I found the end of the customs line and, with all the other travellers, prepared to shuffle slowly forward. The last time I'd come through here they'd barely checked the passports, but today they seemed to be opening every one and scrutinizing the contents. They must, I realized, be looking for someone specific.

I returned to my thoughts. So how could I patch up things with Benson but still maintain some dignity in the process? After all, Benson had had no business stalking off like that. He hadn't even given me time to explain. The line shifted forward.

Maybe I could play it another way, pretend the past had never occurred. I could bargain with Benson as one professional to another using the information I'd gathered. I took another step forward. That was probably the best alternative. The customs agent nodded for me to advance. I gave the woman a reassuring smile and slipped my passport across the counter. She flipped it open. "Anything to declare?"

"Nothing," I said.

"No firearms?"

I gave my head a firm shake. She looked over my shoulder and gave a nod. Two burly customs agents sporting flak jackets and side arms appeared behind me. The woman at the counter gave one my passport.

"You'll have to come with us, ma'am," he said, then they each took one of my elbows, leaving me little choice.

I made a feeble attempt to pull away. "I think you've got the wrong person."

The grip tightened. All the faces down the line were now leaning out to catch the show. My best bet, I realized, was to follow placidly along until someone figured out the mistake. I forced myself to relax and smile. "Lead on," I muttered under my breath.

And they did. Right into an interview room where they plopped me in a chair and left me to stew, the door firmly locked behind them. Half an hour passed, the door opened, and one of the officers swung my bag onto the table, then he left without a word. Fifteen minutes later I got up and began to pace back and forth across the small room. There was no window, just a security camera in the corner. Finally I heard voices outside and the click of the door being unlocked. It swung open and who should walk in but Detective Donald Benson.

"Thank God you're here," I said.

The guard had followed him in, but Benson put up a hand. "I can take it from here. She's not usually violent." The door closed leaving us alone. Except for the camera.

"Very funny, Benson."

He wasn't laughing. He motioned to the chair with a curt nod, then he took the seat on the other side of the table. He unbuttoned his linen jacket (pale beige today), leaned back, and crossed his arms. "You should have stayed in Canada."

So Benson wasn't going to make this easy. Fine. "I like Hawaii."

"But not enough to stay. You were told not to leave the island and you did."

"I had things to do."

"Like what? Obstructing justice? Tampering with evidence in a criminal matter? Lying to an investigating officer? Yeah, you had lots to do."

"And I wouldn't have had to do it if you hadn't been such a pig-headed asshole. Whatever happened to working together?"

"You know, I can have you deported. I'll just list you as ..." he paused. "Undesirable."

I felt a burst of flame in my chest. Jobs were one thing. A personal insult was quite another, but instead of leaping up and ripping out his carotid artery I did something even better. I gave him a cheery smile. "Okay, Benson, do what you think is right." I could see it threw him off, so I sat back and crossed *my* arms, a challenge if there ever was one. His eyes narrowed, then he barked a laugh — a definite *fuck you* laugh — and reached for the phone. He was just lifting the receiver when I said, "You're going to have another murder. Would you like to hear about it now or after it happens?"

He stopped dialing, looked up, and considered the statement, then he shook his head in disgust and starting poking numbers again. I fumbled for my leather jacket, pulled the baggy out of my pocket, and dangled it from my fingers. He'd connected with someone at the other end and he put his hand over the receiver. "What the hell is that?"

"Hang up the phone." His face clouded with indecision. "You can always call back. It's not like I'm going anywhere." He said something softly then slowly replaced the receiver, keeping his eyes on mine. I waved the bag.

"This is what we call physical evidence. The last page of Grenier's diary. Nicely dried and now encased in plastic." I tossed the baggy onto the table. "The answer is there."

He looked down at the bag, let his eyes rest on it, then looked back at me. I could see his mental vacillation. Get rid of her. Pick up the baggy. Get rid of her. Pick up the baggy. He reached for it — took the bait — so now I set the hook.

"You won't figure it out without me. Not in time."

He was holding the bag up peering through the plastic. "What makes you think you're so hot?"

"Fine. Give it a go. But if our guy dies before you work it out you'll spend the rest of your career at a crosswalk in Waimea."

He put the bag down in front of him, gazed at me for a moment just to let me know how pathetic I was, then picked up the phone and punched in a number. Oh well, I'd given it my best shot.

"Okay," he said into the receiver, "you can open up."

The guard unlocked the door and pushed it open. Benson gave me the contented half-smile of a kid pulling legs off flies. "Give me her passport," he said to the guard. The customs agent fished it out of his breast pocket and handed it to Benson. Benson scanned the pages, letting me squirm, then he jammed it into his inside pocket. I was still seated. "Well, c'mon," he said, jerking his head toward the door. "Move it."

I stood up, grabbed my briefcase and bag, and followed Benson out the door. As he passed the customs agent Benson said, "I owe you, buddy," and gave him a playful punch on the arm.

The guy laughed. "I didn't even bring her coffee."

Benson gave me an assessing glance. "She didn't deserve one. See you at poker."

Back in the public area Benson turned left and headed out to the main entrance. I stood there for a second wondering what was going on, then he turned back and flashed his dazzling smile. His SUV was parked illegally in front of the terminal. He opened the door and took my bags.

"Was that all show?" I asked.

He laughed. "Not at all. You're under house arrest. I'm taking you home."

House arrest wasn't so bad. The first thing Benson did was make me breakfast and a decent cup of coffee. I appreciated the effort. The food on the plane had been inedible, my stomach was starting to rebel, and I needed a hit of caffeine to send a signal to my brain that we were going to consider this the morning.

Benson lived in a California style split-level with a view of the Pacific below. I'd wondered what to expect, coming in. Most cops lack taste, but inside I'd been surprised to see a refined decor in beige and white. The floor was a terra cotta tile covered in places with reed mats, there was an expensive looking L-shaped couch in a canvas material, and the furniture was Danish teak. The only flaw was an almost complete lack of warmth. No knick-knacks, no personal mementos, not even a photograph of graduation from the police academy. Too bad. I'd hoped to snoop.

When we arrived Benson went directly to the kitchen, and since snooping wasn't an option I slid open the patio doors and stepped out onto the deck. With its view of the vast Pacific below I could release my mind and let it wander. Only when I heard the clink of cutlery did I reluctantly turn around. Benson had laid out the coffee table with rattan table mats, matching silverware, napkins, and mugs of coffee: impressive for a single guy, not to mention a cop. A moment later he reappeared from the kitchen with two plates. I could see the steam rising from them and I caught the delicate aroma of butter and eggs. My mental free fall went splat against a wall of hunger, and I headed for the couch.

If Benson had done the breakfast thing to soften me up it worked. It's hard to hate a man who feeds you, especially a nice omelet and toast with fresh pineapple on the side. The coffee, too, was dark and earthy. We both ate and didn't say much of anything until our plates were clean, but I didn't want to wait too long. I needed to catch Benson while he was all mellowed out.

"What's going on, Benson?"

He'd flopped back, and his long legs were stretched out beneath the coffee table. He opened one eye, sighed, then struggled to a sitting position. "Grenier's case is closed." Without making eye contact he began to collect the dishes.

I reached out and stopped him. "What?"

"The autopsy results came back. Between the angle of the ligature and the suicide note the medical examiner called it."

"That wasn't a note. It was an e-mail. What about Elizabeth Martin?"

He spread his hands. "Not my case."

"So what was all that at customs?"

At that he turned and his eyes darkened. "Why the frig did you leave without notification? And just so we're clear, this isn't personal. This is business. I got your butt out of a sling and you left me dangling. Don't do that again."

He was right, of course. That is what I'd done, although I'd been spurred on to it by his being such a jerk. Still, it was a good omelet. "I'm sorry," I said.

"If you'd been here I might have been able to keep the case open." He shook his head in disgust, whether at the case or me wasn't clear.

I let a few moments pass then said quietly. "So what happens now?"

He looked at me sideways, his elbows resting on his knees. "You remember what I said a couple of days ago? That maybe we're both being played for chumps?"

I couldn't speak for Benson, but I sure as hell had been taken for a ride, by my best friend Duncan no less. I gave a nod. "I remember."

"Well, you know what?" He stood up abruptly. "I don't like being played for a chump, and even though the case is closed it still smells rotten to me." He crossed to a sideboard where he knelt, unlocked the sliding doors, and pulled out five bulging files and three videotapes. He came back and dumped them on the table. "Copies of Star Boy's forensic files. Let's start back at square one and see what we can find."

We started by my giving Benson a rundown on everything I'd done and discovered in Ottawa. Well, not everything. The part about my deal with Kowalski was definitely off the record. Then we spent the next few hours going through the crime scene report, the list of physical evidence, the witness statements, and the crime scene videos. By the end we were no closer to an answer, but several loose ends had emerged.

We found no corroborating statement for Anthony St. James's alibi. He'd told me that he'd been observing at Gemini the night that Grenier died. We needed someone to confirm that they'd seen him at the Gemini headquarters in Hilo around the time of Grenier's death. Benson agreed to do that.

Then there was Shelton Aimes. I pulled out my notes and compared what he'd told me against the official statement. There was nothing glaring, just annoying inconsistencies. Details like when he last saw Grenier, the conversation they had as they left, the exact place he last saw Grenier. I was more bothered than Benson, who reminded me how notoriously inaccurate witnesses are, but I still wrote a note to update Sylvia on all of this. Shelton Aimes was hiding something, but what?

By two o'clock I was getting antsy with sitting around. We'd been over the reports and crime scene videos at least six times, and frankly, I didn't want to see Grenier dangling from the telescope one more time. We'd also guzzled enough coffee to cause convulsions, and I thought a little rinse of the system was in order. I got up, went to the kitchen, and came back with two glasses of water. I handed one to Benson.

"What's this?" he said.

"It's called water, Benson. Sometimes it's important to branch out."

He glanced back at the video for a minute then clicked it off. The gruesome image of Yves Grenier was replaced by an Asian chef tossing shrimp in a wok.

"There's something wrong with that," said Benson, his eyes on the screen. He wasn't referring to the little crustaceans leaping about the pan. His mind was still seeing Grenier. "There has to be more physical evidence."

Then he clicked off the TV, threw the remote on the coffee table, and headed for the kitchen with his water. As he passed me he grabbed mine and he emptied both glasses in the sink. "You shouldn't drink that shit," he said. His head disappeared into the refrigerator and he pulled out two bottles of spring water, tossed one to me, and twisted the cap off his. "Tap water's full of toxins."

At that moment I had a terrible realization. If I wasn't careful I would fall, and fall hard, for Detective Donald Benson, and I couldn't let that happen.

Benson's priority — to solve Grenier's murder — was not the same as mine. I was here to find those diaries, and the moment I had them I was gone. If we discovered who killed Grenier along the way then it was a bonus, particularly if Kowalski was involved. But bottom line, Benson was just a stepping stone to my ultimate goal: seeing Duncan's children walk free.

I just hoped Benson didn't get close enough for me to catch his scent.

"Let's get going," I said abruptly. I needed fresh air.

chapter twenty-one

Benson pulled into the visitors' lot. He was on duty at three and, given his case load, he wouldn't have time to breathe until sometime after midnight. He pulled the keys from the ignition and threw them into my lap. "Stay out of trouble," he said, and he slid from the seat and headed across the lot.

I opened my door and popped my head over the roof. "Hey, what about my passport?"

He turned, patted the breast pocket of his jacket, and gave me that dazzling smile. "Insurance," he called back. "Have a nice day." A moment later he'd disappeared inside police headquarters.

With Benson out of sight I pulled out Sylvia's phone and called Mellier. The afternoon sun beat down on the truck's roof, and I hung my legs out the open door.

"*Oui*?" Mellier answered.

"Andreas, it's me."

"You're here?"

"In Kona. Can you meet me at the dome in an hour? And you'll need to come dressed for the night. We might be up there a couple of hours."

"A couple of hours?" I could feel him hesitate. "But why?"

I avoided the question. I didn't know who might be standing near him. "Can you get access to the log-in records for the observatory computer the night Yves died?"

"You're asking me to play detective again? What are you looking for?"

"I'm not asking you to do it. I'm just asking if you *could* do it. Theoretically."

"Sure, I think so. You want me to try before I come up?"

I thought about that for a second. There was a risk that someone could trace him. "No. As long as I know it's possible."

When I disconnected from Mellier I checked my watch. By now Sylvia should have made contact with Shelton Aimes and would be waiting for my call. I poked in the number of her newly acquired cellphone and waited. After a series of buzzes and clicks the line connected.

"If it's hot and sunny I don't want to know." It was Sylvia. Behind her I could hear the hum of conversation and the clatter of dishes.

"You found him?" I asked.

"I'm in a café on the Danforth. The house is two blocks away."

The Danforth is a trendy little section of Toronto, home to aging boomers, hotshot young professionals and the city's Greek community. "You're sure he's there?"

"Yeah he's there, but I should warn you, his sister's a lawyer."

"Good, then I hope she can spell extradition. Here's what you're going to tell him. In one hour I will access the log-in records for the observatory computer system. As telescope operator it was Shelton's job to make sure everyone was logged off the computer and out of the dome when he closed up that night. If I find that Shelton logged out but Yves Grenier didn't, then Shelton's story is toast. We'll know that Yves didn't leave with him. Or, to put it another way, we'll know that Shelton left Yves alone in the observatory against all regulations. And we'll also know he lied to the police. I'll take the information immediately to both the observatory's director and the police. Shelton has one hour to call me and set the record straight. If he does, I don't search the logs and it ends there."

"And if he still won't talk?"

"The logs will. It's not a bluff."

"I get the impression he thinks he's protected."

"By Gunnar McNabb? Ask Shelton if he checked Gunnar's identification. Kowalski's a civilian, so my bet is that McNabb's freelance, and if he isn't with CSIS Shelton is on his own. Ask Shelton if he's willing to take that risk. He's got an hour to decide."

With that I got behind the wheel of Benson's truck and headed uphill. I'd just reached the turnoff to the Saddle Road when the "Maple Leaf Rag" chimed out of the cellphone. I drove by the turnoff and pulled onto the shoulder.

"O'Brien," I said.

"This is Cynthia Aimes, Shelton's sister."

Shelton's lawyer, more like it. "What can I do for you?"

She didn't waste any time. "What's on the table?"

"The truth is on the table. Shelton comes clean now and I don't access the logs, but once I do he lives with the consequences."

"He was told if he left Hawaii he'd be immune from prosecution."

"Then you better trace Gunnar McNabb and find out if he's legit, but you better do it fast." I checked my watch. "You've only got twenty minutes."

I could almost feel her considering, weighing Shelton's options, so I tipped the balance. "You know Ms. Aimes, Shelton needs to tell the truth, as much for himself as for everyone else."

There was a scuffling sound and I heard Cynthia Aimes commanding voice. "Tell her."

Shelton took the phone. I actually heard him gulp all the way from Hawaii. "He told me to leave," he said. "I didn't want to but he told me to."

"Yves?"

"Yes."

"And did he give you a reason why?"

His voice dropped. "He was meeting someone. He didn't know what time the person would get there. He didn't want me to have to wait. He told me to go so I —"

"Who was he meeting?"

"He didn't tell me. That's the truth."

"Did he seem concerned about you seeing his visitor? Did he try to hurry you out of there?"

"I was tired. It was my fourth straight night of observing. He just didn't want to make me wait."

"So Yves didn't leave the building with you."

There was a sniff and a reluctant "No."

If Benson had known this earlier the case would still be open. God damn Shelton Aimes, but I couldn't afford to lose it just yet. I kept my voice even. "The last time you saw Yves where was he?"

Now there was a more audible snuffle. "On the observing floor. He wanted to —" His voice quavered.

"He wanted to go up on the lift and make some adjustments to the camera. I told him he couldn't, that it was too dangerous alone. He had to wait until … until …" He sobbed, so I finished the sentence for him.

"— his visitor arrived."

In the background I heard Cynthia Aimes, not the lawyer this time but the exasperated older sister. "For God's sake, Shelton." She yanked the phone away. "We're done here."

"Really? I'm not. Ask Shelton if Grenier had his diary with him on the observing floor."

The question was relayed to Shelton Aimes but I heard no verbal response. A moment later his sister came back on. "He says yes."

Excellent. "One more question. Shelton lied to save his job. Elizabeth Martin is dead. Ask him if it was worth it."

The connection was cut.

I slowly closed my phone and sat for a minute staring straight ahead. True, I was furious with Shelton Aimes. I wanted to wring his scrawny little neck. But the anger, I knew, was fuelled by my own guilt. Who was really responsible for Elizabeth's death? I didn't have to look beyond the seat of this car to find an answer to that question. I put the SUV in gear, pulled a U-turn, and headed up the Saddle Road.

I didn't bother with acclimatization, just headed directly up to the summit and pulled Benson's truck into the dirt lot in front of the dome. The wind slammed the SUV and it rocked on its suspension. I pulled on my down jacket and toque, braced my foot against the truck's frame, and opened the door a crack. The wind grabbed it, but I managed to wrestle control, slip out, and slam it shut. I stood flat against the truck to catch my breath.

It felt like a Winnipeg winter, the wind so sterile and icy cold it seemed to strip the skin from my bones. Below me a great, grey sea of clouds billowed and churned. Above me, high in the jet stream, thin, elastic wisps sped across the sky, their shadows racing over barren rock like predatory birds. If the muscles in my face had worked I might have even smiled. Given the cloud cover above observing would be cancelled for the night. With any luck Andreas and I would be alone in the dome. I pushed myself off the truck, faced the wind, and headed for the entrance.

When I reached the front door I got behind the wind baffle and gasped for air. My head felt light and my vision was slightly blurred. I waited until the dizziness passed then pulled out Elizabeth's keys. To my surprise, though, I didn't need them. When I grasped the knob it turned without the key inserted. Almost reflexively I looked behind me. There were no other vehicles in sight, so who was inside?

I crossed the lobby quickly and opened the door to the hallway. On the magnet board every marker sat resolutely on "out," and the hallway beyond was silent. I had a moment of hesitation then came to my senses. Two people were dead, I could hardly breathe much less fight or run, and my sole armament was pepper spray. My only option was to leave.

I'd just reached the front door when an FCT truck careened into the parking lot and Andreas Mellier hopped out. In a bright red parka with his black hair flailing in the gale, he looked like a South American explorer ready to scale the Andes. In the foyer he smoothed the hair back from his face.

I spoke in a low voice. "The door was open when I got here, but all the magnets are 'out.'"

"That's yours?" he said, indicating Benson's SUV. I nodded. Mellier gave a dismissive wave. "This happens all the time. Maybe somebody called to say they are on their way up so the day crew left the door open or maybe there is someone here, some astronomers or engineers, but they went to borrow something from another telescope. You don't need to worry. Now —" He gave me a searching look. "Are you going to tell me what's going on?"

"The day following Yves's death did you see Elizabeth Martin?"

"You mean —"

I nodded. "Just after his body was found. Did you see Elizabeth Martin either that morning or during the day?"

He gave me a puzzled look. "I thought we were here about Yves?"

"We are, but it's connected. I know Elizabeth came up early that morning just after Yves was discovered, but was she around later during the day?"

He stood for a moment thinking back then said with confidence, "Sure. I was sleeping at the Astronomy Centre when I got the call. I came up here, then not too long after the police arrived and the dome was shut to everyone. We were not allowed back until later that day when we all come up. The day crew, some of the engineers, all the staff astronomers. Because of what happened we had to do a front-end change very quickly and set up the adaptive optics. That means we take off the camera from the top of the telescope and replace it with the secondary mirror. The camera weighs over one thousand pounds and you have to move it very carefully, so an instrumentation change like this can take several hours, but that day we don't have several hours so all the staff astronomers come up to help." He looked away then. "I think, perhaps, it was our way of dealing with the loss of Yves."

"I need you to think back, Andreas, and try to remember everything you can about Elizabeth Martin's movements that day. Was she with you the whole time?"

He gave an exasperated sigh. "You have to tell me what you're looking for. If I know something I'll tell you, but I need to know why you are asking me these questions."

"Elizabeth Martin hid the diaries somewhere up here."

"But surely they're gone."

"I don't think so. We know that Elizabeth took the diaries from Yves's house just after receiving the suicide note. We don't know why, but we do know she did it. We also know that the day Elizabeth died she'd come up here to retrieve the diaries." *For me*, I thought, but I didn't — couldn't — say that to Andreas. "We've assumed that whoever cut her brake lines took the diaries from her, but it's possible they didn't. Maybe the killer cut the brake lines before going into the dome assuming that he'd come back with the diaries, but Elizabeth heard something that spooked her and she fled without them. The brake lines, though, had already been cut. The thing is, of all those people who want the diaries nobody seems to have them." I let a pause hang in the air. "They're still here."

"And you want me to help you find them?"

"I want you to think like Elizabeth Martin. You saw her that day. You're both astronomers. Where would *you* hide a bunch of notebooks?"

He glanced around the foyer. "But this place is immense. I don't even know where to commence."

"At the beginning," I said. I walked over to the doors that looked out across the parking lot. "At Yves's house she put the diaries in her car. When she came up with all the astronomers that afternoon was she in a truck or did she drive her car?"

I could see a flash in Mellier's eyes. "She drove her own car. I remember this because I asked her if she wanted to come up with us. She says no, she'll take her own car so she can leave when she wants, but this is not normal. That road is hell on the suspension."

"Excellent. So once she was here what happened?"

Andreas was now connected. I could see the sparkle in his black eyes. "I was in a truck up front, Elizabeth was behind us, but you know, I was worried about her so when we arrive I waited at the doors for her to come in. She was not carrying anything. I'm sure of that."

"And where did you go from here?"

"To the staff lounge to get a drink. Come. We'll follow our footsteps. Maybe I'll remember more."

Mellier almost vaulted up the stairs. My progress was a little slower, one painful step at a time. At the top I had to stop again and suck back air.

"You need oxygen," said Mellier, but I shook my head. He gave a shrug and moved on down the hall. Halfway to the lounge he stopped and opened an office door. "This is Elizabeth's observatory office. I remember she stopped here but it was just to pick up an extra jacket and maybe leave a purse or something."

I stepped inside. It was a small, dark cubicle, no windows and nothing more than a desk pushed against the sheet-metal wall. A quick look around confirmed my suspicion. There was nowhere to hide a box of notebooks, and Elizabeth wasn't stupid. She'd never choose such an obvious place. From there, said Andreas, they went to the lounge for a power drink then left for the observing floor. Mellier and I followed the path they'd taken, with me keeping my eyes and mind open to everything along the way. In the staff lounge, we each picked up a power drink then headed to the observing floor, still following in Elizabeth's footsteps.

As we stepped out onto the observing floor we could feel the weather had worsened. The wind rattled the aperture doors and the metal dome moaned and creaked under the pressure of the gale. The light in here never seemed to get above dim, and when Andreas flipped a large throw-over switch it seemed, if anything, to make the place more gloomy. He stood for a moment and surveyed the cavernous space, mentally placing objects to recreate the scene as it had been the day Grenier died. He moved forward.

"That," he said pointing to the huge black construction on the floor, "is the camera. It was up there." He pointed to the tip of the telescope high above us.

"That's what you removed from the telescope?"

He nodded.

"Was Elizabeth here throughout the procedure?"

"I'm trying to remember. Give me a minute." He turned and walked slowly around the base of the telescope, muttering to himself and pointing absently to various pieces of equipment, as if replaying the day scene by scene. He looked at the tip of the telescope, followed the trajectory of the lift with his eyes, then looked at the camera where it sat on the ground. Then he followed the whole pattern again. This went on for about five minutes, then he walked briskly back to where I stood. The cold from the floor had risen through the soles of my boots and my feet were beginning to numb. I moved them up and down to keep the blood flowing.

"She was here the whole time. I'm sure."

"She didn't leave even briefly?"

"I'm sure she was here."

Maybe this was all useless. Maybe she came back the following day. She was observing that night and would have had ample time to hide something then. I gave a sigh of disappointment. "Let's follow it through anyway. What happened then?"

"After we finished the front-end change we all go to the lounge to get something to drink and then —" He paused and repeated the end of his sentence with more emphasis. "We all go to the lounge and get something to drink, but Elizabeth leaves. She disappears for maybe ten minutes." He looked up at me expectantly. "Nobody asks where she goes because we all assume she's going to the bathroom. When she gets back I remember thinking that maybe she was crying or sick because her cheeks are very red. We finish our drinks. We're all very tired and sad and everyone, I think, goes home." He gave a little nod, as if agreeing with something he'd said. "Elizabeth was in good shape and the altitude, it had no effect. She could run up and down those stairs and hardly show it. It used to piss me off. I'd be huffing and puffing two floors down."

I could feel myself shiver, whether from the cold or the information I wasn't sure. Where did she go in those ten minutes? It didn't give her much time to get out to her car, grab the diaries, bring them back in, and hide them. "Andreas, think like Elizabeth. If you wanted to hide something in the dome you'd want to hide it somewhere secure, a place where either no one goes or somewhere that only you had access to."

Andreas looked slowly around the observing floor letting his gaze travel across first the floor then up to the struts high above us. "If it were me I would hide them somewhere here on the observing floor, probably with the stored equipment. Instruments become obsolete very quickly, but we never throw anything out. We have pieces of equipment that date back to the opening of the telescope but they haven't been uncovered in ten years." He nodded to the second floor, the wide, open balcony that ran halfway around the dome. "And I'd hide it up there. There's less traffic than down here, less reason to poke around."

As we climbed the open staircase the clang of our boots on the metal stairs mixed with the rattles and howl of the wind, creating a mournful, empty, sound. Once upstairs I could see Mellier's point. Around the edge of the wide floor, up against the railing that looked across the observing floor below, there were a series of amorphous hulking forms hidden beneath tarps and crates.

"You start there," he said pointing to something square covered by a tarp. "I take the old spectrograph. And don't go pulling things apart. These are still delicate instruments. If she hid something around them it would be on top or underneath, not pushed into the electronics."

We began a methodical search under, over, and around all the equipment stored on the second floor. It was good to keep moving because, despite all my clothing, the cold had seeped into my bones and I knew my thinking had slowed. I tried to ignore the discomfort, but by the fourth infrared imaging device I was shivering, my head throbbed, and my stomach was at war with the rest of my body. Andreas, I noted, was still going strong. Wasn't he supposed to get high-altitude headaches? He looked up just as that thought crossed my mind.

"You need to take a break." He stood straight. "We'll go get something to drink and eat and I think you'll have that oxygen now."

I, too, stood up and the world did a little pirouette around me. I reached out to steady myself as Mellier grabbed my elbow. I wasn't so sure about eating, but the oxygen was beginning to sound like a good idea.

In the glorious heat of the staff lounge I slumped onto the couch. Mellier came over with a sports drink and told me to guzzle, then he followed this up with two Tylenol and an oxygen mask. Breathing in the pure, cool gas is the kind of experience that makes you appreciate the finer points of mammalian metabolism. As the oxygen hit my blood and flowed into my organs my thinking cleared, my headache disappeared, and my stomach growled with hunger rather than distress. My body had been slowly deprived of oxygen and now with it flooding into my tissues everything re-ignited.

Since we were going to be here a few minutes I thought I might as well make good use of the time. I pulled the mask away from my mouth. "Have you ever heard of an astronomer named Peter Aarons?" I snapped it back on my face.

"Who's he with?"

Probably God in heaven, I thought, but I said that Aarons had worked in Canada in the early 1960s and had even collaborated with Tony St. James.

"Really?" He leaned toward me and lowered his voice as if there was someone around to hear. He was wearing his impish expression. "Not on the galaxy paper, I hope." I gave him an uncomprehending shrug. "It was Yves who showed me," he continued. "I don't think anyone else around here would even know about it. Tony, you know, he has had a very successful career but there was long ago this one paper —" He gave a Gallic shrug. "But everyone gets one mistake, non?"

Suddenly I felt a jolt up my spine and pulled the mask from my face. "What year was this?"

"Early sixties sometime, I don't remember exactly when, in some journal that doesn't even exist anymore, and perhaps with good reason. Hey, you are feeling better, no?" He handed over a couple of energy bars.

"What was the problem with the paper?"

He laughed. "The problem? The problem was it was wrong. He was looking at the speed of rotation of stars in some galaxy with a very new spectrograph, and the speeds he got were perfect. They followed exactly what we would expect if galaxies rotated with Keplerian motion, like planets do around the sun. The problem is they don't because of dark matter, but in the sixties dark matter was unknown. So how did Tony get those perfect results that turned out to be wrong? In the end it doesn't really matter. The paper was never cited, the journal disappeared, and he never included it within his list of his publications." He gave a little shake of his head. "He was young and we are all human, after all. We see what we want, not what exists."

I felt a sudden burst of energy. "Can you trace that paper? Get me a copy?"

"Right now?"

When I nodded he looked at his watch. "I'll have to go down to the headquarters in Waimea. The librarian, she insists on working only during the day. It is most inconvenient. And you'll have to come back with me. I can't leave you up here alone."

"How long will it take?"

"An hour? Maybe two?"

I stood and pulled on my coat. Between the oxygen, the power drink, and the two energy bars Andreas had passed me, I was ready to take on the world. I felt like I'd just had my first big break.

"You go. I'll be fine."

Now, if I could only find those diaries I'd be home free. Back on the observing floor I stood in the dim light and scanned the boxes and crates. I tried to imagine Elizabeth Martin right here, the box of Grenier's diaries heavy in her arms. Where would I stash them? Then I wondered

chapter twenty-two

I stepped out of the shadows. "I've been waiting for you."

He turned to my voice. "I thought you might be." He walked toward me. As he approached I could see that the travel had taken its toll. Grey bags hung beneath his eyes and the skin seemed to sag from his face. Even his voice was subdued, as if he no longer had the energy to fight. He glanced into the dark enclave. "You think they're still here."

"They have to be. There's no other explanation. Finding them is another matter."

"Then I'll help." He gave me a wan smile. "I have nothing left to lose."

I watched him for a moment trying to read his meaning but gave up with a shrug. "Be my guest." I pulled over a stool, stood on it, and began to hand boxes down to him. He carried them into the light and lined them up. When we had enough to go through I stepped down and opened a box. St. James did the same.

"October 14, 1964," I said. "What happened to Peter Aarons?" He continued as if he hadn't heard. I straightened. "We need to end this, Dr. St. James. For everyone's sake."

He gave a deep sigh then struggled to his feet. I put out a hand but he waved me away. He walked slowly over to the stool and eased himself onto it, a hunched shadow in the dim light. "Simon couldn't take that test. One didn't need to be a psychiatrist to know that, so I took it for him. If that's a crime, to help a friend, then arrest me. I'm guilty."

"Not good enough."

He stiffened. "It's the truth."

"Kowalski would have known and he wouldn't have allowed it. Leaving a known homosexual in a sensitive research position? I don't think so. I need the whole truth."

St. James's voice took on an edge of anger. "Kowalski was desperate to get off that project. That ridiculous thing didn't work, even Kowalski knew it, but after spending all that money the Department of Defence and the RCMP brass refused to accept the truth. To put it bluntly, they needed to catch a spy to justify the expense and Kowalski was under pressure to produce one. If the project failed Kowalski knew he'd be the scapegoat and it would end his career. If he succeeded he'd get a promotion and leave the whole thing behind." St. James raised his hand to his forehead and massaged it. "Kowalski needed a spy and I gave him one."

"You gave him Peter Aarons. Not quite the same thing."

"And how would you know? Were you there?"

"You had evidence?"

"All the signs were there, everything we'd been told to watch for. He was vulnerable — sexually speaking, if you understand my meaning. He often stayed late, and I know he accessed restricted files when nobody was in at night. He always wanted to discuss new technology with other researchers and, the *coup de grâce*, he took up chess."

"That's your proof? He loved technology and played chess?"

"In those days, Ms. O'Brien, Ottawa's chess club was heavily infiltrated by Soviet agents. They used it not only as a place to recruit but also as a way to pass instructions and information. You should do your homework." Now he looked up at me, and his expression was almost pleading. "You have to understand Peter was given a choice, to be tested or not. If he was tested and passed then he would have walked away free, but he refused to be tested. What does that tell you?"

"That maybe he was gay but not necessarily a traitor."

"That's spoken from your perspective in the twenty-first century. If he was gay, as you put it, he was vulnerable. The Soviets targeted anyone with something to hide, and obviously, since he refused the test he had something to hide. The odds of him being blackmailed into passing secrets — if he hadn't been already — were extremely high, and Peter had access to all kinds of information that was worth a great deal to the Eastern Block. It was a risk we couldn't take."

"But you did with Simon Batters."

"Simon was carefully watched, believe me, and I myself made sure he stayed out of trouble."

Stayed out of trouble. Lived in terror, more like it. "So what you're telling me is that you sold Peter Aarons for Simon Batters. Then what? Yves Grenier found out?"

"Yves called me. He hadn't pieced it all together but he was getting close. He'd found out that I was acting director for the brief period when this all occurred and he wanted first-hand information." He raised his face toward me. What little light there was cast the hollows and lines in a soft, yellow glow. "I wanted to tell him the truth. I wanted to make him understand how it had been back then, that you trusted no one. That nothing was what it seemed. He deserved that. His family suffered terribly when Peter disappeared, but to accept that this brilliant man, your great-uncle, was a spy, that isn't easy."

I stomach tightened. "Peter Aarons was related to Grenier?" Which meant he was also related to Duncan.

"You didn't know?" He paused for a beat then seemed to force himself to go on. "I did come here to see Yves that night. I admit it now. While we were talking Yves wanted to make some adjustments to the camera so we took the lift up. It was up there," he nodded to the peak of the dome, "that I told him what had happened. Yves became agitated and, as God is my witness," St. James paused, "he fell. It was an accident, Ms. O'Brien, a terrible, tragic accident, and to my deepest shame and regret I …" His voice faltered and he turned away.

"You covered it up."

"Worse. I called Joseph Kowalski, a man I hadn't seen or heard from in over forty years. But Kowalski had done well. With Peter as a trophy he got his promotion and moved on to a distinguished career in law enforcement. We knew that if the truth came out it would ruin us both. In the current climate of tolerance —" St. James shook his head. "I thought that Kowalski would —" His mouth tightened. "I had no idea what he was capable of. You have to believe me. If I'd known I would simply have gone to the police." He unclasped his hands and let them dangle between his knees. "I'm prepared to do that now. That's why I came back. Yves was right. It's time to reconcile the past."

"It's not that simple. Kowalski is holding three people, a man and two children — Elizabeth Martin's children, in fact — and his ransom is the diaries."

"For God's sake, will it never end?" He stood. "Then we'd better find them, hadn't we."

"You'll testify in court if need be?"

"That's why I'm here."

We worked in silence, me mulling over what St. James had said, him thinking about God knows what. I wanted to believe his story, but there was something that still didn't ring true. On the other hand, if it was a performance it was stellar, but then St. James had done a lot of lying in the past few weeks, in the past forty years for that matter, so maybe he was just damn good.

We'd been working silently for about twenty minutes when that power drink I'd had with Mellier hit the spot.

"Where's the bathroom?" I asked St. James.

He was pulling rolls of cable from a box, feeling around at the bottom. "There's just one for women. It's a bit embarrassing, really, with more women now entering the field, but when this place was built there were almost none. It's a few doors down from the staff lounge."

"You want a sports drink when I come back?"

He gave a nod. "I'll keep at it here."

I wandered down the hall sorting through St. James's story. On the ladies' room door the little skirted icon caught my eye, so absurd in this milieu. How many skirts had ever passed through this door? Long johns and jeans perhaps, but dresses and pumps? Then I took the thought one step further. In fact, how many people in total had passed through this door? There were no women on the day crew, none on the engineering team, and only one astronomer: Elizabeth Martin. She was the only woman in the observatory on a regular basis. Suddenly my words to Mellier echoed in my mind. Where would Elizabeth hide the diaries? *In a place where no one else ever went or an area that only she had access to.* I pushed open the door. So much for thinking like an astronomer.

Nature took precedence over my investigation, but the moment I was out of the stall I scanned the walls and ceiling, looking for anywhere the diaries might be cached. The room was reminiscent of a ship's head with two compact stalls, a mini sink, and a towel dispenser above it. A grimy bar of soap sat on the edge of the sink, doubtless supplied by Elizabeth herself. Like the rest of the observatory the walls were crafted in metal with rivets running up the seams, and there was no door or hole where the diaries could be stashed.

I pulled out my pocket knife and wedged it behind the small mirror, but it was firmly bolted to the wall. I twisted around and surveyed the area above and around the toilet stalls. Just beneath the divider of the second stall I saw the bottom of a cardboard box pushed into a narrow space between the stall divider and the outer wall.

The name of a toilet paper manufacturer was printed in dark pink on the side of the box. I pulled it forward and opened the flaps. The wrapped rolls sat in perfect rows as if direct from the packing plant. Would Elizabeth have had enough time to pull the rolls out and replace them so neatly? Of course she could have done it piecemeal, a little bit every time she went to the can. And who was going question the amount of time a woman spent in the bathroom?

I began to pull the rolls out and throw them onto the floor behind me. By the third level I saw the edge of single notebook, hard-covered and blue, sticking up at the side of the box. I pulled it out and flipped it open. The final page was torn out: Yves Grenier's last diary hastily jammed in the side of the box so Elizabeth could get out fast. She had been spooked, but by whom?

I continued downward chucking the toilet paper behind me. By the time I got to the last row I saw the blue covers of the diaries lining the bottom of the box. I had to give Elizabeth credit. It was brilliant. There was at least a year's worth of toilet paper sitting in the box and only her to use it.

I pulled the diaries out then dumped all the rolls back in. With the diaries in my arms I stepped back out into the hall. I hesitated for a moment. I wanted to haul out, get myself down to Kona and on the first plane off this island, but I couldn't just leave St. James up here all alone.

Back on the observing floor St. James was bent over a box. "No luck yet," he said without looking up.

"I have them."

He raised his head, started to say something, then his eyes flew open and he stumbled back. Before I could react an arm gripped my neck and the barrel of a gun pressed my ear.

"Kowalski knew he could count on you," said Gunnar McNabb. Then he leaned in and whispered in my ear. "You're very thorough."

I released the notebooks and let them slide to the floor. It would complicate Gunnar's life, and the longer I could stall the greater the chance that Mellier or someone else would appear, but Gunnar hardly missed a beat. He tightened the hold on my neck and barked at St. James: "Pick them up."

St. James looked shaken and rose unsteadily to his feet. "I don't think ..."

I kept my voice calm. "Do as he says." I'd seen Gunnar in action and I didn't want to add St James to the climbing body count. St. James came forward, knelt and gathered up the diaries. Then he stood. "These are valuable research documents. You can't —"

All I could see in my mind was Gunnar getting ticked with St. James's defiant chatter and making a snap decision to shut him up with a bullet through the head. I had to stop him talking. Without thinking, I hooked St. James's ankle and toppled him over, sending the diaries skidding across the floor. McNabb didn't like that. He threw me face down on the cold concrete and, with the efficiency of a well-trained cop, jerked my hands behind my back then snapped on plastic cuffs. He did not, however, bind them tightly, which was a bad sign. It meant he couldn't afford to leave marks.

From where I lay on the floor I could see St. James struggle to his feet, gripping one of his shoulders. "What are you going to do with her?"

"The observatory's a dangerous place," said McNabb. "Accidents happen."

At that St. James seemed to come to his senses. He took a step forward. "I can't allow that."

Oh please, I thought, *no heroics*, and I began to struggle against McNabb hoping to divert him from St. James. It worked — a little too well. McNabb planted his knee in my back, raised his gun hand above his head, and prepared to bring the butt down hard on the side of my skull but St. James grabbed his arm.

"No!" he said. "I will not allow it." Then he stepped back and looked down at me. "She's caused too much disruption already. If she has to have an accident take her outside."

McNabb brought his arm down slowly. "Fine. You call Kowalski and tell him we have the diaries." He yanked me to my feet. "I'll be back when I'm done."

Gunnar pushed me down the hall.

"Kowalski won't be happy," I said.

"Your job's done. You're a liability."

"You don't think St. James is going to give you those diaries? You heard him. They're valuable research documents. That's why Kowalski sent me. Because I understand these people and you don't. Take my advice, McNabb, if you want those diaries you better get them now."

I could hear Gunnar breathing hard. Apparently he wasn't acclimatized either. We'd arrived at the front lobby, and I knew that I only had one option: to keep him talking, buy time, and hope I hit upon something that derailed him. "You're freelance, aren't you, Gunnar. You're not with CSIS or the Mounties. You were at one time, and that's how you know Kowalski. You know what that means, don't you, Gunnar? You're not protected. When the shit hits the fan guess who's going to be hung out in front of it. It happens all the time. We both know that."

"St. James can't get very far."

"Don't kid yourself. He's got friends in high places. By the way, I talked to your friend Shelton today. You know, the guy you sent off to Toronto. His sister's a lawyer. Did you know that? She's trying to trace you as we speak, see who you're with. You won't get away with this no matter what Kowalski said."

We'd arrived at the outer door. There were now three vehicles in the parking lot, including Benson's truck. As McNabb pushed me across the parking area a gust of wind hit us from behind and almost threw us both off balance. I thought of running but there was nowhere to go. Where the hell was Mellier?

At Benson's truck Gunnar pressed me up against it and searched my pockets. He found the keys, opened the doors, and threw me onto the floor in the back seat. If he even heard me move, he told me, he'd kill me right there. An extra half-hour of life seemed important at the time so I did as I was told. A moment later we were headed downhill.

"I bet you were a good cop once. When did you go bad, McNabb?"

"I'm on the right side. You screwed up."

"The right side? I'm investigating a murder. Last time I checked that was the right side, or isn't that what they taught you at police college?"

"This is a security operation. We don't always play by the book."

"Is that what Kowalski told you? A security operation? Then you really are stupid." The truck bumped along the washboard road then the nose dipped. We were heading down the switchbacks. "Kowalski lied to you. He sent you out to clean up his mess."

McNabb didn't answer. We came around the first tight turn, way too fast in my opinion, especially since I was running out of bullshit, which was hard to believe. I felt the truck pull into the second tight turn. As it straightened McNabb slowed and pulled over. A car passed us on its way downhill, presumably Anthony St. James. A moment later McNabb swung out of the front seat. I could hear him crunch along the gravel and pause at the corner of the truck. There was a loud pop and a hiss. A moment later he opened the passenger door and pulled me out by my feet.

"Flat tire," he said. He gave me a vicious shove against the truck. "Looks like we'll have to walk."

I thought of telling him that the truck belonged to Detective Benson but decided to keep that information in reserve. It might come in handy the moment before death.

He marched me up the road toward the hairpin turn. Here, in the lee of the summit, we were sheltered from the blasting wind but the temperature was still biting. Above us the sky still raced with wisps of cloud but the sea of cumulus clouds below had disappeared leaving the landscape exposed.

I glanced at the muted lights of the Astronomy Centre far beneath us. A vehicle pulled out onto the road and headed uphill. With no headlights, its progress was marked by the dull yellow parking lights moving against the road. McNabb, too, followed the lights with his eyes then he pushed me abruptly forward.

When we arrived at the lip of the hairpin turn I didn't like what I saw. The mountainside swept down in a steep field of jagged rock. Some twenty metres below an ancient cinder cone rose from the rubble, a black spire, and below it the slope ended in a sheer drop. Gunnar glanced once more at the vehicle grinding its way up the hill then pushed me over the lip onto the field of rubble. At least I'd have a good excuse to stumble, a way to buy time. How long would it take that truck to get here?

McNabb seemed to read my mind. "You'll be dead by then." He jammed the handgun in his belt and, with one hand on my collar and one on my belt, propelled me forward.

"It's not going to work. Too many people know about Peter Aarons." There was a telling pause. I laughed. "Kowalski didn't tell you. You don't have a clue why you're here." He shoved me hard. The cinder cone loomed ahead. If he could get me that far he could hide us behind it. "What did he tell you? That Grenier was selling state secrets? That's why you needed the diaries? You're being played, McNabb."

I felt a hesitation in his stance, the operative's deep-seated fear of a double-cross, and at that moment I pitched myself forward in a loose heap. McNabb overbalanced and came down hard on top of me. A stone dislodged and clattered down the slope. It flew off the cliff and seemed to take an eternity to smash on the rocks below. Gunnar struggled up.

I didn't let up. "He's covering up an old crime and he's using you to do it. What did you do to deserve that?"

That hit home. Gunnar kicked me hard in the ribs, and I groaned and rolled. He hauled me to my feet then brought his knee up sharply. I doubled over, unable to move or even breathe, but it bought me more time. With McNabb distracted the truck continued to climb. It took him a moment to regain control of himself, but when he did he glanced at the road. The truck was now only three switchbacks down. His gaze flicked from the truck to the precipice then back again, gauging the distance. Could he get me over the cliff in time? He grabbed my collar and hauled me up in front of him, but I kicked back hard. My heel connected with his shin, he swore, and his grip loosened for an instant. I made a half turn, threw my shoulder against him, then dove for the ground. McNabb still had to get those cuffs off if he was going to make this look like an accident, and I wasn't going to make it easy.

On the road above a car door slammed. The beam of a high-powered flashlight swung across the slope in our direction. McNabb landed on top of me, covered my mouth, and pressed the gun to my neck, but at this distance, and in this rough terrain, no one would see us anyway. I could feel McNabb's heart pounding through all my many layers of clothes, and despite the frigid air droplets of sweat fell from his face.

Andreas Mellier called my name, and McNabb tightened his grip. The flashlight wavered at the rim of the road, then it swung around and went back toward the vehicles. I should have felt anger or desperation, but instead I was awash with relief. Mellier knew it was my truck. He would know that something was wrong and he'd call Benson. But even more important, he'd get the hell away from here and he wouldn't die with me.

The parking lights went back on and the truck moved off, disappearing around the next curve. McNabb uncoiled. "You could have worked with us, not against us," he said in a low voice. He grabbed my collar and began to drag me toward the cliff. I slumped like a dead weight. He still had to deal with those cuffs. About a metre from the cliff's edge he hauled me up in front of him, pushed the gun into his pants, and loosened the handcuffs. There was nothing before me but a small ledge of stone and a great, black chasm. I was preparing to throw all my weight back against him when a rock dislodged behind us. McNabb swung around. I snapped my hands free of the loosened cuffs and torqued my elbow around. McNabb, though, was too quick, too well trained. He danced to the left and used his foot to hook my left ankle. I teetered and landed hard on my stomach, my legs hanging over the cliff. I could feel myself beginning to slide and I clawed at the stone, searching for a handhold.

The flashlight went on above us, but this time it was much closer. Mellier's voice rang out. "I have called the police. Let her go." The light bobbed down the slope coming in our direction. "Let her —"

McNabb pulled the gun from his belt and aimed at the light. I yelled at Mellier to throw the flashlight, but it was too late. The shot rang out, the light rose and fell in a perfect arc, then was extinguished to the sound of shattered glass. A moment later I heard Andreas Mellier collapse in a tumble of rock.

In front of my face McNabb's shoes turned and took a decisive a step forward. They were so close that I could

chapter twenty-three

Gunnar pitched forward and toppled to my left. He hung for a moment in limbo, an arm dangling over the cliff, then with an eerie slowness he began to slide. First his chest, then his waist, and finally his knees and shoes slipped past me and disappeared over the ledge.

I didn't wait to hear him land. I hauled myself over the cliff and rolled forward, staying low. No little red dot danced in my vicinity unless, of course, it was already sitting right between my eyes. In the darkness beyond, though, I could detect no movement or sound. Who the hell was out there? It wasn't Benson, that's for sure. He would have called out by now. Maybe Kowalski cleaning up a few more messes? And if it was Kowalski was he waiting for me to move? But that couldn't be it. With a night scope and laser sights I'd already be dead.

Somewhere above me Mellier groaned. He was still alive, but how long would he stay that way if he didn't get help? He'd risked his life to save mine. I sprung up and clambered toward the place I'd last seen the flashlight. If someone wanted to shoot me they could do it now. I found the flashlight first, smashed on the ground. Mellier lay just above it. I stood over him for a moment daring anyone to shoot, then I bent down to take a look. He was crumpled on his side with a large pool of blood gathering on the stones beneath him. I rolled him over. He cried out and mumbled something I didn't understand. The bullet had entered his shoulder and probably shattered the joint. I pulled off my scarf and packed it into the exit wound, then used my toque for the entry wound. When I was finished I pulled off my down jacket, covered him, and called 911. By the time I'd hung up they'd patched through to the Astronomy Centre and I could see people running and vehicle lights going on in the parking lot below. I dialed Benson.

"Where the hell are you?" he snapped. "I got a panicked call from the French guy, something about your truck, or should I say my truck, abandoned on the side of the road."

I looked down at Mellier. His breathing was shallow and, when I reached out and touched his forehead, it felt clammy and cold. Which would get him first? Hypothermia or shock?

"What's that noise?" asked Benson. I'd zoned out for a minute and his voice forced me to reconnect. It was a good question. What was that noise? "Is that your teeth, O'Brien? What the hell is going on?"

It was. My teeth were clattering like a locomotive on loose track. "I'm just below the summit," I answered. "How long before you can get here?"

"I'm making the turn up the Saddle Road. Twenty minutes?"

I sank back onto the rocks. "Just follow the flashing lights."

"Frig," he said, and hung up.

I closed my eyes.

Benson hopped down the rocks with the grace of a mountain goat. The emergency team had just finished packing Mellier's wounds and was now transferring him to a stretcher. Someone had woken me up and wrapped me in a down jacket, and I heard the whine of an ambulance from far below. The emergency crew, the driver told me, would get Mellier to the Astronomy Centre then transfer him to the ambulance for the ride down to Hilo. I held his hand as they lifted the stretcher but he'd been unconscious for some time now.

Benson came up behind me, draped a blanket over my shoulders, then helped me to my feet. I watched as six men hefted the stretcher and struggled up the slope. Benson put his arm around me and half dragged, half carried me up to his unmarked car. It felt odd, walking with him like that, like two kids on their first real date.

In the cruiser Benson turned on the ignition and put the heat on high. I huddled in the blanket staring straight ahead. He took one last look at me, then slid out of the car and went to talk with the emergency personnel. Two more police cruisers had arrived and the officers gathered to confer. I watched it all through the windshield, isolated and detached, like seeing a drive-in movie without the speaker in the car.

The stretcher was loaded onto the back of the truck, there were some gestures in my direction and a reassuring nod from Benson. A handshake, a few words, then Benson left them and walked over to his SUV. He squatted and took a good look at the flat tire then came back to the car and slid into his seat. He sat for a moment staring out the front windshield, then turned. "Let's get out of here. We can talk somewhere else." He reached for the shift.

"There's a body at the base of the cliff."

"What?"

"Gunnar McNabb. He tried to kill me."

Benson let his head fall onto the steering wheel and he sat there for a moment, then he slowly lifted it up. "What's going on?"

I turned and looked at him, and for once I could give him an honest answer. "I don't know. At first I thought it might be you. I thought you shot him."

"Someone shot him?"

"McNabb shot Mellier then someone shot him. A high-powered rifle with a laser sight." I paused for a moment trying to grasp what had happened. "Why didn't they shoot me?" I had a sudden memory of McNabb's last moment then remembered St. James. "We've got to get up to the dome."

"You need to go home, take a hot bath, and go to bed."

"St. James was up there." I turned and looked at Benson. "He has Grenier's diaries."

"It's an island, O'Brien. He can't get far."

"He might still be up there." I didn't think so but it was at least worth the trip up.

Benson watched me for a moment longer then gave a reluctant nod.

As we came around the switchback I saw Mellier's truck parked on the side of the road. That's what he'd done. He'd pretended to leave then pulled over and gotten out. He'd paid a high price for his act of heroism, and if he hadn't done it I'd be dead. "Can you pull over?"

Benson gave me another skeptical look but did as I asked. I hopped out of the cruiser and jogged to Mellier's truck. His briefcase was sitting on the passenger seat. I took it and walked back to Benson's car.

When we got to the dome we didn't need to go in. The parking lot was empty, the lights inside were off, and everything was locked up just as I'd predicted. St. James had taken off. I just hoped I found him before Kowalski.

Benson took the direct route down to the water, a road that cut through the back of Waimea and wove through heavy forest in an ear-popping descent. With every kilometre we travelled the temperature rose ten degrees and by the time we hit the shore my shivering had stopped. I'd found a thermos of hot, sweet tea in Mellier's briefcase and guzzled that down. It wasn't like he was going to need it.

Half an hour later we pulled into Benson's driveway. He came around to the side of the car and opened the door as if I'd suddenly become infirm. I stepped out into a balmy night to the quiet rustle of palms. I leaned against the car, savouring the divine heat, then I pulled out Mellier's briefcase as well as my discarded winter clothes and followed Benson up the walk. As I waited for him to open the door I got a whiff of his clean, musky smell. With his head bent over the lock I could just see that line of fine dark hair that extended down his neck. I shivered, but this time it wasn't from cold. Maybe staying at Benson's wasn't such a great idea.

If I was disappointed that Benson walked in ahead of me, switched on the lights, then waved me vaguely in the direction of the living room, I didn't show it. Instead I wandered to the couch and flopped down on it. He headed for the bathroom. A minute later I heard the bath running and cupboards banging open and shut. I peeked over the back of the couch. The bathroom door was closed. I pulled Mellier's briefcase toward me and opened it up. Inside was an article copied from an old journal, Anthony St. James's early publication, and just behind this was a large brown envelope addressed to Dr. Yves Grenier. The return address was Simon Batters.

The bathroom door opened and I slipped everything back in the briefcase. Benson came up behind me and put a hand on my shoulder. "Hot soup or tea?"

"Rum would be good."

"Not in your condition. Hot soup or tea."

"If I have some soup first then can I have the rum?"

He smiled. "We'll see. The towels are clean. Switch on the jets if you're into that."

A whirlpool. I must have died up there on that mountain and by some terrible administrative error been sent to heaven by mistake. "What are you trying to do, Benson? Soften me up?"

He leaned down and put his lips so close to my ear I could feel the heat of his breath. "I'm trying to get your core body temperature back up to 98 degrees. I'd like you to live through the night."

Torpor would be the most accurate word. The jets of water massaged every muscle in my body and after fifteen minutes of bliss I slipped beneath the surface, sound asleep, only to wake up sputtering.

"You okay in there?" Benson yelled.

I wondered if he was certified in mouth-to-mouth. That thought set off other dangerous imaginings so I decided it was time to get out of the water and reconnect to reality, but once out of the bath I discovered that my legs had turned to jelly. I had to hang on to the sink to stand. Finally, when they stopped shaking, I was able to reach for a towel and dry myself off. Benson had left me one of his sweatsuits. Since I didn't have any clean undies I just pulled it on over my damp skin. It was way too big but soft and warm, and the thought of what it had held before caused a rush of heat that made me shudder. This was getting out of hand. I took a deep, controlling breath and opened the door.

Benson appeared at the kitchen door with a steaming bowl of soup. He crossed to the dining room and laid it on a mat, already set with utensils. It smelled divine: a tantalizing mix of garlic, ginger, chicken, and shrimp. I sat down in front of it. A few bright green snow peas floated over a bed of fine noodles.

"I don't deserve this."

I expected a laugh or some banter but all I got was a hard gaze. "You're right. You don't."

Uh-oh. I felt the lust drain away like cream through a sieve. I lifted the spoon, but my hand was shaking. He kept up the steely glare. I put down the spoon and prepared myself for the worst. "Okay, Benson, what?"

"You've had your bath, now come clean."

"I don't know what you're talking about."

"Like hell you don't. What happened out there?"

"I told you. McNabb tried to kill me and someone shot him. That's the truth."

"What do you take me for?"

I didn't think *a big hunk of burning love* was going to do the trick right now so I struggled to find another answer. "Look Benson —" But before I could weasel out of it he stood, went to the couch, picked up Mellier's briefcase, and dumped the contents on the table in front of me. Bloody hell, he was a wily bastard. He'd gone through Mellier's stuff while I'd been in the bath. That's why he'd played Mr. Charming, putting out the clean towels and revving up the water jets. It gave him plenty of time to snoop.

"What is this?" he said, motioning to the contents.

"So I didn't tell you everything. Arrest me."

"Why?"

"Because you're a cop, goddamnit, and I'm up to my ass in cops with this one. How do I know whose side you're on?"

"That's bullshit. I've been clear from the beginning. Start talking."

"Why? You already know what's in there," I said nodding to the papers. Which was more than I could say.

"Damn right I do. So hear this, O'Brien. I may be a dumbass cop and I may not be working with all the information," he looked at the papers on the table, "but I know motive when I see it."

I felt a shiver run up my spine. Motive. The missing link. I reached for the brown envelope, the one that had come from Simon Batters. "I haven't seen this."

Benson's hand shot out. "Not so fast." The prick. He was going to stop me from viewing the evidence, but then he let go of my arm, dipped his hand in a pocket, and threw something on the table. "Not without gloves."

I snapped them on and pulled the envelope over, careful to handle it on the edges. It was addressed to Yves Grenier, the return address was Simon Batters, and it was postmarked the day that Grenier had called both Simon Batters and Helen Keeler. So Batters must have mailed this after he talked to Grenier. Given the speed of mail delivery between Canada and the Big Island it must have just arrived today. The envelope had been ripped open, but by whom? Andreas Mellier? I tipped it and the contents slid out onto the table.

The paper was yellowed, the words on it typed by an old manual typewriter with a ribbon that needed replacing. "Note on irregularities in recent rotation velocity estimates of Andromeda (M-31), Dr. Peter Aarons, Canadian Astronomy Institute." Attached to the article with a rusting paper clip was an equally faded handwritten note penned nearly forty years ago.

Simon,

Comments?

Peter A.

"Bloody hell," I said. I pulled over the copy that Mellier had made of Anthony St. James's early paper. It was titled "Rotation velocity of Andromeda (M-31) based on spectrographic survey of HII regions," then I glanced back at Peter Aarons's paper.

So Peter Aarons had prepared an article for publication and sent it to Simon Batters for review before sending it off to the journal. I glanced through the abstract. "Irregularities" my ass. Peter Aarons's paper was publicly accusing St. James of altering his data. I laid the two articles side by side. I might not understand all the details of the science, but like Benson, I knew motive when it slapped me in the face. Then I thought of something so absurd it made me laugh out loud.

"What?" Benson's voice was sharp.

I realized I must be giddy because it took me a minute to stop laughing and answer Benson's question. "You know Kowalski? The ex-Mountie? He's a victim too. Kowalski is a victim."

Benson sat down beside me. His anger, I could see, was being replaced by interest. "I'm not following."

"St. James conned Joseph Kowalski, not just once, but twice. He used Kowalski's ambition to his own ends. Peter Aarons wasn't a spy, he just got in St. James's way, and St. James used Kowalski to make the problem disappear."

"But why twice?"

Without thinking I put my hand on Benson's arm. "Tony St. James met Yves Grenier in the dome the night that Grenier died. He was there, Benson, up on that lift. That's what St. James told me tonight, obviously thinking that I wouldn't live long enough to tell anyone else."

"Had Grenier found out about these papers? Was he going to blackmail St. James?"

"I don't think so. I don't think he'd pieced together the whole truth, that Peter had been falsely accused. I think at that point Grenier was still searching for answers and he hoped that St. James would have some. By all accounts they were close, Peter Aarons and Tony St. James." I looked down at the two papers lying on the table. "But obviously not close enough."

"So St. James killed Grenier?"

"He said it was an accident." Then I remembered Frederick, the Ident officer's, words about death scenes and added, "But only two people know for sure and one of them is dead. Regardless, he called Kowalski to clean up the mess, that being Grenier's missing diaries."

Benson nodded. "They didn't know how much Grenier had written down." He stood abruptly. "We have more than enough to hold St. James." He left the room. I heard him dial the phone and have a murmured conversation with someone on the other end. Five minutes later he was back and he sat down. "We're not finished yet. What happened up there tonight?"

I looked at Benson, the intelligent face, that soft bristle of dark hair, the slim, hard body. "I'll tell you everything but not right now."

He didn't take his eyes off me as I got up, took his face in my hands, and bent down to kiss him. It was not a timid kiss, not by the end anyway. When I tried to draw away he put his hands on my hips to stop me.

"This doesn't get you off the hook." He pulled me slowly toward him. I straddled him and sank onto his lap. He slipped one hand beneath the sweatsuit and up my naked back. "Don't think for a minute that this gets you off the hook," he said into my hair.

He needn't have worried. I was already landed.

The hot sun streamed through the blinds and I looked at Benson sprawled across the sheets. It was a breathtaking sight, his muscled body, the fluff of dark hair across his chest. I bent over, resisted the temptation to begin last night again, and made do with a gentle kiss on the shoulder. Then I slid quietly out of bed. The sweatpants and sweatshirt were in a heap on the floor so I picked them up and pulled them on just outside the door.

I have to say, I felt fantastic, completely relaxed yet energized. That might change when Benson got up and we had to face post-coital conversation, but for now I just let the feelings linger.

I dumped out the cold soup that was still sitting on the table and rummaged around in his cupboards until I found all I needed to brew some coffee. While it was bubbling to life I went back to the dining room table and picked up the papers that Benson had scattered there, then I picked up the phone and called Sylvia.

"Hey babe," she answered. "Hawaii keeping you hot?"

"Something like that. Are you back in Ottawa?"

"At the Mayflower as we speak."

"I've got something for you."

"Macadamia nuts? I love Macadamia nuts."

Benson emerged from the bedroom wearing only a pair of running shorts. He gave me a bashful grin, scratched his stomach, and headed for the bathroom. I must have been distracted because a second later Sylvia said. "I'm still here."

"Right," I said turning back to the wall. It was safer that way. "I've got some articles I want you to read."

"Oh, that kind of thing. I should have guessed."

Benson emerged from the bathroom and padded toward the smell of coffee. "Hey Benson," I said with the phone covered. "You got a fax machine?"

"In the guest room," he said, pointing to the door off the dining room.

I put the phone back up to my ear. "I'll send them by fax to my apartment. Read them, but don't discuss them with anyone. I'll be back sometime tonight."

"I take it you didn't sleep in the guest room."

"Very funny. Do you have any news on Simon Batters. Is he —" I let the question hang.

"He's doing all right. So is he cute?"

Benson flopped onto the couch. I glanced behind me. "That would be one way to put it. I'll call you later."

"Hey, babe, stay out of trouble."

It was a little late for that.

Sylvia picked me up at the airport, which, considering it was four in the morning, was above and beyond the call of duty. On the other hand, for Sylvia the night was now in full swing. With bandwidth high and usage low a lot could be accomplished online. Me? I was hoping to get an hour of sleep before starting my day again.

When we were out of the terminal and headed down the Airport Parkway Sylvia threw me a glance.

"Your boyfriend called."

"He's not my boyfriend."

"Whatever. He said it was urgent, to call him no matter what time you got in."

When Benson and I parted at the airport I can't honestly say it was sweet. Uncomfortable would be a better word, with neither of us willing to admit that the night before might have meant something other than unrestrained lust. That was fine with me. My life was complicated enough. The thought of adding relationship responsibilities that stretched across the Pacific didn't really appeal, no matter how attractive some of those responsibilities were.

I pulled out the cellphone and poked in Benson's number.

"Benson," he said. He issued the word like an order.

"It's me. I'm back in Ottawa. What's up?"

"Let me just …" I could hear him get up and close his office door. It was eleven in the evening for him, well into his shift. "Last night —" I felt my gut constrict. I hoped we weren't going to get heavy over a satellite link. "That guy McNabb."

I let out my breath. "You found the body."

There was a long pause. "Are you sure he's dead?"

chapter twenty-four

"Benson, I watched the bullet take off half his head. Between that and the cliff, yeah, I'm sure he's dead."

He lowered his voice. "There's no trace of a body."

"That's ridiculous. There has to be neural tissue everywhere."

"Well there isn't. We scraped, we swabbed. Nothing. We'll be trying luminol tonight. No one can clean up completely, especially not in that terrain."

"What about St. James? Have you found him?"

"Another friggin' dead end. He boarded a flight last night to Honolulu before we put out the APB. He had a connecting flight to Toronto but he never got on. Either he's lying low in the big city or he's slipped out from beneath us." There was a third option, but I didn't voice it. "Listen," he started uncomfortably. "I —"

I cut him off. "I'll be paying Kowalski a visit this morning. I'll call and let you know what happens."

I heard the white noise of the satellite link. "Right. Kowalski," Benson finally said. "Yeah, keep me informed." And he rang off.

"Very romantic," said Sylvia. "Exploding heads. That would get my blood moving. So what's this about St. James?"

"He's disappeared. With the diaries."

"Not such a surprise, really. If someone was about to expose something that stupid in my past I think I'd disappear as well."

We were crossing the canal on Bronson Avenue and Sylvia signalled to take the exit ramp onto Queen Elizabeth Drive. "What do you mean?"

"Those papers you sent me? Man, talk about regrets."

"Regrets? What about fraud?"

Sylvia gave me a cryptic smile. "You don't get it, do you?"

I was too bagged to be playing games with someone who was way smarter than me. "That's why I sent the papers to you. I knew you would 'get it.' Why regrets?"

"It's not just that he cheated. If he'd reported his actual results then had the wherewithal to stand by them he would have made one of the greatest discoveries in modern astronomy. Sure, it would have taken a couple of years to figure out *why* his rotation velocities didn't follow Keplerian motion, but he would have been famous, his picture in every textbook. Instead he hid what he saw, published what he thought he should see, and spent the rest of his life hoping that paper would never surface. It's kind of pathetic, really."

"What are you talking about?"

"Dark matter, babe." We'd hit the canal, and Sylvia turned left onto Queen Elizabeth Drive. "That's what St. James saw — the first hard evidence for dark matter — and instead of reporting it he covered it up. That's gotta bite."

In the time I'd been gone from Ottawa the canal's chalky ice had completely melted, leaving nothing but flats of mud and a desultory urban trickle. Yves Grenier had been studying dark matter. Is that why he died? "How did Peter Aarons know St. James fudged the results?"

"Aarons was an astronomer, but he was also an instrument builder. In the early 1960s he began experimenting with the use of image tubes in spectrographs, which, if it worked, would allow astronomers to collect much more precise data. Aarons developed this experimental spectrograph and then let his colleague St. James use it to look at the rotation velocity of stars in the Andromeda galaxy. St. James wanted to know how fast different regions of the galaxy were circling around its centre.

"You've got to understand this was entirely new stuff. Up until that point spectrographs didn't have the kind of precision you needed to do this work, but when St. James got the results they weren't what he, or anyone else, expected. Since these types of galaxies are brightest in the middle, and the brightness decreases as you move out from the centre, astronomers naturally assumed that the mass of the galaxy — in other words the stars — was concentrated in the middle. If the mass is concentrated in the middle and the whole thing is spinning like a disk, the stars closest to the middle will orbit the fastest, and the speed of rotation will decrease as you move out from the middle: Keplerian motion like we see in the planets orbiting around the sun.

"That's what St. James records in his paper, Keplerian motion, but according to Peter Aarons's rebuttal paper, that's not what St. James saw. His rotation curve for Andromeda was flat. To put it another way, the stars on the edge of the disk were moving just as fast as the stars in the center, and that went against all the established theory. So what did St. James do? Instead of publishing his results and saying that he didn't know why it was that way, but it was, he altered the data to fit the accepted theory. He slowed down the outer reaches and sped up the centre. But here's the cosmic joke: St. James's original observations were correct. It took another ten years and a determined woman astronomer for researchers to confirm that most of a galaxy's mass is unseen, and this 'dark matter' sits as a halo somewhere beyond the visible edge of the galaxy. This dark matter acts as a powerful, unseen force that affects everything from the galaxy's motion to its structure and evolution." Sylvia turned left onto my street, pulled up in front of my house, then turned to look at me. "Honestly, Morgan, if I'd been in St. James's shoes I probably would have fudged it too. If there's one thing the history of science shows, it doesn't pay to be at the vanguard. The pioneers get nailed."

"Obviously Peter Aarons didn't agree."

"It was Aarons's instrument. He got a hold of the spectra and he knew the truth. I don't think he had any more idea than St. James what it might mean but that didn't matter to him. As far as he was concerned his spectrograph recorded the truth, bizarre as it was, and that's what had to be published."

I sat there for a minute watching the light from the street lamp play across a scrubby bush in my tiny front yard. Soon it would burst into bloom and fill the street with the heavy scent of lilac, but right now it was no more than dead twigs scratching at the wind. What Sylvia had just told me certainly fit what I knew about Peter Aarons and Anthony St. James: one the consummate scientist with no interests beyond the lab, the other the ambitious researcher working the system for promotion and profit.

There were still several questions left to answer but the pieces were falling nicely into place. I stepped out of the car and pulled my bag from the back seat. I was looking forward to the day. True, I didn't have the diaries but I had more than enough to nail Kowalski to the wall, and by this evening it would be over. Duncan and his children would be free.

At five-thirty, with the sun just beginning to lighten the sky, I was back in my car and headed out to Rothwell Heights. Kowalski, I was sure, would be a morning kind of guy, and if he wasn't his son, Jonathon, would make sure he was. I pulled up into his driveway, strode up the walk, and pounded on the door. Then, just for good measure, I pressed the bell a couple of times. A light went on in the hallway and a shadow approached the door. A second shadow came up behind and I heard voices on the other side, Kowalski's, then his wife's. A child whined. The locks on the front door clicked and it swung open.

"What are you doing here?"

"Surprised to see me?" I held up my briefcase. "I have something for you."

He glanced behind him and made a movement to step out onto the landing but I moved forward, placing myself in the path of the door. "No. We do this inside on the dining room table or not at all."

He hesitated for a moment calculating the risks then called behind him: "Eileen, take Jonathon upstairs."

She came out into the foyer, the child on her hip, and gave him a piercing look. Then she moved toward me and held out her hand. "I'm Eileen Neel Kowalski," she said. "I don't know what's going on but I do know you've upset my husband, and I don't appreciate his work coming into the house. I would ask you to please meet with him during those many hours he spends at the office. However, since you're here now do come in."

"I won't take up much of your husband's time." I looked at Kowalski. "And I'm sure we both hope this won't happen again."

She gave me a curt nod. "Joseph, please get your guest some coffee. Now if you'll excuse me I'll go upstairs and dress Jonathon."

Kowalski waited until she was up the stairs then turned to me. "Let's have them."

"Not so fast. I'd like that coffee."

"This isn't a social call. We're both well aware of that."

"Maybe not, but we can still behave like civilized beings." *Especially with your family in the house*, I thought, *which is precisely why I chose to do this here.*

He turned and headed grudgingly for the kitchen. I followed him as far as the dining room and while he was pouring the coffee I opened my briefcase. When he was back I picked up the mug and took a leisurely sip. It was slosh, just as I'd expected. I put it on the table. Kowalski immediately slid a coaster underneath.

I pulled out Peter Aarons's paper, the one he'd sent to Simon Batters for comments some forty years ago. The one that accused St. James of fraud. I pushed it under Kowalski's nose. "Do you know what this is?"

He didn't even look at it. "Just leave the diaries and get out."

"Just leave the diaries? Very good, Kowalski, but how can I when you already have them?"

His reaction was undisguised surprise. He put a hand on the table to steady himself. "What are you saying?"

"Anthony St. James has them and he's disappeared, along with the body of your friend Gunnar McNabb. There's only one person who could have orchestrated that, and it's you."

Kowalski sank into the chair behind him. "McNabb is dead? I don't believe you."

"Trust me. He tried to kill me first."

He stared for a minute then said, "How?" Then he looked up at me and his eyes held a mixture of defiance and dread. "How was he killed?"

"A single shot to the head. Whoever did it was good."

He took a moment to digest that. "If you don't have the diaries why are you here?"

I threw the paper on the table in front of him. "You've never seen this paper?" He picked it up, pulled a pair of reading glasses from his shirt pocket, and perched them on the end of his nose. "What does this have to do with anything?"

"This has everything to do with everything. Do you know what it is?"

"An article by Aarons, obviously."

"An article denouncing Anthony St. James. Accusing him of research fraud. It would have ruined St. James." I put a hand on the table and leaned into his personal space. "He used you, Kowalski. He used your own ambition against you. Peter Aarons wasn't a spy, he wasn't even necessarily gay, he just got in someone's way."

Kowalski flipped quickly through the pages as if searching for something to prove me wrong. "That's not true," he said. "Where did you get this?"

"St. James used you to destroy an innocent man."

"That can't be." He laid the paper on the table before him, but his eyes were now unfocused. He was seeing something else, a room on Sussex Drive in October 1964, but I didn't give him a chance to examine the past.

"You didn't ask too many questions, did you, Kowalski. You needed out, Peter Aarons was your ticket." I looked around the room: silk drapes, heavy carpets, and polished wood. "And look where it got you." I pulled out my cellphone and laid it on the table. "Don't make the same mistake twice. Don't condemn another innocent man. Make the call."

He seemed to come back from a great distance and looked at the phone lying on the table, then up at me. "I can't do that."

"You have no choice."

"I'll be ruined." He glanced at the stairs. "My wife, my son, they're innocent." Then he gave a forced laugh. "They weren't even born when all this happened."

I looked at the stairs as well. I could hear the little boy's laughter as his mother tried to dress him. How many more innocents would be blighted by this? It grated to say the words, but I forced them out. "Let Duncan and his children go and it dies here."

"But what about Carmichael?"

"You said it yourself. Without the diaries he can't do a thing. He doesn't know the whole story, and I'll make sure it stays that way." I pushed the phone toward him. "Make the call, Kowalski. Do it for the children, yours *and* Duncan's. If you don't I dial the reporter and I blow it wide open."

He stared at the phone for a moment then pulled his cellphone from his belt. He poked the speed-dial. "It's over," he said into it. "Drive them home." Then he flipped the phone shut and closed his eyes. I took the article off the table and slipped it back into my brief-case. I had my hand on the knob when I asked my final question. "What happened to Peter Aarons?"

Kowalski seemed to rouse from a stupor. "He was never mistreated if that's what you mean. He was much too valuable for that."

"What do you mean?"

"They wanted him south of the border."

"You sold a Canadian scientist to the CIA?"

At that his head snapped up. "We didn't *sell* him. We're allies, in case you've forgotten. Dr. Aarons was sent to a secure military facility where he could make a contribution to the war against communism. In return we received valuable surveillance equipment. What would you rather? That we'd thrown him in jail?"

"He was innocent, Kowalski. I would rather you'd left him alone."

I parked in the Civic Hospital lot and swung by the concourse for breakfast. It was still early, and I didn't want to disrupt the hospital routine. I had sausages, eggs, and toast, and when I was sure I could get into Simon Batters's room without witnessing a sponge bath or facing a tray of hospital food I took the elevator upstairs.

The policeman was gone from Batters's door. I knocked lightly and let myself in. Batters lay on the bed, his thin arms resting on top of the sheets. An IV still snaked from his arm, and the bruise on his wrist was now a livid blue-black, but he was conscious and alert. He turned toward me.

"You? Helen said you'd been by, that she'd told you … Well, frankly, she told you too much. Nothing I can do about it now, though, is there?" He turned to face the sunshine pouring in the window.

I walked over to the bed, pulled up the only visitor's chair, and sat down in it. Then I pulled Peter Aarons's article from my briefcase. "You mailed this to Yves Grenier."

Simon Batters picked it up, glanced at it, then threw it back down on the bed. "I should have told him the whole story over the phone but I didn't have the courage. Next thing I know he's dead."

"I need to know one thing. I'm not here to judge, Dr. Batters, but I have to know. Is this," I held up the paper, "how you avoided the test? Did you tell Dr. St. James about it and offer to keep it quiet if you could walk away?"

He turned now and gazed at me, or through me to be more exact. "How little you understand." He picked up the paper and ran his hand over the cover. "I did not betray Peter. How could I betray him? I loved him and he loved me." He looked up quickly. "Although not, unfortunately, in the way I would have liked. As a father figure, perhaps, a mentor, but not in the sexual sense. He was brilliant, a wonderful companion, and I was happy with things as they were. He sent me this paper for critical comments before sending it off to the journal. What you don't understand is that he would have sent it to Anthony too."

"But why?"

"Because first and foremost Peter was a scientist. He only cared about the truth. He didn't give a tinker's damn for politics, abhorred bureaucracy, and would have wanted Anthony's comments. Peter was naive, an innocent soul with a brilliant mind, a tragic combination as it turned out." He looked at the paper. "The night I went for my test I knew I wouldn't pass, but I had no choice. When I arrived at the test room Anthony came out of his office and beckoned me in. He said that he knew I couldn't pass the test and he would take it for me, but only if I promised to leave immediately and tell no one. I asked him how he could make this happen and he told me not to worry. It was like being born again. I was free to continue my work, my life. It was only later when it became clear that Peter had disappeared that I began to wonder, I began to ask myself, if —" He nodded to the paper. "But I owed Tony my job, my life. That's not an easy thing to forget."

"That night after Sylvia — David — and I left your apartment, who paid you a visit? Was it Kowalski or St. James?"

He stared out the window a moment then turned back. "Where is Tony now?"

"He disappeared somewhere in Honolulu. We will find him."

He plucked the edge of the clean white sheet and said almost absently, "I think not."

"What are you saying?"

"You'll think I'm daft." When I didn't comment one way or another he continued uncomfortably. "The night before last I woke during the night. He was sitting right there in my chair, right where you are now. Peter Aarons. I closed my eyes, and when I opened them again he was gone."

I felt this great well of pity open up within me. Here was this fragile, elderly man who had done nothing wrong, but was nonetheless forced to live his life tormented by fear and guilt. "It was the Demerol, Dr. Batters. A dream or a hallucination." I patted his arm. "I'll leave you to get some rest." With that I stood, slipped the copy of Aarons's paper back into the envelope, and left it on the bedside table. "You did the right thing, sending Yves that paper. You had nothing to do with his death."

But Batters hadn't heard my second statement. His mind was still working on the first. "If it was a dream, a hallucination," he asked, "then why had Peter aged?"

When I got home Sylvia was still sound asleep. It would be another few hours before we could go out to a restaurant and get breakfast for her, lunch for me. The message light on my phone, however, was blinking merrily away. I considered not responding — it might be Bob, my boss, wondering when the hell I'd be back at work, but in the end I dialed in. It was Duncan, as I knew deep down it would be, asking me to call him back.

I went into the kitchen, made myself a coffee, then came back out to the living room. When I was sure my emotions were under control I picked up the phone and dialed his number. He answered on the first ring.

"It's me," I said, my voice cool.

"I'm sorry. I really am."

"You damn well should be. You almost got me killed."

There was another long pause. "Are you all right?"

"Did you know Elizabeth had the diaries?"

The silence spoke volumes, but I waited him out. I wanted him to say the words. Finally he muttered, "You wouldn't understand."

"Try me."

"She knew about Peter Aarons. She knew our family was still trying to find him but she wanted joint custody. She was holding the diaries as ransom for Peter and Alyssa. She even told me that Yves would approve, that he felt the children should see her."

"You sent me out there on a custody dispute?"

"It was more than that. I knew that Yves was close to finding out the truth about Peter's disappearance. I'd tried myself for several years, but it became clear that there were people in Ottawa who didn't want the truth revealed. You have to understand that three generations of our family were destroyed by Peter's disappearance. A defector? We knew it wasn't true, but if it wasn't, then what happened to him? Our family needs resolution. We need justice and we need to know the truth, especially with Yves gone. Elizabeth knew that and she took advantage of it. Tell me, what else could I do?"

Honestly, I didn't have an answer to that question, but I also didn't care. What Elizabeth had done was wrong, but so was Duncan's reaction to it. There had to be a better way.

"I have a letter from Elizabeth to her children," I said. "I'll be over in fifteen minutes, I will take the children to the river, I will read the letter to them, then I will tell them everything I know about their mother. But Duncan?"

"I know," he said quietly.

"Too bad. I want to say it anyway. I never want to see you again."

He only let a beat pass. "Do you have the diaries?"

"Fuck you, Duncan." I banged down the phone.

visit in May, although why anyone from Hawaii would come here was quite beyond me.

Of course, there were still loose ends that niggled. Tony St. James and the diaries had truly disappeared. The Hawaiian and Canadian police both continued to search for any trace of him, living or dead, but so far they'd turned up nothing. Pexa, too, seemed to have vanished, and no matter which way Benson dug he ran into a wall. As for McNabb, the luminol showed traces of blood on the edge and at the base of the cliff, but nothing more was found. It wasn't a satisfying end to a tragic affair but it was the best we could all do.

At a newspaper box outside the Mayflower I bought a copy of the Saturday *Ottawa Citizen* and slipped into my usual booth. The waiter arrived with coffee, and I ordered the cholesterol special and flipped open the paper. By the time my breakfast arrived I'd finished my first cup, the restaurant was full, and I'd moved from the front page onto the City section. I was halfway though the sausages when I stopped chewing. A familiar name caught my eye: Joseph Kowalski. I scanned the article. He had, the reporter informed us, been found hanging dead in his garage the day before. Foul play was not suspected. I closed the newspaper slowly and pushed my plate away. Outside the urban athletes in neon spandex jogged and biked by. I suddenly felt sick. St. James had disappeared and now Kowalski was dead. What had I missed?

I hurried down Elgin and turned the corner onto my street. Pexa stood at the base of my stairs chatting with Amadeus, my neighbour's little boy. My stomach cinched. Amadeus looked up and pointed at me. Pexa straightened and gave a single nod. A man sitting on the bench nearby stood and took a step forward. His hair was thin and sandy grey, a little unkempt, and he wore a pair of steel rim glasses on a thin, angular face. Over jeans he wore a green Gortex jacket.

"Ms. O'Brien," he extended his hand. "I need a moment of your time."

I barely glanced at him. I was watching Pexa so uncomfortably close to Amadeus. The man looked over at the two of them. "Oh, he's quite safe. The boy I mean." Then he smiled. "In fact, he couldn't be safer. You should know. Pexa saved your life on more than one occasion."

It took a moment for that comment to compute — the stone hut near the top of Mauna Kea, the attack in the back alley, the dancing red dot — then I turned and looked at the man beside me. "Simon Batters wasn't dreaming."

"A risk on my part," he said. "But well worth taking." He motioned to the bench and took a seat. I sat down beside him. For a moment he said nothing, just watched two crows squawking in the tree above, then he turned to me. "I want to thank you for your work on my family's behalf. Yves. Duncan. I couldn't intervene directly, you understand, but we did our best to keep you safe so you could carry out your investigation. They owed me that much after all these years."

"They?"

He ignored the question. "But my family deserves the truth, Ms. O'Brien. They deserve to know that I didn't defect, and you're the only one who can tell them what happened. Please, do this final thing and end it here."

"I made a promise to Kowalski. It was the price I paid for Duncan and his kids."

He paused for a moment. "But Joseph Kowalski is dead."

At the flatness in his voice I felt a shiver run up my spine. "Tell me, Dr. Aarons, what *is* the truth?"

"What do you believe it to be?"

"St. James said you had a choice but you refused to take the test. Why? Simon Batters told me you weren't gay."

"I was given a choice, that much is true, but it wasn't quite the choice you were led to believe. Tony knew I was close to Simon, and although it was an innocent relationship, who would believe it? Tony said the RCMP were on to me and they'd insisted that I take the test, but as my close friend he'd managed to negotiate a special deal. I could be absorbed into an underground military lab where I'd have an unlimited budget, no administrative duties, and the freedom to pursue my research. The other option was public humiliation, job loss, and possibly arrest. It wasn't much of a choice."

"But why didn't you just take the test?"

"I was in my early twenties, Ms. O'Brien. I'd never been interested, much less involved, with a girl, and I did love Simon in my own peculiar way." He gave a mirthless laugh. "I didn't think I'd pass." Then he held up his hand to display a ring. "I'm married now, by the way. She's a corporal and an engineer. It's ironic really. I didn't choose this life, and yet it's the life I always wanted. The life I always dreamed of. My family deserves to know that. We have to stop it here."

A black car with diplomatic plates pulled up in front of the bench.

"Why don't you tell them yourself? They'd prefer it coming from you."

Peter Aarons stood. "When you carry the secrets that I do you never walk free. Please tell my family what happened and tell them that I'm alive and well. At least that much is now allowed." He turned and moved toward the car.

Then I realized something I'd missed all along. "Duncan's son, Peter, he's named after you." He hesitated for an instant, his hand on the car door. I stood. "What happened to Tony St. James?" He opened the door. I took another step forward. "If you want it to stop here then you have to tie it up."

He half turned and gazed at me over his shoulder. "I've been living underground for forty years. I think it's Tony's turn now."

He disappeared into the dark interior, closed the door behind him, and the car slipped away.

I turned, suddenly remembering Amadeus, but Pexa, too, had disappeared. Amadeus sat reading on the stair. I went back to the bench and picked up my newspaper. Beneath it was a plain paper bag. I looked inside: ten laboratory notebooks, all with blue covers. I pulled one out and opened it to see the tiny scrawled writing of Yves Grenier.

Cold War justice, I thought. *An eye for an eye so we can all be blind*.

I sat down on the bench. One of the crows flew down from the tree, assuming the paper bag held lunch. He perched on the end of the bench and tilted his head, regarding me with bright, black eyes. In making my promise to Joseph Kowalski I'd traded one family for another, but who was the most deserving? If I kept my promise to Kowalski this story would never end, infecting Duncan's children as well.

I sighed and looked at the pile of diaries. It was time to tell the truth, time to forgive both ourselves and others for all our many sins. The future, I realized, can only live when we allow the past to die.

Back in my apartment I dialed Duncan. He picked up right away. "I have something for you," I said, looking at the diaries. "I'd like to come over." When I

acknowledgements

This book could not have been written without the years of friendship, conversation, and support of Dr. James Hesser, Director of the Herzberg Institute's Dominion Astrophysical Observatory, and Dr. Dennis Crabtree, the National Research Council of Canada's Project Leader for the Gemini Telescopes. I would like to state clearly, however, that neither Dr. Hesser nor Dr. Crabtree reviewed the manuscript. The errors, misconceptions, and distortions are entirely my own. If you're an astronomer, don't blame them.

Carolyn Swayze and Barry Jowett provided sage advice and excellent editing. I would like to thank them for their patience and their continuing enthusiasm for my work. Both Jennifer Scott and Jennifer Easter at Dundurn have gone above and beyond the call of duty to make the book a success. Andrea Pruss, also of Dundurn, diligently rooted out my many bloopers and mistakes, for which I am very grateful.

Patricia Montreuil read several early pieces of the manuscript and, along with Sharalyn Hunter and Sylvia Lin, buoyed me up in those particularly hopeless periods. Thank you also to Sarah Herring for several critical conversations along the way. They influenced the course of this book.

Finally, I would like to thank my family: my parents, Joan and Peter Brett, for their continued love and support of a rather challenging daughter; Eva, for her intelligence and irrepressible sense of humour; and Fabie, for being the most wonderful human being to ever walk the Earth.

If you'd like more information on the real stories behind *Cold Dark Matter*, please visit the author Q&A at www.alexbrett.com.